BLOODMONEY

ALSO BY DAVID IGNATIUS

Agents of Innocence

Siro

The Bank of Fear

A Firing Offense

The Sun King

Body of Lies

The Increment

DAVID IGNATIUS

BLOODMONEY

A NOVEL

W. W. NORTON & COMPANY
NEW YORK LONDON

Printed in the United States of America
First Edition

Manufacturing by Courier Westford
Book design by Ellen Cipriano
Production manager: Anna Oler

Library of Congress Cataloging-in-Publication Data

Ignatius, David, 1950–
Bloodmoney : a novel of espionage / David Ignatius. — 1st ed.
p. cm.
ISBN 978-0-393-07811-4
1. United States. Central Intelligence Agency—Fiction.
2. Espionage—Fiction. 3. Intelligence officers—Violence against—Fiction.
4. Women intelligence officers—Fiction. 5. Deception—Fiction.
6. Revenge—Fiction. 7. Retribution—Fiction. 8. Pakistan—Fiction.
I. Title. II. Title: Blood money : a novel of espionage.
PS3559.G54B56 2011
813′.54—dc22

2011003003

W. W. Norton & Company, Inc.
500 Fifth Avenue, New York, N.Y. 10110
www.wwnorton.com

W. W. Norton & Company Ltd.
Castle House, 75/76 Wells Street, London W1T 3QT

1 2 3 4 5 6 7 8 9 0

For Garrett Epps

Revenge, at first though sweet,
Bitter ere long back on itself recoils.

—JOHN MILTON, *PARADISE LOST*

First, you push on your territories, where you have no business to be, and where you had promised not to go; secondly, your intrusion provokes resentment, and resentment means resistance. Thirdly, you instantly cry out that the people are rebellious and their act is rebellion. . . . Fourthly, you send out a force to stamp out rebellion; and fifthly, having spread bloodshed, confusion and anarchy, you declare with your hands uplifted to the heavens that moral reasons forced you to stay: for if you were to leave, this territory would be left in a condition which no civilized power could contemplate with equanimity or with composure.

—VISCOUNT JOHN MORLEY,
STATE SECRETARY FOR INDIA, 1905–1910,
summarizing the anger of Pashtun tribesmen;
quoted in C. F. Andrews, The Challenge of
the North West Frontier, *1937*

BLOODMONEY

MAKEEN, SOUTH WAZIRISTAN

This is Omar's last night in Makeen. He will have dinner with his family and then return to his computer laboratory in Islamabad, and his brothers Nazir and Karimullah will go back to their fighting. Arab guests who have taken refuge in Makeen will share their meal this night, and the malik will visit to say goodbye to "Ustad Omar," as they call him, the wise Omar who has visited places like Dubai and London, which the people of Makeen can barely imagine.

Omar and his youngest brother, Karimullah, have been walking in the high hills above the town before dinner. Omar is nearly forty, and a city man now, whose knees ache as he climbs the rocky escarpment and whose lungs gasp for breath when he stands atop the ridgeline, only the thorny shrubs of acacia for cover. Karimullah is nimble, too much so, his brother thinks, hardened to muscle and bone by the years of war in these mountains. The boy looks like a wolf: narrow-faced, relentless, ravenous for the kill.

Omar looks down from the ridge across the rock-strewn panorama of his valley. The tall pines soften the landscape; they cover the boulders and the ruined fields and the craters where the bombs have exploded. There is the slightest trickle in the riverbed that skirts the hillside; not enough water there to sustain anything except hatred. This is not my land, he thinks. Not anymore. Omar has escaped to another world that regards barren mountains as free-fire zones, and where social networks are not the intimate bond of tribe and blood, but things that come out of a machine.

They are descending the ridge now. Karimullah has his gun, as always, and he takes aim at a bird that has flushed from the brush and is careening toward them. The young man could shoot it in an instant, Karimullah never misses, but he puts the gun down and smiles at his brother: What is our quarrel with this bird?

Omar looks down the hillside again, at the fruit trees and vegetable gardens that his father has worked so hard to cultivate. I am the fruit, Omar thinks. I was nurtured in this place so that I could escape. All those afternoons as a boy, doing number games in the courtyard while his father, Haji Mohammed, wondered if there was something wrong with his oldest son; all those nights when he lay awake with the number puzzles illuminated in his mind like electric lights; all those mornings when he didn't know whom to tell: Those were the signposts to his flight. He had tried to explain it once to an American friend, what it had been like to be a boy in his village, and the man, a mathematician, too, had just laughed in incomprehension.

Karimullah whispers in his brother's ear. He has a secret. He takes the older man down a switchback in the trail, to an abandoned outpost of the Frontier Corps where the young warriors train. They have a simple shooting range to practice with their Kalashnikov rifles, and a room where they do exercises to make themselves strong. Omar tells his brother to be careful. These Americans are dangerous people. The attack on their towers in New York has made them crazy.

Yes, Karimullah knows. He and Nazir are not afraid of these half-men of America. He repeats a Pashtun saying that Haji Mohammed has taught his sons: "Who today is disgraced, tomorrow is lost."

They are almost home. Karimullah is running ahead now to tell their mother that they are back, so that she can prepare the meal. The light is dying in the afternoon. The mountains are pink where the sun hits the ridges and, in the shadows, deep purple and cherry-black. The sky is a cold dark blue; the moon is up, but the stars are not yet visible. Omar looks up by reflex. The sky is empty, he thinks, but then a ray of the disappearing sun catches something in the sky, a ping of light. He shouts to his younger brother, but he is too far ahead to hear now. The guests are already gathering; their trucks are parked in front of the walled compound.

It is impossible, Omar thinks. These demons will not harm my family. I have tried to help them. Even my brothers and the other fighters: What have they done to America?

Omar begins to run. He has been thinking about what he will say tonight to his father and his brothers, but now his subtle mind is no more capable of forming a thought than that of an animal on the run. He can hear the sound: It is the faint throb of an engine and he wants to think it is coming from town, down the road a few miles away, but it is sharper and more persistent. He looks up again, and he knows with the instinctual certainty of the hunted that the sound is coming from the sky, ten thousand feet above.

He cries out to his brother as he runs toward the walls that contained his life when he was a boy, and that now shelter his mother and sisters and the young children. Another truck is arriving for the dinner, kicking up dust, and Omar is wailing for his brother now as loud as he can, screaming for his attention. But it is too late; the light is gone, and each frame of time is too short. The whisper overhead has become the relentless hum of a giant indestructible insect.

Karimullah has stopped. He hears the sound, too, and he is looking to the sky. He raises his gun instinctively, but it is useless and he begins to run. The gates of the compound burst open and members of his family try to dash away, tumbling in their robes, calling on God. They are helpless. They cannot see what is overhead, but they sense it from the sound, and they experience the degradation of fear. Their bowels give way, they stumble and fall; the little ones put their hands over their ears, as if that will stop what is coming. Haji Mohammed does not run. He is a man; he walks slowly and deliberately from the compound, holding the hand of one of his guests.

Omar is on the ground now, and he sees the sudden shadow of a metal arrow darken the orchards. The fire dragon is descending, but he cannot hear its roar. It is moving faster than its sound. It is so quick, this last moment, no more than the blink of the eye and it is too late. The trees bend and the grass goes flat and the animals bellow for help, and the people of Omar's world are stopped in time.

The flash of detonation is white sulfur. The air is sucked into the mouth of the explosion and the fireball rises in an instant to the height of the surrounding mountains. The force of the explosion throws Omar into the air like a clod of dirt. He is unconscious for a time, and at first when he awakes, he cannot hear and cannot see and he thinks he must be dead. The world is white, and he is happy to be gone.

Pain tells him he is alive. Several bones are broken, and he is bleeding from many wounds. He begins to cough up dust and blood. When he opens his eyes, he sees that the world in which he was raised has been destroyed. Where his family compound stood is now rubble dotted by smoldering fires. He can see body parts a few yards from where he is lying, and he hears the cries of the wounded. He tries to stand, but he cannot support the weight.

Let me die, Omar thinks. But in the hours and days and years that follow, he has another thought that comes from his blood and sinews more than his mind: Let me have the honor that is badal, *the insult that answers the insult. He does not mean this in a general sense, but in a very particular way. The people who operate the drones, Omar knows very well, are from the Central Intelligence Agency. He knows too much about them. It is not enough to hate these people; he wants to have power over them and make them afraid.*

He does not take this revenge in the immediate, visceral way that his brother Karimullah might have done. He returns to the National University of Science and Technology. His physical wounds heal, and he does not discuss what happened in Makeen. He continues with his consulting work, too, for the IT departments of a bank in Dubai and another in Geneva. He maintains his other contacts abroad, with the friends he met in California. When people introduce him to foreigners, they say that he is a model for the future of the tribal areas: a gifted man, world-class, you could say, a young man from South Waziristan who shows that it is possible to escape the tribal code.

People address him as "ustad," *the learned one. But truly he is a ghost. He travels to the Persian Gulf and to Europe. He is so thin and fit he might run a marathon, or enter a monastery. He finds new friends who are useful to him. It is still many months before our story begins, but he is motivated by one thought: The people who think they are safe must know what it is to be hunted.*

1

ISLAMABAD

In the softening light of another afternoon, nearly two years later, the façade of the Inter-Services Intelligence headquarters looked almost welcoming. It was an anonymous gray stucco building in the Aabpara neighborhood of the capital, set back from the Kashmir Highway. The only distinctive feature was a ribbon of black stone that wrapped around the front, making it look as tidy as a gift box. Although the building was unmarked, the ISI's presence in the neighborhood was hardly a secret. Pakistanis in other branches of the military referred to its operatives as "the boys from Aabpara," as if they were a neighborhood gang to whom special respect must be paid. Ordinary Pakistanis made it a rule not to speak about the ISI at all.

Inside this house of secrets, facing onto an enclosed garden, was the office of the director general, who in recent years had been a soft-spoken man named Mohammed Malik. On his shoulders, he wore the crossed swords-and-crescent insignia of a lieutenant general. His authority didn't come from his rank in the army, but from his control of information. It was almost always the case that General Malik knew more than the people around him, but he made it a rule never to flaunt what he knew, or to disclose how he had obtained it. That would be insecure and, worse, impolite.

General Malik was not an imposing man, at least in the way of a military officer. He was trim, with a neat mustache, and he was careful about what he ate and drank, almost to the point of fastidiousness. He had soft hands, and a reticent manner. It was easy to forget that he was in fact a professional liar, who told the entire truth only to his commander, the chief of army staff.

On this particular spring afternoon, General Malik had a concern that he wasn't sure how to address. The brigadier who represented his service in Karachi had called to alert him to a potential problem. Now, there were large and small problems in Pakistan, but the very biggest ones were often connected to the words "United States of America." For it was said, not without reason, that Pakistan's life was bounded by the three A's—Allah, Army and America. And in the brigadier's news from Karachi, all three were tied up in one.

It was part of General Malik's aura among his colleagues at General Headquarters in Rawalpindi that he knew how to handle the Americans. This was based partly on the fact that he had spent a year at the Army War College in Fort Leavenworth, Kansas. And if you knew Kansas, people said, well, then, you knew the real America. Malik had actually disliked Kansas, and the only part of America that he had truly loved was the Rockies, where the thin air and the steep peaks reminded him of his ancestral home in the mountains of Kashmir. But he knew how to sham, in the way that is an art form for the people of South Asia, and so he had pretended for years to have a special fondness for Americans from the heartland.

In that spirit of sincere and also false bonhomie, the director general placed a call to Homer Barkin, the chief of the CIA station at the ever-expanding American Embassy in Islamabad. Their regular liaison meeting was scheduled for later in the week, but General Malik asked if his American partner might stop by that afternoon, perhaps right away, if it was convenient. He didn't explain why, for he had found that it is always a good rule to say less than you mean, particularly when you are dealing with Americans, who do the opposite.

"My friend Homer," said General Malik in greeting the chief of station when he arrived in Aabpara forty-five minutes later. He usually addressed him that way, and the American responded by calling him "my friend Mohammed," or sometimes, when he wanted something, just "my friend Mo." General Malik found that especially grating, but he never said anything. He clasped his visitor's hand in the firm way that Americans liked.

Barkin did not look well. His face was doughy, and he looked bulky in his suit jacket, like a sausage ready to burst its casing. General Malik knew why: Homer Barkin had been drinking, and the reason was that he had legal problems back home. He was one of the many CIA officers who had been caught in the boomerang effect of the "war on terror." It was said that he had "crossed the line" in a previous job by being overzealous in targeting the enemy.

Looking at Homer Barkin, his eyes dark from the sleeplessness of depression, his collar button straining against the flesh of his neck, it seemed unlikely that he had ever been capable of zealotry in any form. But this was the "after" picture; he would not have been made station chief in Islamabad if there had not been a "before."

"My dear friend Homer," the Pakistani continued, "I hope you will not mind me saying so, but you are looking a little tired. You must be working too hard."

"You don't know the half of it, believe me," said the CIA officer.

"No, indeed, I do not. Or even the quarter of it. And I am sorry for it, whatever it may be. But I hope that you will take care of yourself in these treacherous times. You are a guest in our house. You are precious to us."

"Appreciate it." Barkin's eyes were flat and his demeanor was impassive. He was not a man who was easily flattered or cajoled. "What's up, General?"

"Let me put it to you, sir: We have had many successes together in recent years, have we not? You could almost say that we are partners. Am I right? And so we like to think that there is a bit of trust between us, even though we are a poor and weak country compared to the United States. We have our pride, you see."

"I never forget that, Mohammed, not for one day."

"Well, then, I have a question for you. Normally, I would not trouble you in the late afternoon with such a detail, but this one is rather important. I hope you will forgive the imposition, and apologize to Mrs. Barkin for delaying your return home this evening."

"Mrs. Barkin lives in Washington, General. I don't know if I can give you an answer, but I won't tell you a lie."

General Malik smiled. Americans did not like lying to others. It made them uncomfortable. Their specialty was lying to themselves.

"Well, now, sir. Here it is: Are you running operations in Pakistan outside of your normal organization? Forgive me for being so blunt, but that is what I must ask."

Barkin cocked his head, as if he had ear trouble and wanted to make sure he'd heard it right. He might be old, but he wasn't stupid.

"Sorry, I didn't quite hear that, General. What do you mean?"

The Pakistani sat back in his chair. He put his hands together and closed his eyes for a moment. When he opened them, he spoke again, louder this time.

"Let me state the question as clearly as I can, sir: Is the United States sending intelligence officers into Pakistan outside the normal CIA cover channels? Is your agency doing it? Or is some other agency doing it? That is what I want to know: Are you running a new game against us? You see, we think that we know you well, but we hear rumblings of something that we do not know. And let us be honest: No ones likes to be surprised."

Barkin's mouth puckered as if he had just eaten something bad.

"Shit, Mohammed. You know I can't answer a question like that. I mean, hell, we run all sorts of operations, declared and undeclared, just like you do. We have agency employees at the embassy who conduct liaison with your service, and you know their names. But if I told you that we had no other presence in Pakistan, and no nonofficial officers, you know I'd be lying. But that's business, right? We don't look up your skirt, and we don't expect you to start looking up ours."

The American gave him a wink, as if they were two old poker players who knew the casino rules. But the Pakistani was not in a mood for professional courtesy.

"I am talking about something different, Homer. I know all about your NOCs. I could name a dozen for you. I know all about your 'forward-deployed military assets.' Perhaps I even know the names of your contractors, including the ones who work for other agencies, which you, my dear friend, are not supposed to know about. But this is different."

"Hey, Mohammed, I'm just a farm boy from Pennsylvania. I'm not getting it. You better tell me what you mean, straight up."

The Pakistani general sighed. He did not like to be so direct. It was awkward. But he had no choice.

"We have picked up signs of a new capability, Homer, with new missions. I cannot be more specific. But we see something coming toward us that we do not like. And I want you to know that. For, you know, we must protect ourselves."

Barkin shook his head again. He moistened his lips, as if to prepare the way for what he was about to say.

"I don't know what the hell you're talking about. We don't have any new capabilities. Not that I know about. Hell, we can't even manage the old ones we've got. You're barking up the wrong tree here, pal."

"I could call Cyril Hoffman at Headquarters and complain that you are an obstructionist and should come home. He would not be amused."

"Call whoever you like, Mohammed. I am telling you the truth."

General Malik studied his visitor, trying to decide whether he was believable. A ruined man is harder to read than a fresh, eager one. His lies could be tucked into the bags under his eyes, or hidden in the folds of flesh below his chin. It was hard to know, but if the general had been forced to make a wager, he would have bet that the American was telling the truth. Whatever was going on, he probably didn't know about it.

The Pakistani changed the subject. The ISI had gathered new evidence of Indian funding for the nationalist movement in Baluchistan. This was a most serious matter. General Malik would be sending a report, for transmittal to Langley. And he was very sorry, the new American requests for visas could not be approved at present. The two men talked for thirty minutes about such details, never returning to the subject that had vexed General Malik.

When the meeting was done, Homer Barkin shook the ISI chief's hand, not quite so heartily as before, and lumbered away. He was at the door when the general put his hand on the station chief's shoulder. Malik spoke quietly in parting, without his usual bob and weave.

"Be careful, my friend," said the Pakistani. "If you stick your fingers in new places, they may get cut off."

"Too late for that, Mohammed," said Barkin. "Whatever this is about, it's already done and gone. And it's not going to be my problem, anyway. It belongs to you, and somebody back home I don't even know."

The general had a walled garden next to his office, with a few square feet of well-tended grass, as green as a cricket pitch, and an honor guard of rosebushes that were soft pastels in the last light of the afternoon. When General Malik had a puzzle to solve, he liked to sit here alone, in a wooden Adirondack chair that he had bought years ago in the United States.

Malik entered his garden now, and installed himself in what he liked to call his thinking chair. He lit up a cigarette, one of the few indulgences he permitted himself. A steward emerged, clad in white gloves and military livery, and asked if he wanted anything to eat or drink, but the general shooed him away.

What were the Americans doing? It was hardly the first time General Malik had asked himself that question over the years, and there were other puzzles marked USA that he was trying to work out. But this time it had a special edge: The Americans were changing the rules of the game. They must think they were being clever in Washington, but they were walking into terrain where nobody could help them—not the general, not his agents, not their clandestine contacts. The Americans would blame Pakistan for their troubles, and in particular the general's own service, but they were the mischief-makers. They would get caught, and it would be their fault.

The general had a rule in life: Do not interrupt someone when he is making a mistake. Let others make their moves first, so that you can react and turn them to advantage. The general had his contacts; he would watch and wait. To say that the Pakistani was playing a double game did not do him justice; his strategy was far more complicated than that.

2

STUDIO CITY, CALIFORNIA

Sophie Marx was up before dawn. She had a phone date with one of her officers in London, a skittish man named Howard Egan who was heading for Karachi and wasn't happy about it. Marx was one of those people who had a knack for waking up just before the alarm sounded, even if it was five a.m., as if her eyelids were wired to a celestial timer. She rolled the width of the mattress to disarm the clock. Her big bed was empty, as usual. She was picky. She was still in her thirties, still in middle school in the secret world, but one of her discoveries as she had grown older was that most things in life didn't measure up to their promise. Many women teach themselves to lie to get along, but Marx wasn't one of them.

She went for a quick run in her neighborhood of Sherman Oaks, striding past the stunted palm trees and the half-green lawns, and then showered and dressed for work. She had a face and body that were easy to take care of: long, jet-black hair that framed a face that was the soft, thin color of skim milk. She had just wisps of eyebrows that arched naturally in a way that looked mischievous, even when she was serious. When she wore her shirts unbuttoned a notch, she looked like a tomboy rather than a tease.

She pulled from her closet a simple pair of jeans and a tailored black-leather jacket from Yves Saint Laurent in Paris that had cost her nearly two thousand euros. She added a pair of black boots; they made her look tall and leggy, even though she was just five-foot-four. She buzzed open the garage next to her small house and climbed into her big car. It was a black Cadillac Escalade with smoked windows, which she called, with relish, the "pimpmobile."

Driving down Ventura Boulevard in the gray light before sunrise, Marx made a mental checklist of what she had to do that day. There was Egan. He didn't like going to Pakistan, but nobody did anymore. She needed to remind him, straight up. This was why the operation in Los Angeles had come into existence: to allow deep-cover officers to go where they couldn't go, and do what they couldn't do. Of course Egan was nervous; that would keep him safe. She rehearsed the speech in her mind.

The light was turning yellow at Woodman Avenue. There was nobody around, but Marx slowed to a stop anyway. She was still thinking about Egan. She would have to hand him off soon to another case officer. He would be upset about that, too, probably. She would wait until he returned from Pakistan to tell him about her promotion. She had been named "chief of counterintelligence," though it wasn't clear what that meant in her little shop. There was no organization chart. Her boss, Jeffrey Gertz, was making it up as he went along. That was what Marx liked about the Los Angeles experiment. It was fresh. They got to make new mistakes.

The light was turning green. In the next lane was a red pickup on struts, with two stoners in the cab who had obviously been up all night drinking. The driver of the truck, an hombre in a turned-around Dodgers cap, was leering at her. Marx gunned the Escalade off the line and didn't look back until she'd made it to Coldwater Canyon.

Marx parked her car in the basement and took the elevator up to the third floor, where she badged in with the overnight security guard. He gazed at her with heavy-lidded eyes; he still had a half hour left before his shift ended, but he looked cooked.

"Wake up, Chuck," she said. "The sun's coming up."

She went to her small office and turned on the lights. On the wall was a framed poster from the movie *Thelma and Louise*, which showed Geena Davis and Susan Sarandon in their convertible, being chased by police cars as they were about to drive off a cliff. Above the image were the words: "Somebody said get a life . . . so they did." On her shelf was a doll wearing sunglasses and a trench coat, with a tag that said "CIA Barbie," which a friend had given her years before when she graduated from the Career Trainee class.

Marx used a Skype connection to call Howard Egan at the hedge fund in London that provided his cover. The name of the firm was Alphabet Capital, and it managed many billions of dollars, but Marx had never understood just how it worked: how much of it was real, and how much was a cover for intelligence operations. She had asked Egan once, and he had said not to worry: The only person who really knew was the owner of Alphabet Capital, a man named Thomas Perkins, and he wouldn't talk if his pants were on fire.

Marx tried to sound enthusiastic as she went through her list of bullet points with Egan. He answered grumpily, giving brief responses to each. When she finished her script, there was a pause.

"I hate this trip," Egan said. "It's insecure."

"It will be fine," Marx answered. "Stop worrying. You are exactly what it says on your business card. So chill out: We have your back."

Egan laughed at the attempt to dispel his anxiety.

"Great," he said. "Now tell me, who has my front?"

He was talking himself into paralysis. Marx had seen it before with colleagues. Once you let yourself start to worry, the floodgates opened.

"Suck it up," she said. "Call me when you're out. Anything else, call the ops center. Are we cool?"

"We're cold," said Egan. "Freezing."

"Out, here," said Marx, as if she were ending a radio transmission. There was nothing more to say.

"Out," responded Egan gloomily.

And that was it. She didn't think about him the rest of the day. He would get through it somehow, because people always did. She thought about writing a note to Gertz, her boss, suggesting that it was time to reassign Egan to something a little less stressful. People began to arrive soon after, and Marx fell into the atonal melody of office life.

The sign out front of the building where Sophie Marx worked said that it was the headquarters of The Hit Parade LLP, a firm that according to its

Dun & Bradstreet profile sold international music and television rights, negotiated licensing agreements and organized trade shows on the side. That explained the office in the Valley, big and roomy, but cheap, too. It explained the contacts with dozens of small firms and their peripatetic representatives, always flying off to strange locations. And it explained the constant stream of international calls and email messages.

"Hit Parade—we've got what's hot." That was the way Marx answered the phone, if anyone ever called her number at the office. The name made it sound like she worked with the Beach Boys and Sandra Dee. She had business cards, too, with a dummy switchboard number that never answered, which she sometimes gave to men in bars who were annoying.

Marx knew the short history of the place, the founding "myth," you might say. Like so many other things about America, The Hit Parade was an aftershock of September 11, 2001. The CIA had been sent off to war, and then a few years later it had been sent to the stocks for a public bashing, when people decided they didn't like the nasty parts of what the intelligence agencies had been asked to do. That left people at Headquarters feeling demoralized and unloved; agency veterans tried to stay out of trouble by doing the slow roll, which only made things worse. Eventually a new administration took office, and the potentates said, in effect, why are we torturing ourselves? Let the old CIA tramp steamer rust away at the dock, and meanwhile we'll launch a stealthy new speedboat.

The White House had called it "new think," as opposed to the witless "old think" that had come before. There was a mantra, among the handful of people who knew about the project: The world had changed; an intelligence service couldn't operate out of embassies when it was trying to recruit people who wanted to blow up embassies. Technology enabled a new clandestine structure. A secure communications system, which used to require an embassy code room, could now be put on a laptop, or even a BlackBerry.

They told new staff members like Marx that the new president loved the idea. He wanted to be a change agent, so he had decided to change the most reviled three-letter acronym in town. The chairmen of the two congressional intelligence committees had signed on, and so had the handful of other people who were briefed on the idea. The few who knew about it accepted the absolute necessity that it be a secret and deniable activity. The old system was a train wreck, so they had created something truly new—floated it free from the wreckage and hid it where no one would ever think to look.

The president turned over liaison with this new organization to his chief of staff, Ted Yazdi, a combative former investment banker who loved secrets and, in another life, might have been an intelligence officer himself. Yazdi managed the operation out of the White House. He never put anything in writing; he never told anyone other than the president what he was doing.

Headquarters didn't like it, but they couldn't stop it. They proposed that the new unit focus on the dirty work the traditionalists didn't much like, anyway—"special activities," otherwise known as covert action. So in addition to the existing stations abroad, an array of new "platforms" was built for a cadre of nonofficial-cover officers and their laptops. The platforms had to connect up somewhere. The old boys wanted someplace close, like Fredericksburg or Rockville, where they could keep the great experiment from getting out of hand. But for once, the advocates of change had their way.

It was decided that the base for this new network should be far from Washington. Consideration was given to Denver, San Francisco, Las Vegas and even Charleston, West Virginia—which just happened to be the hometown of a key member of the congressional leadership. But finally a decision was made to locate the hub in Los Angeles, in a staggeringly ordinary office building in the San Fernando Valley, heretofore famous as the home of America's pornographic movie industry. The building they chose had been the headquarters of a mortgage-lending company that had gone bust before the agency bought it through a series of cutouts.

To keep an eye on this experiment, Headquarters selected one of its crustiest old secret warriors, a man named Cyril Hoffman. He was the associate deputy director, the all-but-invisible number three position in the agency, and a man famous for keeping his head down. Hoffman was an eccentric who liked to collect first editions of British nineteenth-century novels, and whose iPod playlist featured modern operas by Philip Glass. He had a habit of humming when he was on the telephone and, occasionally, when he was in meetings. People who didn't know Hoffman thought that he was a crank. That was a mistake.

Sophie Marx joined up because she was bored with her fancy job at Headquarters—and decided that she liked the iconoclastic man who had been chosen to run the new organization. His name was Jeffrey Gertz, and he was already something of a legend among younger officers.

Gertz had started his ascent in Morocco, making himself indispensable to the crown prince who later became king. Then he had gone into Baghdad in 2002, before the war, under paper-thin cover as an Eastern European diplomat. He had been a one-man station—planting listening devices, affixing infrared beacons to guide the bombers, recruiting and running agents. He had operated like it was 1943 in occupied France and he was working for the OSS. Young officers who were in the loop began trading stories about him: Have you heard what Gertz has done *now*?

The best of it was that he rarely asked permission. As the invasion of Iraq was about to begin, Gertz requested "lethal authority" from Headquarters—meaning that he could assassinate Iraqi targets of opportunity. The seventh floor was in a dither and asked for an opinion from the general counsel, but Gertz went ahead anyway. He had terminated two senior officials when he got retroactive permission, after the president heard about his exploits and said he wanted to give Gertz a medal.

Headquarters regarded Gertz as a troublemaker, but his reputation was made among the field officers. He went to the Counterterrorism Center after Baghdad, where he ran special access programs that nobody ever talked about. To stay out of trouble, he made friends with a few key senators and representatives on the Hill. He gave private briefings to the new president's advisers during the transition. He had pushed all the right buttons, so when the White House decided to launch its bold new experiment, Gertz was in the right position.

Gertz had interviewed Marx in Los Angeles. She was one of several hundred people he tapped as possible candidates for the new unit. It was like being recruited by the CIA all over again. You didn't apply; you were asked to appear at a clandestine location for an interview. When she met Gertz, Marx was initially prepared to dislike him. She had heard tales about his exploits and his reputation for arrogance, and she had known enough CIA macho men to last a lifetime.

But as they talked, she warmed to his pitch. He'd read into her record. He knew what she had accomplished in Beirut, and how she had been pulled out by a division chief who lost his nerve. He told her that she had been vegetating the past two years in a high-status, low-impact job at Headquarters that most other people thought was a big deal.

"You really need a change," Gertz had told her. "If it isn't this job, then I hope you find something else before you go stale."

That did it. Marx knew that he was right. She was becoming a glorified "reports officer," doing the same bland, facile work she had been given when she started at the agency. That was what the agency did with smart women: It made them managers and pushed them up the promotion ladder. It was a kind of repressive tolerance. Pretty soon they weren't fit for real operations anymore, and they weren't given an opportunity. They fell uphill.

Gertz offered the chance to take risks again. In the moment, Marx found that irresistible. A month later, she was settling into her new digs in Sherman Oaks and commuting in the pimpmobile to Studio City.

"Entertainment Is Our Business" was the logo on Marx's new business card, just below the big letters that said: "The Hit Parade." That was a lie, generically. But it was especially untrue on the day that she helped Howard Egan prepare for his trip to Pakistan.

3
KARACHI

In the early glow of the next morning, on the approach to Jinnah International Airport, Howard Egan had a momentary sense of vertigo. The horizon seemed to vanish for an instant, indistinguishable between the blue wash of the Arabian Sea and the white haze of the sky. He stared out the window, looking for the line of separation. This was supposed to be his space, this nowhere land that was like disappearing into a vapor cloud. But today it spooked him. It was too bright outside. The other passengers were looking at him, wondering who he was. And he hadn't hit passport control yet.

Egan had told his handlers in Los Angeles that he didn't want to do the Karachi run again. On his last trip, he had been so sure he was being followed that he had aborted two meetings. Jeffrey Gertz had told him that maybe he should come home, but he didn't mean it. Later, he had sent Egan a message: *There is one thing about winners. They win.* That meant that he should go to Karachi or leave the service.

Egan knew the mantra of invisibility: He did not exist. He had a passport, but it was false. He had distinct features, hair and eyes, but they had been altered. He had a job and business cards and mailing addresses, but they were all imaginary. His cell phones were all clean. He was part of a government organization that could not be found on any chart or budget in Washington. For him, there was only the lie. There was no truth for anyone to find.

And that was how it was supposed to work that spring morning in Karachi: The truth about Howard Egan should have been hidden from anyone outside a tiny circle. The only person at Alphabet Capital who knew his real identity was his nominal boss there, Thomas Perkins.

Egan made his way through the slow chicane of passport control and customs. He didn't look at the customs officers, and he didn't look away, either. There was a momentary commotion off to his left, as an inspector pulled aside an ink-black traveler from Sri Lanka. Egan kept walking, and in a moment he was past the glass and into the snarl of hotel barkers and family greeters who lay on the other side of customs.

In the white concrete atrium of the terminal it was hot and stuffy, with too many watchers and too many opportunities for surveillance. Egan wanted to get to his hotel. He looked for his driver in the host of eager faces and eventually found a man with a sign that misspelled his name: ORGAN. That brought a smile, even on this day of dread. The driver took Egan's bag and wheeled it toward the parking lot with the dignified air of a man who, for a few moments, had a purpose in life.

Egan was a compact man in his late thirties, struggling to keep trim as he moved from hotel to hotel. His appearance changed with his assignments, but the constant feature was his soft mouth, almost a Gerber baby mouth, with lips that turned upward slightly at the corners. The softness should have been worn away, now that Egan had been traveling for more than a year for the new outfit. But he was still raw skin. The more runs he made, the more he was an army of one.

Egan arrived at the Sheraton on Club Road. He had considered staying at the Pearl, a Pakistani hotel that was less obvious. But the Sheraton had a spa and a good Italian restaurant and room service that allowed him to order booze. So Egan had booked his reservation, using his personal expense code. He had stayed at the Sheraton once before, under the same name. That would be a protection, unless they had made him the last time.

At the front desk, he didn't recognize any of the clerks, but eventually a man in a natty blazer came out from the back office and offered a limp handshake and said, "Welcome back, Mr. Egan."

He went to his room and unpacked, hanging up his extra suit and putting his other clothes in the drawers. He was fussy that way, maintaining the same routine in every city. He unpacked his life as if he could control it, drawer by drawer: T-shirts, boxer shorts, socks, all in the right place.

Egan removed the laptop from his briefcase and plugged in the Ethernet cable. He scrolled the news, and then opened the VPN connection to check his email from The Hit Parade in Los Angeles. They had mastered the art of digital camouflage. In the new service, your covert life existed in the cloud of the Internet, to be accessed whenever needed but never downloaded into the here and now.

Sophie Marx didn't have anything new for him. The meeting was still set for fourteen hundred the next afternoon. No change in the ops plan, no change in the security status, no change in the authorities or rules of engagement. Egan logged off and tried not to think about tomorrow. That meeting was in another space, beyond the vertiginous horizon.

Howard Egan had come to Karachi to meet Hamid Akbar, a Pakistani banker who was a nominal client of Alphabet Capital. Anyone who read the emails they had been exchanging would see that Egan was there to promote a new Alphabet fund that invested in distressed real estate assets in North America and Europe. If anyone had asked questions, Egan would have referred them to Mr. Perkins, the chief executive officer of Alphabet Capital.

The real story of Hamid Akbar was more complicated. Twelve years before, he had been recruited as an "asset" by the Central Intelligence Agency. He was spotted when he was an engineering student at the University of Baltimore, and formally pitched a year later, before he went home to Pakistan. He was a Pashtun, which caught the CIA's interest, even back then.

But Akbar had broken off contact with the agency soon after his return. He said that the relationship was insecure. The Pakistani security authorities would easily discover his covert connection, and they would imprison him. His CIA handler was sympathetic: He suggested that the agency might be in touch later, when he had cooled off, but for nearly a decade they had left the Pakistani alone.

Then one day, roughly a year ago, Hamid Akbar had received a visit from an American who had initially introduced himself as an investment adviser, Howard Egan. Egan had proposed a different sort of relationship, with an American entity that had no name or formal existence. It was an offer so lucrative that the Pakistani could not refuse—dared not refuse—and so he had returned to the secret fold.

Where did Akbar's name come from? Gertz had him on a list of prospects; he never said how it was assembled. Gertz gave Egan a Pashtun proverb to share with Akbar at the first meeting: *Awal zaan resto jahan*. First yourself, then the universe. Gertz didn't say where he got that gem, either.

Akbar's value as an asset lay in his family contacts. His uncle was a leader of one of the Darwesh Khel clans that ruled the western border. Like many tribal chiefs, this uncle had become a bit soft and citified, coasting along on rents and levies. The political officer of the South Waziristan agency took him for granted, and so did the Interior Ministry, the Frontier Corps and Inter-Services Intelligence. That made him an ideal target: He was an influential man whose value had been overlooked by others.

"Uncle Azim" was the name Akbar used for his well-connected relative, or sometimes the honorific "Azim Khan." At Egan's request, the two Pakistanis had traveled to Abu Dhabi for a get-acquainted meeting. The American had outlined the financial benefits of a relationship; what Gertz told Egan to request in return was help in pacifying the border areas. Uncle Azim asked for several months to think about it.

And now it was time. Akbar was to arrange a rendezvous spot. Gifts would be exchanged.

Jeff Gertz loved the operation. It was a demonstration of what his new organization could do. Some of the old-timers who had joined The Hit Parade worried that the plan was half-baked, but Gertz insisted that it was solid. Somebody just needed to deliver the loot. He told his colleagues the same bromide he had offered to Egan: The thing about winners is that they know how to win.

Gertz was a winner, for sure. Egan was afraid of him, but he did as he had been instructed.

Egan called Hamid Akbar's office to confirm the next day's meeting. There was a delay as the Pakistani came on the line.

He coughed before he said a word. "I am sorry," said the Pakistani. "There is a problem tomorrow. It is not convenient."

Egan's palm was damp as he held the phone, waiting.

The Pakistani came back, cheerier.

"Could you come to see me tonight at Habib Bank Plaza? It will be cooler." He sounded a bit flustered, or tired, or perhaps it was just Egan's imagination.

"Can we do the business tonight?" pressed Egan. "It can't wait."

"Yes, I think so." Akbar coughed again, a dry cough as if something were caught in his throat. "Wait one moment. I will check."

The Pakistani made a call on another phone.

Egan didn't like it. He wanted to stop, right there. Check out of the Sheraton and catch a flight to anywhere. He hated any changes in the agreed routine.

Akbar came back on the line. His voice was thin, stretched. "This evening is fine," he said. "Come to my office at seven o'clock."

Egan deliberated what to do, but only for a moment. He couldn't just break it off. What possible excuse could he give to his superiors in Los Angeles? Even Sophie Marx would think he had panicked.

"I'll be there, and then, you know . . ." Egan let the words trail off so that the silence encompassed the rest of the plan.

When the call was over, he sent a BlackBerry message to the operations room, telling the duty officer that the timetable had been moved up. It was the middle of the night in Los Angeles. Would anyone at The Hit Parade even care?

Egan took a fitful nap and then went to the hotel gym. He spent nearly an hour on the elliptical trainer, watching a cricket match on the little television to take his mind off what was ahead. It was a one-day international against South Africa. The star batsman for Pakistan looked like a mullah, with a woolly beard and no mustache. He was bowled out, leg before wicket, just shy of his half-century.

Egan went over to the free weights. A fleshy Turk was using the bench, but he went away when Egan picked up the barbells.

His mind wandered as he lay on the bench between repetitions. He was supposed to go to the Lake District the next weekend with his girlfriend. He had booked a room at an expensive inn. Had he spent too much? Should he buy London property before the markets took off again? Was his hair thinning in the back? How many more reps should he do with the barbells to be tired enough to sleep that night?

When Egan returned to his room, he saw that it had been tossed. The hard drive of the computer had been drilled. That, at least, was predictable; they hit the laptops of most Western travelers. Egan showered and lay on the bed in his boxers for a while, watching more cricket. The South Africans were batting now. It was a soothing game, normally, all that green grass and so little action, but today he had the butterflies. His bowels were soft, and he hadn't eaten anything in Pakistan yet.

4
KARACHI

The afternoon was burning itself out in the old quarter of the city known as Saddar Town. The pink hazy light of dusk suffused the stucco buildings, but it would be gone before long. Howard Egan took a taxi to Mohammad Ali Jinnah Road, a mile north of the hotel, and wandered around the market where the old textile weavers hawked their goods. He didn't turn to look for watchers, not even once. That was the hardest part before a meeting, to suppress the instinctual desire to see who might be following you.

Egan surveyed the old stock exchange; garlands of twinkling bulbs were draped from the roof like strings of pearls. To the southeast, past the "salty gate" of Kharadar, a half-moon was rising over the Arabian Sea. Pedestrians were spilling into the road, careening away like gulls at the approach of every car.

On the main streets, under the glare of the streetlights, the merchants and beggars were shouting for attention, and the car drivers were squawking their horns. But in the lee of the traffic, in the old shop stalls, there was a muffled quiet and you could hide yourself, as if in the folds of time.

The briefcase was heavy on Egan's shoulder, and he was beginning to sweat through his shirt. That wouldn't do. He sat in an air-conditioned coffeehouse on Jinnah Road until he had cooled off. At six-thirty he hailed a cab and traveled down Chundrigar Road to the Habib Bank Tower. Once, this had been Pakistan's tallest building; but after thirty years of baking in the sun while other giant buildings sprouted nearby, it had become just another ziggurat of bleached concrete.

Egan sat in the air-conditioned lobby to cool off, and a few minutes before seven, he took the elevator to the eighteenth floor. Hamid Akbar's secretary nodded in humble recognition. Egan had visited only a few months before. Akbar came out of the office to greet him.

"How do you do? How do you do?" Akbar took the American's hand. "Beastly weather."

Akbar was sweating, too. There were damp crescents under the arms of his tan suit, and the top of his shirt collar was moist. Well, why not? It was June. His face was soft and pudgy in the cheeks. He didn't wear a mustache. He looked like the sort of ambitious young man who might join the Karachi chapter of the Young Presidents Organization: a man who wanted to meet foreigners, exchange business cards. He was a generation removed from the heat and dust.

Egan began his patter about Alphabet Capital's new fund. It was called Oak Leaf II. Its predecessor, Oak Leaf I, was doing splendidly. Second-quarter returns could top 30 percent, on an annualized basis. It was an excellent new opportunity for clients such as Mr. Akbar.

"Tip-top," said the Pakistani. "Very impressive, I am sure."

Akbar listened politely to the rest of the presentation, but he was distracted. When Egan finished, there was an awkward pause.

"It's just that I am a bit strapped now," said Akbar. "It's not possible."

Akbar cleared his throat. He opened his desk drawer and removed a piece of paper, which he pushed across the teak desktop toward Egan. It had an address in a suburban district of northwest Karachi. "11-22 Gilani Buildings, Sector 2, Baldia Town." Below that was a time. "2100."

Egan studied the paper and committed the information to memory. He took his pen from his coat pocket and wrote on the note:

"Tonight?"

Akbar nodded. He let the paper sit. He didn't want to touch it. Egan pointed toward the message and crossed his hands in an X. *Get rid of it.* Akbar took the note and excused himself. Thirty seconds later there was the sound of a flush, and the Pakistani emerged from the toilet adjoining his office. He had combed his hair, but you could see the beads of sweat on his scalp.

Egan went back to his investment pitch. He talked about flexible minimums and alternative investments, just to finish out the time for anyone who might be listening. The Pakistani looked relieved when it was over.

Egan took the first taxi in the queue outside Habib Tower Plaza. He settled into the musty cabin of the Hyundai and pulled his BlackBerry from the briefcase. He sent the rendezvous address to the operations room in Los Angeles. They wouldn't like that neighborhood. It skirted Ittehad Town, the district where migrants from the tribal areas had settled.

Gertz's people wouldn't have time to organize surveillance, but at least they would know where he was. Egan typed the coordinates into his BlackBerry and obtained a Google map. The address was thirty minutes away in evening traffic, not counting the surveillance detection run. He would just make it by nine.

The safe house where he would meet Uncle Azim was in a different district, to the east of downtown, near the university. If everything went right, he and the Darwesh Khel clan leader would get there around ten. Bottles of whiskey and cartons of cigarettes had been stashed away in the hideout weeks before.

Egan rode the taxi down Mohammad Ali Jinnah Street past the MCB Tower. A black sedan was cruising behind, two car lengths' distant. It turned when Egan's taxi did. The American exited the cab and walked back to the shopping mall. He entered the lower arcade, took the elevator up one flight, then a staircase down, and then left the building by a different route and flagged another taxi. A few minutes later he stopped and made another switch, using the arcade by the railway station.

Egan was habituated to the manic ballet of these surveillance detection runs: Back and forth, in and out, never looking behind or over your shoulder, or doing anything that betrayed the reality that you were concerned that someone might be following you. An SDR was like the dust baths taken by desert rodents, who rolled themselves in the sand to blot up the grit. It was getting dirty that made you clean.

Egan had authority to break off the run if he sensed danger. They always said that: You don't need proof that something is wrong; someone looks at you cross-eyed, bam, that's enough. Stop the run and skip the meet. The ops plan always had a fallback, and if you missed that, too, so what?

Gertz loved to say it: Safety first, brother. If it feels wrong, it is wrong. Bail out. But he didn't mean it. If you aborted too many meetings, people began to suspect that you were getting the shakes. You were having "operational issues." Which meant it was time to send out someone younger, who hadn't lost the protective shell of stupidity that allows you to believe, in a strange city, that you have vanished into thin air.

Egan tried to will himself into imbecility: Be the taxi. Be the briefcase. But he could hear his pulse in his eardrums, and he was sweating again. His chest was tight, the same way it had been on the last Karachi run. "We need big hearts." That was another of Gertz's admonitions. Egan's heart was ready to bust.

Gertz was right: He was losing it. He had stopped believing and started thinking. He wasn't a winner. He had a small heart.

Egan wasn't supposed to look behind, but he did. He could feel the surveillance, like a laser on the back of his head. And when he looked, he saw the same black sedan that had been following him earlier, near the MCB Tower. The driver looked different now, different clothes, anyway, but they would do that. He knew he should break off the run right there. He had the authority. And it hadn't felt right all day: Pieces were out of focus, or in the wrong place.

Egan's taxi was an old Toyota Corolla with a Koran on the dashboard and baubles hanging from the rearview mirror to keep away the evil eye. The driver was wearing a knit prayer cap, like everyone else in this Allah-dazed city. The seat cushions were threadbare. The metal springs pressed against his bottom.

The driver was lighting up a cigarette. Two boys were cursing each other in the street. "*Gandu*!" said one, using the local slang that means, colloquially, "You faggot!" "*Bahinchod*," roared back the other. "Sister fucker."

Egan was claustrophobic. He told the taxi driver to stop. His forehead was bathed in sweat. He opened the door, then closed it again. The driver was asking for directions. Come on, think: What were his options? He could get out of the car. He could take another taxi back to the hotel, and be on the plane the next morning.

What address? the driver was demanding again. The little bastard wanted his money.

What would it be? Egan closed his eyes. There was no quitting this one, not now. It was too late, too many plans, too much momentum. He formed the words, just as he had memorized them: 11-22 Gilani Buildings, Sector 2, Baldia Town. He rasped out the address to the greedy driver, and the cab pulled away.

Egan never made it to the pickup site. He just vanished. Overhead surveillance didn't have a fix on him in the jumble of traffic. Headquarters confirmed from the reconnaissance log later that he had never arrived at the rendezvous. His contact, Azim Khan, had been there waiting for him, right where he was supposed to be in Baldia Town. Overhead showed the Pakistani arriving a little before nine. He waited until after eleven and then left in his chauffeured Mercedes back to his villa in a posh suburb. What did it mean that the Darwesh Khel leader had shown up for the meet? Nobody could be sure then, or for a while after.

They tried to find Egan all night and into the next day. They mobilized a paramilitary rescue team from Bagram, ready to shoot the shit out of everyone in the effort to find him, but they never got close. The Pakistani police were given the GPS coordinates from his BlackBerry, which indicated that he was in Ittehad Town north of the city center. The police moved quickly into that raw neighborhood, but all they found was the phone. It had apparently been discarded on the run, thrown into a dumpster, where the police fished it out.

They never found Egan's body. It was just gone. That was all you could say. A photo surfaced on a jihadist website, showing a man strapped to a table. There was a cloth over his mouth, and you could see a hand holding an earthen jug, pouring a cascade of water down the man's throat.

They couldn't be sure that it was Egan, or even an American. There was just a glimpse of one of his eyes, contorted by suffering and the instant of agony in which the picture was taken. He was dressed in an orange T-shirt. What you could see of the body were the marks from the cigarette burns and the gruesomely precise cuts of the hacksaw. People who saw the picture never forgot it.

5

STUDIO CITY, CALIFORNIA

Jeffrey Gertz spent his last minutes of ignorance in his car, driving over the mountains to work from an appointment with his dentist in Beverly Hills. That was what made him late. The operations center hadn't wanted to call him until they were sure they had a problem, what with the twelve-hour time difference from Pakistan. And then, when the ops center tried, they couldn't reach him. So he didn't get the news that Howard Egan was missing until he got to work. Gertz fired the watch officer later, as if it had been his fault.

It was a June morning, the air so clear and fluffy it might have been run through the washer-dryer. Gertz steered his shiny red Corvette through the downward slope of Coldwater Canyon, chewing sugarless gum and listening to a military history audiobook on the car stereo. It was just past nine, and the sun was streaming into the San Fernando Valley. He was listening to *An Army at Dawn*, the first volume of Rick Atkinson's history of World War II. When he was done, he would buy the second volume and listen to that, too. Like every warrior, he wanted a good war.

The cassette ended as he neared Ventura Boulevard. The only sound in the car now was the air-conditioning and the murmur of traffic. Gertz let his mind wander. Maybe The Hit Parade needed a motto, he mused. Every successful organization had one, including secret organizations.

"The invisibles: We deliver" . . . or: "The shadow service: Reinventing intelligence." He thought about it, and wondered if maybe he should order up a secret logo, as well, with something spooky like a half-moon or a lightning bolt and no words, no explanation at all.

Gertz had a face that was all angles: raised cheekbones; a firm chin; sharp eyes. He had started wearing a goatee a few years ago, to soften his appearance and make him look less like an Army Ranger. He had short brown hair, trimmed once a month by a stylist in Beverly Hills. He had stopped challenging colleagues to do push-ups on the office floor a few years before, but that was mainly because a superior had advised him it was offensive to women and would hurt his career.

Gertz's nickname had been "Killer" when he joined the agency fifteen years before. People who met him back then weren't sure whether he had acquired the name because he had actually killed someone, or because he was so ambitious. He had tried to tone down his tough-guy image when he moved to Los Angeles, and had even sought the advice of a wardrobe consultant at a clothier on Rodeo Drive. That was characteristic of Gertz. He studied everything. He wanted to get it right.

Today Gertz was dressed in a royal-blue blazer, a blue so bright it reminded you of a Caribbean cruise, with an open-neck black shirt and a pair of light charcoal slacks. He looked like one of the thousands of people in West Los Angeles who prospered through some connection with what was called "the industry." When he gave people his card that said "The Hit Parade: Entertainment Is Our Business," it was almost believable.

When Gertz reached Ventura Boulevard, he turned right at the Ralphs Supermarket. A few shoppers were plodding toward the door. They looked like they hadn't slept all night. He put in a new cassette. The Allies were on their way to Kasserine Pass.

Sophie Marx was at the office when the news came in from Karachi. She had been at home, trying to get some rest, calling the operations room every few hours to check on Howard Egan's progress. The watch officer called her when they got the message about the meeting being moved up a day. After that, she couldn't sleep, so she had come on back. It wasn't a premonition, exactly, but she knew how worried Egan had been about the trip. She had told him everything would be fine, but in the middle of the night, in her bed in Sherman Oaks, she had remembered what it felt like to be alone in a city where people would kill you, for a certainty, if they knew who you were. That was when she decided to come in.

"Call Gertz," she said when it was clear that something had happened. The watch officer tried his cell, but by then he was at the dentist's. It wasn't anybody's fault, but this was a day when things went wrong.

Marx waited for the boss with other senior officers who had gathered outside his office on the fifth floor. She was the most junior member of this group. It was only a week before that Gertz had asked her to run counterintelligence for the little organization. The senior staff wasn't a talky group, even on a good day. They had all spent too many years keeping their mouths shut. The head of Support, a man named Tommy Arden, asked if there was any news yet from the "Death Star," by which he meant Headquarters. Several people answered no.

Gertz emerged from the elevator with his usual fixed smile, but it vanished in an instant. The watch officer was waiting for him, hovering awkwardly by the elevator door. His name was Julian and he wore an earring. The operations chief, Steve Rossetti, was lurking a little farther on, with the nervous eye of a man who didn't want to be blamed, along with Arden, the head of Support. Marx wasn't in the inner circle; she stood farther off. But she was Egan's contact, so in a sense it was her problem.

"What's going on?" Gertz asked. "This looks like a suicide watch."

"It's Howard Egan," said the watch officer.

"What about him? He's in Karachi."

"He's gone missing. He was supposed to be at a meeting nearly an hour ago, but we can't find him."

"What are you talking about? That meet is tomorrow. Isn't that right, Steve?"

He turned to the operations chief, who was older than Gertz by about ten years and whose body was as lumpy as Gertz's was fit. He had been in the ops job three months. The rumor was that he had been sent by Langley to keep an eye on Gertz.

"Change of plans, apparently. Sophie's read the traffic." He turned to Marx.

She stepped forward, toward the boss. She was trying not to think that this was her fault.

"The asset wanted to change the meeting time," she said. "Egan messaged us about six hours ago to say that it had been moved up. He was supposed to be there at nine p.m., Karachi time—nine a.m. our time. But he missed the meet." She looked at her watch. "He's now almost an hour past due."

"Call his BlackBerry. Tell him he's late. Ask him where the hell he is."

"We did that. No answer."

"Flash message?"

"No answer."

Gertz stroked his goatee as he pondered the possibility that this wasn't just a screw-up.

"What about the asset he's supposed to be pitching? The tribal guy."

"The asset is waiting for Egan, at the place they agreed. There's just no Egan."

"Have you called the access agent, the Pakistani who set this up?

"Yes, sir," said Marx. "His crypt is AC/POINTER, true name is Hamid Akbar. And yes, we've tried that. He isn't answering his phone, either."

Gertz shook his head. This day had started off so reasonably. The bad news didn't fit.

"Maybe Egan is spooked," he said. "He got the jitters the last time he was in Karachi, aborted two meetings. Maybe the same thing happened this time. He's just freaking out somewhere, having a drink and looking at shadows."

"Maybe, but we don't think so," said Rossetti, the operations chief. "We're still tracking his BlackBerry signal. It's been on the move for the last two hours, plus. He's just not answering."

Gertz shook his head. The room was quiet. He looked at Rossetti.

"Christ. This is bad."

"I'm afraid so."

Gertz stared at the floor, trying to compose himself. The color had drained from his face. It was almost as if he were embarrassed that something had gone wrong. His people weren't supposed to make mistakes. They had big hearts. There was a dead quiet, which Rossetti filled.

"What's Egan's cover job?" asked the operations chief. It wasn't on his cheat sheet. He was new. He still didn't know most of the network.

Gertz was still looking at the floor, stroking that goatee some more. Marx broke the silence.

"He works for a hedge fund in London called Alphabet Capital. The only person there who's witting is the chief executive."

"Perkins," said Gertz. "His name is Thomas Perkins."

"That's not very secure," said Rossetti. "Why doesn't Egan have his own platform?"

Gertz frowned. He didn't like being quizzed by his operations chief.

"He's a legacy, Steve. Blame your friends at Headquarters. Where's Tommy? He can explain it."

Tommy Arden, who as head of Support was responsible for organizing cover, scurried forward.

"He was a holdover from the old NOC group," said Arden. "We got him from the Global Deployment Center. He'd been working for another investment company in London. We found him a new cover. It seemed to work, until about an hour ago."

"Who knows he's traveling?" asked Gertz. "Does he have a wife and kids?"

"Nope, he's the usual NOC loner."

"Good, that's fewer people to notify."

Gertz was being a hard-ass, but that wasn't right. Not today. To be a leader, you had to take the lead.

"Okay, when London wakes up I am going to call Perkins and tell him that his man is missing. He'll have to put out a statement. Otherwise, zip it. Total radio silence. Understood?"

Sophie Marx nodded assent, along with everyone else. She watched as the group fell away. She wasn't a religious person; her counterculture parents, when they had thought about religion at all, had told her it was lies and nonsense. But as she thought about Howard Egan, gone missing halfway around the world in a frightening city, she asked God to watch over him.

Marx recalled her last conversation with Egan. She wished now that she hadn't told him to "suck it up" when he had expressed anxiety about the mission.

6

STUDIO CITY, CALIFORNIA

Jeff Gertz bulled into his office, Steve Rossetti trailing behind. The others understood that they weren't needed anymore. It was a room with a view, but only of Ventura Boulevard. On the walls were trophies Gertz had collected from various assignments: a rich silk tapestry that the crown prince of Morocco had sent in gratitude after he ascended to the throne; a laughable portrait of Saddam Hussein dressed as a tribal sheikh that he had brought out of Baghdad; a miniature marquee that said, in looping neon script, "The Hit Parade," which he had ordered from a signage company in West Hollywood when his crazy experiment was approved; and behind his desk a picture of the Twin Towers with a long Chinese quotation whose meaning Gertz shared with his intimate colleagues. This was his kingdom, but it was about to be turned upside down.

Gertz sat down in his big black leather chair, and then bounded up again and stared out the window at the traffic heading north on Ventura toward the studios. Part of his problem was that he didn't trust most of his colleagues. He thought they were soft, sapped by an intelligence culture that tolerated weakness and poor performance. They had small hearts. They lived in the visible world. Gertz wouldn't have said it out loud, but he regarded Howard Egan as a weak man; now the strong ones would have to bail him out.

"This is a shit storm," muttered Gertz. "What have we got nearby?"

"In Karachi, nothing of our own," said Rossetti. "There's a consulate, and I think Headquarters still has a base there."

Rossetti spoke slowly and precisely. He was a company man, a slow roller, and he was scared that he would get blamed if things went wrong. But Gertz wanted action.

"Could we send in a traveler, in a hurry? I want to keep this close."

"Sure, but it would be insecure, moving that fast. It's easier to use the guy in the consulate."

"Goddamn it," said Gertz. He hated having to depend on Headquarters for anything. It only confirmed the old boys' wisdom that his new outfit was fine until the chips were down. Then it needed help from the old structure.

"I'll call Langley in a minute," he said. "Let me think. Where's the nearest extraction team?"

"Bagram," said Rossetti. "They're saddled and ready, twenty-four/seven."

"Well, call them. Tell them we may need them in a hurry, but don't tell them why yet."

"Sorry, Jeff, but we need an okay from Headquarters to call Bagram. Those are military assets. We don't have the authority to task them."

"That ask-permission crap was supposed to be over."

"That's not what Headquarters says. You want me to call CTC and find out what they've got cooking?" Rossetti, among other things, was the liaison to the Counterterrorism Center, where Gertz had worked in a previous assignment.

"Ask them what's going on in the Tribal Areas. From what I hear it's the same crazy shit out there. Tell CTC that if they have any Preds up today, maybe this one time they could hold off blowing people away, until we get our guy back."

"Roger. But they won't listen. We do our thing, they do theirs."

"Precisely. Net result, zero." Gertz shooed his hand for Rossetti to leave.

"I need to make some calls. Tell me when you hear from Egan. He's a burnout, that guy, I'm telling you. Too long in the job. He'll show up, and then I'm going to fire his ass."

Gertz closed the office door. He sat back in his big black chair for a moment, trying to think it through, but he couldn't focus. There were too many knots. He had no option but to ask for help.

He picked up the secure phone and called the associate deputy director in Langley, Cyril Hoffman, who was The Hit Parade's official point of contact.

Gertz didn't trust Hoffman; the man was odd: He liked to wear ascots and Panama hats and vests with gold chains. He was from a famous CIA family, which had sent cousins and uncles into the agency for generations. He had started in the Near East Division, like most of his notorious relatives, but a decade ago he had abandoned the family nest in favor of Support—arranging travel and housing and the other humdrum logistical details that allowed the agency to function. In that role, he had amassed an unusual network of power. Nearly everyone at the CIA owed him a favor, as did people in many other parts of the government, as well.

"Bad news?" asked Hoffman when he got on the line. He sounded almost merry.

"How did you know?" answered Gertz.

"Rossetti told me I should expect a call. And frankly, Jeff, why else would you be in touch?"

"I have an officer in Karachi who's AWOL. He missed a meeting an hour ago. That place is the Wild West, and I'm worried."

"Tell me what you need, my friend," said Hoffman. His voice was liquid.

"Rossetti says you have a declared officer in the consulate in Karachi. I need for him to notify the Sindhi police right now that an American citizen is missing, presumed in trouble. Under no circumstances should he suggest any USG connection to the man. I'll send you the alias name and passport number when I hang up. He was covered as a businessman working for a hedge fund in London called Alphabet Capital. He traveled often to Pakistan."

Hoffman made a clucking noise with his tongue, as if he were correcting a pupil.

"I think you mean that the *consular* officer should talk to the Sindhi police, not the base chief, if you want to keep the agency out of it."

"Right. As if the Paks think there's a difference."

"Oh, my, they know us better than you might imagine," said Hoffman. "Can we give the Karachi police a location?"

"We have the GPS coordinates of his BlackBerry. But I suspect that the man and the BlackBerry are no longer in the same place."

"That's unfortunate. Anything else?"

"Find the driver," said Gertz. "That's where the Paks should start. Find the taxi driver who was taking my man to his meet."

"Uh, what's the flap potential here?"

"If he has been captured? Pretty damned big, I'd say. If he's dead, not so big."

"Can we grab him?"

"Sure, if we can find him. That's the other favor I need to ask. Can you get an extraction team from Bagram on the scene, pronto?"

"Yes, but the Paks will get squirrelly."

"Not if you don't tell them. Fly in an extra team from one of the task forces. Put them in a hotel in Karachi. Send some weapons and shit over from the consulate. Have them chase any signals we pick up. If we don't need them, you can send them back to Afghanistan and nobody will be the wiser."

Hoffman paused. There was a reedy noise through the phone that sounded almost like he was humming.

"What about the ISI?" Hoffman resumed. "Should we inform them? They're going to know something is up."

"No. Let them guess. For all we know, they're the ones who did this, them or their friends. I don't think we should tell them a fucking thing."

"The gentlemen from ISI are not stupid, I regret to say."

There was another pause, and that humming noise began again, and then stopped.

"Should we tell the oversight committees anything?" mused Hoffman. "That's what the director is going to ask me."

"God, no. Don't tell them a word. This is a missing American civilian. Full stop. That's all the world is going to know. His identity is secret. Those are the rules of this game, right?"

"Excuse me, Jeff, but it would appear that somebody *knew* that secret identity already. If Egan was grabbed, that means his cover was blown. You might start thinking about how that happened. Before you have another, um, accident."

"What are you going to do?" asked Gertz.

"I . . ."—Hoffman paused and took in a breath, "don't . . ."—another delay, while he blew his nose—"know."

With that, Hoffman rang off.

Gertz told Tommy Arden to send out a book cable to everyone, every officer and every platform that was part of The Hit Parade's network. Report anything suspicious. Avoid unnecessary travel. If you are in a denied area, get out.

It was a big distribution list, more than a hundred people. The cable didn't explain what was wrong, which spooked people in the field. But Gertz was such an operator that people were never sure what he was doing, even when he told them directly. They assumed that if there was trouble, he would take care of it, one way or another.

Gertz believed in lying; that was part of his special aptitude for the job. That was the message of the Chinese quotation framed behind his desk under the big picture of the Twin Towers. It was a passage from Sun Tzu that he had studied after September 11. The translation wasn't written down, but Gertz had memorized it: "All warfare is based on deception. Hence, when able to attack, we must seem unable; when using our forces, we must seem inactive; when we are near, we must make the enemy believe we are far away; when far away, we must make him believe we are near."

Over the past year, Gertz had made a dozen copies of this plaque and given them to trusted colleagues. It was his version of the "commander's coin" that general officers pressed into the hands of the troops. He wanted his people—his new warriors—to understand that lying was absolutely essential to their work. It wasn't an unfortunate consequence of the job. It *was* the job.

Gertz made one more decision that morning, which would affect the future more than he could have realized. He knew that he needed to begin planning for the worst. Hoffman had fired a warning shot, on behalf of the secret barons who managed what was left of Headquarters. The questions would come at them, even if only a few people knew enough to ask. Why had Egan been grabbed? How had his identity been compromised? What else might have come unstuck?

Gertz needed help answering these questions, but only from someone who would be reliable. He trusted almost nobody outside The Hit Parade, and few people inside, either. His principal deputies all were potential rivals, loyal to him in the moment, but ready to switch sides. His operations chief, Rossetti, was a plant from Headquarters. His general counsel spent his time worrying about the inspector general back in Langley. His Support chief, Tommy Arden, was loyal, but he was a mouse.

He went down the list of section chiefs and paused when he got to the name of Sophie Marx. She had just been promoted to her counterintelligence job, but she was smart and aggressive, and she knew the Howard Egan case. What stuck in Gertz's mind was something else: She had done him a favor several months before. An auditor was visiting from Headquarters, and he had taken Marx off site and asked her a lot of questions about The Hit Parade's operations. Marx had spun him, and then she had come to see Gertz later to give him a report.

Gertz had asked her why she ratted out the Headquarters man.

"He asked too many questions," Marx had said, "and he was an asshole about it."

Gertz had liked that. He knew the stories about her operations in Beirut, and how she had escaped an ambush once in Addis. Marx was lucky, that counted for something. And she was still in her mid-thirties, young enough to take risks. The book on her was that she was headstrong and independent. But Gertz thought he could handle her in a jam.

7
STUDIO CITY, CALIFORNIA

Sophie Marx was reading a case file when Jeffrey Gertz peered into her office just before noon. Her glasses were perched on the tip of her nose, and her black hair was gathered in a loose ponytail. She looked up at him briefly, awkwardly, and then back at the file. Gertz had never visited her office before. It was messy. The *Thelma and Louise* poster was askew. On the wall was a framed photograph of two people in sandals and woolly hair, hugging her at her Princeton graduation: The longhairs were her eccentric parents, in from the islands. On her desk was an open bag of SunChips.

Marx assumed that Gertz was on his way somewhere else, but he wasn't.

"Am I interrupting something?" he asked.

"Yes, of course. I mean, that's your job, isn't it?"

He laughed and closed the door.

Marx stood up, shook the boss's hand and then sat back down.

"I'm sorry about Howard Egan," she said, putting the file folder on top of the bag of chips. "That was my case. I should have kept a tighter watch on him. Is there any more news?"

"The Paks just found his BlackBerry in a dumpster. If he's lucky, he's dead by now."

She put her hand over her mouth, and there was a slight tremor of her head, as if she had just hit a blast of cold air. She had made her own runs into dangerous places. She recovered her composure quickly.

"Let me know how I can help," she said. "I feel like this is my screwup, partly."

"That's why I'm here, actually," said Gertz. "I have a problem, and it's about to become your problem."

Her eyes flashed. She wanted to be in the game, but she knew not to rush.

"What do you have in mind?"

"I need someone to investigate how this happened, and in a hurry. Otherwise, Headquarters will take it over. They'll send their own counterintelligence team, and damage-assessment team, and finger-pointing team. I don't want them ruining what we've been trying to build here."

He was leaning toward her, imploring but also demanding. With his lean face and goatee, and that hungry look in his eye, he looked in this moment like a trumpeter who needed a fix.

"And you're free to travel, right?" Gertz continued. "I mean, you don't have a ball and chain here."

Marx understood that the boss was asking, obliquely, about her sex life. She had been married briefly seven years before, to another case officer, but as with so many tandem couples, the romantic attachment was to the work, not the other person. She was always in Lebanon or Addis; he was always in Nicaragua; they were always nowhere.

"I'm free to travel," she said.

"So let's do it. Be my person. Make this case."

She took off the reading glasses and folded her hands in front of her. Gertz was waiting for an answer, but she was still thinking.

"So you want me to get there first. And clean up the mess before Headquarters can make trouble. Is that it, more or less?"

He didn't answer directly.

"I need someone I can trust," he said. "You're it. What do you say?"

"I'm not sure."

"What you mean?" His voice was rising. "One of your colleagues has just disappeared in a garbage dump in Pakistan, and I'm asking you to help and you refuse? Are you kidding me? Maybe you're in the wrong line of work."

"I'm not refusing. Lower your voice. You're shouting."

"I want an answer."

"You're asking me to be your fixer. That's not my job. You just hired me to run counterintelligence for you. Finding out what happened to Howard Egan is what I'm *supposed* to do. It's not a favor to my boss. Even a boss I like and respect."

Gertz smiled. She was fighting for her own space. That wasn't a bad thing.

"Let's start again. I need you to begin a confidential CI investigation of what happened to Howard Egan. You can have access to anything you want in the files, here or anywhere else. You can go anywhere you like. I want you to do it right. But you need to do it fast, or we are going to get blown out of the water. Sorry if I sounded like a jerk before. It's my nature. So what do you say, now that I'm asking nicely?"

"I say yes. When do I start?"

"Right now. Come upstairs in fifteen minutes and I'll show you what we've got. Then I'll take you to lunch."

"Sorry, but I can't make lunch."

"Oh, yeah? Why not?"

"Because I'll be eating at my desk, reading the files you're going to give me."

Sophie Marx moved upstairs to a small office next to Gertz's that had been cleared for her. They worked all that day and through the night, hoping that Egan might make contact. She assembled everything about Egan she could find—his travels, his contact reports, his cover documentation, his roster of agents. She already understood the smooth edges of the puzzle that formed the border of his operational life. Now she would start looking for the jagged ones.

Gertz's secretary, a refugee from Headquarters named Pat Waters, rolled her eyes when she saw that Marx had temporarily joined the front office. She knew enough about her boss's predatory social life to be suspicious of the new arrival. Marx ignored the secretary until she balked at a request for access to Hamid Akbar's 201 personnel file.

"You're not cleared for that," Waters said brusquely.

Marx asked again, as if she hadn't heard the first time, and when she got the same answer she thought of summoning Gertz for help. But that was exactly what the secretary would expect her to do. She asked Waters to step into her small office, little bigger than a closet.

"I am here on Mr. Gertz's orders," she said. "I don't have a lot of time. I'll ask you again, politely, and if that doesn't work, this will get unpleasant for you in a hurry."

Waters didn't answer, but she nodded her head in submission. Marx was good that way: She wasn't a shouter, but she usually got what she wanted.

The watch officer, Julian, came in regularly with reports from the operations center. A flash cable had arrived when the Pakistani police found Egan's BlackBerry. The Paks reluctantly agreed to turn over the phone for forensic analysis. When it arrived at the consulate, the SIM card was missing.

The FBI had a team based in Islamabad, so two agents flew to Karachi to take apart the BlackBerry, along with the local representative from the NSA. They were able to document what everyone assumed: Egan's last communication had been his email message to The Hit Parade with the coordinates of his meeting in Baldia Town. After that, silence. The GPS signal showed movements that were consistent with a normal surveillance detection run until just after eight p.m., when he stopped, or was stopped, in Rasheedabad, a district north of downtown on the way to Baldia. The GPS signal stayed there for about twenty minutes, moving a hundred yards north, then fifty yards west.

Rasheedabad seemed to be where disaster had struck. Then the GPS track moved rapidly north toward Ittehad Town, where it stopped dead around nine. That turned out to be the dumpster, where the Pakistani police found the phone.

Gertz's first priority was to find the taxi driver. Egan would have taken a cab to the meet, probably a string of them. You didn't need special intelligence to find a taxi, you just needed a lot of cops. He had Steve Rossetti work it through Langley, after his initial conversation with Hoffman.

Headquarters sent its man in Karachi a photo of Egan that the consulate could show to the cabbies. The Pakistani police were already pulling in drivers. Once they had a photo to work with, it became routine police work.

The cops quickly located two of the taxis that Egan had taken that night. The drivers confirmed that they'd carried the passenger in the photo. A third driver hauled into the dragnet said he had seen the *gora*, the white man in the photograph, getting into a red Toyota sedan. He remembered it because the passenger had sat in the backseat for a long while, as if he was thinking of getting out, and the driver had hoped maybe he could get the fare instead. But the Toyota had driven away.

Late in the afternoon a call came in from Headquarters. The Pakistani police had found the red Toyota, at three a.m. Karachi time. It was in Orangi, a district south of Ittehad Town where the BlackBerry had been found. The driver's throat had been slit. The police guessed the driver had been dead about five hours, since that was about the time Egan went missing.

Gertz called Thomas Perkins late that night, L.A. time, early morning in London. He wanted to reach him at home before he went to the office. Perkins had been Howard Egan's nominal boss at Alphabet Capital. Sophie was in his office when he made the call, and he nodded for her to pick up the muted extension phone. As he dialed the call, Gertz silently mouthed the word, *Shit*. This was the moment when the bad news would become as real and messy as a turd.

"My name is Mr. Jones," Gertz began. His voice had risen an octave, and it had a nasally sound and a bit of a posh accent. It sounded so different that Marx wouldn't have known it was him if she hadn't been staring at him. He winked at her, acknowledging his impromptu tradecraft, as he continued speaking.

"I work for the United States government. I'm sorry to disturb you at home so early in the morning, but I have some bad news about one of your employees."

"Where are you calling from?" The voice had the fragility of morning.

"From the U.S. government."

"Oh." There was a pause. "This is about Howard Egan, isn't it?" Perkins seemed to know it before Gertz said a word. He had been worrying about this moment for a more than a year, and now here it was.

"Yes, sir. Mr. Egan is missing. He was meeting a client of your fund in Karachi last night, and after that he disappeared. I'll tell you honestly, we are concerned."

"Who is this?" asked Perkins. "Do I know you?" There was a tightness in the hedge fund manager's voice now.

"Sorry, Mr. Perkins, can't say much. I'm Mr. Jones. And your man Egan is missing."

"Fuck! I knew something like this would happen. You need to take care of this."

"We are, sir. We're doing our best. But we need your help."

"No. This is your mess. You clean it up."

Gertz's voice was firmer now. He had a way of establishing control by inflection.

"It's not that easy, Mr. Perkins. Without your help, this will get very complicated, especially for you."

The financier was still angry, but more compliant.

"What should I do? What should I tell people?"

"You need to put out a statement, sir, to your employees and everyone else. That's why I am calling. You need to send a statement to the British police and to the wire services saying that one of your people has disappeared in Pakistan while he was on a business trip for your firm. You should say that you're hoping he's just lost, but you would appreciate any information. You need to do it this morning."

"Okay, a statement. Let me get a pen. What should it say again?" The hedge fund manager spoke with an American accent, even though he had been living in London for almost a decade. He was trying to sound calm.

"The statement should say what I just told you. Howard Egan went missing last night while he was on a business trip to meet with investors in your fund. You are very concerned. Anyone with information should contact the Pakistani police or the U.S. consulate in Karachi."

"Will it get picked up by the media? I don't want a lot of reporters tromping around here. People promised there would be no publicity about . . . this. Ever."

"There won't be. The media won't care about his disappearance. Not unless they find a body."

"A body? You mean he's dead?"

"Maybe."

"Oh, my god. What a mess. Poor Howard."

"I'm sorry. Let me make a suggestion. Why don't I send someone by your house this morning, right now, to help you draft the statement? Would that be a help?"

"Yes, it certainly would. At home, not in the office."

The hedge fund chief was thinking. He was calculating risks, and he didn't like what he saw.

"Can I ask you a question, whoever you are?"

"Sure," said Gertz. "Fire away."

"What happens if Howard gets, um, tortured? And he reveals during interrogation that he, ah, worked for the government. That his work for my firm was, ah, you know, a cover story. What happens then? Because that could, um, destroy my business."

"You deny it. We deny it. We say it's a complete fabrication. Outrageous falsehood. If need be, the State Department spokesman will say it's propaganda to smear an innocent businessman. That's the deal. Total denial. And it goes away."

"Sorry to break this to you, whatever your name is, but people don't believe the U.S. government."

"Well, too bad for them. But nothing bad will happen to you. I promise. And your country appreciates what you have done. Deeply. And we know how to show our appreciation, as you are aware."

"More help from the government. Just what I need." There was a note of sarcasm in his voice now.

"I don't think any of this is going to happen, Mr. Perkins. I should tell you that. I mean the interrogation and all that."

"Oh, yeah? Why not?"

"Because I think that Howard is dead. He would resist capture by anyone. If he was taken, he had ways of, how shall I put this, avoiding interrogation."

"You mean he would kill himself?"

Gertz didn't respond. He waited a moment, and then went on with his speech.

"We'll send someone by your residence this morning to help with the statement. All right? And then someone will contact you as we make a more careful investigation of all this."

"What about the system? Is that going to continue?"

Gertz glanced at Marx. Her head was down. She was reading something.

"I don't know about any 'system,' sorry. Can't help you with that."

"Should I talk with Anthony Cronin? He was my, you know, my regular 'contact.'"

"No. Don't talk to anyone except the people I send you."

"Have I met you?" Perkins asked again.

Gertz ignored the question. He was impatient now. He had done his business with Perkins. He wanted to get off the phone.

"Who are you sending?" Perkins continued. "Because, frankly, I don't want to get in any deeper. This is a mess. I don't need some clumsy, uh, government official."

"I will find a good contact for you," said Gertz. He was looking at Sophie Marx, who met his eye this time. "I have someone sophisticated and sensible, who can put everything back together when the dust settles. We understand your problems. We'll help you get them sorted out. That's a promise."

Gertz turned to Sophie when the call ended.

"How did I do?" he asked. He was vain that way. He wanted reviews.

"Adequately," she answered. "Do you know him?"

"Yes and no."

"What does that mean?"

"Nothing."

He wasn't going to answer, so she stopped trying.

"Poor Mr. Perkins," she said. "I don't blame him for being unhappy. We should never have used a real company as a platform for someone like Egan who could get grabbed. That was stupid. How did it happen? And what did he mean by 'the system'? What's that all about?"

"I have no idea," said Gertz blandly. "Probably he was talking about the way they paid Egan."

"Who's Anthony Cronin?"

"Cronin's an old NOC handler. And you're right about Egan's financial cover. It started before my time. Yours, too. Too late for second-guessing. Perkins will be all right. He's just scared."

It was near midnight, and Marx had many more hours of work to do. But Gertz had said something at the end of the phone call that she wanted to pin down.

"Were you suggesting that I go to London?" she asked. "Did I hear that right?"

"Maybe." He winked. "If you want to."

Her brow furrowed a moment, and she bit her upper lip. She was trying to decide if she should tell him something.

"I would like to go almost anywhere, and especially London. But you should know that I was on the no-travel list back at Headquarters. After I got burned in Beirut and Addis, they thought it was unsafe. I should have told you that before."

"I don't care what Headquarters says. What do you think? Are you still hot? Would it be dangerous?"

She shook her head.

"No. The cover job was insecure. They were on my phone. I have new documentation now. I'm solid."

"That's good enough for me. We can play with your passport some more. But you don't work for the CIA now. You're a private citizen. So fuck it, right?"

She was smiling as she headed back to her cubbyhole. Gertz was a manipulator, but he also knew how to get things done in a hurry.

8
STUDIO CITY, CALIFORNIA

Sophie Marx worked through most of the night, sleeping a few hours in the women's locker room of The Hit Parade's fitness club. She took a walk early the next morning. Her windowless office was claustrophobic, and she needed to breathe. More than that, she needed to think. She had showered and washed her hair, but she still felt groggy. It was as if she were staring into a fogged-up window and couldn't see the face inside. She wanted to do a good job for Gertz, but she needed a starting point.

Out on Ventura Boulevard it was already hot. The Mystic Eye Bookshop had a few early morning customers, and so did the tattoo parlor next door. Sophie wanted breakfast. She passed a Starbucks and a McDonald's until she came to a diner called Hank's. She ordered the "Hank Special"—scrambled eggs, sausage, hash browns, toast. Her father used to make her breakfasts like that when she was a girl back in Florida, when he wasn't too hung over to cook.

Her parents were living in Tortola last she heard, running a restaurant. They had taught her how to keep secrets; maybe that was the only virtue of the crazy, stoned-out life they led: Their daughter learned how to cover the family's tracks as they moved, until the art of concealment became second nature. Oddly, the CIA was the one place she didn't have to pretend. She had confessed it all, her whole crazy childhood, during the first interview. She felt safe. This was a family of weirdos and liars and manipulators, whose only rule was that they weren't supposed to lie to each other.

As she ate her breakfast, Marx thought about Howard Egan, trying to imagine what could have happened to him in those last hours before the meeting in north Karachi. She ordered a second cup of coffee and drew herself a timeline on the back of a napkin. Egan had come to Karachi, checked into his hotel, called the access agent, done a first surveillance detection run, seen the access agent, done a second SDR, and then, disaster. There were many ways this story could have gone wrong, but there was only one place to start. She paid her check and walked back east on Ventura to the big, boxy building with the THE HIT PARADE sign out front.

Marx went first to see Steve Rossetti, hoping to clear a potential obstacle. The operations chief regarded Marx as an interloper. He had wanted to run the investigation of the Egan case himself.

"I need to talk to Hamid Akbar," she said.

"Good luck, kid. Akbar is terrified. He thinks he's next."

"Have you debriefed him?"

"We tried to. I called him, but he didn't want to talk. I told you, he's frightened. He says that if he we try to contact him again, he'll walk."

Marx studied the operations chief. His face was smooth, well shaven. He smelled of Old Spice. He was a man who would rather do too little, tidily, than too much and risk making a mistake.

"That's ridiculous," she said. "Akbar works for us. Who's he to say he doesn't want to be debriefed?"

"Take it to Gertz," said Rossetti, shrugging his shoulders.

"I will," she said, turning back toward her cubicle. "And Akbar is dirty. Wait and see."

Marx called the Office of Security and requested the polygraph record for Hamid Akbar. She had been puzzling over his role since the previous day, when she was digging into the operational files. The Pakistani businessman was the last person known to have seen Howard Egan alive. Why had he moved up the time of the meeting with his uncle? Why had he proposed an insecure location? Where had he gone in the hours immediately after Egan's disappearance?

It took an hour to pry loose the polygraph record from the registry. When the thin file was finally delivered to Marx, it deepened her concern. Akbar hadn't been polygraphed since his initial recruitment in the United States. When he had been re-recruited, Gertz had waived a new test. It was too difficult to bring a polygraph operator on site, according to the file. The result was a counterintelligence officer's nightmare—an agent whose reliability was unproven, in witting contact with a deep-cover officer. Howard Egan had trusted him, but now Egan was gone.

Marx knocked on Gertz's door. This morning he looked like an over-the-hill Chicago sideman. There were circles of fatigue under his eyes, and his skin had a waxy pallor replacing the buff tan. He was wearing a cashmere blazer that was so loosely constructed it looked almost like a cardigan sweater.

"I don't like Akbar," said Marx.

"Me neither. What have you got?"

You couldn't be sure with Gertz whether he had been thinking that all along, or had just considered the possibility when she mentioned it.

"It turns out he hasn't been polygraphed in ten years. Why did you waive a poly on him when you went after him again?"

"It was too cumbersome getting a technician out in the field. And I needed to get to his uncle. The family came well recommended. So I went ahead."

"Who recommended them?"

Gertz shook his head. "Sorry, I can't tell you that. Too sensitive."

She nodded. She knew there were secrets that didn't get shared. That was part of the job.

"Okay, but I have a bad feeling about Akbar. I think he may have set Egan up."

"Maybe. But he has an alibi."

"I missed that. What alibi?"

"He delivered his uncle. The man was at the meeting place, just where he was supposed to be. If it was a setup, why would the uncle have gone to the meet? That's where your theory gets squishy."

"Maybe the uncle wasn't witting. Or maybe the uncle showed up so they would have a cover story when Howard disappeared. I'm not sure, but I need to know more about him."

"Like what?"

"Well, for starters, Egan called Akbar before he went to see him. That call was logged on his BlackBerry. So the NSA should have an audio file of the conversation. I need it. And don't tell me I don't have the right clearances, because you already promised me I could have anything I wanted."

She crossed her arms stubbornly.

"You're jamming me," he said.

"Yes, I am. That's part my job, isn't it?"

Gertz looked at her with an extra measure of admiration. He liked troublemakers, so long as they were on his team.

"How long have you worked for The Hit Parade?" he asked.

"Nearly a year. Ten months, to be exact."

"Do you know where we got the name 'The Hit Parade'?

"No. I always wondered about that. "

"It's from an old-time radio and TV show called *Your Hit Parade*. It started back in the 1930s, lasted for nearly forty years. They played a weekly list of top records, right, which they said was based on an 'authentic tabulation.' But that was all crap. They just made it up. Played what they wanted. Got payola from the record companies, for all I know."

"That's what you liked about it?" asked Marx, raising her eyebrows. "That it was a big con?"

"Yeah, that. Plus I like the idea of hitting people."

She was shaking her head now, but Gertz gave her a playful punch on the shoulder, as if to say, Just kidding.

Gertz got Sophie Marx what she needed. He called Cyril Hoffman, who called the NSA, who called someone in the cryptographic agency's South Asia Division. In an hour the requisite audio file was sitting in Marx's computer queue. She listened to the brief conversation a half dozen times. What struck her was the stress in the Pakistani man's voice—the coughs and pauses, the apology that the planned meeting time wasn't "convenient."

"Can we do the business tonight?" Egan had asked. The Pakistani had made a phone call before he answered. Was he calling his uncle, or someone else? And when he came back on the line, there was that cough—that knot of anxiety.

One of Marx's tradecraft instructors, a decade ago, had told her that "behavior always leaks." He had been talking about how to sense when someone is lying without using a polygraph. There are always clues, he had said—the extra words and phrases wrapped around a simple yes or no, the twitch of a leg, the flutter of an eyebrow, the clutch in the throat, the cough, the pause. Behavior always leaks.

She looked at the photograph of Akbar they'd dug out of the files. He looked smooth, Westernized and insincere. She was convinced that he was rotten. He had sent Howard Egan—a neurotic middle-aged NOC, a man trying to serve out his time until he was pensioned off—into a trap. She was going to squeeze Akbar until the truth popped out.

Marx went back to see Gertz. The door was closed, and the officious Pat Waters made her wait outside until the boss had finished his business. When the door opened, she swooped in and made her request.

"I want to go interview Hamid Akbar, right away. Give him a stress poly. Push him. I listened to the NSA audio file of his call with Egan and I am telling you, Jeffrey, that man is where our trouble started."

"You can't go to Pakistan. It's too insecure. Sorry. Even you can't sweet-talk me on that one."

"Then yank him out. Pull his chain. Have you contacted him?"

"Yes, by phone. Rossetti made the call, and I listened. He's scared shitless. He thinks he's a target, too. Wants to go to ground, break off contact."

"Well, he ought to be scared. He's a bad man."

"Excuse me? Aren't you getting a little overwrought here?"

"That's sexist, calling me 'overwrought.' I could file a complaint with HR, and I'd win, but I'm prepared to compromise. Just let me interview Akbar. Make it happen. Please. Order him to meet me in a third country. Tell him that if he doesn't agree, he really *is* a dead man. Tell him that you'll bust his balls, expose him to the ISI. Come on. This is the door. We have to walk through it."

Gertz smiled, and the tired eyes sparkled for a moment. It wasn't just the tough-girl bit. She wanted so much to succeed.

"Where do you want to meet Mr. Akbar? Assuming that I can get him out?"

"I don't care. Dubai is probably the easiest for him. Tell him Dubai in thirty-six hours. If he won't come out, I'm going in after him."

"I thought you wanted to go to London."

"I do. But not until I have found the man who set up Howard Egan."

Gertz, fatigued as he was, rose from his desk and walked toward her. He put his big hand on her shoulder and began to give her a hug, but thought better of it and shook her hand. He sent her off to Support to scrub her documents and book the next flight to Dubai.

Gertz locked his door. He had to make a call that he had been dreading for the past twenty-four hours. It was to the only person he considered his boss, other than the president himself, and that was the White House chief of staff, Ted Yazdi. He sent a BlackBerry message to costy @who.eop.gov. Hardly an unbreakable code: Chief of Staff Ted Yazdi. The message was just a subject line: *Need to talk*. The answer came back five minutes later. *Call me now.*

Gertz went to the STU-5, the latest model of the Secure Telephone Unit, and dialed Yazdi's secure number at the White House. He answered it personally.

"What the fuck is going on?" asked Yazdi. He had the coarse, corrosive manner of a former Wall Street trader.

"We lost one of our boys in Pakistan."

"So I hear. Is he dead?"

"I hope so, for his sake. But they may have gotten something out of him. That's what I wanted to warn you about."

"Shit. What do we do then? What if it's all over the Internet?"

"Nothing. With respect, sir, don't do anything. If these people issue a statement, have the State Department deny it. The agency will tell you that you have to brief Congress. My humble advice is that you should ignore them. This program is covered under the National Security Act. You have a legal opinion that says so. The congressional leadership has signed off on it. End of story."

"Did the Paks screw us? Is this their hit?"

"Don't know yet, but it's quite possible. This is what they do."

"The president is nervous. He asked me a few hours ago in the Oval if this Karachi thing was going to blow up. I said no, sir. Hunker down. It will go away. That's right, isn't it?"

"Totally right. It's contained."

"These crazy fuckers still want to kill us, don't they? These Pakistanis and Waziris and whatever the hell else. Why do they hate us so much? We're trying to give them money, for god's sake. We're trying to make them happy. What the hell is wrong with them?"

"I don't know, sir. I keep asking my sources that. They keep giving me new names to contact. Eventually we'll get it right. Money talks."

Yazdi couldn't disagree with the efficacy of cash. It was one of his life rules. But still, he wanted to understand why this mission had gone off the rails.

"How did the bad guys make your man? I thought he was superdeep cover and all that."

"It was a lucky shot, probably. If there's a hole, we'll plug it, don't worry. I've put someone reliable on it."

"Not a SWAT team, for Christ's sake. That's all we need is a bunch of people snooping around."

"Not a team, a discreet investigator. But you will have to turn off the CIA director, if he comes knocking. Because he'll want to tell Congress, and then it's out for sure, and we're all screwed."

"What else? I gotta go."

"That's it. Just keeping you informed. Not to worry. Tell the president we have it under control."

"Reassurance from you guys, that will scare the shit out of him. You need to come back here and see me soon, and remind me what the fuck you're doing. Can you do that?"

"Yes, sir. I can come in the next week. I will send you a date and you tell me if it works."

"One more thing, just so I don't have nightmares. There's no USG money here. Nothing that could bite us. It's all clean."

"Yes, sir. It's self-contained financially, no government funds in or out. No paper trail, here or in D.C., all offshore."

"Well, that's something, at least. No more fuckups, please."

"HUA, sir," said Gertz. It was military-speak for "heard, understood, acknowledged." But he was talking to himself. The chief of staff had scurried off to other business.

9
WANA, SOUTH WAZIRISTAN

"Lund te char" **is** a pungent curse in the Punjabi dialect. It means, literally, "hop on my dick," or as an American would say, "Fuck off." That had been the CIA's message to Lieutenant General Mohammed Malik with this business in Karachi, and he did not like it. Nobody wants to be embarrassed in public, but there is a special sting when a man's honor is his most precious possession. So it particularly wounded the general that a previously unknown unit of American intelligence had sent an operative into his country, without authority, and then had gone to such trouble to conceal it.

It was an insult. The ISI chief had considered whether he should do something to hurt the Americans back. That would have been easy enough to arrange, for there were so many ways the Americans, tied down by their expeditionary wars and short of breath, depended on their Pakistani allies.

But General Malik was not a rash or vindictive man. And the more he considered the situation, the more it seemed to him that before seeking to punish the Americans, he needed to understand better what they were doing. He needed to understand, in particular, how this new intelligence unit was choosing its targets. And to do that, it was necessary to travel to the remote territory where the Karachi operation had been aimed. This was not a project he could delegate to one of his case officers, much less to one of the agents on the ISI's string. For, in truth, he did not trust his colleagues on anything truly sensitive, especially involving the United States. So he made the phone calls himself, and sent messages by other channels, to be sure that the ground was prepared.

The general set off with his driver at first light one June morning in his Toyota Land Cruiser. He winced when the SUV passed beneath the illuminated portrait of Mohammad Ali Jinnah and below it the words of the founder's invocation in 1947: UNITY, FAITH, DISCIPLINE. How little Pakistan had of all three, after nearly sixty-five years, but the general was a hopeful man, and at least he could be disciplined.

They rolled along the Grand Trunk Road toward their first stop, the military air base just west of Peshawar. The trucks heading toward the Khyber Pass were decorated like the wagons of the Raj days: The drivers' compartments were made of wood—intricately carved and then painted in rainbow colors and decorated with tiny mirrors and scarabs to ward off the jinns of the hills. In his younger days, the general had found these trucks colorful and charming, but today they seemed just another sign of his dear country's backwardness. He closed his eyes and tried to understand the puzzle of what the Americans were doing.

The general wanted to travel light, with as small a footprint as possible. So he had requested a one-engine Mashaq trainer, rather than the fat Mi-17 cargo helicopter the air wing commander recommended. The pilot still hadn't been told the destination when the DG-ISI arrived. General Malik waited until the little propeller had started to whirl and then put on his headset and spoke into the microphone:

"Do you know Wana garrison in South Waziristan?" he said. The pilot nodded. "Take me there."

The young pilot gave the thumbs-up sign. He was from Gilgit in the north, with the light skin and high cheekbones of the mountains. He had flown the Wana route often enough since coming to Peshawar, usually to ferry officers of the Frontier Corps to their garrison deep in this most remote of the tribal areas. But he had never, in all his flying days, transported a three-star general. The air wing commander filed a hasty flight plan for them, and they were off.

The flight took nearly two hours. They bumped over the low mountain ranges south of Peshawar, toward Orakzai Agency and then south across the ancient princely states of Bannu and Tank, which had for centuries been way stations for caravans coming north from Karachi and the Arabian Sea. At Tank, the pilot banked west and steered the little plane into South Waziristan.

The landscape below was a dry corrugated wilderness: desolate mountains, jagged ridges mile after mile toward the Afghan border. Think of the rolling sea in a typhoon, but with the endless brutal waves formed of dirt and rock. The heat of summer shimmered off these trackless hills, producing a low haze that made it look all the more like the devil's land. It was a place for snakes and scorpions, bugs and vermin. A humble goat would get lost amid these rocks, let alone a human being. The region might be impassable to outsiders; but it was a fortress home to the Wazir, Mehsud and Darwesh Khel tribesmen. Farming was all but impossible in these barren lands, so the natives since the beginning of time had been fierce hunters and brigands.

After the plane crested a last arid peak, almost at the Afghan frontier, a broad valley opened below, and in the middle of this flat ground, improbably neat, stood the town of Wana. Here was a small oasis of cultivation: There were apple orchards and wheat fields, and the fortlike compounds of the residents, each clan living behind high mud walls with gun towers at the four corners to protect them from their plundering neighbors.

Western philosophers might talk abstractly about the state of nature as a war of each against all; but here, it was the simple fact of life. The word "cousin" in Pashto had the same meaning as "enemy."

At the edge of the town was an asphalt airstrip, baking in the sun. The small plane circled the outpost once at high altitude to scout the terrain, and then corkscrewed steeply down to the landing field. When the plane rolled to a stop, the pilot popped the hood. A wind was blowing, so that the heat radiated over the tarmac with the scorching ferocity of a convection oven.

A jeep was waiting to meet General Malik. He drove a half mile to a Pakistani military camp, where he changed out of his uniform into the traditional tribal costume of the Pashtuns, known as a *shalwar khamiz*, with loose cotton trousers and a long shirt. When he emerged from the dressing room, he looked to be a different man. The military starch and polish had disappeared.

Another car was waiting for him; this one was a dusty Land Rover several decades old. The driver was a local man who had been recruited by the ISI from the Waziristan Scouts. The general gave him a map and explained that he wanted to go to a particular compound, some miles outside of town, which was the home of the khan who headed one of the powerful Darwesh Khel clans along the western rim of Waziristan.

The Land Rover rumbled along until the pavement became gravel, and the gravel became dust. As they neared the compound, they encountered a checkpoint manned by tribal militiamen. The driver spoke to one of the guards, who waved him through. The visitor was expected. They stopped at the brown walls of the homestead. They were next door to hell: A few miles farther on began the rough hills, radiating fire-red in the midday sun. But this compound was, if not paradise, at least a place of respite.

The gate creaked open, and a young man bade the general to enter. Inside was an oasis, hidden from the world: There were fruit trees and bright-blooming flowers, and the gurgling sound of water that flowed through a handsome fountain. The general followed the young man to the villa at the far end of the courtyard. As they walked, they could hear the chug-chug of the gas turbine that powered the air conditioners and other appliances. A door opened, and they were welcomed into a room decorated with a fine carpet, patterns woven in rose and turquoise, and red-velvet couches and a table piled high with fresh fruits and sweets.

The Darwesh Khel clan leader, Azim Khan, rose to greet the visitor. He wore his white beard trimmed, rather than in the woolly bush of his neighbors, because he was partly a city man. They exchanged a kiss of mutual respect and trust, and the host professed that he was honored: One of the most powerful men in Pakistan had come alone and unarmed to see him, bringing a blessing to his home. But the host was nervous, too. He feared that the visitor had come to punish him.

Azim Khan lived most of the time in Karachi, where he had land

and villas, and a prosperous nephew who worked at Habib Bank Tower. But for the past week, the old man had gone to ground—returned to his tribal homeland and stayed within the mud walls of his compound. He was frightened and confused, and so he hid.

The khan summoned one of his grandsons to bring tea and a heaping platter of fruits, and then a tray of sweets for his guest. Then, when they had eaten and drunk, he asked the others to leave the room, so that he could talk with the visitor alone.

“Let us not pretend,” began the general. “It is enough for the others to tell lies. But between us, it must be only the truth. One lie and the clear water will become cloudy. Do we agree on that, my friend?”

Azim Khan put his hand on his heart, in a show of sincerity. *“Koag bar tar manzela na rasagei,”* he said, quoting a proverb in the Pashto language, which means, “A tilted load won’t reach its destination.” He translated it into Urdu for the general.

“I know that you were going to meet with the Americans last week,” said the general. “It was wrong, what you planned to do. But I forgive you.”

“Thank you, General Sahib. I do not deserve your mercy.”

“I want to talk with you about the Americans,” continued the general. “I need to understand what they want. Their actions confuse me. How many times have you talked with them?”

“Only once, sir. The second meeting was to take place a week ago. But that did not happen, as you know.”

“What did you discuss before, at the first meeting?”

“We were in the Emirates, sir. The American man asked me to come there, with my nephew. He said that they wanted peace with the Pashtun people, so that we would be their friends. They wanted to begin with the Darwesh Khel people, so that others would follow. All the wealth of America would assist us in this project, he said. I told him I would consider it.”

“Did he offer money personally to you, Azim Khan? Please be honest, my brother. Let there be no grit of lies in this pure brew we are sharing.”

"Yes, General. He wanted to make a gift. Of course he did. I told him our proverb. *Sta da khaira may tobah da, kho das pie de rana kurray ka.*"

"And what does that mean? I am a Kashmir-born man, and I do not speak your Pashto language."

"Sir, the words of the proverb say, 'Don't give me your alms, just save me from your dogs.' I was trying to tell him that I could not help him with his enemies. But he wanted to give me the money anyway. It was a very large amount."

"And what did you decide, Azim Khan, when you had thought about it?"

"Well, sir, I thought, if these foolish Americans want to give money to an old man with a white beard, why not? So my nephew told him that. Yes, I would meet him again and accept his gift. And he was coming to see me, this man, on the night he was taken."

"How much money was he sending you, brother? No harm will come to you if you tell me the truth."

"Well, General, I am embarrassed. But I will tell you. He was sending me two million dollars. It was wired to my account, from a secret fund. And he promised more money, much more, in the future if we worked together. He said it would be ten million dollars, maybe more. He would put it in an account, where I could go visit all this money. And there would be more money for other Pashtun people. I think they wanted to buy peace, sir."

General Malik laughed. He did not mean to, but he could not help himself. He made a dismissive gesture with his hand, as if he were brushing something unpleasant away.

"*Dudh vich mingyan,*" he said, a Punjabi expression that means, literally, "rat turds in the milk." "These Americans are the clowns of the world, are they not, my brother? They drop their bombs from the sky, and then when we get angry, they think of friendship. They think they can make war, and then charm us with money. Really, they bring mirth on a summer day."

"Yes, General. We smile, but we have a saying for this, too, sir. 'A stone will not become soft, nor an enemy a friend.' These Americans think they can change all things with money, even the hardness of the stone. But they cannot."

"So here is my question, Azim Khan, the thing that still puzzles me. How did they know to come to you, an elder of the Darwesh Khel? Are they this clever, that they understand our tribes and clans? Or has some Pakistani person told them on what doors they should knock? I think it must be the second answer, don't you?"

"I am sure I do not know, sir. These Americans have advisers for everything, and perhaps for this, too."

"Now I must ask you another question. It has been troubling me ever since the day this American man disappeared. We know who took him. They are the miscreants, the *takfiris* who hide in these mountains beyond, who think they are God's assassins."

The old man nodded sadly.

"But what I do not know is how these miscreants learned that the American agent was coming. And I am wondering, Azim Khan, I will not play the rabbit with you, I am wondering if it was you who told these miscreants about your meeting. Or your nephew, perhaps it was him."

"No, sir. We did not say a word. Why would we do that? I am not a greedy man. But now my two million dollars has gone. I do not have it. You can turn over every stone from here to Bannu, but you will not find it because I never got it. And the ten million more that they promised, surely that is gone, too. How will I get that now, General? I cannot."

General Malik had taken his chin in his hand, which was something that he did when he was pondering a question and did not have the answer.

"So how did the miscreants know of the meeting, Azim Khan, if you did not tell them?"

"Sir, there are secrets and there are mysteries, and this is a mystery. It is a problem for the Americans. They are leaving footprints that cannot be seen. But someone is tracking them, just the same."

General Malik said his goodbyes. He left presents, as well, gifts that he had brought that, although they were not two million dollars, still brought a deferential nod from the clan leader, and rented his loyalty for a season.

The general got back in his two-seat Mashaq trainer and flew back toward Peshawar through the late afternoon. The summer clouds were forming to the east, hot and sticky, and the plane was buffeted like a shuttlecock, so that the pilot felt that he must apologize to his distinguished guest for the turbulence. But the general barely noticed the rough ride, for he was lost in his puzzle book.

Where did the information come from that drove the American operations? That was what the general wondered, and it had bothered him more each year since September 11, as the Americans squeezed for more from Pakistan. He knew they had their agents, of course they did. The ISI tracked them, and usually it found them out. But this was something more delicate and evanescent. It was as if the Americans had found a window on the culture itself, so that they thought not just about this secret or that, but about the social glue that held the place together.

Who could tell them such things, that was what troubled the general. Who would be smart and subtle enough to see the patterns and describe them to the *Amriki*? If General Malik encountered a person with such a subtle mind, he would want to hire him for the ISI—unless he was a traitor, in which case he would kill him.

General Malik had searched for such an agent, most diligently. He had conducted surveillance, made arrests, interrogated people in the most unpleasant ways, looking for the one who might be opening to American eyes the family secrets of Pakistan.

The general had conducted what the services in the West described as "mole hunts." But he did not like the word "mole." It made these people sound cute and furry. He preferred to call them by the local slang, *gungrat,* which means "dung beetle." For that was what they were, burrowing into the shit of the motherland and then scurrying away to the West. But if there was such a dung beetle, the general had never been able to find him.

He was too smart, this one, too mindful of the ways of intelligence services, and the general had concluded that he must be a man who knew enough to erase his tracks even as he made them. He was out there, for a certainty, and as the little plane bumped over the last ridge of mountains and began its descent toward Peshawar, General Malik made a promise to himself that he would find this man someday, and punish him.

10
LONDON

The sun was just coming up over Hyde Park when Thomas Perkins got off the phone with "Mr. Jones." The first rays were white gold. From the top-floor study of Perkins's house in Ennismore Gardens, he could look across the rooftops to the rust-red bricks of Harrods on Brompton Road, and east across the park to the hotel towers that marked the boundary of Mayfair. The city was changing shifts—some boozy stragglers wandering in from Clubland, a ruddy crew of workingmen mounting the scaffolding that wrapped a building nearby—all bathed in the early summer light.

It was the sort of June morning that had made London irresistible to Perkins ever since he'd set up shop there in the late 1990s. What he had discovered was that this was the best place in the world to be rich. But even that pleasure had its limits.

Perkins told the housekeeper he was going out, and that if a visitor arrived, he should wait in the parlor for his return. He knotted a cashmere scarf around his neck against the morning chill and trundled down the back stairs of his townhouse, slipping out through his garage door onto a mews. He followed this passageway until he emerged at Rutland Gate, where he crossed into Hyde Park.

Perkins was preoccupied. He hadn't liked talking to this fictitious "Jones," the government official who so ostentatiously wouldn't say who he really was. The arm's-length treatment made him feel tawdry, like someone who had gotten caught doing something wrong. That wasn't the way it had started. The "recruiter," for that's what he had been, had spoken of patriotism. September 11 was still a burning memory, and Perkins had wanted to help, like everyone else. And then it had gotten more complicated.

As he strode across the park toward Mayfair, Perkins appeared as a solitary figure, not one of the commodores of finance. Such men are driven by chauffeurs; they do not walk. And when they do venture out, they are accompanied by bodyguards and bag holders—the small army of retainers that exists to minimize contact between the very rich and real life. But in this respect, as in others, Perkins was a somewhat different package.

Thomas Perkins was a tidy man in his early fifties, with small round-rimmed glasses and a thatch of blond hair. He looked boyish; people had been saying that about him ever since he actually was a boy, and it was one of his advantages: It's easy to underestimate someone who seems unmarked by life, to assume that he can't know the same things as people who have visibly lived and suffered.

He was used to being the smartest person in the room, and that sometimes made his boyishness oppressive. Even when he wasn't talking, his eyes darted from speaker to speaker, or to a BlackBerry or computer screen. When doing business, which was nearly always, he would rarely smile or frown. On very rare occasions, when something had especially caught his fancy, you might hear a burst of staccato laughter, ha-ha-ha, followed by a wry comment or question, or, simply, a return to silence.

His lawyer, Vincent Tarullo, had once told him that he looked like Mr. Peabody, the talking dog on *The Rocky and Bullwinkle Show.* Mr. Peabody always knew the answer to everything. Tarullo addressed him by that name even when they were in company, to the point that some people in his Washington law firm actually thought that Peabody was the client's name.

Perkins had another nickname, one that said more about his business life: In the London hedge-fund world he was known as "Pacman" because of his skill in gobbling up assets. The name stuck: Thomas Perkins was the motorized mouth, powering through the maze of finance and eating all the dots in sight, until there weren't any more and he got to start on a fresh screen. He had enemies among his competitors—how could anyone that successful avoid it? But even among the people who tried to follow his trading strategies, Perkins remained mysterious.

Perkins made his way across the Hyde Park meadow, his head down and his thin body in a walk that was almost a run. He walked to work most days from the townhouse in Knightsbridge to his office in Mayfair, and he regarded the park as his front yard. The daffodils that a few weeks ago had displayed a dozen shades of yellow were now mostly wilted and gone. A few tulips were still in bloom, plush lips of color atop their narrow stalks. Even in June, the morning chill left the grass wet so that it matted under Perkins's feet.

Mayfair made the pursuit of money seem like the only rational calling in life. This tiny area, bounded by Park Lane, Piccadilly, Regent Street and Oxford Street, was home to many of London's big hedge funds; it was the place where the world's most talented financial minds had come to make fortunes of a size that could not have been imagined even in the heyday of the British Empire when this district had become fashionable.

Perkins halted at Stanhope Gate. He studied his BlackBerry for the Asian trading news as he waited for the light to change, and then crossed Park Lane and walked into Curzon Street.

This was his favorite part of the journey, watching this little village come awake each morning—the clubs and clothiers, the restaurants and art galleries. It was a ballet of money, choreographed anew each morning. A few refuse trucks were still out in the early morning light, collecting the trading-room litter from the previous day. Some of these lowly trash men were said to be running little businesses of their own, selling hedge-fund secrets to hungry operators who want to slipstream behind the big boys' trades.

Perkins turned right on Stratton Street, and entered a modern building in Mayfair Place. He took the elevator to the top floor, which belonged to Alphabet Capital. At the far end was Perkins's office, with an expanse of windows that looked out across Piccadilly to the Ritz Hotel and, beyond that, to Green Park and, in the far distance, Buckingham Palace.

Perkins opened the main door. It was just past seven, and he had expected that he would find the office empty. But in a far corner of the trading floor, bathed in shadow, Perkins could see one of the young traders who followed the Asian markets. Perkins called out hello and heard a wheezy answer from the trading desk.

Perkins disappeared into his vast office. There was a three-leafed desk, framed by computer screens as big as television monitors. There was a squawk box directly in front of where Perkins sat, with buttons for each of his main traders, so that he could give orders instantly when he saw opportunities in the markets.

Under Perkins's desk, concealed behind a mahogany panel, was a safe. Perkins opened it and removed a tray of documents. Several of the documents bore the name of Howard Egan. Others were from accountants, auditors and lawyers. Perkins gathered them all and took them to the shredder. He ran the contents through once, and then passed the shreds a second time until they were confetti. He went to another safe, secreted in the private locker room behind his office, and removed another sheaf of documents. These, too, were shredded to dust.

Then Perkins picked up the telephone and called his private attorney, Vincent Tarullo, at home in Washington. Tarullo was a former prosecutor at the Justice Department and had run its National Security Section. He had seen almost every kind of trouble a person could get into.

"Sorry to wake you, Vince," he said into the phone.

"No problem. I was just jerking off. That's you, Mr. Peabody, I presume?"

"*Moi-même.*"

"Why are you at work so early?"

"I have a little problem," said Perkins. "Something I never told you about."

"Swell. I always like it when you go solo and exercise poor judgment. It gives me something to clean up."

"Don't try to be funny, Vince. This is not the moment. I have a man who has gone missing in Pakistan. His name is Howard Egan. E-G-A-N. He seems to have been kidnapped. I am going to put out a statement today here in London."

"Why was he kidnapped, for chrissakes? And what was he doing in Pakistan? Does he really work for you?"

"Well, that's the thing. This particular gentleman did a bit of moonlighting."

"For whom?"

"You can guess, surely. Let us say that these people were not unknown to you in your former line of work."

"Oh, Christ. You really are an asshole. Why didn't you tell me?"

"Complicated question. Simple answer: I wasn't allowed to. Anyway, I didn't, and that's that. They want me to put out a statement and sit tight and wait for the whole thing to blow over. Does that make sense to you?"

"I don't know. Do you have any other choice?"

"No. I want you to do something for me this morning. Call your old friends. Not the little guys, but the very biggest one you know, and tell him that I am assuming people will keep a lid on this. Tell him that if they don't, the consequences will be extremely serious, for everybody. *Ooga-booga*. Scare them. You know how to do that."

"Will they know what I'm talking about?" asked the lawyer.

"I rather think so. This is a little, um, difficult for them."

"Are you going to tell me about this, Peabody? Because I think you should. I can fly over tonight. You need help."

"Not now. Maybe I'll tell you later. Right now it's awkward. You would ask questions that I wouldn't be able to answer."

"Hey, level with me, my friend. Are you fucked up here?"

"No. I am the opposite of fucked up, whatever that is. I am just dandy. So long as everyone adheres to their bargains. Then I am fine. That's all I really need you to worry about—that the dikes and levies are secure, and the floodwaters can be contained."

"But I don't know the details."

"Precisely," said Perkins. "You have grasped the point entirely. You don't know the details, so can't give me unnecessary advice. I have to get off the phone now so I can go home and meet one of the 'tidy-uppers.' You make your call, highest level, please, and deliver the appropriate, oblique warning. Then we'll see about getting together. Want to go grouse shooting? I'll be going up to my place in Scotland in August. Let's do that."

Perkins hung up without waiting for a response. He had a few more tasks to take care of, in the part of his computer system that housed the trading records. By then it was past nine a.m., and people were beginning to arrive at the office. Perkins turned off all his electronic systems, triple-locked his door behind him and kissed his secretary on the way out.

He strolled back to Ennismore Gardens at a leisurely pace. He felt easier now that he had done the housekeeping. Back at home, the representative from "Mr. Jones" was waiting in the drawing room, perched on the edge of the couch and looking most uncomfortable. Perkins apologized that he had been out taking his morning "power walk" around the Serpentine, a ritual that couldn't be interrupted, rain or shine.

The visitor introduced himself as Rupert Ogilvy. He was a mousy-looking man, thin as a string and overmatched by his pin-striped suit. He looked like a bank clerk, which wasn't far off. He was an administrative officer at a small support base Gertz maintained out near Heathrow. The young man proffered a business card, which Perkins didn't bother to read because it was surely a phony.

"I have a draft statement that you might want to consider," said young Ogilvy. He removed a piece of paper from his valise and handed it over.

The page had no letterhead or other markings. It was just two paragraphs, stating the simple and undeniable facts: An employee of Alphabet Capital named Howard Egan had disappeared while on a business trip to Pakistan to meet with clients of the firm. Alphabet Capital was requesting help from the U.S. and Pakistani governments in finding Mr. Egan and arranging his safe return.

Perkins read the document carefully and made several corrections in the margins. Then he put it in his pocket.

"Please let us know if you are making any changes," urged Ogilvy.

Perkins laughed. The young man was sweating, even in the cool of the morning. He obviously wasn't happy at the thought that one of his colleagues had disappeared.

"Don't worry," Perkins said, "and don't tell me what to do. I've had enough of that from your colleagues already."

11
QUETTA, PAKISTAN

When Lieutenant General Mohammed Malik was a student in America long ago, one of his military science professors had admonished the class, knowingly, with that old chestnut: “If you sup with the devil, you must use a long spoon.” How right that had seemed to everyone. But they were in Fort Leavenworth, Kansas. That was the land of the guileless, eternal smile. What did they know of the devil? In the unlikely event that they ever encountered the devil, they wouldn’t have supped with him, anyway, long spoon or short. They would have dropped a bomb on him.

General Malik realized when he returned home after his stint at the War College that he did not have the luxury of his American friends. The devil lived in Pakistan. It was necessary to sup with him on a daily basis simply to survive, sometimes without any utensils at all, grabbing it up with your hands.

The devil that concerned General Malik at the moment was the group of operatives that had kidnapped the American traveler, Howard Egan. Yes, he knew who they were. The Americans might not like it, but that was his job. The group in this case was called Al-Tawhid, which means “divine unity,” or, to use the more common term, “monotheism.” The general would have denied to his last breath that he or his service had any contact with these miscreants. But of course that was not true.

They were well known to the ISI, and indeed had been used on occasion to do ISI business over the last few years. That was what intelligence services did. And then, if anyone criticized the contact, they lied about it. Only the Americans tried to pretend that the intelligence business was any different.

The best place to sup with these particular devils was their birthplace and home of Quetta, the capital of Baluchistan on the country's western border. General Malik knew the city well, for he had studied at the Army Staff College there as a young officer, and had returned as "chief instructor," as the deputy commander's position was known, before moving to the ISI.

The general flew to Quetta from Rawalpindi, this time in a lumbering Pakistani Air Force C-130. The plane was not like the gray American versions; it was painted in the colors of the desert, tan and brown, so that it was almost an airborne version of the trucks that plied the Grand Trunk Road. The general sat up top, in a comfortable seat just behind the air crew, not down below with the ordinary soldiers in their web seats slung from metal poles. Three-star generals were not soldiers anymore; they were demigods.

The plane landed at the military air base just north of the Quetta city center. As he stepped out of the C-130, General Malik saw again the austere, arid beauty of the place. The city was like the floor of a rock-hewn amphitheater, a dusty plain surrounded on all sides by reddish gray peaks. Back when he was a student, the young officers at the Staff College had names for these rocky citadels: "Takatu," to the north; "Chiltan," to the southwest; and nearest, to the southeast, the low, graceful cliff whose form they called, in English, "Sleeping Beauty."

General Malik went first to the Staff College. He called on the commander, who was an old friend, and paid a visit to the Officers' Mess, a prim brown stone building banked by cedars. But this visit was really a bit of subterfuge. While there, as was his habit on these trips, he changed into civilian clothes and took a new vehicle; not the army staff car in which he had arrived, but a dirty Hyundai, pitted by the road, in which he would travel to his appointment.

The general headed off again, now in mufti. His frail car passed through the city center, past the knot of people gathered at the four-pillared front of the railway station, and then north toward the red rocks that framed the northern approach to the city. The driver turned off the main road, into a neighborhood that was largely Afghan refugees. For the Quetta police, this was no-man's-land. But for the director general of the ISI, there was no such thing as a forbidden zone. The car zigged and zagged down several byways until it came to a rough-hewn mosque and next to it a walled compound shielding a rambling two-story villa.

General Malik called a number on his cell phone and spoke to an ISI case officer inside the villa, to advise that he had arrived. A metal gate swung open and the Hyundai turned into the compound and parked, while the gate was quickly closed and relocked. The general walked toward the villa, its rough concrete blocks topped by the rust-red protruding rods of the steel reinforcing bars.

The young ISI officer met the visitor at the threshold of the villa. He was dressed in the garb of Pashtun tribesmen: a turban around his head, a long vest, loose trousers billowing in the breeze. The general entered the building and was escorted into the salon. It was curtained against the midday sun, but in the low light the prize was visible: Seated on the couch was a fierce-looking young man, a warrior prince, he seemed, with a grizzly black beard and long hair under a white turban.

"Commander Hassan," said the general, extending his hand. The young man took the general's hand in both of his. There were no kisses on the cheeks; these were men who, but for the ritual hospitality of the meeting, might shoot each other.

The others retreated from the room, including the ISI case officer who had arranged the meeting, and even the young commander's bodyguards, who were present with him always and everywhere. There remained just the distinguished Pakistani general, his mustache finely trimmed as always, and the fearsome tribal warrior.

"It is a pleasure to see you again," said the general. "You have been busy. We hear about you. But we do not see you."

The young fighter responded with appropriate reticence, by quoting a Pashtun saying. "*Da khali daig ghag lor de,*" he said, which means, "An empty vessel makes much noise." This vessel, real and full, was silent.

General Malik answered in his own ritual phrases, proverbs rather than declarative sentences. To have done otherwise would have seemed barbaric.

"You are a *mojahid,* Commander Hassan. It is said that cowards cause harm to brave men, but clearly there are no cowards among you. It is said that fear and shame are father and son, but you do not know these emotions. You are from another family, I can see that."

The young fighter bowed his head at the compliments and offered thanks to God for his success.

"Now I must ask you a question, Hassan. For that is part of why we talk, you and I, so that I can ask and you can tell."

"Yes, *badshah,* I understand." He paused then, and unwound his turban slowly, so that his long hair was free. It was rich and lustrous, even in the heat of the house. He swept it back from his face. He was a young lion, this one.

Hassan spoke another Pashtun phrase: *"Wrori ba kawu hesab tar menza."* This one was unfamiliar to the general, so he asked what it meant. The young man translated into Urdu: "We will behave like brothers, but we shall know what is yours and what is mine."

"So then I will ask: How is the American man, the one who disappeared in Karachi?"

"He is dead, General. He died several days ago."

"Did he die badly?"

"Yes, General. He would not talk at first, so we had to use methods. Then it becomes hard. It must end."

The general nodded. He had used torture himself, but he did not like it. He turned back to Commander Hassan.

"What did you learn from the American? I think he had many secrets, this one. Perhaps you can tell me."

"Ah, *badshah,* we have our secrets, too. We cannot tell you everything. You are our enemy, sir, when you are not our friend. But I will tell you a little."

The general put his hand on his heart. It was a dignified way to say that he was grateful.

"The American worked for the CIA. You know that. But it was a part of the CIA that was not the CIA. It was something new and evil. A new way to spread lies."

"What was he doing here?" The general thought he knew the answer, but he wanted to hear it, just the same.

"He came with money, to give to a traitor from the Darwesh Khel: a soft Pashtun man, not a fighter. The American was going to bring him more money, and more money, until he had bought up as many of our people as were for sale. That was his mission. They know they are losing, you see. They want the war to be over, so they hope to buy peace. It is always this way with the *gora*." They run up the hill, but they do not know how to get down."

The general nodded. He waited for the young man to say more about Azim Khan, but he didn't. Instead, he spat into a bowl beside his chair.

"Did the American confess how his organization operates?" asked the general.

"Yes, as much as he understood. It hides inside of businesses. It has a big headquarters. He said before he died that it was in Los Angeles, but how can we check? He pretended to work for a finance company in London. They sent him on his travels, as if he were one of them."

"And will Al-Tawhid pursue other members of this CIA that is not a CIA?"

"Forever. We are not finished with the Americans, or with the Pakistanis who have been so misguided that they chose to help the Americans."

The general didn't take the bait. He nodded again, and then spoke more softly, so that the young warrior had to lean toward him to hear.

"I have one more question about this incident, Commander. Then we can talk of our other affairs. And my question is this: How did you know that the American was here in Pakistan? How did you know that he was working for this CIA that is not the CIA? That is a very big secret. How did you discover it?"

"This, sir, I cannot tell you."

"Why is that, Brother Hassan? Is it because you do not trust me? For I tell you, this is the most important thing, what I have asked. I want you to answer me."

"It is true that I do not trust you, *badshah*. But that is not the reason I will not tell you."

"Why, then? When I have humbled myself and told you that I want this information especially, only for you to shame me in this way?"

"Because I do not know the answer. We have a friend who gives us this information. He is our teacher and guide. But how he obtains it, I do not know. Nor do I know his identity. We never see or hear him. We received an electronic message about the American in Karachi. We did not ask more questions. As we say in our Pashto language, *Chi na kar, pa hagha the sa kar.* When it is not your business, stay away."

"Why does this mysterious guide help you, Commander Hassan?"

"I cannot say, General. Why does the scorpion sting when he is disturbed, or the wolf devour his prey? He has a reason, this man, but I do not know what it is. He is our ghost."

General Malik reflected a moment. He sensed from the man's demeanor that he was being truthful. The commander did not know this secret of how the American's deep-cover identity had been cracked, but perhaps he could find out. And if not him, perhaps it could be discovered by one of the ISI's other contacts in the brotherhood of Al-Tawhid.

"So what did you learn from this experience with the American, Commander Hassan? Not the little things that we have discussed, but the big thing?"

Hassan thought a moment. He ran his fingers through that long hair once more, and then spoke in his Pashto tongue.

"*Da maar bachai maar wee.* This is what I know: The baby of a snake is also a snake. This new CIA is worse than the old one. Its money is more dangerous than its rockets. For that, General, you must beware."

"Grant me another request, then, so that I will not leave with anger. For many years I have heard in these lands of 'the professor.' But this man is unknown to me."

The commander looked at his visitor suspiciously. "I do not know who you are talking about."

"Yes, you do. We have listened to your talk. Some call him the professor. Others call him *ustad.* We think maybe he talks with the Americans, maybe he works against them. We hear his footsteps, but we cannot find him. Where is he?"

The Pashtun man emitted a low guttural sound that might have been a snort or a laugh.

"Nowhere, sir. That is where he is. He does not exist. You have been dreaming, I think. There is no such man."

The conversation continued in the Quetta hideaway for another hour, as the two men exchanged information and offered reciprocal promises. The general wanted help in planning operations against other Muslim groups, ones that Al-Tawhid despised. These other groups targeted their operations against the "little enemy," the Pakistani army and state, rather than the "big enemy" of America. Commander Hassan shared information. Of course he did. That is how people survive in the East. For it is said: Friends are serpents; they bite.

General Malik did not offer information himself. He left that to his ISI case officer, a pudgy colonel whom he summoned late in the meeting. This man did what could not be done.

While General Malik paid a visit to the toilet, the colonel provided names, cell phone numbers, ISI contacts who would be helpful. He advised which villages in the tribal areas to stay away from, because they were on the American target list. He handed over new communications devices, whose frequencies were not tracked by the Americans. He was helpful, in all the big and little ways that are part of the secret world.

General Malik flew back to Rawalpindi that night in the cold, throbbing body of the C-130. He wanted to go to sleep, for he was tired after the long day, but he found that he could not. He was turning over in his mind the information that Commander Hassan had provided. More than that, he was thinking about the secrets the young warrior had not divulged.

But General Malik understood: Somehow, the brotherhood of Al-Tawhid had found its way inside the American compartment. It knew when a secret agent arrived in Karachi and whom he met. These simple men in their *shalwar khamiz* had not cracked the American code themselves, but someone had helped them. How was this possible? General Malik did not know the answer yet, but he set his mind to discovering it. What he would do with this secret, once he learned it, he did not know.

The plane bucked and shuddered as it skirted the summer thunderstorms of the Indus Valley. The general was somewhere else. He was thinking of his biggest unsolved mystery from his early days as director general. It dated back to 2005. The Americans were working their antiterrorism traces very hard in those days. They were pressing everywhere for information that they could load into their computers—to follow money flows and communications links and all the other strings that would lead them to Al-Qaeda. Of course, the Pakistanis were trying to help officially, just enough, but they had held something back, too.

It had become obvious to General Malik in the course of 2005 that the Americans had obtained the identities and communications protocols of several of the ISI's most sensitive contacts with Al-Qaeda. This was evident because the Americans began targeting these men, and eventually killed two of them. What troubled the general was that only someone with an intimate knowledge of ISI tradecraft and Pakistani dialects could have uncovered these links. They had been disguised by codes within codes. That was when the general had begun to worry that a *gungrat,* a dung beetle, was loose in his stores of information.

General Malik had paid an unofficial visit that year to Washington, where he had called on the man in the CIA he knew best, a rotund and genial officer named Cyril Hoffman, who always understood more than he said.

"Are you inside our tent, Cyril?" the general had asked.

They were sitting in the CIA cafeteria, surrounded by signs warning agency personnel that a foreign national was in the area. Hoffman had leaned toward his Pakistani friend.

"Of course we are," the American had whispered, his voice as soft as spun sugar. "But you can't see us, and you can't feel us, and you'll never find us. So my advice is to stop worrying about it. You'll only make yourself unhappy if you go poking around."

Perhaps that had been the right advice, but General Malik had launched his investigations anyway, silently at first, and then more openly. He was looking for a Pakistani who understood signals intelligence, someone with the intellectual creativity to disassemble an elaborate puzzle. They called in a dozen suspects—military and intelligence officers, a senior executive of the leading wireless telephone company, several professors, a retired ISI officer who had been living in India. The investigators ruined the careers of most of these people, with their rough and stupid questions, but it couldn't be helped.

Eventually, sometime in 2007, General Malik had given up, just as Cyril Hoffman had advised. The Pakistani leak seemed to have dried up, that was part of it. But Malik had concluded that Hoffman was right. This inside source was too well hidden. Perhaps the truth about this source would emerge one day, on its own, but tearing up the garden to try to find him was unwise.

Malik's own private name for the case was "the Cheshire Cat," because he could see the grin, but not the cat itself. It made him mad, still, to think that the Americans could vex him.

When he arrived at his office in Islamabad the next morning, General Malik summoned Homer Barkin, the CIA station chief. He told him that in four hours the Foreign Ministry would send a formal statement to the embassy declaring him and two other members of the CIA station at the embassy persona non grata because of their intelligence activities. They would be ordered to leave the country. He advised Barkin to leave that afternoon, to avoid unpleasant consequences at the airport.

Barkin was bewildered. He had met in this office with the ISI chief only a few days before. They had talked of friendship and trust.

"What the hell is going on?" he asked. "What is this all about?"

General Malik shook his head. He had a distant, wistful smile, as if remembering better times.

"It seems that you really do not know."

"Know what?" asked the station chief.

"My poor, unfortunate Mr. Barkin: Your expulsion is a message to whoever in Washington thinks it is acceptable to send secret warriors with bribes into the territory of an ally. If it is true that you did not know about this operation in Karachi, then that is the greatest outrage. I suggest that you resign, sir, when you get home. These actions will have consequences. That is what you should tell Langley."

Barkin, still astonished, sputtered a response.

"I protest, on behalf of my agency. We have done nothing wrong."

"Thank you, Mr. Barkin. This is nothing personal, I assure you. Now you should leave. I fear that Pakistanis will be very angry. I would not be surprised if there were demonstrators tomorrow at the entrance to the diplomatic zone near your embassy, expressing their outrage. The embassy should take precautions, I think."

12
DUBAI

The Dubai Airport had a hungover, half-deserted look when Marx arrived. She made her way past bleary-eyed South Asians in transit, who were wandering up and down the corridor like weary birds looking for a place to alight. The customs hall was nearly empty, except for the Filipina "Marhaba" girls who were arrayed to greet any VIP visitors who chanced to arrive. The city beyond had the look of a new luxury car, its seats still wrapped in cellophane, standing in an empty showroom with no customers in sight.

"Things are looking up in Dubai," insisted her taxi driver, an Indian from Kerala. He offered to show her an apartment that she could sublet, half price, no, quarter price. Marx took his card and then told him to be quiet. As the driver weaved along the airport road across the new downtown, they passed a dozen dazzling apartment towers that appeared to have few if any tenants. Would anyone ever live in them, or would they gradually decay into ruins of chrome and glass, with blowing sand caking the entryways and the elevators creaking to a halt for lack of maintenance?

Marx checked in to her hotel, a vast place made to look like the architect's fantasy of an ancient Arab city. It had been immaculate a few years before, every surface of brass and wood polished and sparkling, so that if you rubbed one of the urns that decorated the lobby, you might expect Aladdin himself to pop out. Now the mahogany furniture was losing its stain, and some of the fancy carpets were discoloring from the sun and the foot traffic.

Marx loved Dubai the way earlier generations of intelligence officers had embraced Beirut or Hong Kong. It was a city that existed at the margins, between East and West, between the imaginary and the real. Plus it had good air service, and you could drink the water. She liked it even more now that the bubble had burst and the place had come back to earth. The hotels that were never full, and the parking lots that were still sprinkled with Mercedes cars that had been abandoned when their owners couldn't make the payments.

She showered and changed, and lay on her bed for a while staring at the ceiling, thinking about how she would handle the interrogation of Hamid Akbar. An hour before the meeting, she rode the elevator down to the ground floor, which opened onto one of the ersatz canals that linked the buildings in this imaginary Medina. She took a seat in the stern of a dhow that served as a water taxi; behind her loomed the towers of a make-believe Arabian fortress.

She was dressed in a black pants suit, her hair pulled tight in bun, sunglasses masking the fatigue in her eyes. She turned her head toward the breeze blowing in off the Gulf. A gust caught a few strands of hair and pulled them loose. She had taken a pill to sleep on the long flight, and then another. Now that she had arrived, she felt groggy. She gave her cheek a gentle slap to wake herself up. With the sting came a bit of color.

The turbaned boatman tried to be friendly. He was a poor fisherman from Dar Es Salaam who couldn't support his family running a boat back home. He spoke about fish. Sophie Marx didn't want to make small talk, and she didn't have any dirhams to give him a tip. She told him in Arabic to keep his eyes on the water or she would report him to the hotel manager.

The boatman deposited her at the Villas, the meeting place that Gertz's support staff had arranged on short notice. The polygraph operator was already there. Gertz had dispatched him from Prague, where he nominally worked for an electronics company. Dubai station had a resident polygraph technician, but he reported to Headquarters, and Gertz vetoed that.

Marx stepped gingerly off the prow at the landing. The polygraph operator opened the door for her. He was a big, powerfully built man, well over six feet, with tattoos decorating his biceps. Marx was glad to see him.

"Hey, my name's Andy," he said, extending a forearm as thick as a log.

"Where did you come in from?" she asked.

"Ashgabat," he said. "It was the quickest flight from Prague. I had to sleep in the transit lounge in Turkmenistan. Too hot. Glad to leave."

"It's hot in Dubai," she said.

"Not when you're in the pool." He smiled. This assignment was a vacation for him.

Marx looked around the villa. It was too fancy for the task ahead: It offered a fine view of the water and beyond it the Burj Al Arab, billowing like the sail of a dhow forty stories tall. Marx closed the curtains and turned up the heat in the room till it would raise a sweat. She made herself a pot of coffee and waited for the Pakistani.

"Break him," she told herself. "Make him talk."

Hamid Akbar knocked gently on the door as if he were afraid that he would wake the neighbors. Through the intercom, he spoke the phrases of the recognition code. He retreated a step when Andy, the technician, opened the door. The American was so big. Akbar peered inside and saw that the CIA officer awaiting him was a compact and well-tailored woman. He bowed slightly in her direction and said, "Madam."

"Welcome, Mr. Akbar," she responded. "Please sit down. This will be a long visit, I'm afraid. I have many questions for you. Would you like some coffee?"

The Pakistani was waiting politely for her to sit down before seating himself.

She motioned sharply for him to take his seat, while she remained standing, her arms folded. She knew that she must establish dominance from the beginning.

"I am sorry about Mr. Howard Egan," said the Pakistani, placing his hand over his heart. "It is most unfortunate that he is missing. I do not know what went wrong."

The Pakistani sat awkwardly, his knees together primly. He looked like he hadn't slept in a week. There was perspiration above his lip.

"We are all sorry, Mr. Akbar. But we need to know how this happened. People in Washington have questions about your role. I must warn you of that, so that we understand each other."

The Pakistani arched his neck. He looked offended.

"Why me, madam? I have done nothing wrong, I assure you. It is I who am in danger. Next they will get me."

Marx had been about to deliver to him the coffee she had promised, but she thought better of it. She set the cup down.

"I don't think you get it, Mr. Akbar. You are a suspect. That is why you are here. You were the last person to see Mr. Egan. We need answers from you. My friend here is going to strap you to a machine that will tell me if you are lying. The reason we are doing this is because we have power over you. You must understand that."

He looked at her warily. She was a woman; he was a man. But she was giving him instructions, and the big American with the tattoos was there to back her up.

"I can leave," he said. He was trying to be assertive, but the way he formed the words it sounded more like a question.

She heard the weakness in the voice. It was the same voice she had heard on the NSA audio file.

"No, Mr. Akbar, you are wrong there. You cannot leave. You have taken money from the United States, and now, to be honest with you, we have power over you. Do you realize that? You could try to leave. But my friend Andy and I would stop you. And then we would tell people in Pakistan about your contacts with us, for all these years, and they would take care of the rest. So don't talk any more about leaving, please. Are we clear?"

There was silence, so she repeated the question.

"Are we clear, Mr. Akbar? Otherwise, I am going to instruct Andy to take you into custody."

He nodded. The sweat beads were rolling down his forehead now. He wiped the dampness away with his sleeve.

"And don't call me 'madam.' It's a name for someone who runs a brothel. Tonight I am your control. You can call me that. Miss Control."

The little lines around his mouth crinkled. He had been nervous when he walked in the door. Now he was frightened.

"What is my name? Say it, please."

"Miss Control."

"Thank you." It sounded strange, even to her, but she nodded approval. One of her tradecraft instructors had admonished her years ago at the Farm that an interrogator was like a jeweler working on a precious stone. You had to tap it at the right points, to make the rough bits fall away so you could see what was really there.

"Let's get started," she said, motioning to the technician to begin attaching his wires to Akbar's body. The Pakistani fidgeted. He didn't like to be touched, but there was nothing he could do about it.

"First the technician is going to ask some baseline questions, to measure your normal reactions. You do have normal, right?"

"Yes."

Andy went through a string of simple questions: name, place and date of birth, passport number. As the Pakistani answered, he became confident again, leaning forward in his chair. Marx listened for a while, struggling to think of a way to establish primacy. When there was a pause, she broke in.

"Are you a homosexual, Mr. Akbar?"

"My goodness, no. Of course not. How can you ask that?"

She looked at Andy's monitor.

"You're lying. Let me ask it again. Have you ever had sex with a man?"

"No. This is a most gross insult. I am leaving now." He began pulling at the wires, and then stopped when the big American seized his hand.

Marx looked to Andy, who studied his computer terminal and shook his ahead.

"You're still lying, Mr. Akbar. Three strikes and you're out. That's what we say in America. Now tell me the truth. Have you ever had sex with a man? When you were a boy, perhaps? Women have an intuition about this, I'm warning you."

"I do not have to answer," he said. His eyes were becoming moist at the edges. He was humiliated to the core.

"I'll take that as a yes," she said. "Not a problem with me. All I care about is that you tell the truth. If you don't, I'll find out. Is that clear? Okay. Continue, Andy."

She sat back, confident now in her dominance. People from shame cultures were so vulnerable if you pushed the right buttons.

The technician asked more questions, alternating soft ones and hard ones. He stood behind the Pakistani, who couldn't see him and heard only his questions, one after another. When the machine indicated deception, Andy would ask the question again until he got an answer that registered as truthful. After forty-five minutes he nodded to Marx that he was ready for her to begin.

Her task now was to break him. This man had set Egan up. She had become convinced of that as she pursued her investigation. Now she had to prove it.

"We will begin the serious part, Mr. Akbar. I can tell you that your life depends on your giving me the right answers. Do we understand each other? This is life or death."

The Pakistani nodded.

"Let's go back to the night Howard Egan disappeared. In addition to your uncle, someone else knew that you were meeting with him. Is that right?"

He shook his head. He paused a moment, looked around the room, and then said quietly, "No one."

Marx turned to Andy, who nodded. The answer had produced no sign of the anxiety associated with a lie, which meant that it had to be considered true.

"Let me ask it again, Mr. Akbar. You told someone else you were meeting with Egan, right?"

"No. No one."

Andy nodded again.

Marx loomed over the Pakistani man. Her face showed a blush of anger.

"You are a liar! Tell the truth, or you won't make it to the next Eid.

You told someone else about your meeting with Howard Egan. True or false?"

His voice was thin and strained by fear. He was sweating. But he gave the same answer.

"I told no one."

Andy again signaled that the machine had not registered deception. Marx stepped back from the Pakistani. She motioned for Andy to join her in the bathroom, where they talked for several minutes. Then she returned.

"Your contact in the Taliban told you to move up the meeting time for Howard Egan. Is that right?

"No. That is not true. I don't know anyone in the Taliban."

Andy nodded.

"Are you lying to me now?"

"No. I wanted to hide the meeting. It was dangerous for me. Why would I tell anyone?"

"I'll ask the questions, Mr. Akbar. Who told you to move up the meeting?"

"My Uncle Azim. He said he had to go back to Waziristan the next morning for the funeral of someone in the tribe. That was why he had to do it that night."

"Is that statement truthful?"

"Yes."

"Have you talked with your uncle since Egan disappeared?"

"No."

Andy's face was suddenly animated, as he shook his head to indicate that the machine had registered deception."

"You are a liar. I am warning you, we will not tolerate this. Now let me ask you again. Have you talked with your uncle since Egan disappeared?"

"Yes." The man's voice was so small, the word sounded as if it had been blown through a tube. The sweat covered his forehead.

"I talked with him the night the meeting was supposed to happen. He called me. He asked why my friend had not come to the address we had agreed. I said I did not know. He called me again and said that he was going to leave and go back to Waziristan right away. He was frightened. That is all."

"Why did you lie before?"

"Because I was afraid that you would be angry with me. I was not supposed to talk to anyone about anything. But I talked with him."

Marx nodded. She went over to the thermostat and turned it down, until the air conditioner was blowing full-tilt.

"It's too damn hot in here," she muttered.

Marx started again, probing around the edges of Akbar's story. She asked him for details about his initial recruitment and handling, about his past meetings with Egan, about his payments from the agency. She kept looking for a route into the deception that she had been certain was there when they started. But try as she might, she couldn't find an opening in his story.

After another hour of frustration, she decided that the only explanation was that she had been wrong: Hamid Akbar had not blown the operation. The compromise had come from somewhere else.

The Pakistani looked spent—sweated and chilled, poked and prodded until he had no reserves left. He wasn't deceiving her, but there was still a missing piece. She nodded to Andy that she wanted to continue a little longer.

"We're almost done, Mr. Akbar," she said. "I have just a few more questions, okay?"

"Sure," he said. His face was drained.

"Have you been in touch with another intelligence service?"

"When?" he asked.

"Ever. Have you ever been in touch with another intelligence service, besides ours? Or any other contact that you've never told us about."

"Not that I haven't told you about. I always told the truth."

She looked at Andy. He nodded. The machine said he wasn't being deceptive.

"Why do you say, 'Not that I haven't told you about'? There's nothing in your file about contact with another intelligence service. Who have you talked to?"

He opened his palms wide in a protest of innocence.

"It was only the police. The Intelligence Bureau at the Ministry of Interior. I told that to my case officer."

"To Mr. Egan?"

"No. The one before him. As soon as the police contacted me, I told him. It wasn't important. They talk to everyone. They are police, like I said."

"How often did you meet with them?"

"A few times. Six, or eight. I am not sure that I can count. They visit people who have studied abroad, like me. They visit everybody. It is Pakistan, madam. It is not Baltimore."

"Did you tell the police about your contacts with us?"

"Oh, no, madam. Certainly not. I knew that would be wrong."

"And they believed you?"

"Oh, yes, I think so. They never said they did not."

"Did you ever talk to the Inter-Services Intelligence, the ISI?"

"Oh, no. Not ever. They are quite dangerous. In Pakistan, we make an effort not to talk with them."

"How about your uncle? Did he ever talk to the ISI?"

"That I would not know. It is not something that I would ask, or that he would answer."

Marx looked at Andy. He shrugged, out of sight. It all registered true.

"Please, madam. If you doubt me, check your files. I explained it all. I have never told a lie."

"How recently did you meet with the police?"

"The last time? It was six months ago, perhaps. We met at my office. They came round, to stop and talk."

"And they never asked about Mr. Egan?"

"No. They knew about my investments, all right. The ministry has a section that monitors foreign accounts. But they did not ask about Mr. Egan."

Marx thought a moment, trying to see how the pieces fit.

"Have you ever had your office swept, Mr. Akbar? To check for microphones or cameras?"

"Oh, no. Why would I do that?"

"Just to be safe," she said. She closed her eyes.

She offered Hamid Akbar a cigarette and a glass of whiskey, while Andy unstrapped the wires. He accepted both. She opened the bottle and poured a drink for everyone. They'd had a couple of shots each when Marx pulled her chair up a little closer.

"We're friends now, right? So I am going to ask you a question, friend to friend. How do you think Howard Egan was discovered, then, if you didn't tell anyone?"

"I am sorry," said the Pakistani. "It is not for me to say."

"Go ahead. Tell me what you think."

He closed his eyes, and spoke a sentence in Pashto. *"Da cha, pakhpala. Gila ma hawa dab ala."*

"Sorry, but that's not very helpful."

"It is a saying of my Pashtun people. It means: 'These are self-inflicted wounds, not from others.'"

She was startled. "What do you mean by that?"

"I think that you have a problem, madam. The problem is not me. Mr. Egan's job was very secret. The people who have taken him, I am sorry for that, but they would not have known who he was unless someone told them. There is a leak. They are inside your house. It must be that. I am sorry to say it. That is why I am frightened. What this leak might be, I cannot say, but I hope that you will find out. Yes, truly I do."

Sophie didn't answer him at first. She didn't want to start telling lies herself. Eventually she spoke. It was the voice of a tired combatant on an ill-lit battlefield.

"We will protect you," she said. "America has great power. When we look weak, that is an illusion."

The Pakistani nodded respectfully, but inwardly he smiled. How could these Americans protect anyone, when they did not know who had stolen their secrets?

13
ISLAMABAD

A few days after the expulsion of Homer Barkin, an unusual American visitor arrived in Islamabad. The man came in a Gulfstream jet, unmarked except for the tail number, and he took a suite at the Serena Hotel, at the crest of a hill overlooking the diplomatic quarter of the capital. The gentleman was dressed more flamboyantly than a normal Western traveler, in a double-breasted summer suit that enfolded him like a tent and a Panama hat with a parrot feather, of yellow and blue, stuck in the black satin hatband. The traveler had long maintained that the best disguise was to be so visible that people would take you as a public personality, albeit undefined, and overlook the possibility that you had a separate and secret life.

The traveler's name was Cyril Hoffman, and he was, in fact, associate deputy director of what remained of the Central Intelligence Agency.

Hoffman had come to pay a quiet visit to Lieutenant General Mohammed Malik. It was not a normal liaison trip, of the sort CIA officials frequently made, and for that reason Hoffman had not informed the U.S. Embassy or the acting chief of station. He had discreetly consulted a Pakistani source he had developed over the past decade, a man who had helped him to understand the nature of the insurgency that was devouring Pakistan and the Tribal Areas. But otherwise he had kept his own counsel, waiting to deliver his message to the ISI chief.

General Malik was a family friend, of sorts. The Pakistani had been befriended by Cyril's flamboyant cousin Ed, during his years as chief of the CIA's Near East Division. And the young Mohammed Malik had been friendly with Cyril's uncle, Frank, after he retired as chief of station in Beirut and set himself up as a consultant and fixer in Riyadh. It was the personal touch that mattered in this part of the world, Cyril Hoffman had told the director in proposing his off-the-record visit to Islamabad. He would be back in the office in forty-eight hours, he promised.

The Serena had the empty feeling of a mausoleum. The floors were waxed and buffed to a high gloss, which never seemed to lose its shine because so few feet traversed the lobby. Hotels had been targets for suicide bombers in Pakistan the last few years, and the American Embassy directed most visitors to anonymous "guesthouses" whose locations, it was thought, were unknown to the jihadists. To Hoffman, the fact that the Serena was avoided by Washington visitors made it the ideal place to hide.

The morning of his arrival, Hoffman took his breakfast in the chandeliered dining room, at one of the tables that were arrayed around a marble-clad fountain. There was only one other diner in the room, a businessman who was shouting details of his commercial plans into his cell phone. Hoffman placed foam-rubber plugs in his ears to block the noise, and went to the breakfast buffet.

Hoffman had one breakfast, a heap of scrambled eggs and turkey bacon and buttered toast. And then, for good measure, he returned to the buffet table and had a second breakfast, this time a big bowl of bran flakes and fruit that would aid his digestion. There were also donuts, small and lumpy and dusted with confectioner's sugar, and he took two of these, to eat with his coffee. He installed himself at his table and devoured this feast, reading the English-language newspapers, *Dawn* and *The News*, until it was time to go calling.

General Malik had proposed that they meet in Rawalpindi, at a guesthouse on the compound of the military's General Headquarters. That would be a more confidential setting than the ISI's headquarters in Aabpara, the Pakistani general advised. He sent his own limousine to pick up Hoffman, so that the American would not be bothered by awkward questions at the GHQ gate.

When the car arrived at the Serena, Hoffman gathered his billowing suit jacket around him and took a seat in the back, behind a smoked-glass partition. He put the buds of his iPod in his ears and clicked on a recording of *Così fan tutte*, one of the library of operas and musical comedies that he carried with him to maintain a sunny mood, even as he traveled long distances. He hummed to himself as the car made its way through Islamabad's western suburbs.

The entrance to General Headquarters was a reminder that the Pakistani military was a living remnant of the British colonial army. There was an emerald cricket pitch just outside the gate, with a pavilion where the players could retire for tea in the late afternoon. Batsmen in white trousers and cable-knit sweaters, impervious to the summer heat, were practicing their strokes in the batting nets as Hoffman's car passed. The entry gate itself looked as if it hadn't much changed since imperial days; it was a banked by green lawns and ceremonial cannons, and walls of marble and granite.

General Malik was waiting for Hoffman at the guesthouse. He embraced him and kissed him on both cheeks, and the American reciprocated, and not with air kisses, but with the soft smack of lips puckered against skin. Since Hoffman had never married, it was occasionally rumored about the agency that he might be homosexual. What he told people, in the rare moments when they ventured into his private life, was that sex of any kind was a bore and a distraction: It was too hot and wet and uncomfortable.

The Pakistani had turned up the air-conditioning, so that it was positively chilly in the small sitting room. A steward in white gloves arrived with tea almost as soon as they were seated, and then with little sandwiches on white bread whose crusts had been removed.

"Well, sir, I can see that we have gotten your attention," said the Pakistani general. "Such a speedy journey! Perhaps we should expel your station chiefs more often, to hasten your visits to our poor country."

"It is always a pleasure, Mohammed, but you needn't take such extreme measures. Just pick up the telephone and call me next time you're peeved, how about that?"

"Most assuredly I will do so. On the promise that the next time you send someone here on a most secret and nefarious mission, you will call me first to ask permission. Otherwise it may strain our relationship, you see. We do not like surprises."

"We didn't do it, old boy. That's why I am here. This was not a CIA operation."

"Bosh! My dear Cyril, I do not wish to bicker with an old friend, or play semantic games. There will be time to discuss our differences. But here, have a sandwich." He handed Hoffman the plate, and the American removed a tasty chicken sandwich with sweet mayonnaise and a dusting of black pepper.

It was hard to say which of them was more polite and indirect, as they felt each other out. General Malik asked about Hoffman's family, and he, in turn, asked after the Pakistani's only child, a daughter who was attending medical school at Emory University in Atlanta. Hoffman had subtly assisted her admission, though he had never said so to the general. They talked of music, for both were opera buffs. They talked of books. General Malik was an admirer of Philip K. Dick, whose science fiction novels he had begun to read when he was a young officer posted to Fort Leavenworth, Kansas.

"He is very bleak, don't you think?" said the general. "All that talk about authoritarian states of the future. I recently read *Flow My Tears, the Policeman Said*. I thought it might have been about my poor country. And yet, I could not stop reading."

"Try *Dr. Bloodmoney*," said Hoffman. "You'll feel like taking a suicide pill."

Hoffman would normally have been happy to continue with this civilized exchange for a while longer. It was a way of clearing the throat before getting to the point. But he had only so much time before he had to get back on his Gulfstream jet, so eventually, after eating two watercress sandwiches and a small chicken kebab dipped in hot sauce, he got around to the purpose of his visit, which was to deliver a warning. But even then he did it in a most peculiar and roundabout way.

"I wonder if I could tell you a story, Mohammed," Hoffman began. "Would you mind that?"

"Not at all, Cyril. I am most fond of your stories. They always have a moral, which sometimes is not immediately obvious. That is the way we like to tell stories here in my country."

"Well, sir, this story is a true one. And it's about soldiers. People like yourself. I am a civilian, working for an agency that, let us be honest, has seen better days. But this story is about the flower of our youth, so to speak—the young men and women who, like yourself, wear the uniform. As a matter of fact, you could say that it's about just that: The uniform."

"Ah, Cyril. The uniform. How apt. I am sure I will find this story most instructive, once I hash it out."

"If you please, my friend, I want you to think about the uniform that a U.S. Army officer wears. A desert combat uniform, tan, with the camouflage markings. The kind that would be worn by a soldier who is fighting our common enemies in Afghanistan, let us say, or in Iraq, or Somalia—any of the places we have been lately, or may yet be. Do you have it in your mind, that uniform?"

"Oh, yes, indeed. Clear as a bell."

"Do you see on the arm the little American flag? It's made of shiny plastic material. Do you see that just below the shoulder? That's what the soldier wears when he's in a combat zone. Not the regular embroidered flag on a nice piece of cloth, but a plastic one. Can you see it in your mind's eye?"

"I do, for a certainty. And I have often wondered why they wear that one, and not the finer cloth one."

"Have you, now? Have you wondered that? Well, this is your lucky day, because I am going to explain it. Our soldiers wear that little flag because it can be read by an infrared beam. It distinguishes them as U.S. forces—friendly forces. And they wear it so that our pilots and troopers and riflemen will know not to shoot at them. It's a special piece of protection, you see? To keep our men and women out of harm's way. Don't you think that's a smart idea?"

"Of course. It is so American, to use the technology so adeptly, to mark your people as your own. I wish we could be so advanced in our poor country."

"But see, here's the problem. And this is the reason I wanted to tell you the story, Mohammed. I am sorry to say that our enemies, Taliban fighters in Afghanistan, and Iranian Revolutionary Guards in Iraq and people on other battlefields I won't name, have been *tricking* us. If they are lucky enough to kill a U.S. soldier, they will strip off his plastic American flag and take it away with them. And they will keep these, you see. Gather them up, and at the right time, stick them to their own clothes. So that when the helicopter gunship comes after them, or the unmanned drone, it will look as if they are Americans. They will trick us, you see? They will deceive us. And they will use their trickery to survive and kill us when we are most vulnerable. What do you think of that?"

The American folded his arms, which weren't quite long enough to reach across the span of his rounded torso. Hoffman watched the face of his Pakistani host. "Do you like my story?" he asked.

The Pakistani didn't answer at first. He stroked his mustache with his index finger, gently aligning the hairs.

"I am not sure that I understand it, really, Cyril. I always like your stories, but what is the meaning of this one? And why have you come all the way to Pakistan to tell it to me?"

"Well, sir, this is a story about the difficulty of distinguishing friends and foes. The people who are really your enemies will try to make themselves look like your friends. And when they do that, they are especially dangerous. Do you see?"

The Pakistani was becoming peeved now. For all his politeness and his natural reserve, he could not disguise it.

"Yes, of course I see. I am not an idiot, sir. But what does this story of trickery have to do with me, and with my country? Why are you insulting me in this way, by suggesting that we are not friends, but foes who are playing tricks on you? For that seems to be the intent of the story, unless I misunderstand you."

"You never misunderstand anything, Mohammed. You are a very smart man. And I have always admired you, truly I have, as a fine gentleman and a patriot. Yes, indeed."

Hoffman adjusted his round form in the chair, tilting himself toward his host, as if to make sure that his voice was heard.

"But I want you to realize, my old friend, that there are people in America—some of them pretty high up, too—who think, to be blunt, that you are diddling us. That you are not playing straight with us. That you tell us you're our friend and ally, but at the same time you're helping the people who kill our soldiers and even, perhaps, our unarmed civilians. You are playing us, in other words. That's what these people think. And I want you to know—from me, a friend who respects and admires you—that this is a problem. You need to stop this behavior."

The Pakistani was shaking his head. On his face there was a mournful look, a look that said: *How could it have come to this? How could this man come to my country, to look me in the face and insult me in this way?* He did not say those things, though they were plain enough in his manner, but instead said something that was much more direct and, in that sense, out of character.

"Look here, Cyril. There may be politicians in America who say these things, but as we say in our Punjabi language, they are *dala* and *randi*. Pimps and whores. Let us cut the bullshit. Shall we do that? Cut this bullshit? I know why you are here. And I know why you told me the fairy tale about the flag."

"Oh, do you, now? Well, that's a relief. Pray tell."

"Yes, let me tell you about the real story, Cyril, not the make-believe one: An American was kidnapped in Karachi a week ago. We are very sorry for it. As I am sure you know, our police have been working to help."

"Yes, yes. Thank you for that." Hoffman nodded his big head.

"Now, this man appeared to be a businessman. But we are quite certain that he was something else. That he was an intelligence officer, to be blunt. But we didn't understand who he was working for. He did not appear to be working for your esteemed organization, Cyril, not for any part of it that we know, but for some other entity, which we do not understand. We do not like that, not at all. It is you who should apologize, sir, not me. This is a most gross violation of our sovereignty. It required a response, and so it was farewell for Mr. Barkin."

Hoffman shrugged. He folded his arms across his chest. He looked like Humpty Dumpty in a summer suit.

The Pakistani was angry. His pride had been injured, and that was not an easy wound to salve. His voice was sharper now.

"I did not expect a comment. I did not ask for one. But I must tell you, this turn of events bothers us. We do not like it when our 'friends' play games in our backyard. In that respect, my dear sir, we are just like you.

"What I dislike especially, Cyril," he continued, "is the implication in your comments—and in the fact of your visit—that we had something to do with this poor man's disappearance. That is truly offensive to me. After all that we have done and suffered, all the terrorist bombs, all the dead, to be accused of murder. This makes me angry."

Hoffman put up his hand, bidding the Pakistani to stop. He spoke more gently now.

"It was not my purpose to offend you, Mohammed. Truly it wasn't. And of course I can't comment on this fanciful story you just told me about the disappearance of a gentleman who, if memory serves, was working for a financial firm in London. But let me simply say, to my dear and esteemed friend, that if we thought your service was in any way connected with the disappearance of an American citizen, under these circumstances, we would take that most seriously. Yes sir, most seriously, indeed."

"We did not do it, Cyril. We know nothing about it." He spoke gravely, as people do when they are telling a most serious and important lie.

Hoffman stared unblinking into the eyes of his host.

"Heck, I never said you did."

"Let me repeat: We did not do it. We have no contact with these people whatsoever. If you think we do, you are mistaken."

"Well, that's nice," said Hoffman. He smiled. But his tone made clear that he did not believe his host. There they were, two old friends, each making statements the other was quite sure were false.

The Pakistani opened his arms, palms out, in a gesture of frustration. How could it have reached this point of impasse? He took another sip of his tea, now cold, and closed his eyes for a moment to clear his head.

"Now, Cyril, I will tell you something, because we are friends," said the general. He spoke softly at first, but his voice gained strength.

"You are looking in the wrong place. You are making a mistake that is characteristic of your country. I am surprised to hear you make it, because you are smarter than most of your fellows, but there we are."

"I'm listening, Mohammed. What's the mistake?"

"You do not realize your vulnerability. You do not realize that your adversary could do to you what you have been doing to them. There is a leak, my dear. I cannot say what it is, but it is for you to discover. I am sorry. Although you have been very clever in this new covert business, whatever it is, somehow they have found you out."

"Old Cyril is a little slow today. You better explain more."

"I cannot, sir. That is my point. I do not know. But someone knows. That is what you must consider."

"These riddles are giving me a headache, Mohammed. Why don't you tell me what it is you have to say?"

"Why should I? How can I? You have just accused me, more or less, of murder. Why should I think that you will listen to anything I say?"

"Do me a favor. Just say it. Tell me how we've been busted. Come on, say it, goddamn it."

The general shook his head. He did not like to hear profanity, especially in the sanctuary of his own quarters.

"I have already told you the essential fact, Cyril. They are on to you. The fact that you did not understand me illustrates the problem. You ask me for more, but there is no more. Perhaps you will think about it as you fly home. Maybe you will think about it, at greater length, when you are home. Maybe you will do something about it. I cannot say. It is not my problem. It is yours."

The general rose. The meeting was over. He shook the American's hand, and then, feeling that this was not enough, kissed him again on the cheeks. This time, Hoffman did not reciprocate. And it was a cold hand that he offered, for he was certain that the Pakistani, for all his fine words, had been false with him.

The Pakistani looked at his visitor, his face registering at once anger and injury.

"He's dead, by the way, your man in Karachi. The body cannot be recovered, but I do not think you would want to see it. His passing was a blessing, under the circumstances. Our police will say that he had an accident. He went trekking. Fell off a cliff. That will save us both from embarrassment. We will put something in a coffin and send it back to London. You can worry about the rest."

Cyril Hoffman nodded. How very like the Pakistanis, to tidy up the mess. What he thought, as he walked back into the heat of the Rawalpindi morning, was that his dear friend General Malik could not possibly know about the death of this American intelligence officer unless he was working with the people who killed him.

14
ISLAMABAD

Dr. Omar al-Wazir parked his car along Scholar's Drive and mounted the concrete steps to his office at the National University of Science and Technology. It was located west of Islamabad, in an otherwise desolate quadrant of ground off the Kashmir Highway known as H-12. It was as if the authorities wanted to quarantine science and keep it at a safe distance. The palms at the entrance were so wilted they were bent nearly double, and the potted plants that lined the walkway were just so many stalks and clods of dirt in the midsummer heat.

Dr. Omar was holding office hours today at the School of Electrical Engineering and Computer Science. He was a research professor, a coveted position, since the only responsibility, other than his own work, was to supervise a few graduate students. He closed the blinds against the sun so that his office was almost dark. The whiteboard at the far end of the room, scribbled with notations and algorithms, was the only object that picked up any light.

Dr. Omar booted up his computer and waited for the screen to come alive. He didn't do his sensitive communications here, but on another machine in the computer lab whose IP address was easier to mask. But there were puzzles he could solve in the office, too. He took off his suit jacket and put it on the hanger that hung from a hook on the door. He was neatly dressed, in a white shirt and lightweight summer suit that was the color of tobacco. His face was clean-shaven, not even a mustache, so that even with his big nose and dark complexion, he looked more Western than Pakistani.

There was a knock at Dr. Omar's door. A young man with a scraggly beard peered into the room. His name was Tahir and he was a doctoral candidate under Dr. Omar's supervision. His thesis topic was promising: "Traffic Analysis for Network Security using Streaming Algorithms and Learning Theory." When it was completed, the army would probably decide to classify it, and then Tahir would be stuck, but for now he could dream.

"Excuse me, professor, I am sorry to bother you," said the young man. He looked like he hadn't eaten or slept in a week.

"Come in, Tahir," said the professor, taking the student's hand and pulling him gently into the room. "It is office hours. You are not bothering me. I belong to you today. What is it that you want?"

"I was wondering, Doctor, if you had heard from Stanford or Caltech?"

Dr. Omar had contacts in the computer-science faculties of both those schools, from his own days as prodigy in computer security. Tahir had asked for his help in arranging a postdoctoral fellowship at one of the California schools.

"I did talk to them, but I am afraid it is not good news. They cannot take you next year. They have already made commitments to people with similar research topics. *Koi baat nahin,* I tell you. Never mind. There will be other chances to study abroad. The university has many exchanges with China now."

The young man shook his head sorrowfully. He did not want to go to China, but to the United States.

"What about Iowa State?" the student asked. "Or the University of Central Florida?" The National University of Science and Technology had official links with both those schools, too.

Dr. Omar laughed at the thought of little Tahir, scrawny as a she-goat, trying to make his way in the wilds of Orlando.

"We'll try," he said. "I don't know anyone at either place, but I will send the abstract of your dissertation with a nice note, and you never know."

"Thank you, professor." The graduate student gave a little bow and backed out of the room, as if he were leaving an audience with a medieval prince.

Dr. Omar smiled as Tahir was leaving. They all wanted to go to America, these boys, even with the visa problems and the expense and everything else. The professor could understand it well enough. He had been much the same at that age, wanting to escape a world where you were bound to live with your mother until you had found a wife, who then behaved as if she were your mother, too.

Dr. Omar did not have that problem now, though it gave him no comfort. He had lost his mother nearly two years before, along with most other members of his family, and the memory was as bitter to him as if it were poison. Sometimes, when he closed his eyes, the world went white again. He did not talk about it, ever, and few people even knew of it. He had one surviving sister, who had been away with her own family on that terrible day. She lived in Peshawar, where Dr. Omar visited her occasionally and sent her money to help pay for her children's schooling.

The professor went back to his research, waiting for the next earnest student to knock at the door. His main project these days, at least officially, was in something known as "computational neuroscience," which focused on the algorithms of the human brain. It was hopeful and uplifting, the idea that computers could mimic the processes that took place in threads of neurons, and in that sense it was a relief from the other work that Dr. Omar hid from everyone. He had told his contacts at the Military College of Signals in Rawalpindi, who reviewed his work, that computational neuroscience was the future of warfare, because it would someday drive robots. They liked that, and approved a handsome grant.

Dr. Omar kept his hand in computer security, too, to make everyone happy. He wrote occasional papers, and did consulting abroad, and gave lectures in Rawalpindi at the MCS when they asked. His original work as a graduate student had been in a specialty known as "pseudorandomness," a technique that used algorithmic techniques to produce numbers that were indistinguishable, in a technical sense, from random values. Dr. Omar had always been fascinated by numbers, ever since he was a little boy in Makeen when the solutions to number puzzles used to light up in his head like the display on a carnival arcade.

It had turned out that this topic of "pseudo-randomness" was a very hot one when Dr. Omar had gotten his doctorate in the late 1990s. A team at Stanford was doing similar work, and they had invited Dr. Omar to give a paper on his research. That was how he had met the Californians, and a lot of other people, too. The visiting analysts sitting in the back of the lecture hall had studied the Pakistani's formulas, and found uses for them that were far beyond what the young man had imagined.

Omar al-Wazir, nicknamed "the Waz" by an Indian friend he met that summer, stayed in Palo Alto for a month. He lived in a suite in the graduate student housing behind the law school, but he spent most of his time in the computer science library in the Math Wing of Memorial Hall.

When Omar went to Peet's Coffee & Tea nearby, the California girls often tried to pick him up. He was tall and exotic-looking, and he had the endearing manner, even then, of a young professor. A girl named Debbie finally succeeded in taking Omar home to bed. She lived in a big California ranch house on Page Mill Road. She had the biggest breasts Omar had ever seen or could imagine. They made love every day after that until it was time for him to fly home. She said she would write, but she never did; he was a summer romance.

Omar made many other friends that month in Palo Alto, who did stay in touch and continued to ask about his research. The Pakistani authorities queried him when he returned home, but they were proud of him, too. He did some consulting for the government, and as he began to be invited to conferences abroad, he always reported back on them—not all the details, and not every conference, but enough to keep everyone satisfied. Because of his tribal upbringing and his gentle ways, Omar al-Wazir was regarded as a man above reproach.

There had been a time several years ago, before the disaster in Makeen, when the Inter-Services Intelligence had invited him—commanded him, in fact—to pay them a visit in Aabpara. They were summoning a lot of professors in those days.

He was quizzed by an unpleasant man who called himself Major Nadeem. This interrogator took him through all the byways of his life.

"Why did you go to Cadet College at Razmak?" the major had asked.

"My father sent me. He said I would be useless as a hunter or a fighter, because I was always thinking about numbers. Don't ask me how, but I knew which ones were primes and which ones were divisible by nine, or twenty-seven, or one hundred twelve. My father decided it was a gift, although a strange one. He said I should go to a real school. Here, you can call him and ask him."

Dr. Omar had handed the major his cell phone.

His father was still alive then, a craggy old man trying to survive in a South Waziristan that was becoming, more each day, a shooting gallery.

The major shook his head. The last thing he wanted to do was talk to an old Pashtun grandfather living among the rocks.

"What did you do at Razmak?" the major had demanded.

"I studied math and engineering. I won all the prizes there, two years before I was supposed to, so they got me a scholarship to study at the University of Peshawar, where they had a computer science department. I lived in one of the hostels and joined the Khyber Islamic Culture Society. You can check."

"Did you know any Americans then?"

"No. I wanted to. I had a picture on my wall of Bill Gates when he was young. He looked no better or smarter than any of the Pashtun boys in the hostel. We all wanted to be like him."

The major nodded. Bill Gates was acceptable. He asked about the Stanford trip. Who had been interested in the research?

"So many people, I did not know them all. They studied my work. They asked me questions. I told the ISI about it when I got home. A major like you, he was. You can check."

The major did not want to make more work for himself. And it was true, the story as it had been narrated and understood was all in the files.

"Why did you go back to America?" he demanded, looking at a sheet of paper.

"I was invited to present a paper at a conference that was cosponsored by the Institute of Electrical and Electronics Engineers. It was a great honor for me, and for my university. You can ask them."

He held out his cell phone again, so that Major Nadeem could make a call to verify, but the major shook his head.

They spent several more hours like this, going through the major episodes of Dr. Omar's career. When they came to his most recent work on computer-security algorithms, Dr. Omar apologized that he could not talk about this work in any detail because it had been classified as "top secret" by the Pakistani military.

The major found nothing of interest. Dr. Omar was very careful, then and always. The major asked him to sign a paper, and to report any suspicious contacts, and Dr. Omar assured him that he would. The Pakistani authorities never came after him again. That was three years before his world went white.

Omar al-Wazir had multiple binary identities, it could be said. He was a Pakistani but also, in some sense, a man tied to the West. He was a Pashtun from the raw tribal area of South Waziristan, but he was also a modern man. He was a secular scientist and also a Muslim, if not quite a believer. His loyalties might indeed have been confused before the events of nearly two years ago, but not now.

Sometimes Dr. Omar grounded himself by recalling the spirit of his father, Haji Mohammed. He remembered the old man shaking his head when Omar took wobbly practice shots with an Enfield rifle, missing the target nearly every time. The look on the father's face asked: *How can this be my oldest son, this boy who cannot shoot?* But Haji Mohammed had taught him the code of manhood, just the same.

Omar had learned the catechism from his father: Wars begin with *badal,* an assault on a man's honor and self-respect. A proud man must avenge this insult, measure for measure, or he would suffer the greatest shame. That was why there were ceaseless wars in the tribal areas, Haji Mohammed had explained. It was the Nang-e-Pashto, the tribal code of honor, which required people to seek vengeance for the injustices inflicted by their cousins, neighbors, rival tribes, foreign invaders. A man would vow to sleep on the ground, or eat with his left hand only, until he had taken revenge, and only then would he let himself relax.

"To my mind death is better than life, when life can no longer be held with honor," Haji Mohammed had said one night after a long talk under the stars.

"Please, Father," Omar had implored, thinking that the old man might put a gun to his son's head at that very moment. But Haji Mohammed had laughed and explained that he was just quoting a passage from Khushal Khan Khattak, the warrior poet of the seventeenth century, and that it was the same now and always.

This was a code that understood war, but it had been tested by the great wars that shook the red-rock hills like a long, echoing chain of explosions.

When Omar was a little boy, the Russians were still over the border and his town was a staging ground for the Afghan holy warriors. Omar remembered how they would parade through town with the guns they had received from the Americans and their Pakistani agents. When the Russians finally left, the holy warriors became ordinary warlords and it was a world of anarchy. Then when Omar was a teenager, there were the fierce young men who called themselves Talibs and demanded justice. They marched through Makeen, too, on their way in and out of Khowst and Kandahar.

But all this was just a prelude to the big war that had come after Omar had left home to pursue his studies—when Al-Qaeda came to South Waziristan with its money, and then the Americans came after them, and brought all the hell there is on earth. Dr. Omar had wondered then if he should return home, but he knew that was impossible. He had pleaded with his mother and father to leave, but that was impossible, too. They were rooted in the rocky soil like two prickly cactus bushes.

Omar had thought for a time that he could end the war if he helped make Al-Qaeda go away, so that the Americans would go away, too. But that was beyond his powers.

There was a shadow that followed him, as it follows every Pashtun man, and that was shame. It was not enough to be successful; what was essential was to be an honorable man. That was why he had gone home two years before, to see if he could escape the shadow. But another shadow, a shame that was shameless, had darkened his world.

Omar had always wondered what he would do if something bad

happened to his parents. And then, on that terrible day, he had discovered the answer.

Dr. Omar waited for more of his graduate students, but none came by for the rest of the morning. He locked the door of his office and went to the computer lab, a squat two-story building a hundred yards away, where he preferred to do his communications for reasons of concealment. He had a number of different email accounts that he visited and, it might be said, a number of different personalities that inhabited these electronic spaces.

Most times, Omar felt that he was living behind a mask. But oddly, when he did this work under a variety of assumed names, he felt something close to peace.

15

STUDIO CITY, CALIFORNIA

Sophie Marx was numb from fatigue when she returned from Dubai. She hadn't slept well on the outward leg because of worries about the meeting ahead. She had hoped to collapse into her seat on the way home, but she slept only fitfully: Her body was too heavy for slumber, and her mind was too hot. She had taken on responsibility, on behalf of Gertz and the whole team, for investigating the disappearance of a colleague. But she was coming home empty-handed. Her theory had been wrong. She was still baffled about how Howard Egan's cover had been broken, and she didn't know who else in her organization might be vulnerable. It was an oppressive sense of failing in an assignment where she had badly wanted to do well.

She tossed back and forth on the couchette of the Emirates jet, trying to get comfortable. But sleep didn't come, and she thought about ways she could answer her questions. Part of her problem, she concluded after many hours, was that she didn't understand the context for these events: Why was Egan in Pakistan in the first place? Why was he paying money to tribal emirs? What was the mission for which Gertz had risked this man's life?

Marx went to the office, tired as she was, after a brief stop at home to shower and change. She wanted to begin querying the files to see if she could answer these questions. Jeff Gertz was away on one of his mystery trips, which made it easier. She figured that she didn't have to ask his permission to pull the operational files, because he had already granted it.

The Hit Parade's most sensitive information was not in the computer system, but kept in hard copy only, in a large room called "the Vault" on the ninth floor. The keeper of this archaic library was a retired military officer who had formerly worked for the National Security Agency's military cryptology branch, known as the Central Security Service. He was a fussy man who had helped protect some of the country's biggest secrets for several decades. He was always called "the Colonel," even though he had retired from active duty ten years before.

Marx took the elevator to the ninth floor and walked to the colonel's lair. The door was closed and he didn't answer at first, perhaps hoping that the visitor would go away. She knocked again, harder, and this time the door opened and out stepped the Colonel. He was a short, balding man, little taller than Marx herself, with a florid face and a bulbous nose. His actual name was Samuel Sinkler, but people rarely used it; he preferred rank only.

"Sorry to disturb you, Colonel, but I need to look at the Pakistan operations files."

She showed him her badge.

"Nope," he answered. "Sorry, you can't have them."

"But Mr. Gertz personally authorized me to look at all files I needed to investigate the Howard Egan case."

"He didn't tell me that." The Colonel had a thin smile. He liked saying no.

Marx shook her head. She was tired and didn't like being jerked around.

"I need those files, Colonel. I can't do my work without them."

"That's not my problem, miss. You could get Mr. Gertz, but he isn't here." He smiled again.

She pondered what to do. He obviously expected her to give up if he said no often enough.

"I'm not leaving until I see those files. Will you give me access if Steve Rossetti says it's okay?"

"That's a hypothetical," said the Colonel.

She picked up a phone on the nearest desk and dialed Rossetti's extension.

"Steve, it's Sophie. I'm back from Dubai and I have an emergency. I need access to some files on the ninth floor and Colonel Sinkler says he needs someone's permission. Can you come up now?"

There was a pause, while Rossetti temporized on the other end. He didn't like making decisions.

"I really need help now, Steve," she said. "Otherwise I'll have to call Jeff. He won't be pleased, but I have no choice."

That did it. Rossetti arrived five minutes later and personally signed the necessary piece of paper for the Colonel. Neither man was happy.

"Thanks, gents," she said breezily. The Colonel marched her back to the Vault and unlocked the steel door, while Rossetti retreated to his office.

It was cold in the stacks. The Colonel was one of those men who believed that people worked more efficiently at lower temperatures. Marx was wearing a long-sleeved blouse, but she was shivering after thirty minutes. She descended to her office and returned with a cardigan sweater, which she buttoned to the neck. It was dark among the racks and cabinets, so she asked the Colonel for a flashlight, which he grudgingly provided. He seemed to think that darkness, too, was part of good security.

Marx started with the paper records of Egan's travels. These were more detailed than the computer records she had consulted before. They showed a total of five trips to Pakistan over the previous thirteen months. Two of those journeys had been to Karachi, two to Lahore and one to Islamabad. To see what Egan had been doing on those trips, Marx had to consult two other sets of files. The first was his personal 201 file, which recorded the active cases he had been managing, but using cryptonyms to conceal the true names of his contacts. At the time of his disappearance, he was the case officer for four agents, all of whom had the digraph "AC," which was The Hit Parade's notation for Pakistan, borrowed from an old CIA cryptonym.

To learn the real identities behind those code names, Marx had to consult a separate registry inside the Vault, which was locked and guarded by video surveillance. Here again, the Colonel initially said no. Marx summoned Rossetti back, and he signed another piece of paper that allowed her access.

"I hope you find something," said Rossetti. "If this turns out to be a wild goose chase, Gertz will be pissed off."

"I'll worry about Jeff," she answered. "Not your problem."

Rossetti walked back to elevator, muttering as he went, "Get some sleep."

The Colonel told her to turn her back while he punched the proper code into the cyber-lock. The door clicked open. She fumbled for the light switch and set to work.

Marx began matching crypts with true identities. She first found the name of the man she had interrogated in Dubai, Hamid Akbar. She knew he would be one of the four. Egan had met him four times over the thirteen months, twice in Karachi, once in Istanbul and once in Abu Dhabi. The second name was Azim Mohammed al-Darwesh, whom she assumed must be Akbar's uncle. Egan had met him just once, four months before the kidnapping, in Abu Dhabi, on the same date as the meeting with his nephew, Akbar, who evidently had accompanied him to an initial get-acquainted meeting outside the country. This much was simply confirmation of what she already assumed.

Then came the surprises.

The third name listed was Lieutenant Colonel Hassan Chaudhary. He appeared to be a serving officer in the Pakistani military. Egan had met him three times: once in London, once in Beirut and once in Lahore. Marx ran traces on Chaudhary's name and discovered that he served in the office of the chief of Combat Development, which was the branch of the Pakistani military that had overseen its nuclear weapons program. He was from a prominent Punjabi family, and he was the third generation to have served in the military.

The fourth name was Professor Aziz Mukhtar. He was the rector of Mohiuddin Islamic University in Azad Kashmir. Traces on the professor showed that he was a leading activist for the liberation of Kashmir from Indian control. Egan had met with him twice, both times in Dubai.

It was an unlikely mix: A banker, a tribal leader, a military officer from a great aristocratic family and a Muslim activist. Marx was confused. These might be foreign-intelligence operations, designed to gather information about Pakistan's plans and intentions. But Marx doubted that. FI collection was still the province of the old CIA structure. This looked like something different.

Marx knocked on the Colonel's door. He assumed she was finished for the day, and extended his hand to receive the flashlight. But she had come with a new question.

"If you please, Colonel, I would like to look at the disbursements register," she said. "I need to see what we've been paying the agents whose names I've been pulling."

"You can't," answered the security officer. The blank, unhelpful look on his face shaded toward a smile. It gave him pleasure, once more, to say those words of refusal.

"Let's not go through this again. I can go back downstairs and get Steve Rossetti a third time, and he can come up and tell you the same thing as before. But, honestly, Colonel, that's a waste of time. Why don't you just say yes?"

"I can't. It's not possible to see those records."

"Why the hell not?" It was a relief to be able to swear at this cranky old man, but she wasn't expecting his answer.

"Because those records aren't here, that's why not. And watch your language."

"Where are they, if they aren't here?"

"Mr. Gertz has them. I don't know where he keeps them. And I know for certain that nobody has ever accessed them, because if they had, they would have asked me first, just like you did. But it's a waste of time. The disbursements are off-line. When I have questions about money, I ask Mr. Gertz. So should you."

Sophie Marx returned to the Vault, more confused now than before. She still wanted to answer the basic question: What were The Hit Parade's objectives in Pakistan? But she wondered now if she might have been misjudging the program's scope. She had assumed that Howard Egan was the only officer handling Pakistani cases, but that might be wrong. She took up her flashlight again and went prowling in the main personnel and travel files. Because the data wasn't computerized, there was no easy way to do a search and cross-tab for anyone who had visited Pakistan or handled a Pakistani agent. It all had to be done by hand.

Marx went back to the registry of cryptonyms and looked for all the cases with the AC digraph, which marked the agents as Pakistani. It took her the rest of the afternoon to pull together the information, but it was worth the trouble. She realized that she had been looking at a piece of a larger Pakistan operation.

There were fully nineteen cases, including the four that had been handled by Howard Egan. The others had been run by case officers who were based in Paris, Beirut, New Delhi, Cairo and Amsterdam.

Armed with the agents' code names, she went back to the inner file of true names and began to assemble the picture. The Hit Parade had recruited senior officials from all three major Pakistani political parties; it was paying money to the leaders of four more tribes in the frontier areas, two in North Waziristan, one in Orakzai and one in Malakand. It had two more agents from Kashmir on the payroll, and three prominent Pakistani clerics.

A new operation was scheduled soon, according to the files. A young case officer based in Amsterdam was about to meet for the first time with a new prospect, a young Pakistani diplomat from a well-known family who was serving in the Pakistan Embassy in Moscow. The name of The Hit Parade officer from Amsterdam stuck in her mind. It was Alan Frankel: He was the guy with red hair who was writing a blog as part of his cover. She had met him six months ago, when he was getting some new tradecraft training. She had thought at the time that he was cute, and had half hoped he would ask her out, but he hadn't.

What Sophie Marx had found looked like a broad network, of the sort that back at Headquarters might have been handled by the Special Activities Division. In theory, all such covert operations were supposed to be driven by a strategic plan, which was reviewed and updated periodically. But there was no trace of such strategic guidance for Pakistan operations. Where did these projects come from? How were they tasked? Who suggested the names?

She went to the Colonel one last time before turning in her flashlight for good.

"I'd like to see the Special Activities finding for Pakistan," she said. "And don't just say, 'You can't.'"

"You can't."

"Oh, please! Why not?"

"Because it doesn't exist. Not on paper at least, not that I've seen."

"Well, where is it? There has to be a plan. We don't just send people all over the world willy-nilly. There's a directive, a finding."

"It's in Mr. Gertz's head. He's the boss. Maybe he writes it down, and maybe he doesn't, I wouldn't know about that. I'm sure he reviews it with somebody, but I wouldn't know about that, either. So what you're going to have to do, Miss Marx, is wait to see Mr. Gertz when he gets back."

For once, the Colonel had it completely right. There was no choice now but to wait for the boss to return.

Marx stopped by Rossetti's office on her way out, to thank him for his intervention. He was still there, gazing at his computer screen, when Marx stuck her head in the door. Rossetti looked nervous at first, thinking she had come to ask him for something else, and he was relieved when she said she was packing it in for the night.

"You don't give up, do you?" he said. "Are you always like this?"

The question caught her off guard. She was so tired, all she could do was answer honestly.

"I'm persistent. At least, I used to be, when I was in the field. I got lazy when I was back at Headquarters. It's all in my file, if you want the details."

"I know," he said. "I've been reading. I got curious."

"So you know I got in trouble in Addis Ababa?"

"Yeah, but why? That wasn't clear. They always leave the good stuff out of a 201."

"I got burned, that's what happened. I was covered as a UNESCO officer in Paris, which gave me a reason to visit U.N. offices in Lebanon and Ethiopia regularly. I was working developmentals mostly, going in and out of Beirut, working out of the UNESCO office in Mar Elias. I nailed a recruitment there that got us inside the Hezbollah communications net. I was thinking I was pretty cool. But then it got nasty."

"What happened?"

"They made me on my next trip to Ethiopia. It was bad."

"Tell me the story. I was in Addis for a few months in the nineties."

"Okay, so I picked up surveillance my first day. I thought I saw a chase car following my taxi to U.N. headquarters. I didn't worry too much, and I didn't report it. Addis wasn't a high-threat assignment, and there were friendlies all over, and I didn't want to scratch the trip. So I went out a second day, this time in a UNESCO staff car, a nice big Mercedes to visit a demonstration project in Debre Zeit."

"That was a mistake, I take it."

"Big time. Two vehicles shadowed us as soon as we left the international zone. We kept going until we got to a Muslim district called Saris, where the Somali refugees lived. The road narrowed. No friendlies around. Bad scene. Ambush zone."

"What saved you?"

"Luck, frankly. I screamed at my driver as the cutoff car was coming toward us. I told him to floor it, and that if he slowed down, I would shoot him. It turned out that he driven a taxicab in America. That was our salvation, the fact that this Ethiopian knew how to drive like a crazy man. He gunned the car onto the shoulder. The chase cars tried to follow, but he was driving a Mercedes that could do over a hundred, no problem, and their cars were crap. So we outran them, basically."

"No shit." Rossetti was shaking his head. He was impressed, despite himself.

"I called the emergency number at the embassy, and the police showed up a few minutes later, and that was that."

"And nobody got hurt?"

"Not physically. My cover was gone. Even I knew that. I put in my resignation papers at UNESCO, gave up my super-gorgeous Paris apartment and came home to Headquarters, where I was vegging out until Gertz rescued me."

"How did the bad guys make you?" asked Rossetti "Did CI ever figure it out?"

"Nothing official. But I think it was a technical hit, some kind of data mining, back in Lebanon."

"Come on!" Rossetti shook his head. Insurgents weren't smart enough to do data mining.

"I'm serious. It was my cell phone calls. The Lebanese government, meaning Hezbollah, had accessed my call records. When they matched up the call data with calls made by other people they were watching, I was busted. They passed the information to their friends in Addis."

"You really think they're that smart?"

"They don't have to be smart, Steve. They just need to have the same stuff we do: data-mining software; pattern analysis, link analysis; watch lists. They could be stupid as mules, but they could still nail the old CIA. That's why The Hit Parade exists, right? To go places where they can't find us."

"I hope that still works," said Rossetti.

Marx was going to say something upbeat in response, but it wasn't in her.

Jeff Gertz's mystery trip was to Washington, D.C., perhaps the least mysterious city in the world. He went there to meet with the president's chief of staff, Ted Yazdi. It was an unusual encounter nonetheless. It took place in a private home in Bethesda that belonged to one of Yazdi's assistants, who had vacated the house at the boss's request. It was like an agent meeting in that respect, though it was hard to say who had recruited whom.

The safe house was a big suburban estate up on a hill. It looked like the clubhouse of a country club, with a big portico and a façade of brick and stone, and well-mowed grass on all sides. The floodlights were on, and a man in a bulky suit was standing in the driveway, scanning the street.

Yazdi was waiting in the living room when Gertz knocked on the door. He was wearing dark glasses, even though the curtains were drawn, and was chewing on a piece of gum. He sat on the edge of the couch, anxious for the meeting to begin. There are civilians who are easily seduced by secrets, who chortle over the details the briefers throw in about foreign leaders' sex lives or health problems, and Yazdi was one of them. He was eager to enter an otherwise forbidden world.

Yazdi had asked for an update on The Hit Parade's operations. Nothing on paper, for obvious reasons. The president was preoccupied with his legislative agenda, and the chief of staff didn't want to bother him, so he was holding it in his head. It was hard for him to keep it all straight.

"I get paid to be nervous," he began. "That's what I do for a living. So I need to know all your shit. It's on me if anything goes wrong. I'm holding the bag."

"Nobody's holding the bag, sir, because there is no bag. As I told you when we agreed to set up our capability, we don't exist. We are self-funding, and self-liquidating."

Yazdi took off his sunglasses. He had a narrow face and a mouth that was always parted slightly at the lips, as if ready to bite.

"I don't believe you. How is that possible? I worked for an investment bank. Money has to come from somewhere."

"Don't ask me, Mr. Yazdi, please. You don't want to know. We have a system. It works. We have more than enough money."

"Okay." Yazdi nodded. He hated not having every last secret. "Tell me the list."

Gertz ran through the list of countries where they had operations. It had all the names you would expect: Lebanon, Syria, Iran, Egypt, Pakistan, Afghanistan. And it had a few names that you wouldn't expect, such as China and Russia and France.

"Pakistan's the biggest, right?" asked Yazdi. "That's the hardest one, isn't it? They've got two hundred million pissed-off people, plus nuclear weapons. Scary shit."

"The Paks are our main target right now, sir. That's where we have put the most effort, in people and money."

"Is it working?" asked Yazdi. "That crazy shit in Karachi when your guy vanished scared me."

"It will take time. But money does wonders when you spread it around. I don't know anyone who doesn't want to be rich. Even in Pakistan."

"How do you get your names? I mean, how do you know who to bribe?"

"People tell us things. Old friends, new friends, throw in some secret ingredients. Put them all together, cook it in the oven and, voilà, it's a soufflé."

"I hope so, buddy. This is 'Project Pax.' That's what I told the president. We've spent enough time fighting our enemies. Now we are going to buy them off. It's time for 'global green,' meaning money. We are going to have a leveraged buyout of all the people who have been trying to fuck us over. That's my line to the boss, just so you know. That's right, isn't it? That's the strategy."

Gertz nodded. Strategy was not something that interested him. He was an operator; he usually left the big-think stuff to others, though in this case there wasn't really anyone to leave it to, other than the gum-chewing White House chief of staff, who had only the vaguest notion of what they were doing.

Gertz didn't worry about it. His job was to serve the president, and if the president wanted to hose the war zone with money so people would stop killing Americans and he could get reelected, that was fine. Gertz wanted to get the job done. He found the right people, assembled lists of names, developed capabilities and covers. And soon the activity had taken on a life of its own; it had been set in motion and now it was hard to stop.

"Project Pax," said Gertz, nodding his head. "That's great. I like that. The president will get a Nobel Peace Prize, and you and I will be the only people who will understand how it happened."

16
MOSCOW

Alan Frankel had every reason to think he was safe. His surveillance detection run had stretched across two countries by the time he got to Moscow. He had flown from his home in Amsterdam to Berlin to meet some potential clients for his advertising firm, Kiosks Unlimited, which despite its grand name had just one salesman, him, and a secretary. Then he had traveled to Prague for a day, meeting another prospective client and sending a string of text and Internet messages. In each city, he had posted an entry to "Admonitions," his blog about the global media market. His cover was backstopped and integrated at every level; the deeper someone went on the Internet to check him out, the more confirmation they would find for his identity.

And now Alan Frankel was in Moscow on the last leg of his trip. He was staying at the Volodya Park, a new hotel on the south bank of the Moscow River, just below the old Red Square. It wasn't as fancy as the Kempinski or the Four Seasons, not by half. But the little hotel was just right for a young ad-sales representative who was pushing into a free-wheeling market with his laptop and lots of hustle.

Jeffrey Gertz thought of Frankel as one of his up-and-comers. He sometimes referred to him as "Blogger Boy" in meetings with his senior staff in Studio City. Frankel was the new-age operations officer who could go anywhere in the world he wanted because his cover was impenetrable.

Sometimes Gertz posted his own comments to "Admonitions," under the screen name "Ironman23." He would opine on publicity campaigns for new movies and music releases. Occasionally he would post a subtle word of praise for Frankel following an especially good operation, disguised in what he imagined was blogger language and signed, *Ironman23.*

Russia was a hard place to operate, even Gertz admitted that. The Russians had total control of the environment, with fixed surveillance everywhere: They saw you coming in and going out; they watched as you waited for a Metro train, or crossed the street, or sat in the hotel lobby. It wasn't worth the trouble arranging meetings in Moscow, anyway, the old pros said. It was so easy now for Russians to get out of the country. Let them fly to Croatia or Majorca with the other tourists and meet you there.

But that no-go logic was for losers, according to Gertz. There was no such thing as a denied area in his world of mobile platforms. The Hit Parade could operate anywhere and everywhere—getting its people in and out before the local service had a chance to notice their passport stamps, let alone rumble their missions. In his operational atlas, Moscow was no different from Munich or Montreal.

Alan Frankel had come to Moscow to meet a Pakistani diplomat who had been posted to Moscow a year before. He was from a prominent Punjabi family in Lahore, whose members included the leaders of the political party that dominated the province, some of whom had a history of making trouble for America. Frankel was going to offer him a lot of money—so much money that in the old, pre-Gertz days, it would have been authorized by a covert action "finding." What the Pakistani would have to do in return was steer his family away from the anti-American virus that infected Punjabi politics.

Gertz had gotten a tip from one of his sources that this Pakistani was ripe for recruitment. Frankel's job was to close the deal.

Frankel kept living his bulletproof cover when he arrived in Moscow. He made an appointment with TanyaTech, an ad agency that did political work for the Kremlin. They had lavish offices in an old mansion along the river; inside the door were pretty young Russian girls to greet visitors and show them to their appointments. In other lives, these long-legged, silken-haired women might have been oligarchs' girlfriends, or worse, but here they were decorative office ladies.

Frankel had asked to see the boss, Lev Lieberman. He was out, or so claimed his secretary, a woman with striking white-blond hair and purple eye shadow. Frankel charmed and pestered this woman into making a call, and a few minutes later the director trundled down the hall.

The Russian listened sleepily to Frankel's presentation, staring at his iPhone most of the time. He perked up slightly when the American said that he could rep TanyaTech for one-quarter of the price that the fancy advertising firm in London was charging. But then he shook his head—impossible!—and went back to tapping out messages on his phone.

The Russian finally got rid of Frankel by sending him to NovyaBank, a financial company in Moscow that was part of the same business network. When the American asked for a contact there, the Russian rolled his eyes and called a friendly underling at the bank, who reluctantly agreed to see Frankel that afternoon at his office east of the city center.

The NovyaBank headquarters was a gray slate building that, in the harsh summer light, had the sooty look of an unwashed truck. The traffic was a knot on the way out of downtown Moscow, so Frankel was fifteen minutes late. When he arrived and asked the doorman to call upstairs, he was told that his contact was out. The man's secretary said in broken English that the gentleman in question had left two hours ago—not long after Lieberman had called to make the appointment.

Frankel spelled his name twice for the secretary and gave her his telephone number and email address. For good measure, he left his card with the doorman. All he wanted was embellishment for his identity, which he had achieved simply by going to the bank's offices.

Frankel never once looked for surveillance. That was the virtue of a three-country SDR. If anyone became suspicious along the way and began asking questions, they would find only reinforcing pieces of the cover legend, place to place and meeting to meeting. It wasn't a legend, really; it was a true lie.

The meeting with the Pakistani diplomat was set for ten that night, at a bar near the Moscow hills where young couples went to get their wedding pictures taken. Gertz favored that kind of open meeting place; he believed that once your cover was established, it was best to hide in plain sight. What drew attention were the attempts at concealment.

Frankel had six hours to kill. He went back to his hotel and dropped off his briefcase. Near the hotel was the Tretyakov Art Gallery, which he had missed on his earlier trips to Moscow. That was a plausible stop for a visiting American businessman, and it was better than sitting in his hotel room.

He walked the few blocks to the gallery, still housed in its nineteenth-century palace. The collection was an ark of the Russian past: The paintings on the walls conveyed all the contradictory yearnings of the Russian elite—their French manners and fashions, their awkward enjoyment of privilege born on the backs of serfs who were no better than chattel slaves, their forays into intellectual terrain that more cautious Europeans barely dared to imagine. Room by room, with its portraits of pallid aristocrats and fierce, bearded peasants and desolate winter landscapes, the gallery conveyed a foreboding of what lay ahead for Russia.

Frankel paused occasionally to savor the paintings; he sat for a good minute looking at a Kramskoy portrait titled *Unknown Woman*, haughty in her carriage, a white feather in her sable hat. He doubled back to an earlier room, to see the brushwork of a portrait painted fifty years before by Borovikovsky of a similarly haunting Russian beauty. That was when he had the first inkling that he was being followed. A dark-browed beetle of a man he had noticed on his way into the gallery had appeared again, he was certain. This time the dark figure was wearing sunglasses and a red-checked beret.

Frankel made no sign he was aware of surveillance. But having glimpsed it once, he saw other signs. A woman loitered in one gallery when he entered and stayed when he left. Among the members of the guided tour that moved from room to room, there was a mottled face that was too hard and unblinking to be believable as a normal gallery visitor.

Was he spooking himself? That was the trouble with operating far from home, at the end of a long string of false names and meetings: You began to see shadows even when they weren't there.

When Frankel exited the Tretyakov in the afternoon sun, he sat down on a bench and composed a BlackBerry message to The Hit Parade's dummy address, using veiled language. "I may have competition for the Moscow account. I'm hoping they will give up, so I can relax and enjoy my evening. Let me know if you have any business tips." But after a minute's deliberation, he deleted the message, rather than send it. Gertz would think he was a pussy. And what could they do to help him, anyway?

Frankel walked toward the Moscow River, not too fast, and then along the banks to the Kamenny Bridge. He crossed into Red Square, pausing at St. Basil's Cathedral, and then at Lenin's Tomb. The marble façade of the tomb looked dirty, as if it hadn't been polished since 1989. He couldn't see anyone now, but in a big open space like this, surveillance was so much harder to detect. He walked down the narrow footpaths of the Alexandrovsky Gardens and then back along those same walkways through the square and toward the Tverskaya Street.

He saw faces that looked familiar, but he couldn't be sure. Even in the chill of the late afternoon, as the sun disappeared behind the low clouds, he was sweating.

He crossed the square to Tverskaya Street and walked half a block to the grand old façade of the National Hotel. It was a fine building, with salmon-pink brick interlaid with white all the way up to its crenellated roof. Under an awning stood the front door, gleaming wood with polished brass handles, framed by stone carvings of flowers and grapes. Standing guard was a doorman in his summer uniform, hat and vest.

As Frankel moved toward the entrance, the doorman stopped him and asked if he was a guest. There was a private function that evening, he said. No visitors.

Frankel needed to get away. This was the wrong place to be. He heard commotion in the hotel lobby and a throng of people pushed out the door toward the noisy arcade of the street.

Just outside the hotel entrance stood a man with a shock of black hair, chewing on one of his fingernails as his eyes fixed on Frankel. He looked like a proper Moscow gangster, with a pin-striped suit and pair of thick, black-framed sunglasses. He was moving toward Frankel now, pointing to a car parked along Tverskaya Street with the door opened, motioning for him to get in. Two more men were approaching from behind.

The man shouted out something to Frankel. He spoke with an accent, so it was hard for passersby to understand what he was saying. *The Moscow News* reported the next day, quoting people who had been on the sidewalk, that he said "addition," or perhaps "rendition." But that made no sense. The other papers said he had just growled out a curse.

Frankel lunged away and sprinted up Tverskaya. The black-haired tough followed him, and then another man, faster and stronger, who was gaining ground. The boulevard was crowded with early evening shoppers. Frankel weaved among them: Nobody would fire a gun into such a crowd; there were too many people.

Frankel looked back and saw the two men following close behind. He was too obvious, shirttails out, arms churning. He tripped on a loose brick as he headed up the street, and he stumbled for a moment. Even if they didn't shoot, this was a sure path to disaster. If he kept running amid this crowd, the police would arrest him even if his other pursuers peeled away. He would be busted either way.

He saw an opening to his left, Nitinsky Street, and peeled off toward it. The two men followed. As Frankel ran up the street, he saw a third man coming toward him to block his escape. He ducked into a dark alley that was lined with trash bins from the neighboring buildings.

The police found Frankel's body in the alleyway a little after six p.m. He had struggled when his pursuers tried to drag him off, people in offices and apartments above told reporters. As he tried to flee, he was shot point-blank, three bullets, a silencer on the gun.

The newspapers described two of the killers: dark features, swarthy, they all but announced they were from Chechnya. But like so many crimes in the new Russia, this one remained unsolved. The assassins disappeared into the lawless second city of the capital, where they owned the police. The spokesman for the Moscow prosecutor's office said it looked like the work of the Chechen mafia, but people always said that about unsolved crimes.

17
STUDIO CITY, CALIFORNIA

Jeffrey Gertz was watching *Morning Joe* in the bathroom, trimming his beard and wondering what jacket to wear, when he heard the news bulletin that an American businessman had been shot in Moscow. They didn't give a name, and it didn't occur to him that the victim might be one of his own people. Gertz had just returned to Los Angeles from Washington the night before, and was thinking mainly about whether to go to Las Vegas that weekend. As he was dressing, the phone rang. It was Albert, the new watch officer in Studio City. There was a hitch in his throat, and he had to cough before he could speak.

"Sorry to bother you at home, Mr. Director." He had only been in the job a few days and addressed Gertz as if he were a cabinet secretary.

"What is it, Albert? I'm getting dressed."

"An American has been shot in Moscow. It's on the wires. Mr. Rossetti thinks he may be one of ours. He said you would want to be informed."

"I just saw that story on television. That's our guy? What the hell?"

Gertz was unsteady for a moment, and sat down on the leather bench in his dressing room. He had a towel wrapped around his waist, but it fell away. He muttered, more to himself than to the watch officer.

"Christ, it must be Frankel."

"Roger that, sir. The embassy has someone at the morgue. The Russians have ID'd the victim as Alan Frankel, birthplace Denver, date of birth May twenty-sixth, 1980. His business cards say he runs an ad agency in Amsterdam named Kiosks Unlimited. Headquarters called Mr. Rossetti a few minutes ago, and he called me. I checked. All that information matches our operational files. What should I do?"

"Nothing. Wait for me. Don't talk to Headquarters until I'm there. And don't talk to Mr. Rossetti, either. He's not your boss, damn it."

There was a pause on the other end. The watch officer wasn't sure what he was allowed to say.

"People are kind of upset here, Director. We've gotten two messages from the field already, asking what's up. What should I tell them?"

"Tell them I'm on my way in. Tell everyone to chill out for a few minutes. This may not be what we think it is. No messages to anyone until I get there."

"Yes, Director."

Gertz felt better giving an order, even if it was just to shut up and sit tight. He thought a moment. The story was moving so fast, he needed to backstop the cover right away.

"One more thing," said Gertz. "Call Tommy Arden in Support and tell him to make sure someone in Europe is answering the Kiosks Unlimited phone in Amsterdam. This person should confirm Frankel's cover biography, but that's it. Express shock, grief, 'How could anyone have done this to Mr. Frankel,' et cetera. Do that now, and tell people to stay cool. I'll be there in thirty minutes."

Gertz finished dressing, a plain blue blazer instead of the summer-weight plaid he'd been planning, and a tie, too. He stood for a moment staring out the window, trying to collect his thoughts.

His apartment was on the top floor of a building on the eastern edge of Beverly Hills, almost to West Hollywood. One bank of windows looked across Doheny Drive toward the leafy suburbs and the hills.

Another looked down Santa Monica Boulevard toward the sprawl of downtown, half hidden by the smoky mist of the morning. He took a Red Bull out of the refrigerator, and then popped one of the energy pills his homeopathic counselor had recommended.

Gertz threw his briefcase in the Corvette. Though it was a sunny day, he left the top up. He turned on the local NPR station and listened until they mentioned the Moscow shooting. Then he turned the radio off. He didn't want to hear.

Gertz knew how to take a punch. That was part of why he had risen so quickly in the agency. He had been ready to take risks when other people were worrying about whether their legal insurance was paid up. When people had decided the CIA was so messed up it was time to start over, Gertz had been there, the resilient one, ready to take the enterprise deep underground.

This was a combination punch: Two members of his organization had been targeted in two weeks, and he didn't know why. He felt bad about the people, in a generalized sort of way, but he barely knew them. He felt worse for himself. If he didn't draw a tight circle now and control information, the structure he had created would begin to wobble. People would ask questions, secretly at first, but that would lead to other questions. The garment would begin to fray along the seams, and then—if people really began to pull—it would come apart.

It was the same as with any flap, Gertz told himself. The best solution was to hunker down and wait for it to go away.

When Gertz arrived at the office block on Ventura Boulevard, the façade was bleached white in the morning sun. Inside, there was a hum of anxiety: People had been waiting for the boss to arrive, and now they wanted him to give orders. There was a low-level panic. The news had spread rapidly; how could it be otherwise? People worried that their invisible organization had somehow come under a spotlight, and that they all were vulnerable.

Gertz did the one thing nobody would have expected, which was to act normal. He said hello to the secretaries by name, and then went into his office to read the message traffic. He summoned Arden for a report: The calls to Kiosks Unlimited in Amsterdam were being answered by the reports officer who worked with Frankel as his secretary; she was quoted in the latest news reports expressing shock and sorrow. The dam was holding, at least for the moment.

Gertz placed a call to Cyril Hoffman at Headquarters. Hoffman didn't know much, either, but he agreed that in a situation of uncertainty, the best thing to do was for everyone to keep their mouths shut. The best damage control policy, in this case, was to do nothing.

"What was your man working on in Moscow, anyway?" asked Hoffman. "Odd spot to visit."

"Pakistan. He was meeting a diplomat."

"Do I know about this?"

"Of course you do. You know about everything. If you want details, check the White House."

"Why was he killed? This sounds like another Karachi problem. He's dead, by the way, your man Egan. Confirmed. Roger that. I think this second one was a mafia hit."

"You're joking, surely," said Hoffman.

"That's what they're saying on television. Chechen mobsters."

"But surely that's untrue."

"Maybe. But it's convenient. Don't rock our boat, Mr. Hoffman. That's my advice. I am trying to keep a lid on. I hope you are, too."

"Be careful about Pakistan. My sources say people there are rather upset with us. They don't like being vaporized from ten thousand feet. And they don't like having money thrown at them by the CIA, even in the benign and invisible form you like to imagine that you have created."

"My sources tell me that when people are shooting at you, you buy up their guns."

"Does that refer to us or the Pakistanis, I wonder?"

"Both, sir."

"Bold words: I will send you a soapbox."

"Hey, Mr. Hoffman, if you're unhappy with me, just say so."

"Heavens, no. Following your adventures is one of my few pleasures.

But perhaps a little more contact with the home office. The personal touch. What say?"

They talked for several more minutes before the associate deputy director said, "Cheerio!" in his usual, incongruously upbeat voice, and rang off.

When Gertz finished his conversation with Hoffman, he called Steve Rossetti and said he wanted to hold a senior staff meeting in the secure conference room.

The group gathered on the third floor. People dropped their cell phones in the locker outside the room and trundled in. There were about twenty people, the heads of all the main operational departments and their deputies, plus a few other key staff members. They nodded stiffly at Gertz as they entered. They had liked being part of his great experiment, but most of them didn't know him very well.

Sophie Marx entered the room and took a chair at the far end. She was wearing a black suit, well tailored but somber. She was tired, with the sallow look that agency officers sometimes described as a "safe house tan." After the quick trip to Dubai she had labored for many hours in the Colonel's files. She needed to talk with Gertz. She had sent him a brief memo about her polygraph of Hamid Akbar and asking for a meeting to discuss her plans, but he hadn't answered.

Marx was settled in her chair, wishing she had worn more makeup to hide her fatigue, when Gertz walked toward her. He passed all the way around the conference table to her place. She had wanted to talk to him, but not now, with the senior staff listening.

"How was Dubai?" he queried, shaking her hand. "Good trip?"

"Yes and no," she answered. "It demolished one of my theories. Now I have to start over."

"We all do," said Gertz. "Come see me later today, when this Moscow business is sorted out. We'll decide what to do next."

Everyone in the room heard the exchange. People moved in their chairs, or cleared their throats, or otherwise signaled their unease. They could see, if they hadn't known already, that Sophie Marx had a special role in this crisis, and that whatever Gertz was doing to contain it, she was his partner.

Gertz waited until everyone had arrived, and gave them a little more time after that, until there were no more coughs and whispers.

"I want to confirm what most of you have already heard," he began. "Today in Moscow, one of our officers was killed. He was shot downtown, near the Kremlin, three times at close range. I am told that he died on the scene."

There were groans around the room. For all the bravura of people in the intelligence business, things like this didn't happen to them. They weren't soldiers, and they certainly didn't expect that their colleagues would be gunned down, Mafia-style.

"Let me say a few words about our colleague Mr. Frankel. He was operating under very deep cover, unknown even to some of the people in this room, and he was an unusually capable young officer. He epitomized what our new organization is about—secrecy, speed, daring. He was one of the best. Unfortunately, the world will never, ever know that. He took his cover with him to the grave. He would want us to keep it there. I trust we are all clear on that."

In the silence, Steve Rossetti spoke up. He was wearing his blazer with the American flag pin on the lapel. He was known to be close to Headquarters, so people listened to him with special attention.

"Can we still maintain that cover?" Rossetti asked. "I mean, won't the NSC want to look at this? And the inspector general at Langley? And the congressional committees, won't they have some issues here?"

"No, no, and no," answered Gertz. "We are not going to open our doors for anyone. There's nothing to disclose. This is a personal tragedy, and there are some operational issues we have to address. But that's our business and nobody else's."

"So what do we do?" asked the operations chief.

"We maintain radio silence. And we do nothing—I repeat, nothing—that would suggest any link between Mr. Frankel and this organization or its parent in Langley. Remember, we do not exist. We have been given a license to operate as a true clandestine service. That is very precious, and we have to guard it, especially now."

Rossetti pressed ahead, even though it was obvious to all that his intervention was not welcomed.

"But we've lost two officers now, sir. I'm worried about the safety of our people. Around this building, people are asking what's going on."

Gertz could sense the uneasiness in the room—the fear that can turn into revolt, and disorderly retreat, and failure. He had to give them something.

"Thank you, Steve, for raising that. I want to address it directly. The case of Howard Egan worried us all. He was taken by people who evidently knew that he had a secret role separate from his business cover. We believe he's dead, which is perhaps a blessing. As you may know, I have asked our chief of counterintelligence, Sophie Marx, to conduct an aggressive internal investigation to figure out what happened. The case of Alan Frankel is quite different. I have talked with Headquarters, and we think this is unrelated to the other attack."

"What is it, then? Who hit Frankel?"

"From what we've seen so far, this looks like a Russian mob hit. It was not the sort of thing that terrorist operatives do, much less intelligence services. Too bloody, too much out in the open. I'm guessing at this point, but I think Chechen businessmen ordered the hit. They were worried that our young man was pushing into their territory."

"Why would they think that?" asked Sophie Marx from the back of the room. "So far as anyone knew, he was just a kid selling ads, right?" It was the first time she had spoken in a big staff meeting. Her tone was hardly deferential.

"Within this room only, let me explain why local mobsters might have been upset: Mr. Frankel met in Moscow with representatives of a publishing company owned by one of the Kremlin's pals. That may have been his mistake. My guess is that somebody thought he was muscling in on their territory. Or maybe the Kremlin got nervous. But the point is, there's no reason to think that his cover was blown."

"Except that he's dead," said Sophie. She was pushing him, in a way that even Rossetti wouldn't have dared. That was the advantage of being the boss's pet.

"Listen, folks, I am trying to level with you. I know this is hard on all of us. But this looks to me like a mafia hit. That's what the initial reporting on Moscow television is saying. And that's what I told Headquarters a few minutes ago."

"What does Cyril Hoffman think?" asked Rossetti. He was skeptical that the associate deputy director would buy into this explanation quite so quickly.

"Hoffman thinks it's our case," answered Gertz. "He trusts our judgment."

The meeting broke up, with the members of The Hit Parade's leadership team a bit calmer than they had been an hour before, but still not sure they understood what was going on.

Gertz had left out only one thing in his valedictory mention of Cyril Hoffman. Although the associate deputy director had deferred to Gertz's handling of the Moscow case, he had also asked him to come back to Washington promptly for a visit to talk things over, one on one. The personal touch.

That afternoon, before he left for LAX to catch the red-eye to Washington, Gertz stopped by Marx's cubicle. He looked gray, worn out by a day of treading water.

"Let's take a walk," he said. "Get an ice-cream cone."

"Sure, but I don't eat ice cream."

She went to the ladies' room and put a little more masking cream under her weary eyes and joined him at the elevator.

Studio City looked particularly seedy that afternoon. There was a low sticky heat, not the usual dry desert feel of the Valley but something more like the humid Atlantic Coast. Gertz took off his tie and threw his blazer over his shoulder. The cars were whizzing by on Ventura Avenue, providing the only bit of breeze on the hot day.

"Were you really as confident as you sounded in there?" asked Marx.

"No," he answered. "I needed to buy some time . . . for you. So you can investigate this, quietly."

"Do you believe that line to the staff about how the Moscow killing was a mafia hit?"

He looked at her blankly. His eyes were so hard to read.

"Maybe it's true. I don't know what to believe. That's why I have you. You're going to figure it out and tell me."

"So this is my problem now?"

"And mine. But you're the person who's going to figure it out." He put his arm around her shoulder. She pulled away, but gently.

"I thought Alan Frankel went to Moscow to meet with a Pakistani diplomat," she said. "This wasn't about Chechens."

That shot hit its mark. Gertz took a step back, as if to regain his balance.

"How on earth do you know that? I didn't say anything about what he was working on."

"I went to the files. That's what you told me to do. So I did it. I checked all our Pakistani cases. Alan Frankel was running one of them. He was meeting someone from one of the big political families."

Gertz narrowed his eyes for a moment, then his face went back into neutral.

"You're sharp," he said. "That's why I wanted you for this job. Yes, he was working on Pakistan. So are some other people. We are moving mountains there, or trying to. But be careful. There are things involved here that nobody—no-*body*—knows about back at the Death Star."

She was puzzled.

"Who knows about it, if Headquarters doesn't? I don't get that."

"It was approved by the man we work for, the president of the United States."

She stood on the sidewalk of Ventura Boulevard while the cars revved their engines a few yards away.

"Is that why there's no record of Pakistan disbursements in the file? And no finding or mission directive?"

Gertz's eyes flashed again, then he laughed.

"What a little snoop you are. Well, knock it off. If there's something I think you need to know, I'll tell you."

"How do you plan these missions, Jeff? How do you know what doors to knock on?"

Gertz shook his head. This time he wasn't smiling.

"You are asking too many questions. This is out of your lane. Don't outsmart yourself."

They walked on for another fifty yards in silence, until they neared a traffic light. Gertz had said his piece, and Marx waited for the tension to pass. She needed as much information as he was willing to give her. She was operating outside the wire.

"Did you read my cable from Dubai?" she asked.

"I skimmed it. I gather that Akbar passed his polygraph."

Marx nodded. "It wasn't just that. He could have finessed the poly. It was more the feel of the guy. The more we talked, the less likely it seemed to me that he was working with the bad guys. He's a chump, a scared rich boy who went to study in America. I was barking up the wrong tree."

"So how was Egan blown, if it wasn't Akbar?"

"I don't know. I worry that we have a bigger problem, but I don't know what it is."

"Well, I hope you figure it out before another of our people gets waxed."

"So you *don't* believe that fairy tale about the mafia in Moscow."

"Hey, lighten up. For general consumption, I believe it. Between us, I am agnostic."

She stopped walking and studied him. His face was hard, with that bristle of goatee giving him a look that, for a moment, reminded her of a poster of D. H. Lawrence. What was real, in all his tough talk and secretiveness?

"Can I ask you a question?"

"Sure. Good luck."

"What are we doing in Pakistan? Help me out. I mean, what was Egan trying to set up when he got kidnapped? I don't think Hamid Akbar had a clue. But what is it?"

"Sorry, but you are pushing me where I cannot be pushed."

His face had gone to stone.

"Was it intelligence-gathering, or Special Activities? I found a receipt in Egan's operational file for gold bars that he took from the depository for one of his earlier operations. It was over fifty pounds, nearly a million dollars. What was that for? We don't pay any agent that much."

He took her wrist and held it, not a gentle touch, but a hard squeeze.

"These are questions I can't answer, and you shouldn't ask. We do things that are very secret, and this is one of them. Don't ask me again, because you'll get the same answer."

"I'm trying to do my job.

"You're pushing too hard. You'll rupture a disk. Like I said, lighten up."

A Baskin-Robbins was just ahead: pink, gaudy, an incongruous relic.

"You want an ice-cream cone?"

"Ugh." She shook her head. "You can get me something else, though, if you're in a generous mood."

"What is it? I'm always in a generous mood with you."

"A ticket to London. I want to meet Egan's boss, the guy who runs the hedge fund. I want to understand how they do business, how many people there knew about Egan's travels. The bad guys must have pumped poor Howard about where he worked. They know more than I do."

"Thomas Perkins." He spoke softly, enunciating each syllable. There was on his face an odd look of suspended animation. He had been caught off guard.

"Right, Perkins. Alphabet Capital. You told him that I might be coming to visit. Well, I want to do it, as soon as I can."

"This is a complicated relationship. There's a lot of baggage, not all if it ours. Maybe it's better to leave this one to me."

"Hey, Jeff, if I can't do this, I might as well leave the whole thing to you. What's the point? Maybe you should have someone else do your investigation."

She was threatening him, subtly. He had little choice but to accede. She was his best hope for keeping the lid on.

"You *have* to be careful. Do not go turning over rocks when you don't know what's underneath. Remember, madam: You are a snake handler, not a snake charmer."

"Don't worry." She put her arm through his, a feminine version of his arm around the shoulder. "I'm always careful."

18

CHARLES TOWN, WEST VIRGINIA

It would be wrong to say that Cyril Hoffman was a dandy. He was too big and substantial a man for that. But he dressed in a way that suggested another time, the 1950s perhaps, when CIA officers wore suits with vests, and hats that were not baseball caps, and senior agency officials acted like members of the very best club that ever was. On this evening, the man had a straw boater banded with a regimental stripe. He flourished the hat when he saw Jeffrey Gertz enter the restaurant.

Hoffman was a master of the details that other people forgot. That had been his secret when he ran Support. He organized a small army of covert logisticians who would find safe houses in a hundred cities around the world, and put reliably discreet renters in them so they didn't have the telltale empty look. He organized what amounted to a string of private airlines, and schemed to find ways to keep them flying when other nations got pissy after the scandals about rendition and torture.

Hoffman kept the balls in the air, as best he could, but even he had understood that the old days, in which the Hoffman clan and their mates were a law unto themselves, were over. Real life had caught up. Sensing the hurricane that menaced the family business, Hoffman had wanted a safe place where he could ride out the storm, a "lily pad," as they liked to say in the agency. He was rewarded with the position of associate deputy director—formerly known as executive director, until it was sullied by a predecessor—which was reckoned to be the third most powerful job at Headquarters.

Hoffman had used that position to fight for the agency's self-preservation at a time when most of official Washington wanted it neutered. Sometimes that meant acceding to ideas he wouldn't have chosen himself. Indeed, that was how he had come to be Jeff Gertz's point of contact and seeming patron: Hoffman had understood that the new administration wanted to conduct this experiment with a new clandestine service far from Langley and the old culture. He would never intercede. But he wanted to keep an eye on this new creation and its headstrong, charismatic boss. Gertz was the sort of man, in truth, who embodied everything that Hoffman was not.

Despite Hoffman's genial, flaccid exterior, he disliked such "hot-shots" more than anyone realized. He was reassured by the knowledge that they always made mistakes. He had the deep, abiding anger that a man feels when he watches others take the credit and win the glory, over many years, for things they couldn't have accomplished without his help. But he had mastered the art of containing this rage in the most genial possible package—making himself appear an object of mirth rather than of envy or threat.

Hoffman had proposed that they meet at a modest restaurant called the Anvil, just past Harpers Ferry, West Virginia, and about ninety minutes from Washington. It was an eccentric choice, and Gertz assumed that Hoffman had selected it for security. But that was only part of the reason, as it turned out.

Before coming to dinner, Hoffman had visited the racetrack in Charles Town, a few miles farther down the road. He had won more than a thousand dollars, thanks to tips from a former agency officer who had bought a stable in the vicinity and claimed to know, for a certainty, which horses were reliable bets and which ones were clunkers. Hoffman was still glowing from his winnings, and his smile initially suggested to Gertz that this would be an easy conversation.

"Welcome to the Anvil," said Hoffman grandly, gesturing to the nearly empty restaurant. “To an anvil, everything looks like a hammer, to coin a phrase. Are you an anvil, Jeffrey, or a hammer?”

“I am definitely a hammer, sir.”

“Not a very effective one of late, I’m afraid. You keep hitting your thumb, or someone does.”

“We’ve had some bad luck these last couple weeks, for sure. But we’ll get our mojo back.”

“What in the Sam J. Hill is going on out there? If you don’t mind my asking, or even if you do.”

“We’re working it, but obviously we have a problem.”

“Yes, I think that would be a fair statement. Losing one officer is unlucky. Losing two is, well . . . you tell me: What is it?”

“It’s a mess. But like I told you on the phone, maybe the two aren’t related. Maybe one is an operational problem, and the other is gangster stuff: Moscow rules. That’s what I told my people.”

“Well, it’s preposterous. Don’t insult my intelligence by saying it again.”

“Yes, sir.”

Hoffman wagged a fat index finger at his guest.

“You seem to think you can bluff your way through this, my boy. That is a big mistake. You have a serious problem. Your officers are supposed to be invisible, but evidently they are not. Someone knew their movements. That is dangerous, my friend. What if you have a serious leak? What if all your operations are insecure? Then you are bleeding, hemorrhaging. Are you not?”

“That’s not going to happen. I have someone working it. We’re doing an investigation. We’re going to find the leak, if there is one, and close it.”

“Oh, *good*. There should always be an investigation. That way, if it blows up and people get the willies, you can say, ‘Sorry, but we can’t discuss it. It’s under *investigation*.’ And who is conducting this no-holds-barred inquiry for you, please?”

“My chief of counterintelligence. Her name is Sophie Marx.”

Hoffman took from his pocket a white index card and a fountain pen, and wrote her name in neat script.

"Is she the cute one, with the ponytail, who was in Beirut, with the hippie parents?"

"Correct. She's very good. And she knows how to keep a secret."

Hoffman peered at him, his eyes narrowing almost to a squint.

"Are you 'doing' her?"

"No such luck."

Hoffman brandished the barrel of his silver and gold S. T. Dupont and wagged it at Gertz.

"Don't dip your pen in the company inkwell, my boy. Those days are over."

"Don't worry. I'm using a ballpoint. Never needs ink."

"Has Miss Marx discovered anything that would shed light on what happened in Pakistan?"

"Not yet. She just went to Dubai and fluttered the access agent, who was the last man to see my officer before he disappeared. She thinks he's clean. We're still trying to understand how the bad guys knew our man was in Karachi."

Hoffman tapped his nose with his index finger, as he habitually did when he was thinking about something.

"I am worried about our Pakistani friends, the ISI," said Hoffman eventually. "That's one of the reasons I wanted to see you. I am worried that they are being less than completely honest with us. No, I will be more explicit than that: I think they are lying to us."

"What makes you think that?"

"I paid a visit last week to one of my old friends. Rather high up. It did not inspire confidence. He claimed they were innocent: white as snow. But I'm afraid I did not believe him. I think they are on to you, my boy. They hear your footsteps. They see you in the shadows. You need to be very careful."

"Have you got anything I can use? Anything I can give to Marx?"

"Nothing but intuition, I'm afraid. The Pakistanis, in my experience, are habitual liars. They are so aggrieved by past slights that they think that any sort of behavior is acceptable. But I am perplexed. I will tell you that."

"Why, Mr. Hoffman?"

"Because I've had our stations put a watch on ISI officers in all major posts, including Moscow. I tasked the NSA, too, and the NRO and all the other behemoth agencies that you no doubt find tedious now that you are so lean and mean. They've been at it for nearly a week. And to my surprise, they have come up with nothing unusual. I am fairly certain that ISI officers in Moscow, declared and undeclared, had nothing to do with the killing of poor Mr. Frankel. That is why I am perplexed."

"What should we do?"

Hoffman wagged his finger, once, twice, three times.

"Be . . . very . . . careful."

They ordered dinner. Hoffman, though a big man, ate sparingly, just picking at his steak. He ordered a bottle of wine, too, but only sipped occasionally from his glass. It was as if eating and drinking were private pursuits that couldn't be enjoyed fully while someone was watching. Hoffman talked over dinner about his rare-book collection, and about the opera, in a pleasant, singsong monologue. When the dinner dishes were cleared, he got serious again.

"How are things going out there? I mean, besides all this messy business. Are you getting it done? I know this is between you and your friends at the White House, but I thought you might give your Uncle Cyril a peek."

Gertz smiled broadly, for the first time that evening.

"Things are going great, actually. We are pushing everywhere we can. The things that can't be done—well, we're doing them."

"And you have enough money for all your operations? Don't tell me what they are, because I didn't ask."

"We're rolling in money. We have some, let us say, 'novel' funding mechanisms. You would love them, frankly."

"I don't want to know. Not now, anyway, when I can be subpoenaed and sued and publicly castrated on the George Washington Parkway. No, thank you. That's why you are there: To think the unthinkable. And do it, too."

"Heard, understood, acknowledged."

"Can we tell Congress anything?"

"Don't even consider that. That would undermine everything we've been trying to do."

"Gadzooks, boy! Don't go telling me what to do. I've already informed the director. He didn't understand what I told him, fortunately. But he's an ex-senator himself, for goodness' sake, and he doesn't like it when things get messy. If he understood that someone has been killing our deep-cover officers, he would say that we need to share the news—merely for reasons of self-protection."

"It's too risky. If it leaked that these men were U.S. intelligence officers, then people would ask what part of the agency they were working for. Then you would have to admit to your friends in Congress that you've built a whole new capability the public doesn't know anything about. And at that point you can kiss the new clandestine service goodbye."

"You are preaching to the choir here, Reverend." Hoffman held up his hand, but Gertz continued.

"And then people would ask what we've been *doing*. What operations have we been running? Was the president aware? How would the White House like to answer that one? 'Deaf and dumb' won't work if this hits Capitol Hill."

"Yes, yes, I know all that. But there is this pesky matter of the law. The director read me the executive order on intelligence the other day. He helped write it, as a matter of fact. It gave me indigestion."

"People talk too much."

"Ah, that they do. I am afraid that God was not an intelligence officer."

"With all due respect, that's your problem, Mr. Hoffman. Read the director the National Security Act of 1947. It says the NSC will authorize 'such other intelligence activities as may be required,' and it doesn't say how, which is good enough for me. But just don't leave me hanging, if you decide to do a striptease. You and the director would regret that. I promise you."

Hoffman's eyes brightened.

"Oh, a threat! I like that. Yes, I do. I can't tell you how that warms an old bureaucrat's soul. You would lose in such a fight, my friend, quite disastrously. You would be blown into so many pieces that people would not know where to find them."

"Don't screw me, Mr. Hoffman. That's all I'm asking. You'll take a lot of other people down with you."

"This is becoming tedious," said Hoffman. "I need another drink."

He scooted away from the table, with a big man's delicate, small steps. It was almost a dance the way Hoffman walked, with something of the cadence of the old-time comedian Jackie Gleason. He returned from the bar with a shot of tequila for Gertz and, for himself, a mai tai with a tiny paper umbrella floating on the surface.

19
LONDON

Thomas Perkins invited Sophie Marx to join him for dinner the night she arrived in London. He proposed that they meet at nine-thirty, his preferred dinner hour because it was after the New York markets had closed. He provided an address on South Audley Street and, when she asked if the place was formal, he laughed and said it was annoyingly stylish. She chose a simple black dress and a string of pearls. As she was about to leave her London hotel room, she decided to take her hair out of the ponytail and let it fall against her neck.

When Marx arrived at the appointed address, she found an unmarked door and, inside, a black velvet curtain. There was a hum of noise, more like the sound of a private party than a normal restaurant. There were no markings in the entryway to suggest that the establishment had a name. "What is this restaurant called?" she asked the hostess, who eyed her skeptically.

"It is a dining club, madam. It is called Edward's." The hostess softened when Marx said that she was a guest of Thomas Perkins and asked to be shown to his table.

Heads turned as she made her way down the long aisle toward Perkins's table in the back of the room. It wasn't just that she was attractive—that was true of most of the women here—but that she had a physical bearing and authority. The men and women scanning her lithe body might have guessed that it came from show-jumping or tennis. They would not have imagined that she had been trained to shoot automatic weapons and jump from airplanes.

There was a buzz in the place, everyone talking as they pounded down their drinks. It had the energy of a trading floor, which was where most of them had been an hour before, closing out that day's bets of fifty million or a hundred million dollars, or in a few cases far more. Mayfair had found its legs again; even the people who had been wrecked pretended that they hadn't, and nobody really knew, except from the size of their order flow. The one thing that everyone in the room thought they knew was that Thomas Perkins was on top of the world, especially as the elegant woman in the black sheath sat down at his table.

Perkins was reading a summary of that day's trading, so he didn't see her approach. When she reached his table, he looked up with surprise. It was like a blind date. When Anthony Cronin had called and asked him to meet a woman who was a colleague of Howard Egan's, he had not imagined that she would arrive in quite this package. And she, in her own way, was also pleased: She had expected someone with a hard edge, but Perkins just looked intelligent. He was dressed in the clothes that rich men wear, hand-tailored and of finer fabric than is found on any rack. He looked studious in his glasses and also youthful, with that unlikely curl of blond hair.

People were still watching. This was too much attention. She leaned toward him and said that her name was Sophie.

"I read once that a spy should have a face that a waiter forgets," Perkins said. "I think you flunk."

"Thank you, if that's a compliment." She smiled, but it vanished in an instant. She leaned toward him and spoke in his ear.

"We are sorry about Howard Egan's disappearance. It must be a shock for your people. We are grateful that you have been so helpful."

"I didn't realize that his work was so dangerous."

"Neither did we. That's why I'm here."

Perkins pulled his chair closer. This was a noisy place, with more traders bursting in the door every few minutes from South Audley Street. They were pumped with testosterone—loud and vulgar, boasting of their big trades. They tried to hide their anxiety, but this was a world where people got destroyed in a day: A trader made bets that went sour, borrowed money to cover yesterday's mistakes, and then more for today's, and then, pow—the risk manager walked over to his screen and closed him down. And then he went to Edward's to pretend it hadn't happened.

"Are these people all billionaires?" asked Marx, looking around the room.

Perkins shook his head. "They all want to be, and some of them will be, but nobody knows which ones will get lucky. That's what keeps the juice flowing."

They drank some wine, making small talk, and then ordered food. She asked what "dressed crab" was, and he answered that it was the opposite of undressed crab. She ordered that, and risotto with white truffles. He ordered the same thing, to make it simple, and bottle of a 1990 Cheval Blanc, a first growth from Saint-Émilion, which at over five thousand dollars was the most expensive wine on the list.

Eventually they got around to business. He asked why she had wanted to see him. She told him the truth, more or less: She worked for the same part of the CIA as Howard Egan, and had been asked to conduct an investigation into his disappearance. She hoped she could spend some time at Alphabet Capital, reviewing Egan's trading files and communications, and spending time with his colleagues.

"What are you looking for?" asked Perkins.

"I don't know yet. But somehow Howard's cover was blown. The people who kidnapped him knew he wasn't just working for a hedge fund. I need to find out whether there was a leak."

"There's always a leak," said Perkins, taking off his glasses and looking into her eyes, a few inches away. "Half the people in this room are trying to get inside my computer system right now, trying to figure out whether I am long Argentine government debt or short, or buying Hong Kong equities or selling."

"This leak is dangerous, Mr. Perkins. We need help. We have to find it and turn it off."

Perkins nodded, trying to match her seriousness. His forelock fell across his forehead, making him look improbably young.

"I'm game. What am I going to tell my people about you? I mean, if you're going to spend time on our trading floor, they're going to wonder what the hell is going on."

"Tell them I'm a tryout," said Marx perkily. "Tell them you're thinking of hiring me as an analyst. I couldn't pass as a trader, but anyone can be an analyst, right?"

"What are you going to analyze? This work isn't completely mindless, you know."

"I used to work in Beirut. I know about oil. So tell people that's what I'm doing. I'm on a tryout as an energy analyst. Then you can fire me when I'm done."

"Well, you can't have too many energy analysts, right? What did you do in Beirut?"

"I don't know you well enough to answer that," she said, with a look halfway between shy and sly. "Let's just say you would have found me entertaining. Spectator sport, except you wouldn't have understood the game."

"That's tantalizing."

"It's all you're going to get."

Sophie Marx couldn't have explained why she was flirting with him. Perhaps it was the wine, or the fact that he was better-looking than she had expected. Maybe it was that he was so rich. Sophie had grown up poor with her screwball parents, moving from beach shanty to boat to day hotel, one of them always running off with someone else. There was something inescapably pleasurable about money.

As they were eating dessert, a big, drunken Irishman stumbled toward the table. Sophie had seen him at the bar when she arrived, already inebriated and making too much noise. As he neared Perkins's chair, he plopped his large bottom on Perkins's lap and began to moan.

"Oh, it feels so good. Oh, it's getting hard." He was trying to be funny.

"Hello, Seamus. Get off my fucking lap." Perkins gave him a shove.

The big man stood up and bowed unsteadily in Sophie's direction.

"Sorry, miss. Inside joke."

"Get lost, Seamus, now. Don't embarrass yourself any more than you already have."

"You know, Perkins, you really are an ungrateful cunt. Did you know that?"

Perkins stood up. The bartender and a burly waiter had arrived by now, to escort the loudmouth to the door.

"Go home, Seamus. Stop making an ass of yourself. Come back tomorrow and try to make some money."

The Irishman wobbled off, flanked by the bouncers. "You are a *cunt*," he said again loudly. "A selfish, ungrateful cunt."

Perkins shook his head. "I'm sorry about that."

Sophie leaned toward him and put her hand on his arm.

"What was that all about?" she said. "Why did he use that language?"

"He's just a loser, that's all. He's ruined. His fund is shutting down. Nobody will lend him any more money. He thinks it's my fault."

"Why does he think that?"

"Who knows? Because I'm still solvent and he isn't. We were on opposing sides in some trades. I won and he lost. He asked for a loan, and I said no. His problem is that he is untalented and unlucky, in that order."

"Well, I must say, that was entertaining: a floor show. You didn't really get hard when he sat on you, did you?"

Perkins laughed out loud, to Sophie's relief. He ordered a bottle of Château d'Yquem to drink with dessert.

Toward the end of the evening, she got serious. She didn't want to break the mood, but she had to give him some news so that he could begin making plans.

"There's something I have to tell you," she said.

"Something nice?"

She shook her head.

"Howard Egan is dead," she said quietly. "The Pakistani police are issuing a statement. They're saying he died in a hiking accident. They will send the coffin here, and we'll take care of the rest. You'll want to tell your people. There will be stories in the newspapers, probably. We need to get ready for that."

She removed a piece of paper from her purse and handed it to him. It was the text of the statement that the Pakistanis would be issuing.

Perkins glanced at it and lowered his head. When he looked up, Marx could see that his eyes were moist, not quite tears.

"I really liked Howard. You know, he didn't want to do your job anymore. He wanted to stop. He told me that the last time I saw him. He asked me if he could have a real job at Alphabet Capital, instead of a fake job."

"What did you tell him?"

"I said he would be bored. I told him that all we did at Alphabet Capital was make money."

Perkins's car and driver were waiting outside. He invited her to come back to his townhouse in Ennismore Gardens for a nightcap, or visit Annabel's in Berkeley Square. She was tempted, even though she had just flown across the ocean and knew for a certainty that it was a *bad idea*. She said she would take a rain check.

Perkins insisted on driving her to her hotel. It was an old pile near Marble Arch that had been remodeled by an American hotel chain. Its virtue for Marx was that it wouldn't bust her per diem. Perkins feigned shock when the driver opened the door at this most ordinary address.

"This won't do. Not for you. Tell your boss that I won't talk to you anymore unless you move to someplace more appropriate. This place is insecure: Nobody working for me in real life would ever stay here. It's a dead giveaway. I suggest the Dorchester. It's near my office, and it's where you would stay."

She moved to the Dorchester first thing the next morning. They gave her a grand room overlooking Hyde Park. Mr. Perkins had called ahead.

20
LONDON

The trading room at Alphabet Capital was a hedgerow of computer screens, two and sometimes three to a desk. It wasn't a tidy office. Nobody on the floor wore a tie, one man was dressed in shorts and sandals, and several of the men had ponytails longer than Sophie Marx's. It didn't matter what you looked like, evidently, so long as you made money. There were a lot of Asian faces on the trading floor, many Indians and some Pakistanis, it appeared. That was a worry now.

Marx arrived at nine-thirty dressed in a blue suit and a white blouse, much too sensible an outfit for the trading floor. Perkins's secretary, whose name was Mona, walked her over to see the director of Human Resources. He found her a desk at the far end of the floor where the analysts sat. It had just one computer screen. The morning was spent in tutorials on the Bloomberg Terminal.

Perkins sent out a system-wide message in midmorning asking everyone to gather on the trading floor. He emerged from his office in shirtsleeves, head bowed. It was obvious to everyone that something bad had happened.

Perkins said he had just received a call from the U.S. consulate in Karachi. Howard Egan, their missing colleague, was dead. He had fallen during a trek in the mountains near Karachi, and the Pakistanis had finally discovered his body. He read the police statement. He said that Egan's remains would be returned to the States, where the family would hold a memorial service. He was about to head back into his office, somber business done, but he stopped and turned toward the dozens of employees, most of whom had known the deceased only slightly, if at all.

"Howard Egan was a decent man; much too nice for our business. He loved his work. He was a risk-taker, always. In this case, he took a bigger risk than he could handle."

He paused for a time, looking at the floor, as if he were going to say more. But the words didn't come, and he turned abruptly and retreated to his Bloomberg screens.

They stood there for a moment, trying to take in the news. Someone in the back said, "Hear, hear," as if Perkins had given a toast rather than a eulogy. People slowly dispersed back to their desks to begin once more the roar of trading, which didn't take a break for anyone.

Shortly after his little speech, Perkins called Sophie Marx in the HR training room and invited her to lunch. He proposed to meet her at a restaurant called L'Oranger in St. James's Street at one. That sounded reasonably discreet, so she said yes.

She felt mildly guilty about having a good time in London when her colleagues were in danger, so she emailed Gertz telling him that everything was going according to plan and that she hoped to have some answers for him soon. Gertz responded promptly. She wondered why he was still up; it was nearly three a.m. in Los Angeles. He told her to go someplace where she wouldn't be overheard, so he could call her cell phone.

"Perkins likes you." That was the first thing he said. She wasn't sure from his tone whether he was pleased about it. She asked how he knew that so quickly, and he explained that Perkins had messaged his agency contact, Anthony Cronin, and that Cronin had told him.

"We have a delicate relationship with this guy," Gertz continued. "I'm glad he's opening the door, but be careful. This is a china shop. You touch the stuff and you're going to break some of it. And then you're screwed. We're all screwed. So walk softly. Be professional. And don't take too much frigging time. I need something to give to Headquarters soon, or we're all going to be sitting on the crapper full-time."

"How much time do I have?"

"A week, two weeks at the outside."

"That may not be enough. This is complicated. And if I find a lead, I'm going to need to follow it. Don't you think?"

"Sure, sure. Just get it done in two weeks. I've told Cyril Hoffman that you're working on this. You, personally. You know what that means?"

"That it's my ass."

"Precisely." He told her to have fun in London, and not to run up too big a bill at the Dorchester. Apparently Perkins had confided that to Anthony Cronin, as well.

The restaurant was deep in Clubland, at the corner of St. James's and Pall Mall. Marx took a taxi, hoping to get there first, but when she arrived, she saw Perkins's car idling outside. He was nestled against the banquette, reading the latest trading report as he did habitually, wherever he was. The entirety of the fund's life seemed to be summarized by those numbers: What positions it had taken that morning, which ones it had sold. He put the market manifest aside when she sat down. She pointed to it and asked him why he found it so riveting.

"Trading is a narrative," he said. "You can describe it on this piece of paper, but it's more like a book. One part of the story is connected to all the rest. Right now we think the European Central Bank is going to start tightening again at the next meeting, which means Eurozone interest rates will go up. So we're buying euros and selling European equities. As the euro gets stronger against the dollar, oil prices will go up a bit, so we're buying oils. But if the dollar is off, that's good for U.S. exporters, so we're increasing our position in some large-cap U.S. equities, too."

As he talked, he pointed to the trades that morning that had been driven by the "narrative," as he'd put it. She tried to follow along, and occasionally nodded as if she understood what he was talking about. But most of the markings on the sheet just looked like very big numbers and she didn't follow the trading logic, up or down.

"Let's go back to the start," she said. "How do you know the European Central Bank will start tightening at its next meeting?"

He smiled sheepishly, and she thought at first that she had asked a dumb question. But it wasn't.

"That's the secret sauce," he said. "I can't explain that. It's how we make our money. When you know things, the bets aren't so risky. Otherwise, it's just a casino. If I wanted to gamble, I could do that in Las Vegas, without hiring all these people."

They ordered lunch, and it was delicious, of course. This man only seemed to eat good food and drink the best wines. In this case, it meant pumpkin soup with cognac, served with chicken livers on toast, followed by a *navarin* of lamb. She waved off the sommelier, but Perkins said that it would be criminal to have the lamb without a glass of Margaux, so she relented.

Sophie had first-day questions about Alphabet, and he answered them genially. He told her that perhaps a half dozen of his employees were of Pakistani origin, including several in the IT department, and one in accounting. He promised to get their names and pull their files. And he explained Howard Egan's routine: He had made his travel arrangements through Perkins's secretary, Mona, and he drew on his own operating account when he was traveling; it was one of several accounts Alphabet maintained at Fédération des Banques Suisses, but had its own routing number and depository arrangements. Normally, Egan and a private banker at FBS named Felix Stern were the only people with access to these records, but Perkins said he would try to get them, too.

She listened attentively, and took some notes in a wire-bound pad she had brought in her purse. As he talked, she recalled another conversation, several weeks before, when she had first heard the name Thomas Perkins. She had been sitting in Gertz's office in Studio City, listening in on one of his phone calls. Perkins had asked, "What about the system?" but Gertz had blown him off. She had wondered about that at the time.

"I have a question," she said. "What's 'the system'?"

There was a little flutter of one of his eyelids. He tried to cover with a smile and another tug on his Margaux.

"What are you talking about? I don't know about any system. What system?"

"That's what my boss said when you asked him about 'the system.' 'Mr. Jones,' that was the name my boss was using. You remember: He called you to say that Howard Egan was missing. Toward the end of the conversation, you asked him, 'What about the system?' And he said he didn't know what you were talking about, just like you said a minute ago. So, being a curious girl, I want to know: What's this *system* that nobody seems to know about?"

He shook his head. "How on earth did you overhear that conversation?"

"I was listening on the extension. Don't be angry. My boss wanted me to hear the call. I think he knew we were going to be friends."

Perkins had drained his wine and was starting in on his mineral water. He was trying very hard to act normal.

"I can't talk about it, Sophie. I'm sorry, but it's not my secret to share."

"What does that mean?"

"It means that if you don't know about it already, then there's a reason. And it's not my business to go blabbing about it. Surely you understand that. This is your world, your rules. I'm a bystander."

"Will you check with Anthony Cronin?" she asked.

"I certainly will." The easy smile had returned, not just a million-dollar smile, but a thousand times brighter. "You can count on it."

Perkins proposed that they walk back to the office. It was a fine summer afternoon, with little flecks of cottony cloud padding the blue sky. He seemed to want to tell her about himself, to explain who he was and how he had gotten to this pinnacle: He had been a professor of economics long ago at MIT, he said, teaching students about efficient markets and portfolio theory. He had been a prodigy, in academic terms: the youngest among his peers to get a doctorate, the youngest to get a tenured teaching job, the youngest man, as one of his friends needled him, ever to turn thirty. All he had ever wanted was to be a professor, but once he achieved that goal, he found to his surprise that it bored him.

He stopped Sophie on the sidewalk and took her arm; he seemed especially to want her to understand why his life had turned toward business, and how the money had begun to shower down on him.

"My academic friends all thought it was a betrayal, going to Wall Street. There weren't any hedge funds back then; people disapproved of making money. But I thought to myself: Why is it better to lecture about the financial system as a professor than to be part of it? That was when I first thought about starting a fund of my own. It wasn't that I wanted to be rich. I just wanted to be an active person in the world, not a passive one."

He seemed to want validation, to need approval from this woman who had risked her life in faraway places.

"I was insecure, the way professors are," he continued. "I didn't know if I was tough enough to make it in the real world. That bugged me."

"So are you? Tough enough, I mean."

He flinched. The question wounded him.

"I'm sorry," she said. "Of course you are. You're a natural. That's obvious, even to me. You make it look easy."

They were passing Jermyn Street and were nearly to the Ritz Hotel. They were walking the richest square mile on the planet, and he wanted her to understand.

"It's *not* easy. What you are seeing is an illusion. Markets are not a gentle ride, they are a hurricane. They can destroy you. They almost destroyed me a couple of years ago."

She laughed. She thought he was joking.

"You? You're the golden boy. That's what everyone says. You're the one who came through the bad years without getting whacked. You're the Pacman. You eat everyone and everything."

"That's all crap. I was nearly destroyed. My creditors were lining up all the way to Trafalgar Square. I survived that, but barely. And I could be wrecked tomorrow. Looks are deceiving, my dear. All that glitters may be gold, but that doesn't mean it's yours for keeps. You have to make arrangements, visit the pawnshop. You need to have friends. You are forced to play the game."

"Everyone does that, right? Behind every great fortune, there's a crime, as somebody said."

"It was Balzac, and it's true. And do you know what? It makes you vulnerable."

"Sorry, Tom, but I have no idea what you're talking about."

He took her arm again.

"When I was on the edge in 2008, I cheated. It was the only way to stay afloat. And the people who knew what I'd done had a handle on me after that. I was not a free man."

"Who were they?"

"None of your business. Well, that isn't exactly true. It is your business. But I don't want to talk about it."

"You don't sound very happy, for a multibillionaire."

The look on his face confirmed her intuition.

"I'm trapped," he said. "I know that sounds crazy, but if I could escape this world, I would do it in a minute. But I can't, so I try to collect the things that money can buy, to help me forget about the things it can't."

Sophie wasn't sure what he was talking about, and now, having said so much, he stopped talking. He was quiet the rest of the way back, almost taciturn. His step didn't seem quite so light and carefree. Sophie felt sorry for him, though she couldn't say why.

Perkins went into his office when they got back and began making phone calls. Sophie had another Bloomberg tutorial scheduled for three o'clock. When she got back to her desk at five o'clock, there was a one-sentence message from Jeff Gertz: *We need to talk.*

She took the elevator down to Curzon Street and walked north until she found a private spot. It was a small park off Mount Street that was enclosed by grand brick apartments. She took an empty bench and called Gertz. He was angry, you could hear the effort in his voice as he tried to control himself.

"Where are you?" he began. "And don't say London. What street?"

She gave him the address of the leafy park and said it was off Audley Street, behind a public library. The phone went dead, and she knew instantly that Gertz was there, in the city, must have been there since she arrived, shadowing her. As she waited, she watched the squirrels dance across the tree branches, so nimble, so certain where they were going, limb to limb. Lucky squirrels, that they could do it on instinct and didn't have a consciousness that could visualize the idea of falling.

In less than five minutes, the familiar form entered the park; the lean body, almost gaunt; the lupine face, hard-cheeked, softened with the goatee. He was dressed in one of his California outfits: black shirt, black trousers, as if he were going to Dan Tana's to meet his Hollywood friends. Gertz scanned the park and the surrounding buildings for surveillance and then took a seat next to Sophie Marx on the wooden bench.

"Well, madam, you really did it this time. You really shot the pooch." He was shaking his head.

"Hi, Jeff. Good to see you, too. What the hell are you talking about?"

"I kept telling you to be careful, not to go sticking your pinky into whatever looked tasty. But you were too smart for that. You had to ask Mr. Lucky to tell you *everything*, and in the first twenty-four hours, too. And now you've put him and me and the whole goddamned enterprise at risk, and yourself, too, by the way. You really are a piece of work, Sophie."

He stood up, as if he couldn't contain his consternation sitting down, walked a few paces and then came back to his seat on the bench. She watched, waiting for him to calm down.

"What on earth are you talking about, Jeff? Obviously you're furious at me, but I don't know why. What have I done?"

"Give me a break. That sweetie-pie stuff may work with Perkins, but he doesn't lie for a living, and I do. You deliberately compromised me by asking Perkins about a confidential comment that he made to me on the phone two weeks ago. And don't pretend that you don't know what I'm talking about. I know that you pumped the guy for that information today at your fancy bullshit lunch."

"You mean when I asked Perkins about 'the system'?"

"Of course that's what I mean. I can't believe that you would do that. That is lame-ass judgment. That would normally be a CEI. You know what that is? A career-ending incident."

"Slow down." Her mind was jumping backward and forward in time as she tried to understand her boss's rage.

"So Perkins called Anthony Cronin already? And Cronin called you? That was fast. You people don't waste any time."

"Jesus, girl, how dumb are you? I *am* Anthony Cronin. I have been Perkins's case officer for the last few years."

"Oh." She felt manipulated, but more than that, she felt stupid.

"So here's what we're going to do, now that you have pushed your way into the part of the china shop marked DO NOT ENTER. I am going to explain 'the system' to you. And then you are going to help me keep it going. Because if you don't, your job will end, effective immediately, and I will do everything I can to make it impossible for you to work anywhere else for a long frigging time. Are we clear?"

"Yes, we're clear."

He smiled, for the first time since his cyclone had blown into the park. His teeth were so white and sharp they seemed to sparkle in the summer sun. He had her now: She was in his loop again, and he was relieved.

"That's better."

"For you, maybe. What's the system?"

"The system in question is actually quite simple. For it is based on the clearest precept of human life—the golden rule of reciprocity—which is, 'Do unto others as you would have them do unto you.' That means Thomas Perkins helps us. And we, in turn, help Thomas Perkins."

"How do we help him?"

"We give him the coin of the realm, my dear, which is information. We know things that move markets. We tell him. He makes money. Some for him, and some for us, thank you very much."

"What do we do with our share?"

"We spend it. If you hadn't noticed, we have agents all over the world who are paying people large stipends: Bribes, to be blunt. Where do you think the money comes from—given that we don't exist? Well, I'll tell you: We make money the old-fashioned way. We *earn* it. Thomas

Perkins provides the structure. We provide the information. Put them together and you have a money machine."

"That's the system?"

"Yup. And starting this minute, you are a part of it."

Marx surveyed the tidy park. The grass under her feet was emerald-green. Within a half-mile radius was perhaps a trillion dollars of wealth, in constant invisible motion.

"Can I ask a question?"

"No. The part where you ask questions is over. Now it's the part where you follow orders."

"I'm going to ask the question anyway, Jeff. Is this legal, what we're doing?"

He put his arm on her shoulder, not roughly, but in a way that was meant to reassure.

"Yes. The Hit Parade was created under the National Security Act. It has powers and authorities to do things that other organizations are not permitted to do. That's what allows us to operate. By other rules, we may be illegal, but we have our own rules. Does that help?"

"Not really, Jeff. You managed to say yes and no at the same time."

"Well, then, you got it right. That's where we live."

21

MAKEEN, SOUTH WAZIRISTAN

Dr. Omar returned home to South Waziristan on the second anniversary of the day when hell came to earth. He told no one. People said it was too dangerous in the tribal areas now, and few of his university friends even knew that he was a refugee from that world. But memories of the place haunted him, especially of that last afternoon. When he closed his eyes, he saw the metallic gleam in the sky ten thousand feet above; he saw the flash-click, like the pop of a flashbulb and the opening and closing of a camera shutter—that transformed life into death; he watched as his family vanished in a pulse of light. Sometimes it was all he saw.

He had dreamed of leaving this place forever. His exile had begun when his father sent him away to school in Razmak, up the road in North Waziristan. When he left, Omar had only the tendrils of beard. But even then he wanted a life that would not be bounded by the primitive triad of *zar zam zamin*—gold, women and land. He was the bright boy who excelled in mathematics, the one destined for college and engineering school. Omar had embodied the possibility of escape. But he had come to understand that this was an illusion. There is no escape from the tribal code that defines who you are.

People called him Dr. Omar, or "professor," and religious friends used the Islamic honorific *ustad,* or "learned one." The handful who knew he was from the Tribal Areas spoke of him as the hope for progress and reconciliation. His black hair was trimmed by a barber; he shaved his face every morning with an electric razor; he dressed like a college professor, in a sports jacket and open-necked shirt. His hands were soft, too. He did not believe in violence as a way of life; for him the code of revenge was learned and, in that sense, unnatural. That was why he needed to go home: to remember and recommit.

Dr. Omar told friends in Islamabad that he was going away for a bit of holiday up in the mountains. People thought he meant Gilgit or Chitral, in the far north. He borrowed a friend's Toyota and headed southwest toward Bannu, where he stopped at the ISI office to get the necessary papers and permissions. He showed them his identity card, which listed his birthplace. He was visiting home, he said: Peace was coming to his native region, thanks to the ISI, and he wanted to see the place again and tell people about the new world that was waiting outside these barren hills.

The road west into the mountains was treacherous, better traveled by animals than cars. Omar took his time; he wanted to see every tree and hillside. Driving down the dusty road from Razmak toward Makeen, he went so slowly that the other cars honked and raced past him, calling out names. He didn't care. The distant landscape hadn't changed: the low hills rising from the narrow valley, dotted with pines and scrub brush, and beyond, the slate-gray hillsides of the dry mountains. And everywhere the rocks, as if God had made this land his slag heap for the pieces that wouldn't fit anywhere else.

As he got closer to home, Omar began to see the scars of the war. The big compound in Makeen where the young fighters had done their training was shattered by bombs. He stopped the car and got out to look: He saw corrugated metal from what had once been a roof; and the collapsed walls, chunks of concrete pierced by steel reinforcing bars. These were the big targets that had been hit by the Pakistani air force; they were the visible wounds. There were new stores in the market center; bright signs that advertised cellular telephone carriers and Japanese automobile tires and laundry powder from Lahore; there was even a new red sign that read, COCA-COLA.

Omar turned off the main road toward his family's compound a few miles distant from Makeen center. The road sloped up now, winding with the curve of a dry riverbed that was strewn with rocks on this summer day. He remembered this river in springtime when it was engorged by the runoff of the melting snows from the mountains to the west, near the Afghan border. On a sunny day, he would come here with his younger brother Karimullah, rolling an inner tube that they would ride through the surging waters, clinging for dear life. Looking at the dry bed now, you could not imagine that water had ever flowed through it.

The road curved away from the stream and he saw a row of apple trees. This was the southern edge of his family's property. Once this orchard had been neatly tended; his father had sent him out with a scythe to cut down the low brush; now it was overgrown with weeds and scrub. A few early apples that had fallen from the trees were rotting on the ground, infested with worms.

He had in his mind a picture of what he saw as a boy when he returned from the orchard with a basket of apples on his shoulders. He would take the path toward home, this one just ahead, and he would see the family compound snug against the hills. The walls would change color with the light of the day: red-hot in the summer sun, dappled on a cloudy day. When he banged at the gate and the servant boy opened the heavy wooden barrier, he would enter a special place in which food was always cooking, and people were laughing, and there was always a cool spot to rest in summertime and a warm one in winter.

Omar rounded this last curve and looked: There was nothing at all. Even the rubble had been stripped. You could see where the walls of the compound had been and bits of debris that were useless even to the scavengers. There was nobody to live here, and nobody even to rebuild it.

He closed his eyes and tried again to imagine the way it had been, but this time the image would not come. It was gone, with his family. The pieces of their flesh had decomposed into this ground. He bent down and kissed the earth. The dust caked his lips, but he kissed the ground again and wept. For a long time, he could not stand up. There was no power in his legs, because of the sadness and the emptiness of loss. What gives us the strength to move? It is anger.

Across the vale he saw the home of his cousin Najib. The compound was still standing. He walked the half mile to the gate and knocked on it until a gnarled man emerged, his beard gray, his faced creased by sun and suffering. It could not be that this wizened man was his cousin; they were nearly the same age. His eyesight had gone, and he did not recognize Omar. He welcomed the stranger in the Pashtun way, invited him into the courtyard, sat him down with a drink. He had a satellite television, powered by his generator, and he turned on the picture, to be polite, while they talked.

Cousin Najib wanted to know who this visitor might be. The professor explained that his relatives had lived in Makeen long ago but moved away. They lived in Quetta now; that was where most of the refugees had moved during the decades of war. The visitor named a family who lived a mile or so away, and said they were his people. He asked about neighbors who had been friends of his father and brothers.

What about Hakimullah from across the valley? Dead, with all his family. And Majid, what about him? He was dead, too. His wife had survived but she had moved away after the drones attacked. She lived in Peshawar now, or maybe Bannu. And Ahmed Wali? He survived the drones, but he was killed in the mountains. His boys swore revenge, but they were dead now, too. This was a land of ghosts, said the host. The people were all gone; the ones like him who pretended to live, they were ghosts, too.

Cousin Najib put on his glasses. He studied the face of his visitor—short-haired, beardless, his face seemingly unmarked by this harsh world.

"I know you," said the bearded man. "You are Omar. We played together when we were boys. Your brothers were Karimullah and Nazir. Your father was Haji Mohammed. I know you."

"You are mistaken," answered the visitor. "Omar is dead. He died with his family in the drone attack. I am another."

When he returned to Islamabad, the professor went to the head of his department and asked for a few weeks' leave. He said that he had a promising research project on which he needed to concentrate. He didn't trust the security of the computers at the university, so he bought a new one, into which he could plug his flash drive and parse the names and numbers that he had assembled so painstakingly. It was a jigsaw puzzle of vengeance. You had to fit the pieces together just so, and then you glimpsed the pattern and the picture was revealed.

In the culture from which Dr. Omar had emerged, there were rules as precise in their way as the symbolic logic of computers. There was *itbar,* which meant trust, and was the bond between equal men and the foundation of dignified life. There was *nang,* which was honor, and *badal,* which was the personal code that required that a blow to that honor to be answered by an equal blow, bloodshed by bloodshed. Without this reciprocal balance, the world would have no order and life would be meaningless.

A special obligation for revenge was applied in the case of *meerata,* which was the annihilation of the male members of a family. In such cases, the tribe would set the houses of the culprits afire and drive them from the country and kill them, one by one, until the score was settled. The *tor,* the black of shame, could only be converted to *spin,* or white, by death. The cycle was one of purification, and it would end with the peace known as *melmastia,* the generous spirit in which the just man was able to forgive the wrong done to him. But not until the balance of honor had been restored.

The professor knew very well who had killed his family and ravaged the other clans that made up his world. It was the Central Intelligence Agency. They had devised this means of assassination from the sky; they did it in secret, so they claimed, though they boasted about it all the while. The worst of it was that they took these actions from the safety and security of great distance. They were cowardly: They never looked their victims in the eye; they never heard the screams. This was inhuman, the professor thought; it required a calculated response.

And so the professor had pondered how he might make these assassins feel the same fear that the people of his valley had felt for all these years. He was not at war with the world. He was a Muslim, but he was not passionate about his faith. He did not want to be like the jihadists who boasted of their violent deeds in videos and on the Internet. They were no better than the Americans; they thought they were God's chosen ones. They talked about the virgin girls who awaited them in heaven, how they would be "rocketed to paradise." When they looked at pornography, they said they were getting ready for the joys of martyrdom. The professor might use these jihadists because he had no choice, but he did not admire them. They did not understand the balance of honor, the *gundi*, which makes civilized life possible even in the terrible wilderness of the Tribal Areas.

The professor had begun his work, but it was not finished. He understood that when he kissed the ground on which his family had died. There was more *saz*, more blood money, still to be paid. He knew that it would have to end someday, just as it had started, but he didn't know how. When was the *saz* enough? He wished his father were still alive to explain it to him.

He traveled to Europe once more, to contact a friend in Belgium. It was a short trip, only two nights. He stopped in Paris on the way back and spent a day consulting for a French bank that had invested in a large agricultural project in the Sindh and was having difficulty repatriating its profits. He even gave a thought to visiting the American Embassy, off the Place de la Concorde, just to look into the eyes of the employees. But they might see him, too, and photograph him, and that would reopen a file somewhere. So he sat on a park bench off the Avenue Gabriel, a hundred yards from the embassy entrance, and watched the people come and go through the heavy metal door.

22
LONDON

Thomas Perkins invited his new energy analyst to the morning meeting where he planned each day's trading strategy with his lieutenants. Through his windows, the London morning sky was royal blue, accented by the few thin clouds that scuttled west to east across the expanse of glass. The south end of Mayfair was arrayed below, with the shops of St. James's Street to the east and the silky lawns of Green Park to the west. It was like inhabiting a cocoon spun of gold thread, this penthouse office. To remain atop this fine building, a person would consider any reasonable offer of assistance, especially if he were assured that his actions would be legal and, more than that, a service to his country.

Perkins was at his desk. Facing him were four big screens, mounted two-by-two on the wall, chronicling the U.S., British, Japanese and European markets. Bloomberg trading screens surrounded his desk on three sides: the left screen displayed Alphabet Capital's order flow for that day's trading; the middle one showed graphical information about securities and markets of special interest; the right screen displayed a half dozen instant-message chats, with securities dealers who handled the firm's business and with other useful informants.

The "system" that Perkins had constructed with the man he knew as Anthony Cronin was invisible, though it most assuredly was in place. It would have been impossible for an outsider to distinguish any special bits of information from the torrent that flowed in from the multiplicity of screens. That was why it was so lucrative. A slight advantage at the margin could produce a very large difference in outcome. If you knew for a certainty, say, that the Bank of China would be raising interest rates later in the next trading day, you could make a great deal of money. But most people assumed that sort of trading advantage was impossible: You would need to have your own spy within the Chinese bank, or a hidden microphone, or a code break that allowed you to read their encrypted communications. No private trader could hope to do any of that; but someone who had government help . . . that was a different matter.

Perkins rose from his desk and moved to the conference table. He introduced his team of analysts to the new tryout on the energy desk, Sophie Marx. She was appropriately nervous. She had spent a day preparing for the meeting, tutored by Jeffrey Gertz, who wanted her to make a splash her first day. She still wasn't sure she could pull it off; mercifully, she didn't have to go first.

Marx looked at her notes. Gertz had arranged for her to do some quick "energy research" with Janko Spellman, a Serbian with a shaved head and big ears who had been a CIA asset during the Kosovo War. He traveled Eastern Europe now, picking up information for Gertz as if it were so much lint on a blue serge suit. He had just returned from a particularly useful trip to Ukraine.

"Talk to Janko," Gertz had said. "He has the goodies."

"I don't like this," Marx had answered.

"Too late for that. Second-guessing is for losers."

And he was right. If you wanted a job where you only did things you knew were right, you should look for another line of work.

Perkins clanged his water glass with his pen as if it were the opening bell on Wall Street; it was time to make some money.

"What's happening in the debt markets?" he began. "It feels like time to sell anything French. Banks are weak, GDP growth is weak. Their bonds haven't been downgraded yet, but I bet they will be soon. Sell France. Am I right, Fiona?"

Perkins turned to a British woman in her mid-thirties, who was one of his banking analysts. Fiona was wearing thick glasses, and her hair was in a bun. She looked ferocious.

"*La chute*," she said. "The spread between LIBOR and the French interbank rate has been widening for a week. But the market is confused. The spread was forty basis points as of this morning, down five basis points from yesterday."

"Confused." Perkins repeated the analyst's comment with relish, for this was his favorite of all possible market conditions. "People are assuming that the Germans are coming to the rescue. But they aren't. Why should they clean up France's mess? They aren't weaklings, like Greece and Portugal, they're supposed to be coequals. The French spreads are going to widen. Go tell Cameron we want to short every debt or equity issue that says France. Will you do that? Right now, please."

Fiona scrambled out of Perkins's office onto the trading floor, where she found Cameron Cummings, the lead trader in Eurozone markets. He wore blue-framed glasses, which made him look like a model in *Men's Vogue*. But he was a killer, like most of the people on the floor.

While Fiona was relaying the boss's orders, Perkins had thought of a further refinement. He pushed a button on a microphone in front of him, which activated the squawk box; he punched two more buttons, so he was connected directly with Cameron's desk.

"Do this carefully, please. Don't scare the market. Do it in small bites this morning, not all at once, so the dealers don't get it. If people see what we're doing, they will all want to sell. Can you use a cutout, Cameron?"

"Morgan Stanley owes me. They'll do the first fifty bucks on their account," said the man who managed the Euro debt portfolio.

"Brilliant." Perkins disengaged the squawk box and turned back to his market strategists. "What do we know about the ECB, Dominic? Anything new?"

Dominic Caprezzi, the balding, well-fed analyst who followed the European Central Bank, spoke up.

"I met last week with George Paternoster, the deputy chief economist at the ECB. He didn't exactly say so, but I think they're going to start tightening again."

Perkins shook his head. "Paternoster is getting fired. I have it on good authority. I meant to tell you. What about the German yield curve? Did he say anything about that?"

Heads nodded around the table. German interest rates were one of the big market plays in hedge-fund land right now. Short-term rates had gone up so much recently that the curve was flattening. Many traders were betting that long rates would begin to rise, too, to restore the traditional upward-sloping curve.

"Long rates have to rise," said Dominic, echoing the conventional wisdom. He got a bit pedantic at that point, reminding everyone that higher long yields were rational, and thus inevitable, because they were the commensurate reward for the risk of holding money for a longer period.

"Nope," said Perkins, cutting him off. "It's not going to happen. Here's the narrative: Flat yield curve; ECB happy with it; wants long-term rates low. End of story. Our bet is a flat yield curve."

"Are you sure?" asked Dominic warily. Perkins encouraged his analysts to challenge him, though they were never convinced he meant it.

"That is an epistemological question, which I cannot answer. What is certainty? But I think I'm right. And that's enough."

He got on the squawk box and called for Cameron again. "Watch your Eurobond maturities, please. And keep buying at these prices, even if everyone else is selling. They're wrong."

Perkins turned to Sophie Marx. She had been watching this drill with intense interest—not simply in appreciation of how finely the instrument was tuned, but because she was curious where the information came from: How much was normal market intelligence, how much was guesswork and how much was secret information—telephone and email intercepts, or well-placed agents inside central banks—that had been acquired by U.S. intelligence and passed on to Perkins? It was impossible to know, and that was the point.

"Do you have anything for us, Miss Marx?" he asked. "You're the new kid, but don't be bashful."

"I do have a little something." She smiled coyly. These people didn't know her. She was the tryout.

"Delicious. Tell the class, please." The Pacman's mouth was open, ready to chomp another new asset before it was time for lunch.

"This would be a good time to buy oil and gas in the commodities markets, raw stocks and futures both." She spoke slowly in a voice that quavered slightly with the anxiety and uncertainty that a newcomer would feel.

"Do you think so?"

"Yes, sir, and it would also be a good time to short the stocks of Russian oil and gas companies and any foreign majors that market Russian supplies."

"And why is that?" asked Perkins. She hadn't briefed him in advance, and he was genuinely curious. "Most people have been going the other way. They think energy prices have peaked for a while. And they like the Russians. Why do you think different?"

"The Russians have pipeline problems." She spoke so quietly that people at the far end of the table had trouble hearing her.

"Is that so? Well, I haven't heard anything about them. And I follow the energy market pretty closely."

"It's not really public yet, Mr. Perkins. But there was a rupture of the Russian gas pipeline in western Ukraine two days ago. They shut it down yesterday, and it's going to take quite a while to fix. I think."

Everyone was silent. This was big, market-moving information if it was true.

"Well, fancy that," said Perkins. "I like it. In fact, I love it. Let's do what the new kid says. What say, Ivor?"

Ivor Fyfe, the firm's chief risk manager, was skeptical. He dealt in probabilities, and it was highly improbable that this new analyst, whom nobody had ever heard of, could come up with such a scoop. He enforced the firm's self-protective trading rules, which mandated that any trader whose account was down 5 percent be put on watch, and the account of any trader who lost 10 percent be suspended. Now this neophyte, fresh off the street, was proposing to gamble with the capital of a firm she hadn't yet been invited to join. It offended him.

"Not to rain on the parade," said Ivor, "but how do you 'know' this, Miss Marx? I mean, did a little Russian birdie tell you?"

"I have a friend in Ukraine," Sophie answered. "He just visited Lviv, near where the pipeline has one of its transit stations. He heard about the problem yesterday. They're trying to hush it up, but people in the town know about it. He says it's a big deal."

Perkins goaded her.

"And why is it such a big deal, please?"

"It's big because the rupture came just after the point where the two feeder pipelines, Soyuz and Brotherhood, join up and form the Trans-Gas line. I checked this morning. The pipeline throughput into Poland has stopped. They say it's just routine maintenance. But it isn't."

Perkins's eyes were flashing. He was excited.

"So tell us, Miss Marx: Should we make a big bet here?"

She nodded vigorously. Her ponytail flapped against the back of her neck.

"Ivor? Last chance to be a skunk."

Fyfe looked glum, but he nodded and said, almost inaudibly, "Okay."

"Let's do it, then. Call Stan in here, someone. He can coordinate the trades."

Stan Ferber was summoned: He followed Russian securities, and he helped plan the trading strategy for the day. They would move decisively, but veil their hand wherever possible, taking positions before the information got out and the markets turned. The oil and gas positions were long; the Russian equity positions were short.

Sophie went back to her desk to watch the action. There was an animal intensity on the trading floor. The whole room seemed to know within sixty seconds that they were about to make some very large bets on the strength of a tip from a newcomer who had just walked in the door.

Perkins ambled over to her desk, amid the controlled pandemonium of the trading preparations.

"I've corrupted you," he said. There was a curious look on his face.

For most of that day, Alphabet Capital got killed in the markets. Gazprom put out a statement that it was conducting routine maintenance in Ukraine and Poland, and most traders accepted it at face value. By noon, the firm was down over two hundred million dollars, on paper, and by early afternoon the losses had risen to over three hundred million and were still increasing.

Ivor Fyfe went to see Perkins at one-thirty. The risk manager's job was to do just that—limit the firm's exposure to large market swings—and he didn't like what was happening. On a typical day, Alphabet Capital made or lost half a percentage point on its portfolio. If it limited its risk to one point a day, it stood to make a solid 16 percent return annually, in good markets and bad. If it risked three percentage points, it could make a much more exciting 48 percent return. But Perkins was blowing out even that risk-reward formula, based on the musings of a pretty new analyst, and Ivor wasn't happy.

After the risk manager's visit, Perkins summoned Sophie to his office. The losses were still mounting, and the whole firm watched her travel the floor, as if she were a prisoner heading for the hangman's noose. But she walked out several minutes later with a big smile, and Perkins followed her a few moments after that and instructed his traders to double down their bets. A jokester in the back of the room sent an IM to his friends: *office pool: did miss energy just give the boss (a) a blow job, (b) a rim job, (c) a spanking?*

The markets began to turn that afternoon, just after two-thirty when the New York exchanges opened. Word was out that Alphabet was making some large bets, and traders were spinning rumors. A little after three o'clock, Bloomberg carried a story saying there were reports that the Russian pipeline problem might be more than regular maintenance. At four, the first story appeared citing rumors that the pipeline had ruptured. Gazprom still wasn't commenting, but anything Russian was getting pounded now, as the markets began to bet the rumors might be real.

Gazprom issued a statement at eight forty-five p.m., London time, as the New York markets were about to close, confirming that its main supply pipeline to Europe had ruptured. Full repairs might take three weeks to a month. There was a global trading frenzy. Alphabet's positions, which at midday had been down three hundred million dollars, were now up by nearly three times that amount.

Sophie Marx had just made Alphabet Capital nearly a billion dollars. Stan Ferber, the chief Russia trader, went over to Marx's desk with a bottle of champagne after the Gazprom announcement moved on the wires. He poured a glass for his new energy analyst, to applause from the traders nearby.

While Sophie was drinking her champagne, Perkins emerged from his office. People thought he had come to join in the celebration, but his face was tight. When he reached Sophie's desk, he spoke into her ear and asked if she might be free for dinner that night, as soon as the closing bell rang in New York. He looked oddly glum. Ferber and the others pulled back and returned to their desks.

"What's wrong?" she asked. "You're a winner."

"This used to be more fun when we were making real bets," Perkins said quietly. "It's too easy playing with a marked deck."

"So quit," she said.

He stared at her for a long moment, as if he didn't think that were possible.

23
LONDON

Perkins wanted to get out of London. He proposed flying to Paris in his G5 for a late dinner. He would call Jean-Marie at Taillevent, who would hold a table for them. Sophie thought he was joking, but she didn't understand: She had just made Perkins's firm a billion dollars. If she spent a million dollars a day, five days a week, it would take nearly four years to work through that stash. Why shouldn't she fly on a private jet to Paris for dinner? Money truly didn't matter when there was so much of it. That was unnerving for Sophie, who had grown up wishing for the things that money could buy. But as she was packing her overnight bag in her room at the Dorchester, her phone rang. It was Perkins.

"It's too late," he said. She wasn't sure at first what he meant. "My pilot says we can't get a landing slot in Paris until tomorrow morning. He thought I was daft."

They settled on the River Café, which was outside central London, but only barely. It was a stylish place on the Thames, up near Hammersmith. The interior was shades of blue, a sea-bright carpet and an aquamarine wall, set against the gleaming stainless steel of the open kitchen. Perkins was a regular; he went to places he liked, where risk of a bad meal was low.

Perkins took off his jacket and rolled up his sleeves, and in the low light of the restaurant he didn't look quite so much like the Pacman. Sophie had been wearing a tight, tailored jacket over a blue blouse. She threw her jacket over a chair, too. One thing about being rich, momentarily, was that you could afford to be untidy. She was a handsome woman: supple, bright-eyed, her face always on the verge of a mischievous smile. And on this evening, relaxing in the afterglow of a successful day, he was a handsome man: shy in the way that famous people are, looking for the things in life that didn't have a price tag.

Perkins knew the menu, and he ordered everything he thought she would like: roasted yellow peppers; bruschetta with wild oregano; risotto with white peach; and grilled fishes whose Italian names, *spiedino* and *branzino*, made them sound much tastier than monkfish and sea bass. He couldn't resist ordering another lovely bottle, this one from the Alto Adige. It wasn't like Sophie to allow herself to be spoiled, but she acceded quite happily in this case, and devoured what was put before her.

"Tell me about Sophie Marx, if that's permitted," said Perkins. "I don't know anything about you, except that you seem awfully good at your job."

"'The CIA—we make a world of difference.' That's the slogan the recruiters use."

"And does it? Make a difference, I mean."

"Enough to keep me interested. I'm sort of an action junkie. And I like keeping secrets. I've had lots of practice."

"You still haven't told me anything. Where did you grow up? Let's start there. That's not classified, is it?"

"In Florida, mostly. And then in St. Croix for a while. And then I ran away from home. Just your normal childhood."

"I think you're going to have to explain yourself, madam."

"I *never* explain myself."

But then she did. In the flush of that summer evening, she told him the story that she never told anyone outside work. She trusted him, for reasons she only half understood. She sensed that he was caught, like her, in a world in which he was successful but not entirely happy. He was chasing a glowing filament that receded even as he advanced. Perkins was a good listener, and he let her tell the tale.

"My parents were hippies, sort of," she began. "They were on the run. I was never sure who from, the cops or the FBI, or just from normal people. And they pulled me along with them. We had a lot of things we couldn't talk about with anybody. I guess that's how I got started with the secrecy thing."

"What was your mother like? She wasn't a spy, I take it."

"Do you really want to know? This is private, and it's sort of embarrassing."

"Yes, I really want to know. I want to understand what makes a woman turn out like you."

"My mother was a rebel. She looked like those sixties pictures you see of beautiful girls at Woodstock, or Joni Mitchell album covers. And she was a daredevil. If you told her she couldn't do something, then she had to do it. Unfortunately, she had a habit of wandering off. I thought she wanted to get away from me and my father, but she said she was just a free spirit. When she was having a good time, she forgot about going home."

"Would she come back?"

"Usually, but sometimes it took a while. I had to take care of things while she was gone. Cook, and do the shopping, and pay the bills. And take care of my dad when he was blue. I was like Junior Mom. No wonder I'm weird, right?"

"You're not weird in the slightest. I'm sorry to break that to you. What was he like, your father?"

"He was a dreamer. A romantic, I guess. He was very handsome, sort of impulsive. He did his share of bed-hopping, too. His big problem was that he wasn't very well organized. He had gotten busted for selling LSD in New York when he was still at Columbia, and then he violated his parole, so we had to move a lot, and sometimes he used false names, and it was a big mess every fall when I had to go to school and we had to fill out all the forms."

"Where did you live?"

"We started on the Gulf Coast, in Naples, then in Daytona Beach on the Atlantic side, and then in Key West. In the summers I would sometimes go up north to stay with relatives. But the school thing was a problem every September. That's why we moved to Christiansted in the islands. Some of my parents' screwy friends were setting up a private school there, so that their children could be freethinkers and not have to study reactionary subjects like spelling and grammar. We lived on a houseboat in Christiansted Harbor. It was the only thing they could afford. I hated it. Every day was like the cast party for *Hair*."

"How did you end up so normal, Sophie? I don't get it. With a childhood like that, you should be in a mental hospital."

"I have a nonstick coating. What saved me was that I ran away. I knew I couldn't live like that anymore, and my parents weren't going to change, so finally I just left. I was fifteen. I had a rich aunt, my father's sister, who lived in Chicago. She took me in."

"Is that where the Marx family came from? Chicago?"

"Not exactly. Marx wasn't our real name. My father changed it to that when he was on the run. The family name was Devereux. My aunt wanted me to change it back when I came to live with her, but I said no. The next year she arranged for me to go to a boarding school in New Hampshire. That's where I learned how to act normal. But believe me, I'm not."

"You could have fooled me. From the moment you walked into Edward's, I thought you were Greta Garbo."

"I'm a good pretender. That's one of the survival skills I learned. And having lived that crazy life, I knew things the other kids didn't, so I was popular. And I did well at Exeter, too. Somehow, all those years of bad schools and listening to my parents' dopey ideas hadn't made me stupid. So I was a 'success.'"

"I still don't get the CIA part. How did you end up there? With that crazy childhood, I would think you'd want to do something utterly ordinary—work in a bank, or an insurance company."

Her eyes were alight. She was getting tipsy, on the wine and the company.

"Isn't it obvious? The CIA was the only place where people understood me. I found a whole government agency full of people who lived on the run, and had secrets they couldn't tell anyone, and were always pretending. It was a building full of weirdos like me. I told the agency recruiters everything about myself. I had to. It was the first time I had told anyone the whole story. And do you know what? They loved it."

"Come, now, Miss Devereux. Are you *always* pretending? Like now, for example."

"Every minute, and especially now. I'm always afraid someone will expose me as a fraud. I have dreams about it. And my name is Marx."

Perkins took her hand. It was an unusual thing to do, even in the midst of this intimate conversation.

"You probably won't believe this, but I have the same anxiety. I think I'm going to be found out. The world I've built is going to come crashing down, and I'll spend the rest of my life trying to pick up the pieces. I'm scared, all the time."

"You? That's ridiculous. What do *you* have to be afraid of?"

"Failure, collapse, bankruptcy. When you're playing with so much money, it's easy to get in trouble. That's why I agreed to help the agency. I tried to explain this to you. At the time we got seriously connected, I was on the ropes. My investors didn't know it, and the Street didn't know it. But your friends did. They understood that I was vulnerable. That made me a perfect recruit. Isn't that what you people say?"

"Yes, that's what we say."

She looked at Perkins across the table. He wanted to explain, and she was truly the only one he could tell.

"How did it happen?" she asked. "How did we recruit you?"

So he told her the story. It was a peculiar play, where the audience seemed to understand the story as well as the actor.

"You know Anthony Cronin, the man who introduced us?" he began.

She nodded. Yes, she knew him. That was all she wanted to say, for now.

"I first met Cronin in New York five or six years ago, I can't remember. That was the easy part, before the squeeze began. The meeting had been arranged by a hedge fund manager I knew. It was obvious that he had intelligence connections but he never explained them."

"He was the spotter," Marx said with a wink. "That's what we call them."

"Okay, so he called one day and said he had a friend in the government named Cronin who was a big deal, and that we should meet the next time I was in the States. And I thought, sure, great. A lot of people in finance were helping out after 9/11 and I thought I should, too. So I telephoned the number he gave me for Cronin and left a message saying that I would be in New York in a week. Cronin called back the next day. He suggested we meet at the Athenian Club, where I guess he was a member."

Marx smiled at the thought of such a rendezvous. She had visited the club herself, with one of her professors, when she was an undergraduate at Princeton. It was a handsome beaux arts front on West Forty-Third Street, with a white marble façade, elaborate carvings and moldings and a club flag flapping in the breeze next to Old Glory.

"A perfect place to take an ex-professor like you," she said. "Old paintings on the wall, books in the library shelves, rooms with bathtubs and no showers: old school. Nothing bad could happen there."

"Cronin was waiting upstairs, sitting in a leather chair and sipping a martini as if he owned the place. He rose as soon as I entered the room. He obviously had a picture of what I looked like. The waiter arrived, and I thought, what the hell, do the James Bond thing, so I ordered a martini, too. I took a sip, we talked for a while. He told me about how some famous names in finance were helping: This man got them a new building on Fifth Avenue, pronto, after the New York station went down on 9/11. That one used his company as a front to catch a terrorist from Pakistan. All very impressive."

"So the hook was in."

"Definitely. After a while, he popped the question: 'How would you like to help your country in a time of need?'"

"We call that 'the pitch.' What did you say?"

"I told him of course I would. I had decided that I would say yes on the flight over. I asked him what it would involve, and he said little things, until we got to know each other better. And that's all it was, the first few years. Little things: Can you tell us about your foreign contacts?

Can you help us facilitate a payment overseas? Can we use one of your houses as a meeting place? Easy stuff."

"That's 'development,' by the way, the part where we watch you and see how you're doing. When did it get nasty?"

Perkins looked down at his plate. As much as he had wanted to tell the story, it got harder at this point.

"They caught me cheating. That was the start. I had a man inside the Bank of England. He was giving me information about the Monetary Policy Committee. I was paying him five hundred thousand dollars a year, to a bank in the Cayman Islands, and making twenty times that off his information. But the transfers got picked up by the U.S. money-laundering snoops, and my guy panicked. He thought he had been caught by the Inland Revenue for tax evasion."

"So you asked for help?"

"Exactly. I told Cronin about it. I didn't exactly ask him to fix it, but he knew that's what I wanted. Case went away. Poof. No more questions."

"And you were relieved. And you thought, these intelligence friends of mine are pretty helpful."

"Just so. But then it turned. The markets began to go screwy, and I was in trouble. Like a lot of people, I had bought fistfuls of credit swaps that I thought could never go bad, I mean, how's Morgan Stanley ever going to go bust, right? But everything turned to shit in a couple of weeks, and I was desperate to raise cash."

"And you got a call from Cronin?"

"You know the script. Cronin called and said he had a great idea. He'd heard I was in a little trouble and he knew the perfect way out. We should do what I had been doing with my guy in the Bank of England, but on a global scale. He would supply the inside information, I would trade on it and we would split the profits."

"'The system.'"

Perkins nodded. "And now you're part of it. That's my fault."

Marx shook her head. "I'm a big girl. I know what I'm doing. And this guy Anthony Cronin isn't ten feet tall. Believe me. If you really want a way out, you'll find one."

Perkins wanted to order cheese, but she said no, at the end of so much heavy talk she wanted something sweet. *Dolce*, she said, but not *dolcissime*. He ordered *panna cotta*, a delicate dessert of cooked cream, served with grappa and baked *nespole*, an Italian fruit that looked like an apricot and had a taste between sweet and tart.

"Tell me about Beirut," he said, as they were drinking the last of the dessert wine. "You said that you worked there, but you didn't tell me what you did."

"Of course I didn't. Don't be silly. That's a no-no."

"I don't mean the details, just generically, sort of. Make it up, as if it were a spy novel."

"Okay. Imagine an international civil servant. She works for UNESCO in Paris, at least that's what her card says. She travels regularly to Beirut. She stays at the Phoenicia, on the corniche. She spends her days at UNESCO's office out near the airport, but she has free time at night and on the weekends. She goes to restaurants. She has a chalet at the beach. She's always meeting people. Sometimes they're her agents. Sometimes they work for Lebanese intelligence, or for the Syrians, or the Iranians. Sometimes they exchange information for money. One of them tells her a big secret about how Hezbollah communicates with its operatives. They have a private telephone system. He tells her where the cables are buried."

"Is she in danger, this woman?"

"Not usually, if she does it right. It may sound like she's taking big risks, but she knows how to operate, she's just another pretty girl in Beirut. But then people worry her cover is too thin, and she has to get out of Lebanon in a hurry. And then a bad thing happens to her, in Addis Ababa, and it's obvious she has been burned. They make her go home. She gets a fancy job, but she's bored stiff. She hates success."

"You see! That's why I like you so much. We're the same person."

"But I escaped success, Tom. I went back in the trenches. You're still a billionaire."

He shook his head. He loved her story, but it couldn't be that easy, even for a woman who had mastered the covert life as a young girl, for whom lying was part of survival.

"Is that true, what you told me, more or less?"

"Not a word of it," she said. She closed her eyes. "I'll make up more stories another night."

They were in Perkins's car, heading back to Mayfair. The food and wine had sent her into low-earth orbit in the restaurant, but now she had come back to ground.

Neither of them spoke for a time, and in the silence Sophie recalled the events of the day. Whatever else you could say about it, the trading that had made a paper fortune in a few hours was illegal. Normal people went to jail for insider trading.

That wasn't a stopper, in itself. What the agency did, routinely, was to break the laws of other countries. If a job were simple and above-board, then some other entity of the government could take care of it. Intelligence officers were supposed to do the twisty things, and that was especially true of the new service for which she worked. But even by these debased rules, she sensed that what she and Perkins had done was over the line.

"It was fraud, what we did today, wasn't it?" she said. "Trading on private information, and making all that money. That's against the law."

"How can it be illegal, if the government told us to do it?"

She nodded. That was the right answer. That was what Jeff Gertz would say. But it was a mistake to confuse Gertz with the United States government.

"You want some advice from your new energy analyst?"

"Of course I do. I want to know everything you're prepared to tell me, about every subject."

"Okay, then, if my colleagues ask you to do something, and they say it's legitimate, then get in writing. That's my suggestion. Don't go on a patriotic speech and a handshake. In our business, those don't mean much."

"I tried that already. I asked Anthony Cronin. He told me it wasn't possible. He said, 'Trust me.' So I did."

"Oh, Jesus." She shook her head, and then she laughed. It was funny, really, when dishonest people told you to trust them.

"Let me ask you something," she said. "Do you think you can get out of this, if you decide that it's wrong?"

Perkins thought a long moment. He took her hand, and then let it go.

"It would be difficult now. When your people came to me, I had borrowed a lot of money. I had emptied the tank, pretty much, and was running on fumes. They helped me pay off the debts, and then once the system began to work, we were rolling in money. But they have a call on it. They take their share of the profits."

"You mean they own you?"

"They call it partnership. And it's so much money now that I don't really care. I mean, it's north of ten billion dollars, heading for twenty billion. Even if they take three quarters of it, I'm still absurdly rich."

"Read the fine print, Tom. These people are killers. That's what they do. Whereas you're a nice person, so far as I can tell. I don't want you to get caught."

Perkins took off his glasses and rubbed his eyes. He didn't look quite so young now.

"I *am* caught, Sophie. That's the point. We have an expression in economics, *ceteris paribus*. It means 'all other things being held constant.' It allows you to make assumptions and build models. But in this case, all other things aren't constant. What's been done can't be undone. I don't like what's happening. It scares me that Howard Egan got killed. If people found out he was a spy, they can find out other things about my business. And then the whole thing will come down."

Marx took his hand and gave it a squeeze. She wanted to say something encouraging, even if she didn't fully believe it.

"I don't know anything about economics. But when I was a girl, my dad liked to tell me, 'The only way you can be free is by working for yourself.' In his case, that basically meant doing nothing, but he was right. You've got to find a way to get free of this. Maybe I can help you."

"Smart man, your dad; smart daughter, too. I'm trying. I'm looking for ways to dig out. Maybe we could share a shovel."

As they neared the Dorchester, Perkins asked, once more, if she wanted to come back with him to Ennismore Gardens for a nightcap. She answered once again that it was a nice idea, really nice, but no, she would not.

24

MALAKAND, PAKISTAN

The people of the Tribal Areas have a fondness for proverbs, and there is one that sounds like this in the Pashto language: *"Khar cha har chaire hum law she, bia hum hagha khar we."* The literal meaning is that a donkey will remain a donkey, no matter where it goes. Or, to put it more elegantly: Nature cannot be changed.

When Lieutenant General Mohammed Malik first heard this saying from one of his Pashtun case officers, he knew that it expressed a truth about the people of the frontier region: They were what they were; they could be pushed and prodded, but not changed. Money, flattery, pressure, guns—these might convince the donkey to move a little to the left or right, but they did not change its character. The people lived by their Pashtunwali, their tribal code. Its pillars were personal honor, the obligation to avenge an insult, and the chivalry that allowed the stronger man to be generous toward the weaker one.

General Malik recalled these tenets as he traveled toward Peshawar on his way into the Pashtun heartland. He had received a call the day before from one of his ISI officers in the field. A member of the Al-Tawhid brotherhood had been captured in Bajaur Agency in the far northwest. He was carrying an unusual piece of information that the local case officer did not understand. The man seemed ready to talk, but he was not yet talking. The ISI case officer did not want to pass the information up the chain of command. He wanted General Malik himself to come to Malakand Fort, to interview the Tawhid courier and see his documents.

General Malik set off at dawn in his Land Cruiser. He traveled in a small convoy this time, one vehicle ahead and one behind, with bodyguards armed against an ambush. He planned a stop in Peshawar on the way, to meet with the major general who headed the Frontier Corps, the constabulary force that was supposed to keep the peace in the Tribal Areas and sometimes did.

As the Grand Trunk Road neared the outskirts of Peshawar, a great reddish mound became visible. From a distance it looked like a small hill with a garrison arrayed across the flat-top summit. This was the Bala Hisar fort, which since the sixteenth century had controlled the entry to the Khyber Pass, thirty miles to the west, and thus the gateway between Afghanistan and the great Indus Valley that contained the modern nations of Pakistan and India.

The general's convoy was waved through a checkpoint and took the steep road up this man-made hillock. In the courtyard atop the fort, a company of Frontier Corps guards mustered for his welcome. They wore the tunics and daggers of the British Raj, and their units were still called by the same names: the Khyber Rifles, the South Waziristan Scouts, the Bajaur Scouts and a half dozen others.

The corps commander greeted him. He was a big man, well over six feet, with a large belly and a growth of stubble on his face. He was a Pashtun himself, the descendant of the princely family that had ruled the ancient trading city of Bannu, a stopping point between Peshawar and Quetta. He knew how to run the frontier in the old-fashioned way, but he was not a man suited for the ISI's intelligence game. If he encountered an adversary, his instinct was to shoot him, rather than recruit him.

General Malik pumped for information about Al-Tawhid. Was the group still growing in Bajaur and the Waziristans? Was the Tawhid content to attack the Americans and their Afghan allies across the border, or was it threatening Pakistan? The general would never have admitted it to the outside world, but the ISI was prepared to tolerate the Tawhid so long as it didn't directly challenge the government. A double game was manageable, but not a triple game.

The Frontier Corps commander answered as best he could: Al-Tawhid lived village to village, operation to operation. It had not attacked the Frontier Corps yesterday, or for six months of yesterdays, but it could do so easily tomorrow. Its operatives were here on the frontier, but they were in the settled areas, too: in Karachi and Lahore and Quetta, and in Islamabad itself. General Malik nodded his agreement; he knew the reach of this "brotherhood" too well.

"These Tawhid are cocky buggers," said the corps commander. "To rule the frontier, you need a big wallet and a big gun. These miscreants have neither, and they have been punished by the drones. But still they think they can take on America. I do not see it. Under their turbans, they are just men. They pretend to know, but what can they know? They are little men with big Korans."

The corps commander, with his protruding gut and his rough speech, had unwittingly stated the problem that concerned General Malik. What did the Tawhid know? Where did these "little men" get the information that allowed them to poke the giant? The ISI had picked up the chatter, about a learned professor and his secretive ways. But the analysts didn't understand what it meant, and that troubled the general. There were so many professors on the ISI payroll already; was this master miscreant one of them?

The ISI chief continued in his convoy toward Malakand. They traveled north through the dusty plain of Mardan, lined with roadside stalls and small shops. The general smiled every time he saw a billboard depicting a Kalashnikov rifle. It was the insignia of a laundry powder bearing the same name. Only the Pashtuns would make an assault rifle the symbol of cleanliness.

As they pressed on, in the lee of Mohmand Agency to the west, the road began to rise toward the mountains. The gaily decorated trucks, laden with their cargos, slowed nearly to a crawl and the general's convoy weaved back and forth on the two-lane road, narrowly missing cars in the descending lane. As the switchbacks grew steeper, the traffic sometimes halted altogether, while the general's driver beeped indignantly on his horn and muttered Punjabi curses.

They eventually reached Malakand Pass, and just beyond it they came to the old fort that guarded this portal through the mountains. It was a tidy garrison, little changed in the sixty-five years since the British had left. The convoy drove past a company of infantry soldiers mounting their vehicles for patrol and continued on to a small brick house at the edge of the compound. A man in civilian clothes was waiting. This was Major Tariq, the local ISI officer who had summoned General Malik.

The major led his boss over a hill and down a path lined with blue pines and cedars. On this downward slope, the view opened to a magnificent valley in the distance: the Panjkora River rushing south through Dir District to meet the Swat River. It might have been an alpine vista in summer: the peaks framing the lush ground; the riverbanks lined with graceful alder and willow trees; the farms rich and green.

The major continued down the hill till he reached a pair of red-brick buildings. This was the local ISI station and, next to it, the combination guesthouse/stockade, depending on whom it contained. Today it was a stockade, and inside it was the man General Malik had come to see.

"Haj Ali" was the name the prisoner had given to Major Tariq. He had been captured in Bajaur two days before, trying to make his way across the frontier into Afghanistan. When he had searched the man, Major Tariq had found a flash drive, a portable data-storage device that could be plugged into the USB port of any computer. The major had installed the device on his laptop and examined the information. He hadn't understood what it meant, other than that it looked important, so he had summoned the chief of his service.

General Malik entered the building that served as the local ISI station. On the wall he saw his own picture, neatly framed, along with portraits of his recent predecessors. Directors came and went, but the ISI was a permanent fixture in these parts; visitors to the major's office might have been recruited by different ISI regimes, but the message was that they were all knitted into the same web.

Major Tariq unlocked the secure area at the rear of the room, where he kept his sensitive materials, and bade the general enter.

General Malik took a seat before the computer. The flash drive was already installed, and in a few moments the screen was alight. The drive contained just one brief document, an Excel spreadsheet that was designated "Registry."

The general clicked on this document and the screen displayed four entries each with a difficult string of letters and numbers. There were no markings at the top to identify what each column represented, and they presented a confusing array.

The four entries were divided into two pairs and read as follows:

1) BANK JULIUS BAER BKJULIUS CH12 0869-6005-2654-1601-2 BAERCHZU 200 71835

BANK ALFALAH ALFHAFKA 720 34120

2) BARCLAYS BANK BARCLON GB35 BARC-4026-3433-1557-68 BARCGBZZ 317 82993

AMONATBONK ASSETJ22 297 45190

General Malik studied the short document, making a few notes to himself on a pad. At length, a puzzled general turned to his subordinate.

"What is this *hallahgullah,* Major?" he asked, using a local slang word that means confusion. "Is this what you brought me all the way to see? This is just numbers and letters. It is a banking directory."

"Yes, sir." The major bowed his head submissively. "But it means something, I am quite sure."

"Everything means something, *babu.* But what? Have you questioned the man who was carrying it?"

"Only a little, sir. I was waiting for you."

General Malik printed a copy of the document. Then he logged off the computer and removed the flash drive to take back with him to Islamabad. He asked the young case officer to stay behind while he walked to the other building in the compound, where the courier was confined.

The ISI chief stooped to enter the low-ceilinged room. It had the musty animal smell of a century of prisoners. The general swung open the shutters, and a bright shaft of light illuminated the form of Haj Ali. He was a young man, handsome even in the suffering of his confinement. He had an unmistakable Pashtun face: prominent nose, hard cheeks, thick black hair and beard and sharp, hooded eyes. He was shackled, his hands and legs bent tight against the frame of a wooden chair.

General Malik took a chair next to the window, so that the prisoner had to squint into the sunlight to see his visitor. For a long while, perhaps five minutes, the general didn't speak. The captive courier strained against his shackles, making the muscles of his neck, face and arms taut with his resistance.

The general's first word was a call to the major to come and unlock the metal cuffs. When the prisoner's hands and feet were free, he stood for a moment, arched his back and then sat again in his chair with dignity. Major Tariq asked the general if he wanted a guard for protection, and the general said no, that he wanted to be left alone with the man.

The silence resumed, and as it continued, five minutes, ten minutes, it was the Pashtun man who became restless. He looked away, he cracked his knuckles, he coughed, he scratched his head. He was the one finally to speak.

"Nikka," the prisoner began, using the Pashto word for grandfather. He quoted a famous warrior proverb, which the general had heard from other tough mountain fighters: "When I die, let it be in the way of a brave man, so that that everyone feels grief, not like a scorpion or a snake whose death brings to all relief."

General Malik did not answer. The silence returned so that it filled the low room. At last he addressed the prisoner. He spoke in a low voice, not of menace, but authority.

"Who are you, brother?" asked the general. "What are you doing here?"

"I am Badal. That is my name. I am vengeance. What am I doing? Until I was caught, I was traveling to Afghanistan to take revenge on my enemies, the American spies."

"Achaah," said the general. It was an Urdu word that could mean assent or skepticism. "And how were you going to do this, Mr. Vengeance?"

"We know them, Nikka. We understand their secrets. We know

where they go and who they meet. We will use this information to kill them, one by one."

"I do not like these Americans, either. But I am smarter than you, brother. I do not announce it. I think you must be weak, to talk so defiantly but to have only your little arms and legs to carry you. I will get farther, I promise you. And do not call me *nikka*. I am not your grandfather."

The young man shook his head.

"That is a lie, Nikka. You do not fight the Americans. You are their friend."

The general ignored the taunt. He let the silence build again, and spoke after another minute had passed.

"I feel sorry for you, brother. You are a foolish young man. Those who know do not speak. Ask your superiors in the Tawhid. They will tell you. I think I am finished with you. You have not earned my respect."

The courier studied the general. This was not what he had anticipated. Every fighter expects to be beaten if he is captured, and he tries to prepare for torture. To be treated as a dangerous man is a mark of honor. But the fighter's dignity had been challenged by the general's scorn. He puffed his chest and thrust his chin up like a fighting cock.

"We *know* their secrets," the courier repeated. "We will take them down, just as we did their agents in Karachi and Moscow. We see everyone and everything."

"So that was your operation, then, in Moscow?" asked the general, inclining his head forward in a bow of respect.

"Of course, and there will be more to come, thanks God. Wait and you will see. It is not a lie. We know everything."

General Malik sat back. He studied the prisoner and then shook his head.

"No, I do not believe it. If you were as important as you say, you would be carrying documents across the frontier. But we have looked at that little thing, that little chicken prick that you were carrying in your pocket. We have studied it, brother, and we know that it is just a few numbers and banks. If that is your big secret, then you are *kutti da putr*, as we say in the Punjab, the son of a dog."

Now the courier was truly upset. He had been insulted, and he reacted in the way the general knew he would.

"You are wrong, Nikka. The proof of my words will come soon when more American agents are dead. Why do you think I was carrying the computer stick? Because I am taking the knowledge that it contains to my brothers in Afghanistan, and they will take it north, to Dushanbe. If I am caught, what of it? There are others on the road, and not just to Kabul. They travel to Cairo and even London and Paris. Soon the whole earth will be aflame and the American spies will not be able to walk upon it, anywhere."

"The document has the names of banks in Afghanistan and Tajikistan. Are the banks part of your plan for vengeance?"

"Ah, sir, that I do not know. I am a fighter, not a clerk. I do not study this computer stick, so I do not know what is on it. You are unlucky, sir. You have captured me for nothing."

The general fell silent again, and not just for effect. He was thinking carefully about what the courier had said and trying to fit it with other things that he knew. After another long minute, during which the young man became restless again, the general posed a new question.

"Tell me about the man you call the professor. Do you know him?"

"No, Nikka, I do not know this man."

"But you have heard of him. Do not lie, because I will find out and it will be worse for you later."

The young man shrugged. "Of course I have heard his name. He is our sword, the professor. He is the one who knows. But I have never met him. Nobody meets him. He is the ghost. And now I am happy that you are asking, because it means you do not know who he is."

"Do you think your computer stick comes from him?"

"Perhaps. Why not? I do not know. But it has the secrets, so maybe it comes from the professor. But I will never know. Nor will you, old general."

"Are you lying to me, Haj Ali?"

"I am a fighter. I am Badal. I am taking vengeance for the death of my brother and my uncle and restoring the honor of my family. Why would I lie? You can beat me for a week and a month and a year, but you will learn nothing more than what I have told you."

They did try to beat it out of him, of course. But, true to his word, he did not give up any more of the secret. General Malik observed the first interrogation session, back in Aabpara where they brought the prisoner, hooded for questioning. The general did not watch after that. He didn't like torture, but more than that, he knew that in this case it would do no good. The man was just a courier. He didn't understand the secrets of the letters and numbers himself. He only knew that they were deadly to the United States. They couldn't let the courier go, after all that had happened. He died on his way to a prison in Lahore.

General Malik wondered whether he should share with the Americans what he had learned. He decided against it. It was not his job to protect intelligence agents of the United States, especially ones who were acting illegally inside his country. A simpler man would have set the Tawhid loose so they could bloody a few more *faranghi* spies, and gone off to the mosque to say his prayers. But General Malik was cursed with a Western trait: He brooded about his mistakes; he felt guilty about what he had left undone.

What did he really know? He had a four-item spreadsheet of numbers and letters. He would ask his analysts to explore what this intelligence meant, and then he would consider what to do with it. But it was not his problem. He would say to the Americans, much as they had said to him, *lund te char.* Hop on my dick.

25
DUSHANBE, TAJIKISTAN

Everyone loved Meredith Rockwell. She was Istanbul's answer to the Junior League. She was a pretty girl, with flowing blond hair, so flamboyant and social that nobody wondered when she went jetting off to Dubai or Casablanca for the weekend. She had quickly become a fixture in the American community in Istanbul, organizing lunches and dinners, séances with local artists and boat trips up the Bosporus. She was a widow, she told everyone, children going to boarding schools back home; a big trust fund from her late husband to help her travel and entertain. Colorful stories about her had spread in the year she had taken residence in her fancy apartment in Beşiktaş. She was having an affair with a French count; no, it was a Saudi prince, or, in a third version, a Russian oligarch. All the while, she kept partying with her friends and traveling to exotic places, coyly refusing to explain where and why.

She was found dead on a street in Dushanbe, the capital of Tajikistan, where she had gone for one of her famous trips. She had taken a suite at the new Dushanbe Hyatt Regency, the fanciest hotel in Central Asia. The staff recognized her; she had been there before. Her luggage was still in the room, two Louis Vuitton bags, one of them still unpacked. The local authorities let the embassy tidy things up.

The police report said she had gone to find a bank on Rudaki Avenue and then taken a walk in the city park near the hotel. She had met a man there; she seemed to know him, witnesses said. She brought him back to the hotel and up to her room, and then he left. The hotel staff members were not scandalized. They expected that sort of behavior from Western women. The man was Tajik, witnesses said, or perhaps Uzbek or Pakistani. Nobody got a very good description. The doormen and porters looked away politely when the couple arrived.

Next she had taken a taxi, north along the Varzob River and then right on Somoni Avenue. She got out near the presidential palace but walked the other way, away from the crowded boulevards and the traffic and down a quiet street. It was a Russified neighborhood, still bearing the remnants of Soviet days: wood frame buildings painted salmon pink; signage of twinkling lights that formed Cyrillic script; high-cheeked Tajiks strolling in their summer T-shirts and jeans. Through this cityscape passed the American woman. She seemed to be going somewhere, from her deliberate pace, but there was no evidence that she had planned a meeting.

The assassination was a professional job. A car with darkened windows pulled alongside Rockwell as she was making her way down a lane a half mile from the city center. The assassin opened the door and fired two shots with a silencer. People didn't realize they were gunshots at first; nobody would have paid attention at all, if she hadn't screamed so loudly in English as she fell. The police tried to talk to her in the ambulance on the way to the hospital, but she wouldn't answer their questions. They thought she was in shock. She died in the emergency room as a Tajik doctor tried to stop the bleeding.

Jeffrey Gertz was awake when the call came in the early morning. He flinched when the watch officer gave him the news. He'd had an affair with Meredith Rockwell. She was a party girl in true name, as well as alias. He went back to the office, driving way too fast through the canyon, not caring about anyone or anything except keeping a lid on his little organization.

Steve Rossetti was already at the office when he arrived. The operations chief lived in Encino, a few minutes closer. He looked relieved to see the boss. He didn't want this to be his problem.

Gertz took him by the shoulders and looked him in the eye.

"We are at war, and we don't even know who with. We are not going to give this enemy any more targets. That's order number one. I want everybody to get in a hole and pucker up until we understand what's coming at us."

Gertz told Rossetti to work out the details and report back in an hour. That wasn't much time to organize the message traffic and the operational changes, but Rossetti got it done. He was efficient, when he was told what to do.

They went to ground, no halfway measures this time. Gertz issued an immediate stand-down order to everyone, every officer in every clandestine platform around the world. Nobody was to move; no operational travel; no agent meetings; no movement at all outside home unless absolutely necessary. People were allowed to come home, but that was it.

Gertz called his sources abroad, to see what they knew. He got much commiseration, but no facts. This network of consultants and friends, which he had assembled over the years, was his privy cabinet. They provided the tips and suggestions that shaped Gertz's operations. He had one special informant in the shooting gallery of South Asia who usually knew something, but this time he was dry as dust. Whoever it was had left no tracks, the informant said.

Rossetti ventured that maybe the media would miss the story in faraway Dushanbe, but Gertz knew that was impossible. This was the kind of news that was made for cable television and gossip magazines: American socialite gunned down without explanation in one of the armpits of the world, leaving her millionaire wardrobe back at the presidential suite.

The media lit up in a way they hadn't with the two previous deaths. Meredith's friends from Istanbul were on camera within that first news cycle, talking about her charity balls and society dinners and shadowy love life. It was irresistible. Who was the blond mystery woman? What on earth had taken her to Dushanbe? Why had she been murdered there so brutally, in a manner that could not be blamed on purse snatchers?

Gertz had his people call reporters with tips that Meredith Rockwell had been leading a double life—that she was a coke-head who had gotten involved with international drug cartels. Several news organizations assigned reporters to cover that angle the first day. It was an axiom of journalism that you could not libel the dead.

The few people in the U.S. government who knew the truth were frightened. Cyril Hoffman called; the White House chief of staff called. They wanted to know what the government should say. Gertz gave them all the same answer as always: Don't say anything. Don't acknowledge or even hint at any U.S. government connection. This was a senseless attack on an American citizen. It had no connection with any other event. The victim obviously had a complicated personal life. Shit happens.

The cover story, threadbare as it was, might well have held up in the same way it had for the previous two deaths. But people had other ideas this time. They wanted credit.

Late in the afternoon on which Meredith Rockwell was murdered, a telephone call was received at the Associated Press bureau in Islamabad. The caller was known to the bureau chief as a member of the Islamic underground. He said that a statement would be posted in one minute on a jihadist website, sent by the Muslim group that called itself Al-Tawhid. He said that the statement was legitimate, and that the Associated Press should disseminate it immediately.

The message appeared moments later on the Internet, as the caller said it would. It was in English, and it read as follows:

> *In the name of the Prophet Mohammed, peace and blessings be upon him:*
>
> *Today, the Brotherhood of Al-Tawhid, which celebrates the oneness of God, announces that it has executed an agent of the American CIA in Dushanbe, Tajikistan. This agent was delivering a bribe to a leader of the Islamic Movement of Tajikistan, to bring him into the camp of capitulation and shame, but this plot failed. For this crime, the agent received justice.*
>
> *The Brotherhood also announces today that it was responsible for two previous operations against American agents. The agent Howard Egan was seized in Karachi, Pakistan, where he*

was seeking to bribe a tribal leader. The agent Alan Frankel was seized in Moscow, where he was seeking to bribe a Pakistani diplomat. For these crimes, they were executed. The Brotherhood delayed its campaign in the hope that these actions against Pakistan would stop, but they have continued.

We make this declaration of war. There are other secret American agents and they will be killed, one by one, until the United States withdraws from Pakistan and all Muslim lands. We will choose the time and place of our attacks. The American people should ask: Who are these agents who bribe and kill Muslim people far from home? Why do they seek to destroy Pakistan and other free and democratic Muslim nations?

We affirm the oneness of God. God is Great.

—Ikwan Al-Tawhid

Despite frantic requests from the news media, the White House waited two hours before authorizing a response. So few people knew the details of the case that it was difficult to assemble the proper team for discussions. In the end, a secure videoconference was held that included just four people: the president, his chief of staff, the associate deputy director of the CIA, and a CIA officer in Los Angeles who was called "John Doe," even in this confidential meeting. After this session ended, the chief of staff instructed the State Department spokesman to issue this statement:

The allegation by the group that calls itself Ikwan Al-Tawhid is an absurd and baseless attempt to claim credit for the tragic deaths of three Americans abroad in recent weeks. Contrary to the claims of Al-Tawhid, the three individuals were not employees or agents of the United States government. Detailed public information confirms that one was a businessman in the financial sector, one was an advertising salesman, and one was involved in international philanthropic work.

The statement by Al-Tawhid is a cynical attempt by a previously unknown group to use these deaths to gain publicity. The United States condemns this action. The Federal Bureau of Inves-

tigation and other agencies are working with the governments of Pakistan, Russia and Tajikistan to identify the real killers of these three Americans and bring them to justice.

The State Department spokesman repeated this line when asked about the Al-Tawhid statement at the press briefing later that day. He told reporters in the off-the-record "gaggle" that followed the formal briefing that the FBI was pursuing evidence that the death of Meredith Rockwell may have been drug-related. It was possible, the spokesman said, that the other two deaths also had involved international criminal gangs, and that the "absurd" Al-Tawhid statement might have been an attempt by the mafia network to conceal its role.

The CIA public affairs chief, meanwhile, contacted the reporters who regularly covered the intelligence beat. He assured them in the strongest terms, speaking as a "U.S. official," that the three people who had been killed had no connection whatsoever with the CIA. Weirdly, such denials had more credibility when they were not for attribution, and in this case it could be argued that the spokesman was telling the truth. Certainly it was true as far as he knew. The head of the National Clandestine Service personally called the reporters from *The New York Times* and *The Washington Post* and told them that the three dead Americans were not on the agency payroll. He could vouch for it personally.

The denials made it through the first news cycle intact, and the story held up over the next few days. There were some breathless exposé stories in the Pakistani press, but they were always making wild claims about American intelligence activities, so nobody paid much attention. The ISI press cell in Islamabad was unusually silent, and the reporters there assumed that was because the ISI itself must have links with Al-Tawhid. That was true enough, though even the ISI knew less than it would have liked. The reason for silence was more complicated. The director general of the service, Lieutenant General Mohammed Malik, was trying to decide what to do.

Jeff Gertz responded in character: He toughed it out. He maintained his composure and confidence, and looked for ways to project it to others. He held a "town hall meeting" with his staff in Studio City late that first day and reassured them that their security was his primary concern. He arranged protection details and armored vehicles; he provided counseling to help employees deal with stress; he hosed The Hit Parade and its global staff with money and perks.

Gertz called Sophie Marx in London and told her that she was running out of time. Unless she came up with something in a few days to explain to the White House why America's most secret warriors were being killed, he would bring her home and send someone else. He needed the frame of a story, quickly; they could fill in the details later, when they had more time.

26

DOHA, QATAR

Cyril Hoffman did not make the mistake of believing propaganda, least of all when it came from his own government. After the videoconference about Al-Tawhid with Gertz, the president and his chief of staff, the State Department had issued its statement, which Hoffman knew to be a bald lie. The claims by Al-Tawhid were essentially correct: The United States was running a covert-action campaign against Pakistan aimed at bribing key leaders and perhaps, over time, halting actions against America and gaining control of that country's nuclear weapons.

It wasn't that Hoffman thought these were bad ideas, necessarily, but he didn't like the fact that the project had been assigned to a jury-rigged start-up agency behind the CIA's back. It worried Hoffman, too, that Al-Tawhid had somehow penetrated the supposedly perfect security of The Hit Parade and was killing its operatives. That had to be stopped, but the magnificent Gertz seemed unable to find the leak.

Hoffman had been keeping tabs on Gertz for years, and more so since he had set up shop in Los Angeles for The Hit Parade. But despite Hoffman's efforts to contain the experiment, it had morphed and grown to the point that it posed a risk to the U.S. government as a whole, including the CIA, which Hoffman was sworn to protect. American agents were getting killed; jihadist groups were issuing statements; the spill was widening.

One of Hoffman's vanities was the idea that, when the Gertzes of the world had made a mess, people like him would have to clean it up. He had a favorite poem by Rudyard Kipling, which had been given to him years ago by his Uncle Frank, another cleaner-upper of other people's disasters. It was called "The Gods of the Copybook Headings," and Hoffman kept it in his desk drawer, to reread whenever he encountered something particularly stupid. He turned to the poem now and reminded himself of the power of these gods to outlast the ambitious do-gooders:

As it will be in the future, it was at the birth of Man—
There are only four things certain since Social Progress began:
That the Dog returns to his Vomit and the Sow returns to her Mire,
And the burnt Fool's bandaged finger goes wabbling back to the Fire;

And that after this is accomplished, and the brave new world begins
When all men are paid for existing and no man must pay for his sins,
As surely as Water will wet us, as surely as Fire will burn,
The Gods of the Copybook Headings with terror and slaughter return!

How to stop the terror and slaughter? That was becoming Hoffman's responsibility now, too. If Gertz could not stanch the flow, then Hoffman would have to help. He thought back over his conversations with Lieutenant General Mohammed Malik. The ISI director had been trying to tell him something when he had visited Islamabad. But Hoffman had been so intent on delivering his own message that he hadn't listened as carefully as he might have.

The Pakistani general had protested about the operation in Karachi. Well, fair enough, of course he would. Countries never liked it when other countries conducted unilateral intelligence operations on their territory. But there had been something else that the general had wanted Hoffman to understand. There was a leak of information; the kidnapping of Howard Egan wasn't an accidental bit of good luck for the "bad guys," but something more fundamental.

Hoffman had done the obvious things after he returned from Islamabad. He had talked with the top Pakistan analyst at Langley, and contacted his own most sensitive private sources, but he had come away with nothing. He wondered now why had he not listened more carefully to what the Pakistani general was trying to tell him.

It is never too late to apply good sense as a corrective to stupidity. The call to arms, as it were, came to Hoffman late on the night after Meredith Rockwell's death. It was early morning in Islamabad, the time when Mohammed Malik would be having his morning tea in the office, and reading his cables, and planning what to do next. So often, Hoffman's prescription was: When in doubt, do nothing. But he had a different instinct now, and he knew there wasn't any more time to waste.

Hoffman picked up the phone and called Malik's private number at ISI headquarters. The general himself answered, on the first ring, with a starchy hello.

"This is your friend Cyril Hoffman," he began. "I think we need to talk. What do you say to that?"

"Talk or shoot, it must be one of the two. Your boys have been very naughty, Cyril. The Tawhid statement has set the cat among the pigeons. We are angry, I must tell you that, sir."

"Let's try talking. And they're not my boys, or girls, either. That's part of what I want to talk about. It will be worth your time, Mohammed, I promise you. And just for the record, it's your boys who have been doing the shooting, not mine."

"Where do you suggest that we have this talk, Cyril? The telephone would not be a good idea, for either of us. And I regret to say that I am not able to welcome you here in Islamabad at present. The mood is a bit sour, as you can imagine."

"Let's meet tomorrow in the Gulf, neutral territory. I'll fly over to wherever you like. Just name it."

"Not Dubai. Your service owns Dubai. I would suggest Doha, if I were prepared to say yes."

"Come on, old boy. Don't play games. We need to do this. People are getting killed, and it's going to get worse unless sensible people get involved. This situation is dangerous, my esteemed brother."

"I am glad that I am still included in your club of 'sensible people,' Cyril. And I am amused that you choose to call me 'brother' at such a time. It is either a sign that you are sincere, or that you are an unprincipled rascal."

"You know very well that I'm a rascal. That's why we get along. Now, say yes. Meet me in Doha tomorrow night. I'll be staying at the Four Seasons. We'll have dinner, my treat. Do we have a date? Come on, now, don't make me beg."

The phone was silent for several moments, as General Malik considered the situation, both the aspects that Cyril Hoffman understood and those that he didn't.

"Yes," said the Pakistani. "I will meet you tomorrow night in Doha. Please come alone. I will do the same. This is not a meeting that I am prepared to acknowledge in any way."

"Don't you worry. Uncle Cyril is going to use a clean plane, with virgin tail numbers. And I would be most grateful, dear friend, since we are talking about discretion here, if you didn't share my itinerary with the gentlemen in Al-Tawhid, should you chance to encounter any of them. I'm not saying that to pick a fight, just being honest."

General Malik was going to protest, but with three American intelligence officers dead, it was not an unreasonable request.

Hoffman made a second call that evening, to Jeff Gertz. He asked for a summary of the investigation that Gertz's shop was conducting into the leak of information that had led to the attacks on Howard Egan and the others. Hoffman recalled that the probe was being conducted by that nice young woman, Gertz's chief of counterintelligence, the one who'd been stationed in Beirut, with the peculiar family. How was she getting along?

"Sophie Marx is the officer's name," answered Gertz. His voice was clipped. He didn't want to be answering questions from Headquarters now.

"And where is Miss Marx, pray tell?"

"She's in London, investigating the hedge fund where Egan worked. She's headstrong, and she hasn't found the magic bullet yet. If she doesn't figure it out soon, I'll get someone else who will."

"A bit hard to manage, is she? Knocking on too many doors?"

"Yes," answered Gertz. "Something like that. Plus, she isn't getting me any answers. Just more questions. She keeps asking about the big picture. This is a detective job."

"I take it you mean Pakistan, when you speak of the big picture."

"I mean the big picture. Things she isn't cleared for, but wants to know anyway. We need to get to closure here. People are getting killed and we don't know why. I need to put more people on it, maybe next week. Right now, nobody is moving."

"How do I reach this difficult woman? I might like a progress report of my own."

"Sorry, Cyril. You can't. She works for me. I'm not ready to declare open season yet. We'll call you when we have something, and you can talk to her all you want then. But not now."

Hoffman rang off a few minutes later, cheery as always. The moment he ended the call, he initiated another one to Steve Rossetti, who gave Hoffman a cell phone number for Sophie Marx and her secure email address.

Hoffman thought about calling her, but it was the middle of the night in London, and he didn't need to speak with her now. He had already ascertained the only thing that mattered to him, which was that Marx was independent and restless enough to make Jeff Gertz nervous. He didn't know if she was trustworthy, but you never really knew that about anyone until you took the risk and found out.

The two intelligence barons arrived in Doha the following afternoon in their unmarked private jets and went to the Four Seasons on the Corniche in West Bay. The hotel was an example of the instant luxury that had enveloped the tiny, absurdly rich nation of Qatar. It was a modern high-rise, sprinkled with bits of Islamic kitsch to reassure the locals: mirrored domes atop the two hotel towers, and an ersatz desert fort out front to house the parking attendants.

In the heat of high summer, a vaporous shimmer rose from the waters of the Gulf. The palms that ringed the hotel were drooping, despite the perpetual irrigation. The hotel lobby had the grand, empty look of a showroom: Any Qatari with sufficient money had fled the summer heat of the Gulf for the mountains of Lebanon or the Côte d'Azur.

Cyril Hoffman took the cheapest room they had. He didn't have the director's approval for the trip, and he didn't intend to tell him about it. He had commandeered the plane on his own authority, but he might have to eat the hotel bill.

Hoffman sat in his room waiting for dinner, watching Arab girls in bikinis play in the pools below before returning home in their formless black cloaks and veils. What an odd part of the world this was: Hoffman reminded himself to be tolerant that night if the Pakistani general said something that he knew to be a lie; it was a matter of cultural dissonance.

They met in the private dining room of an Italian restaurant called La Fortuna, on the ground floor. Hoffman went down early and gave the waiter a hundred dollars and a credit card in the alias in which he had registered at the hotel. He told the waiter not to enter the private room unless he was summoned.

General Malik arrived at eight o'clock on the dot, dressed in a blue blazer, white shirt and a red-and-black, regimental-striped tie. He looked like a military officer even when he was in mufti. Hoffman was already there, luxuriating in a summer suit of white linen, with baggy trousers and a blousy double-breasted jacket. In place of a tie, he was wearing a paisley ascot. He looked like an art-history professor at Sarah Lawrence College.

Hoffman had ordered a fancy bottle of wine and an array of appetizers. They were on the table when General Malik entered the room. Hoffman told the waiter to go away and leave them alone. He poured his Pakistani friend a glass of the Brunello.

"Ain't life grand?" said Hoffman, clicking his glass against that of his guest.

"No," said Malik. "It isn't grand at all. It is rather a mess. Chin chin."

"No small talk, then? No foreplay? No 'how's the family?'"

"I think not. I am flying back to Rawalpindi tonight." Malik looked at his watch. "In three hours, to be precise."

Hoffman took a long sip of his wine and put down the glass.

"Let me get to the point, then. I came out here to tell you one big thing. I could get arrested for what I am going to tell you, put in jail for passing secrets to the enemy. So I want you to listen carefully. Will you do that?"

"Of course, Cyril. Why do you think I have come, if not to listen, and perhaps also to talk?"

"The operations that you and your Al-Tawhid friends have uncovered are not run by the CIA. They are being run by a new organization that has gone haywire. They are conducting a covert-action campaign against Pakistan without any legal authority, and it will fail. I say that because I am going to make it my personal business to take it down. This new organization has gotten the White House to play along, but that's just because they're inexperienced. I'm working on that, too."

Malik shook his head. "This is poppycock. I know your tricks, Cyril. This is another cover story."

"I thought you might say that, so I brought you a little something to establish my bona fides." He took several sheets of paper from the pocket of his white suit and handed the document across the table to the Pakistani.

"What is this?"

"It's a letter to the general counsel of the CIA from the White House counsel's office. It's dated two days ago. When you boil down all the legal verbiage, it says that the White House takes responsibility for all statements that will be made about the Al-Tawhid accusations. The agency will be 'held harmless,' as the lawyers say. It's not their baby."

"What does that prove? I am a military man, not a lawyer."

"It proves what I just said. This is not a CIA operation. There is no official agency campaign to do anything to Pakistan. There is a crazy-ass operation run by some drugstore cowboys who have figured out a way to finance their activities without going to Congress, and who temporarily have gotten some hotheads in the White House to go along. But like I said, they are going down. I guarantee it."

"Why are you telling me this, my dear? It is most unlike you to volunteer anything. I cannot ever recall a similar moment of generosity, with you or any of your famous cousins and uncles. What's the 'catch,' so to speak?"

"I need your help, pure and simple. We have a nasty little war on our hands. Three people have gotten killed. Any more, and people will start to panic. They will take action to protect themselves. That gets ugly, real fast."

"What can I do about it?" asked General Malik, with a shrug. "I am not a member of the Ikwan Al-Tawhid. I am not shooting any Americans. I am a victim, not a perpetrator."

Cyril Hoffman wagged his finger at the man across the table. "But you *know*. Of course you do. That's your job, and you're good at it. You know the people who are doing the killing, and I have a feeling that you even know how they are doing it. They are getting information that helps them track the movements of people in this new organization that I was talking about. We've been looking for the leak, and we haven't found it yet. But I'll bet that you have."

"You give us far too much credit, my friend. We are the ISI, not MI6 or the Mossad. And if you say that we are running the Tawhid, that is a lie, sir. A most despicable lie." He pounded the table.

General Malik was protesting more heatedly than was necessary, or wise. For in the silence that followed his retort, Cyril Hoffman was able to look into his eyes and, in the uncanny way that Hoffman had, to read from his expressions a narrative.

"You can't fool me, brother. I see that little smile under your mustache, Mohammed. I see that twinkle in your eye. You've got something. Yes, you do. And we need it. I will be frank with you, even though that's not my nature. This could get dangerous if we don't find a way to work together. I need you to help me out. Tell me what you know."

The Pakistani did not answer at first. He was never a man to rush.

"Let us eat something, shall we?" he said.

General Malik reached for the plate of beef carpaccio, and slowly ate one of the paper-thin slices of meat, savoring the taste while he contemplated the situation. He helped himself to some foie gras, too, putting a generous lump on a piece of toast and chewing it, bite by bite.

Hoffman buttered his bread. He tried not to let his impatience show.

The Pakistani finished his little snack and dabbed at his mouth with his napkin.

"You're right, of course. We do know a bit about the Tawhid, as you would expect. And you are also correct that we know something of how they are doing their targeting."

"That's my man. Come on, now. Tell me. You came here to say it. You know you did."

"It involves banks. We just obtained some computer material that we took off a Tawhid courier. But I will be honest, I do not understand it. I have been trying to find the computer genius who put it together, but frankly, I have failed. I have been nervous about the material. It could be misused. So I have been sitting on it. But perhaps I could have one of my analysts take another look."

Hoffman buttered his bread some more and then put it aside. He took a sip of the fine red wine. He was searching for different possibilities, but he kept coming back to the thought of Sophie Marx at the hedge fund in London. She was the one working this problem, and she was the most likely to crack the code that Malik had described.

"What if I sent someone to help you?" asked Hoffman. "She's one of our best counterintelligence officers, and she is the person on our end who has been trying to understand the leak of information about our man in Karachi, and now the others. She's smart, and she knows how to keep her mouth shut."

"What is the name of this wonder woman, please?"

"Sophie Marx."

General Malik took out his fountain pen and wrote her name in small, precise script in a black notebook he kept in the pocket of his blazer.

"You won't find a whole lot about her in your files, or anyone else's," said Hoffman. "But if you asked the right people, you would discover that this young woman ran a very professional operation in Beirut that opened up to us Hezbollah's communications network. She recruited a woman in one of the Lebanese telecommunications companies, and a man in the Ministry of Telecommunications. It was quite dangerous. We think very highly of her."

"What would be the understanding, in the event that I were to receive her?"

"She would help you analyze this targeting information. She would investigate it. And then she would use the information to protect our people from further attacks."

"She would uncover Al-Tawhid's network of informants, in other words."

"Well, sure, if that's what it is. She would help you take them down. Or we'd take them down ourselves, if that's easier."

The general helped himself to another tasty glob of foie gras. He had barely touched his wine, up until now, but he took a healthy drink.

"What is in it for us, Cyril? I am sorry to be crass. But this is a human business, after all. In exchange for giving you this very important piece of intelligence, what do I get in return?"

"Well, now, fair question, entirely legitimate. First, you avert an open break with the United States of America, which despite its puny political leadership is still the strongest country on earth and can make life very difficult for countries it doesn't like. Second, you have my promise that I will stop the covert action that has been undertaken against Pakistan. Stop it, cold. And if I don't, you are free to go public with whatever the hell you want, and take me down, along with a lot of other people."

"That's very nice, but not tangible, Cyril. There are people in Pakistan who would argue that I am betraying an ally, which is Al-Tawhid, to assist an enemy, which is the United States. As you know, I am a moderate man, and I find that sort of thinking abhorrent, but there we are."

"Look, my friend, if Al-Tawhid is in a position to kill our officers, they can kill China's and Russia's—and even your own ISI men. I don't know what this secret surveillance capability is, but if they can use it against us, they can use it against anybody. That's dangerous—but especially to you, brother, dear. So we will be doing you a big favor."

"I am warming to this idea. But I still do not see a benefit for us commensurate with what we are giving up."

"Hey, Mohammed, we're talking about the fate of the world, and you're haggling as if we're in the spice bazaar. But that's okay, because I love you. So let me say this about that: America would be very grateful for this help. I know that you would never ask me for any personal reward. But I would feel compelled to offer you one, in the quietest way possible. This rogue operation has been generating billions of dollars. And when we shut it down, some of it is going to fall off the truck. Do you follow me?"

General Malik smoothed the hairs of his mustache and patted his lips with his napkin, even though he had eaten little.

"I have no idea what you are talking about," he said.

Cyril Hoffman smiled. "Forgive me, even for mentioning it."

"Why don't you send this woman, Miss Marx, to me in Islamabad? Have her contact me on my personal phone when she arrives. We will see what is possible. More than that, I cannot promise."

They finished the appetizers and the wine. Hoffman was going to order the main course, but General Malik said that he needed to get back to his plane and go home. People would ask questions if he were late in returning. So Hoffman ordered a jolly dinner and instructed the waiter that it should be sent up to his room, where he ate it while watching Fashion TV.

27
LONDON

When Cyril Hoffman's Gulfstream jet landed at RAF Mildenhall for what was supposed to be a refueling stop, he went to the distinguished visitors' lounge and called Sophie Marx on her cell phone. It was morning in London, and she was at the office in Mayfair starting a day of investigation. The caller's number was unfamiliar to her and she didn't answer at first; the only person who called on this phone normally was Jeff Gertz. But when a second call came in immediately from the same number, she answered it.

Hoffman was groggy from travel, but he tried to sound cheery.

"You don't know me," he began, "but my name is Cyril Hoffman. I am the associate deputy director of your parent company, so to speak."

"I know who you are," Marx answered. "We all do. You're famous."

"Oh, good! Well, I am in Britain, passing through, and I thought perhaps you could meet me for breakfast or lunch, or whatever meal people are supposed to eat at this hour. I have been traveling, and I am a bit mixed up."

"Where are you, Mr. Hoffman?"

"Essex, or Sussex, or something like that. It's an air base. I can get a car and be in London in an hour. We need to meet somewhere, um, quiet, where nobody will have any idea who we are. I will book a room at the, let me see . . . Holiday Inn. I am looking on my infernal BlackBerry for the right one. 'Holiday Inn Express Limehouse.' That sounds dreadful, doesn't it? It's in the East End, in between you and me. I'll see you there in an hour. Ask for 'Fred Smith' and come up to my room. Don't worry, I'm quite harmless."

"I'll be there. I hope there isn't a problem."

"There most definitely is a problem. That's why I want to see you. But it's not your problem, if that's what you mean. Just come to the hotel, and don't tell anyone, please, including your mates out in Los Angeles, especially not them."

The desk clerk at the Holiday Inn gave Sophie Marx a dubious look when she requested the room number of Mr. Smith: He called on the house phone to make sure that the guest was expecting a visitor. When "Mr. Smith" confirmed that he was in, the desk clerk gave a sorry shake of his head, as if he pitied them both for the encounter that was about to ensue.

Hoffman was waiting in a small room on the eighth floor that overlooked a parking lot and, beyond it, the architectural foothills of the City of London. He was wearing a navy cashmere sweater that gave him the soft, round look of a blue marshmallow. His eyes were rimmed with the pouches of fatigue. His reading glasses were dangling from his neck on a braided lanyard.

Marx hadn't time to change into something fancy, so she was dressed informally, in the slacks and denim jacket she had worn to work. They made a most unlikely pair.

Hoffman shook her hand warmly, as if they were old friends, and thanked her for coming on such short notice. He motioned her toward a bright red couch on the other side of the bed, and settled his bulk into a matching red desk chair. He took out his cell phone and removed the battery. She did the same.

"You look familiar," he said, eying her. "Have we met?"

"You spoke at the graduation of my Career Trainee class. You wouldn't remember that. And then when I came home from Beirut, I was part of a group that briefed you on telecommunications tradecraft. You probably wouldn't remember that, either."

"I don't, but I remember your face, from somewhere or other. And I have read your file, so I feel as if I know you. You have a very good record, I must say. People like you. They have confidence in you. That includes your current supervisor, Mr. Gertz. He expects you to unravel the mystery of who has been killing his officers, although I think he is becoming a tad impatient. How is it coming along, then?"

Marx looked at him warily, uncertain of how to proceed. Hoffman wasn't her boss, and she wasn't authorized to talk with him about her work, even though he was a senior CIA official. But he was a celebrated figure, and he conveyed an authority that transcended the nominal rules. She decided to answer.

"My theories have all been wrong so far, sir, but I'm working on it. If Jeff is impatient, so am I."

"What does your intuition tell you? Be honest with me. I need to hear your ideas."

"I think this isn't a normal counterintelligence investigation, Mr. Hoffman. Usually we look for an inside source who has penetrated our operations—a rotten apple in the barrel. But that doesn't fit the facts: The people who have been killed were based in different locations. They didn't know each other. The only thing they had in common was that they were working on the same target. The only person who knew the details of what they were working on was Mr. Gertz, and he's not a suspect."

"So what does that leave as an option? Where's our leak?"

"I don't know yet. But if I had to guess, I would say that we have a technical problem. Someone is reading our mail. They are tracking our digital footprints. But that's hard to believe. These groups in Pakistan are smart, but they don't have the surveillance or intercept capabilities that a government does. At least we don't think they do. That's why it's a puzzle. Does that make any sense?"

Hoffman nodded vigorously. There was a smile on his face. He had wanted to make certain that Sophie Marx was the right person for the plan he had set in motion, and he was reassured.

"Just so," he said. "Someone is reading our mail, or, to be more precise, our financial records. That is how they are targeting us. They are inside the banking system in a way that allows them to see our people and where they are going. That's how they have been killing our officers."

Marx looked at him curiously.

"How do you know all this, Mr. Hoffman?"

Hoffman patted his stomach. He was smiling again.

"I have a source. And he's about to become your source, if you will agree to help me."

"What do I have to do? Just tell me."

"It's complicated. I need to ask you some questions. Are you hungry?"

She shook her head, but Hoffman called the front desk anyway and ordered two plates of french fries and two beers, both of which he appeared quite happy to consume himself. When he had placed his order, he turned back to Marx.

"Now, then, for starters, are you frightened? Personally, I mean. With three people from your organization dead, this is obviously risky business. Jeff Gertz says he has issued a no-travel order, with everybody grounded to their home base. But you're still here in London. Why is that? Aren't you worried?"

"Of course I'm worried. But I'm not about to go home. I don't scare easily. If you read my file, you know that I had an unusual upbringing. All the scary things have already happened to me."

"Are you willing to travel to places that would be more dangerous than London?"

"Sure, in principle. Where do you have in mind?"

Hoffman closed his eyes. He clasped his hands and put them under his chin. He looked like an overfed monk.

"Pakistan," he said. "I want you to see someone in Islamabad, if you're willing. You will have to meet him in person, and on his turf, I'm afraid. Otherwise we cannot obtain the information that he says he is prepared to offer."

"Who's the source in Islamabad, if you don't mind my asking?"

"His name is Malik. He is the director general of Inter-Services Intelligence."

"Well, fancy that. Good for you, Mr. Hoffman."

"Thank you," he said ceremoniously, with a small flourish of the hand that was meant to signify a bow. "But you understand what this means. My source is in contact with the people who have been killing your colleagues. That is the nub of our problem. He tells me that he is prepared to help us, and I believe him. But you are the person who will take the risk."

"That doesn't bother me. People in that part of the world are always playing a double game. It goes with the territory. I learned that in Beirut. So, sorry, if you're trying to frighten me off, it won't work."

"Good girl. Now I have another question for you, if you please. What do you think about Jeff Gertz?"

"That's not an easy question. He's my boss. I report to him. He gave me this job and a chance to exercise responsibility, so I'm grateful. He's never done anything to harm my career."

"Yes, yes. But that's not what I'm talking about. Do you trust him? That's what I want to know."

She tried to think what the right answer was, politically speaking, and concluded that there wasn't one. She just had to say the truth.

"He has powerful friends, Mr. Hoffman. That's what people say, anyway. So my answer may get me in trouble. But no, I don't trust Jeff fully. I don't understand his agenda. He has a tight hold on our organization, but I don't always understand what he's doing. Maybe I shouldn't say that, but it's what I think."

Hoffman had closed his eyes again while she was talking, so she couldn't read his reaction. He didn't say anything for a few seconds after she had finished her answer, but then he spoke up.

"You have it exactly, precisely right, as far as I am concerned. That's why I am going to ask you not to tell Gertz anything about your trip to Pakistan, or what you learn there. I want you to report back to me, and then we will figure out what to do."

"I'll get fired, Mr. Hoffman. Jeff won't tolerate disloyalty. I know that about him. He'll find out, because he always does, and then I'll be out the door. You're asking me to commit career suicide."

"I don't think so," said Hoffman slowly. "I am actually offering you a means of escape from professional ruin. But there's no way for you to be sure, is there? The reality here is that you will have to take my word. I cannot offer you any assurance that would be credible. In the end, it's like everything else in our business. It is about trust."

Marx looked out the window of this antiseptic hotel, toward the clustered buildings of the City of London. She had always hoped there would be a moment in her career like this, when someone would offer her the chance to do something really important. But now that it had arrived, it was so fragile, no more than a thread between two people who, until an hour before, had never talked.

"I trust you," she said. "Let's talk about the details."

They spent another hour within the four bland walls of the Holiday Inn Express. Hoffman ate his french fries, both plates, but Marx had one of the beers. He explained the procedures for contacting Lieutenant General Mohammed Malik through his personal email address and his private cell phone number. Hoffman said he would send the Pakistani general a message advising that she was coming.

With that transmission of information, he warned, the real danger would begin. For it was a certainty that General Malik had been in contact with the people who were killing Marx's colleagues, and he might do so again if he decided it was in his interest. And even if General Malik didn't breathe a word, the trackers from Al-Tawhid might be able to follow Marx anyway, through their own surveillance, just as they had the other operatives of The Hit Parade.

They talked, finally, about what Marx would say to Jeff Gertz about her absence. She proposed the cover story: She had uncovered something important for the investigation in the files of Alphabet Capital: Howard Egan had met with someone in Dubai on his way to his fatal visit to Karachi. She needed to debrief this person immediately, and there hadn't been time to check first with Gertz. She would apologize in an email that she would send from the airport, as she was about to board her plane.

"Will he believe that?" Hoffman asked.

"Probably not. But it will be too late for him to stop me by then. And you'll protect my back when I return, assuming that I return."

Marx meant that last line as a bravura joke, but neither of them laughed. This was a situation in which it was impossible to be sure that she was not walking into a trap.

That afternoon, when Marx returned to the Alphabet Capital office in Mayfair to make her travel arrangements through Perkins's secretary, she received a "book cable" message from The Hit Parade in Studio City that had been sent to all personnel abroad. It stated that an officer of The Hit Parade had been killed in Afghanistan that day while on his way to a covert meeting. That made four.

The cable repeated, more emphatically, the earlier directive that no officer of The Hit Parade should travel without explicit permission. There was a global lockdown. Every foreign officer should take immediate precautions to ensure personal security, varying their routes, procedures and communications practices. They should stop using all credit cards and cellular phones, including those issued to them in alias names.

Sophie Marx ignored the message. Mona, the secretary at Alphabet Capital, had booked the initial leg of Marx's flight to Islamabad via Dubai for that evening. She knew that if she didn't leave immediately, she might not be able to do so at all. She knocked on Perkins's door to say goodbye, but Mona said that he was out of the office, visiting his lawyer. She tried to write a note, but gave up after several tries in which she said either too little or too much.

When she got to Heathrow, Marx sent a message to Jeffrey Gertz, as planned, saying that she was on her way to Dubai. She was sitting in her seat waiting to take off when her phone rang. She moved to turn it off, fearing that it was Gertz, but she recognized Perkins's number. When he came on the line, his voice was enthusiastic, almost breathless, as if he'd just made a big decision. He apologized that he had been away from the office. He had been doing some thinking, he explained.

"I'm not going to keep working with these bastards," he said.

"Good," she answered. "Don't."

"But you're one of them."

"Not anymore. I'm out."

They were closing the door of the plane. The flight attendant was telling people to buckle their seat belts and turn off their cellular phones.

"What are you, then?" asked Perkins.

"I'm not sure."

The flight attendant was walking down the aisle. Marx pretended to turn off her phone and when the attendant had passed, she put it back to her ear.

"Where are you?" asked Perkins. "It sounds like you're on an airplane. Where the hell are you going?"

"I'm in a good place," she whispered. "I can't say any more now. Don't ask."

"Don't go. I want to see you. I want to be with you. I'm the only one who knows your real name."

"Don't be a sentimental ass," she said, which made him laugh. "And don't do anything self-destructive. I like going to good restaurants."

"Come back," he said.

But she was gone. The flight attendant had threatened to take away her phone and have her removed forcibly from the plane if she didn't stop talking immediately. She turned off her phone and removed the battery, so that nobody could track her GPS movements while she was away. Then she sat back in her seat and closed her eyes.

28
ISLAMABAD

They say the safest airline is the one that has just had a crash, because the crew takes extra precautions. On that theory, Sophie Marx decided that she would stay at the Marriott Hotel in Islamabad, which had been the target of a catastrophic truck bombing some years before and was for a time off-limits to U.S. diplomatic personnel. She reasoned that if it was officially regarded as dangerous, the hotel would be the safest place in Pakistan. She was traveling in alias, and she was not normally a fearful person. But on her way into town from the airport in the late afternoon, the air heavy with the heat of summer, she thought about calling her parents, with whom she hadn't talked in more than a year.

It was dark by the time Marx arrived, and an improbable array of blue Christmas tree lights twinkled along the length of the hotel's front security barrier. It was a horizontal concrete block decorated with faux-Oriental arches, topped by the too-red Marriott emblem. The design said "America in Pakistan," once a selling point but no more. The façade had been rebuilt after the attack, with double-thick walls that were now advertised by the hotel as "bomb-proof."

Marx was tired from the flight and wanted to remain anonymous for a few more hours. She took a swim in the hotel's indoor pool and then dined alone in the Japanese restaurant. She told herself that this was just another operation; there was an element of danger whenever she traveled; this time it was just more palpable. She took a pill before going to bed, but she awoke in the middle of the night. She finally drifted off toward four o'clock with the television on.

The next morning, before breakfast, she sent a text message to the cell phone number she had been given for General Malik, saying that she had arrived. She described herself as *Mr. Hoffman's friend.* Thirty minutes later, the phone rang and it was the general himself, inviting her to pay a visit later that morning.

"Gentle lady," he said solicitously, "I will send a car to the Marriott at ten o'clock to pick you up."

"How do you know I'm at the Marriott?" Marx hadn't told him where she was staying, and she was supposed to be traveling under clean cover.

"Please, madam, this is my country. There is very little here that I do not know. Let us not get off to a bad start before we have even met."

Marx said that she would be ready at ten. She knew then for a certainty that she was in danger. Her identity had been compromised within hours of her entry into Pakistan, and she had no good way to protect herself. If she tried to leave the country now, the ISI could stop her; if she tried to seek protection in the U.S. Embassy compound, the ISI could block her way. The Pakistanis could arrest her anytime they wanted. Her security was in the hands of someone she didn't know and had little reason to trust.

The general's Land Cruiser arrived at ten o'clock as promised. When Marx emerged from behind the security wall, the driver jumped out of the vehicle and opened the passenger door. She was dressed in a cloak and scarf in deference to local sensibilities, but the driver seemed to know who she was by her appearance. Was there anyone in Pakistan who didn't know that she was coming?

Marx wished she could leave a trail of bread crumbs to find her way back home, as in the children's fairy tale. The moment she entered the car, she was effectively General Malik's prisoner.

They headed south on Ataturk Road, in the direction of the ISI's headquarters in Aabpara. But rather than turning right on the Kashmir Highway toward the office, the driver continued south into Shakarparian Park, a lush expanse of green that bordered the city center. He left the main avenue for a gravel road that wound through a grove of trees and came to a security checkpoint, where a guard waved him through. The Toyota stopped at the road's end at a guesthouse on the banks of a large body of water, which Marx knew from her maps must be Rawal Lake.

In the heat of midmorning, nothing was stirring. The surface of the water was smooth as glass, and the air was thick. The trees were barely green, more a light tan, their leaves baked like chips in the oven. Even the birds had gone silent. The driver escorted Marx to the guesthouse and opened the door, beckoning her to take a seat on the couch. The room was cooled by a noisy window box that throbbed and rattled against the heat. The driver brought a cool drink from the pantry and set it before the guest. Then he retreated out the door and locked it from the outside.

Marx waited for more than an hour before the general arrived. She searched for something to read and found only one book, *The Defense and Foreign Affairs Handbook on Pakistan*. She opened to the first page: "Pakistan is, indeed, a nation on the edge. Many of the critical challenges facing Pakistan today, however, are not of its own making." It was America's fault, India's fault, somebody's fault. She put the book aside.

She debated calling Cyril Hoffman to tell him where she was, but decided against it. The call would surely be monitored, and there was nothing Hoffman could do now, in any event. It was easier simply to admit that she was helpless.

Rain clouds gathered, and there was a brief shower, the raindrops falling straight down into the water on this windless day, perforating the surface of the lake with tiny dots. The shower ended as quickly as it had begun, and in an instant the bright sun returned. It was like being in a terrarium. Her hair felt wet and matted against her neck; she pinned up her ponytail so that it formed a bun.

General Malik arrived just after noon, accompanied by an aide carrying a laptop computer. The general was a courtly man, trim in his uniform, handsomer than Marx had expected. The aide placed the laptop on a table at the far end of the room; he plugged it into the wall, powered it on and then disappeared out the door.

"I am so very sorry to be late," began the general. "It must appear that this was a deliberate slight, but I assure you it was not intentional. I was talking with Cyril Hoffman, to be quite frank with you."

Marx nodded but said nothing. It was always a mistake to be ingratiating, especially for a woman. Better to let the general say what he wanted. When she didn't answer, the general arched his thick black eyebrows curiously and then continued.

"I was talking with Cyril about you, as a matter of fact. I am a bit worried, you see."

Marx kept her silence for another moment, but she needed to understand what he was telling her.

"Why are you worried, General? Here I am, ready to do business."

"Because I think it is possible that others know you are here in Pakistan. To be more specific, madam, I am concerned that your presence here is known to the Tawhid organization that is responsible for the deaths of the other American intelligence officers."

Marx studied him. This clipped and controlled man was famous for his dexterity at lying, but in this case she thought he was being truthful.

"How could they possibly know I am here? You must have told them."

"Certainly not, madam. That is why I called Cyril. I wanted to inform him of this danger, you see, and to assure him that I had played no role in disclosing the fact of your visit. No, I am sorry to say that they learned of your travel quite on their own. That is the problem, you know. They have found you out."

"How can you be sure they know, if you didn't tell them yourself?"

"Please, Miss Marx. Do not let us trifle with each other. I know because it is my job to discover the secrets of these miscreants. I have agents among them. I overhear their conversations. I watch and listen. And I am telling you, with the greatest of regret, that based on this intelligence I am quite certain that they are aware of your travel to Pakistan."

"Can you control them? Can you keep them from harming me?"

"*Achaah!*" He tapped his forehead with his hand. "That is what you Americans can never understand. To know is not to control."

Marx thought a long moment. She didn't want to be panicked or rushed. She watched the general's eyes. They were dark brown, with a sparkle of light at the center. It was an intelligent face, if not quite an honest one.

"I believe you, General," she said.

"Thank you."

The tightness in his cheeks eased. He tried to smile.

"So I must ask you," she continued, "how do they know that I am here? What is this methodology that allows them to monitor our movements? Mr. Hoffman told me that you have ideas about how they are targeting our officers. He said that it involves our financial networks. He said you would help. That's why I came. Now the matter is a little more personal. I am quite in your protection."

"You touch me, madam." He put his hand on his heart. "Come, sit down with me at the computer and I will explain what I can."

He gestured for her to join him at the table at the far end of the bungalow, where the screen of the laptop was glowing faintly. She rose and followed him across the room. He removed a small object from the pocket of his uniform. It was a computer flash drive. He fumbled with the drive, attempting to insert it in the USB port at the back of the machine.

"I am not very good at this, I am afraid. That is the problem with being a general. There is always someone younger and cleverer to do such things for me."

Eventually he got the drive in place. He sat down at the computer and manipulated the mouse until he had clicked open the file from the external drive. A four-line Excel spreadsheet came up on the screen.

"This is what I wanted you to see," said the general. "Mumbo jumbo, you will say. But look, please, and then we can talk about what it all might mean."

He turned the computer screen toward her, so that she could read the document more clearly. It displayed the four strings of letters and numbers:

1) BANK JULIUS BAER BKJULIUS CH12 0869-6005-2654-1601-2 BAERCHZU 200 71835

BANK ALFALAH ALFHAFKA 720 34120

2) BARCLAYS BANK BARCLON GB35 BARC-4026-3433-1557-68 BARCGBZZ 317 82993

AMONATBONK ASSETJ22 297 45190.

He handed her a piece of paper that contained the same brief burst of information. That was his gift, for which he had summoned her, at considerable danger, from across the sea.

Marx studied the screen, trying to break the code. At length, she turned back toward the Pakistani officer. She was shaking her head.

"I want to understand what this means, General, but I am having trouble. It looks like bank routing numbers. Can you decipher it for me?"

"Perhaps I can," he answered. "Not because I am smart about such things, which is very far from true. But I have a young major on my staff who is quite the computer buff. He has been helping me, you see, so that I could make some sense of this bloody nonsense."

She took his hand and held it for a moment. It was a forward gesture for a woman in a Muslim country, but it was spontaneous and genuine.

"Please tell me whatever you can. I don't mean to be overly dramatic, but it's a matter of life and death."

The general nodded, in deference to the woman's distress.

"I will tell you everything, then, madam. I was not sure that I would do so. This is a complicated business for us. I do not need to explain. But now that I see you, and understand the risk you have taken to come here, I am quite ready to be helpful."

"You are very generous. Thank you."

"The first thing you need to know, madam, is that I obtained this computer device from a Tawhid courier we captured in the Tribal Areas just over a week ago. He was on his way into Afghanistan. During interrogation, he stated that the information on this device would help his group to kill American agents.

"The American agents are dead," she said. "The latest victim was just killed in Kabul. I was notified before I left London."

General Malik bit his lip. He shook his head. He appeared sorrowful, but that was only to hide his feeling of guilt. He had been warned that such an attack was coming and he had done nothing to stop it. That was the fact. He leaned toward her across the table.

"I am sorry for this, but it could not have been helped."

She kept silent for a moment, but she was angry. The operative in Kabul had been her colleague. He had a wife and children.

"Yes, General, it could have been helped. You could have stopped the people who killed him. Or you could have told us. This is a strange friendship, where you watch our people get killed and don't do anything to prevent it. We deserve better than this, don't you think?"

He put his hands up, palms extended limply. "Please, please. This is not the time for recriminations. We have much for which we could reproach you. This is a tricky game, you know. We are not playing cricket on a nice green lawn. Perhaps I should go away. What is the use? It is the same old story: You blame us, we blame you."

He pulled back his chair and rose, as if he were preparing to leave.

"Please stay, General. Talk with me. I am trying to be honest with you. It is a measure of my respect. We must understand each other, for it is a fact that we need your help."

He bowed his head, not quite in deference. He was still standing.

"Please," she repeated.

"Very well," he said, taking his seat again. "We will not think about the past, but the future. Let me continue with my story. We intercepted this courier fellow. He was carrying the computer drive that I have shown you, containing the information that is on the screen there. He told us that there were others on the road carrying the same information. We did not understand it at first."

"But now you do?"

"Yes. My clever major thinks he does, at least. These are bank codes, just as you say. They are numbered, one and two, for two American agents that the Tawhid was tracking. Let us look at the first line." He pointed to the first line of code on the screen:

1) BANK JULIUS BAER BKJULIUS CH12 0869-6005-2654-1601-2 BAERCHZU 200 71835.

"So here is what we think: This is the coding for the bank account from which a payment originated. It is Bank Julius Baer, a private bank in Zurich, which is known as 'BKJULIUS.' What follows that is a twenty-one-character code, beginning with 'CH12.' We believe this is the International Bank Account Number for the originating account. This is called the IBAN, I am told. The final entry, which begins 'BAERCHZU,' is what is known as the SWIFT code. I had always assumed this was a reference to making haste. But no, my major tells me that it is an acronym for Society of Worldwide Interbank Financial Telecommunication, which manages this system for wire transfers. I hope that makes sense, perhaps just a bit."

"It makes perfect sense, General. And let me make a guess. The second line is the recipient account." She pointed to the second line on the screen:

BANK ALFALAH ALFHAFKA 720 34120

"You are the clever one, madam. This is the account that your operative in Kabul was using to receive the payment for the gentleman he intended to, what shall we say, to bribe. It does not include an IBAN designator because Afghanistan is not part of the IBAN system. But it does include a SWIFT account address with the 'AF' and 'KA' notations to signify Afghanistan and Kabul."

"What about number two? I assume it's the same pattern, originating account and receiving account." She traced the two lines with her finger:

2) BARCLAYS BANK BARCLON GB35 BARC-4026-3433-1557-68 BARCGBZZ 317 82993

AMONATBONK ASSETJ22 297 45190.

She looked at the end of the string for the SWIFT code of the recipient bank. "TJ" was the country designator. She groaned and shook her head. That stood for Tajikistan. This was the address of the bank in Dushanbe that had been receiving money for Meredith Rockwell, now deceased.

Marx closed the laptop. She did not want to look at the ghostly glow of the screen anymore.

"I knew the recipient," she said. "This message was her death sentence."

"Yes, it was. I am sorry to say so. These miscreants are very smart. They obtain the routing numbers, you see, and then they recruit people in the banks, simple Muslim boys who are clerks. That way they learn who controls these accounts. When a payment arrives, they know the paymaster is coming soon, and they know the name, the work name, you see. And there are other things, I think."

"What other things are those, General Malik?"

"Credit card numbers, perhaps, airplane reservations, patterns, signatures. Who can say? Whatever is on a computer. All the things that you think are confidential. That is how they know that you are here, madam. They start with a few pieces of data, and then they connect them. They highlight the person who buys the ticket from London to Islamabad using the same telephone number or wire-transfer procedures as someone already on their list. They follow the patterns, you see. Like any clever idea, it is really quite simple. You just have to be smart enough to think of it."

She put her head in her hands. She had been trying to solve this puzzle, piece by piece, and at last she could see the picture: It was a system that had been constructed as if in a mirror image.

"My God. It's so obvious," she said.

The Pakistani general looked at her curiously, waiting for some explanation of her outburst.

"Do unto others," she said.

"I beg your pardon, madam."

"We call it the Golden Rule: Do unto others as you would have them do unto you. Well, now they're doing it unto us."

He looked at her dumbly, as if this were all too complicated for a simple Pakistani.

"I am sorry, Miss Marx, but I do not understand your golden rules and riddles. If you want my help you will have to explain it more clearly."

"I am sure you understand very well, General. You probably figured it out long ago. And it is no riddle at all, just good tradecraft. We built a system to capture terrorists. We watched their bank transfers, their money flows, their phone calls, their credit-card purchases; their movements. Then we used computer programs to look for links and patterns, so that we could identify our targets. And then we killed them. Sometimes you helped."

The general coughed.

"And now they are using the same tools against us. That is what has happened, isn't it?"

The general smoothed the skirt of his uniform jacket. It was awkward to have to answer such a direct question.

"I think you may be on to something there, madam. Very well said, I think. They have taken your book of plays and made a copy, turned it inside out, rather. Yes, I think you have smoked it out now."

He was playing with her and she didn't like it. She reached out her hand again for his, but he withdrew his arms from the table and folded them, his long fingers intertwining.

"Who is this smart, General Malik? Who has organized this system? Do you have any idea?"

He stared at her, blankly at first, his face a mask. But then he softened slightly; his lips turned up at the corners and his eyes relaxed.

"Tell me," she pressed. "Too many people have died."

"Very sensitive, this one is. Not easy to talk about."

"But you must help me. Mr. Hoffman said you were the only hope. I risked my life to come see you, General. I implore you." She extended her hand again. She did everything but cry.

He sighed and smiled. Perhaps he had intended to tell her all along, but he acted as if it were a gesture of gallantry for a damsel in distress.

"Ah, Miss Marx, how can I refuse you? It is easier to be cold-blooded with a man, but a charming woman melts the heart."

She disliked this playacting, but it obviously appealed to the general's vanity.

"You are a gentleman," she said. That brought a look of solemn satisfaction to the Pakistani's face.

"Here is what I can tell you: There is a man we have been trying to apprehend for some time. He has many names, as you might expect. Usually people call him 'the professor,' or '*ustad,*' which means the learned one. We think that he is the one who has solved these technical puzzles. We have made many investigations. But we do not know who he is. He covers his tracks very well. Perhaps he is already known to us, but we cannot see it. Maybe he is even known to you."

"Where is this professor? How can we find him?"

The general shook his head slowly. "That is the difficulty, you see. He is a ghost. We have tried very hard to find him, you must believe me. We have summoned many professors over the last few years, I assure you. But we have not been successful. He has a network of associates, some known to us and some unknown. But even they do not know his identity; we see only where he has been, not where he is."

Marx drained what was left of her water. She wanted to trust the general, but it was hard to believe that the ISI could not locate such a person, using its own pervasive net of contacts.

"Is this professor the leader of Al-Tawhid? They issued the statement taking credit for the operations he has enabled, so I assume he is their emir."

"No, no. We suspect that he works with the Al-Tawhid. He uses their people. But he is not really a member. I do not think he is very comfortable with the jihadists' ideas. He is a modern man, to know so many things. They are too primitive."

"Then why would he do this? If he's not a jihadist, why would he work so hard to kill American intelligence officers?"

"Ah, madam, I could tell you. But I am not sure you would want to hear the answer. It will be upsetting."

"Of course I want to hear it. Don't be silly. Tell me."

"Perhaps it is a matter of revenge, madam. So many people have died in these wars, you see, and it is an insult that is felt by our whole nation. Perhaps the professor knew some of the dead, I cannot say. But I suspect it is a matter of personal honor for him. You said it yourself a moment ago: Do unto others."

She was silent. There was nothing, really, to say. He went out to fetch his orderly and have him make some tea.

29
ISLAMABAD

Sophie Marx opened the door of the guesthouse onto the cloying heat of the afternoon. It was claustrophobic inside and she needed a walk. The stillness of midday had broken: The surface of the lake was thick now with bugs, and every few seconds there was a ripple as a fish broke the water in pursuit. A lakeside path had been carefully planted with a border of rosebushes in shades of red and pink and yellow; their petals were limp in the humid summer air. The grass was patchy, bleached by the light, more dirt than lawn.

Marx ambled along, lost in thought, until she heard a voice ahead call out sharply, "*Rukiye!*" which means "stop" in Urdu. It was a Pakistani soldier brandishing his automatic weapon. Beyond him was a chain-link fence. She raised her hand apologetically and turned and headed back to the bungalow. So this was the limit of her freedom: fifty yards.

General Malik was waiting for her when she returned. He offered her a cup of hot tea that had been brewed by his orderly and sat her down on the couch, installing himself in a big easy chair next to it. The furniture was faded green velvet, topped by embroidered white doilies; like everything the Pakistani military touched, it conveyed a faint nostalgia for the bygone Raj. The general sipped his tea and ate one of the sweet biscuits that had been set out by his batman. The air conditioner chattered in the window.

"You shouldn't go walking off on your own, madam. It isn't safe for you."

Marx didn't answer. She was surely in jeopardy, but it wasn't clear whether the general was her protector or her jailer. The Pakistani took another biscuit and sipped his tea. He seemed contented, which was not good. She spoke up.

"What are we going to do, General? I need to contact Mr. Hoffman soon. What am I going to tell him? We can't do nothing."

The general chuckled. He found her impatience amusing. He had resolved to help, but not quite yet.

"Do what? That is the question, you see. You Americans always want to do something. That is your nature. But the something that you do often makes things worse, whereas doing nothing would at least provide a neutral course of action. This is your problem, I think."

"Maybe so, but I still have to do something. I'm in danger. You said so yourself. I need to take action, but I don't know in which direction to go."

"You really are quite brave, madam. I must say that. Cyril Hoffman chose a good emissary. And I want to be helpful, truly I do."

The general reached into the pocket of his jacket and withdrew a piece of paper, edged with a red border.

"I have something more for you. Perhaps it will be useful."

Marx took the paper from him. It had a classification marking at the top of the page and appeared to be an intelligence report in English. It began with a date, which was just over two months earlier. Below that there were two telephone numbers, identified as "Bhut 1" and "Bhut 2," and the transcript of a brief conversation:

BHUT 1: "Perihelion."

BHUT 2: "Aphelion."

BHUT 1: "Hello, there. This is your friend from the New World. I hope it is not too cold for you in Brussels."

BHUT2: "Hello, back. It is the same here, always. It is Belgium."

BHUT1: "I have new numbers. I am sending them to you at the same address as before."

BHUT 2: "You want all the transfers for these?"

BHUT 1: "Yes."

BHUT 2: "It will take some time. There are new rules now. It is Europe: Privacy, privacy. I have to be careful."

BHUT 1: "How long?"

BHUT 2: "A week. It has to be normal business. Is that too long?"

BHUT 1: "No. That is soon enough. I want to have everything ready before we start."

BHUT 2: "Okay. I can do that."

BHUT 1: "Thanks, buddy. Perigee."

BHUT 2: "Apogee."

Marx put down the paper and shrugged.

"Very interesting, no doubt. But what is it?"

"This is the transcript of a conversation we intercepted a couple of months ago."

"Who are Bhut 1 and Bhut 2? The first man sounded like he must be an American, with the talk about the 'New World' and the 'buddy' stuff."

"Very clever, that. It was meant to throw off anyone who was listening. But in fact, we believe that Mr. Bhut 1 is the gentleman I was describing before, 'the professor.' We have lost this link, I am afraid. He never used this cellular number again. But the person of immediate interest, for your purposes, is Bhut 2."

"And who might Mr. Bhut 2 be? I take it from the transcript that he is in Brussels."

"We believe that he is a Belgian national named Joseph Sabah. He is an employee of the Society for Worldwide Interbank Financial Telecommunication, also known as SWIFT, which you will recall plays a rather important part in the scheme of your adversaries. I suspect that he is what might be called the 'inside man.'"

"Have you done anything with this intelligence, General Malik?"

"Not until now."

She looked at the paper again, more intently now. She wanted to understand every word.

"Why did they talk about 'perihelion' and 'aphelion' at the beginning, and 'perigee' and 'apogee' at the end? Is that a code?"

"A recognition code, I would say. It's science talk. My smart major tells me that these words are used by physics students studying celestial mechanics. The first pair of words refers to orbits around the sun, the second to orbits around the earth. Or perhaps it's the other way around. They must have common academic interests, although we haven't been able to find the link."

"And what about your crypt 'bhut.' What does that mean?"

"Ah, madam, it means 'ghost' in Urdu. That is our problem. We are dealing with Ghost 1 and Ghost 2. But perhaps you will do better in finding them than we have."

Marx studied the paper, as if she might read a deeper meaning between the lines. It was just a wisp of information, a few brief seconds of intercepted conversation, but it suggested the outlines of a meticulous structure of intelligence. How had such a powerful network been created out of such meager raw material?

"This man is very clever, this professor of yours, whoever he is. We've had thousands of people working for nearly ten years to develop money traces and link analysis, and your guy puts it together in his garage."

"He is not 'our guy,' madam. You must put aside this CIA fantasy. It is a delusion."

"Who is he? That's what I'm asking. How can anybody be that smart?"

"Ah, now you are truly asking me a riddle. How high is the sky? How deep is the well? We cannot say."

"But he must have learned all this from somewhere. People can't do this sort of thing on their own. It's not possible. They need help from an intelligence service."

"I must protest. If the implication is that we taught him, you are wrong. Dead wrong, if you will forgive that phrase under the circumstances."

"Then who taught him? Where did he learn how to use these techniques? These are things we thought only the CIA knew how to do."

The general cocked his head sideways and gave her a look that was knowing, scolding, taunting.

"Well, then, madam, perhaps you have your answer. Perhaps this is the echo of the master's voice."

"Oh, don't be silly," she said. "Why are Pakistanis addicted to anti-American conspiracies?"

General Malik could only laugh. "Why indeed?" he said. "It must be part of our backwardness. Yes, I am sure of it."

Marx looked at the intercept transcript one more time. "Do you have the coordinates of Ghost 2?" she asked.

"Of course."

He reached into the jacket of his uniform once again and handed her another piece of paper. On it was written the name, phone number and address of Joseph Sabah in Brussels.

"Well, that at least gives me an itinerary. They say that Brussels is lovely this time of year."

"Are you quite sure it's wise for you to travel there? Perhaps Mr. Hoffman could send someone else."

"Perhaps, but I'm greedy. I want all the fun for myself. Plus, I'm stubborn. And how dangerous can it be, really? Nothing ever happens in Brussels."

"Do not joke, madam. They know that you are here. I told you that when we began talking. We monitored a circuit last night in which they discussed your arrival at the airport. They do not yet seem to know where you are staying, but they will. And if they have seen you come, they will see you go."

"Not if you stop them, General. You can turn off their eyes and ears. You can distract them. The ISI owns Pakistan. That's what everyone says."

"I wish it were that simple. Truly I do. But it is not. To know what they are saying inside the tent, you must have someone of your own inside the tent. And we have done that, I am not embarrassed to say so. But that gets complicated, doesn't it?"

"Playing both sides? Yes, it certainly does. Maybe you should stop."

He smiled in that courtly way that said yes but meant no.

"I am playing *your* side, madam. I hope I have made that abundantly clear, to you and to Mr. Hoffman. I do not think it is wise for you to travel to Belgium. I think you should go home. But that is not my decision."

"No, it's not. No disagreement there."

"To assist you, madam, and to demonstrate my good faith, I have one last gift. I obtained this from someone 'inside the tent,' as it were. I am sorry that I cannot give it to you, but I am prepared to let you take a look."

General Malik shouted for his orderly, who was out back behind the kitchen. The young man appeared in an instant, thinking they might want some more tea, but the general ordered him to go get his briefcase from the car. He returned a moment later with the leather case. The general turned the dial of the combination lock and popped the top. He removed a sheaf of pages bound with a metal clasp and handed it to Marx.

"We obtained this from a confidential source. I cannot say more about the document, I am sorry. And I cannot let you keep it. You should start by looking at the heading."

At the top of the first page were the words "ALPHABET CAPITAL," and below that a subhead that read, "FBS Correspondent Accounts." There were nearly a dozen pages, dense with listings.

Marx tried not to show any emotion as she turned the pages. Through its account at Fédération des Banques Suisses, Alphabet Capital had done business with banks in London, Paris, Milan, Moscow, Tokyo, Hong Kong, Dubai, New York, Los Angeles and a dozen other money centers. At the top of the list was a Bank of America branch in Studio City, California. The four banks referenced in the file on the flash drive were all on the list.

"May I take notes?" asked Marx.

"No," answered the general. "But my dear madam, the point is that there is no need for you to take notes. This information is available to you and your colleagues already. Unless I am mistaken, it is in fact *your* information."

"How did you get this?"

"I cannot say. But I hope you can see now why I am advising you to be very careful. To some very dangerous people, you are an open book."

General Malik sent her back to the Marriott in a different vehicle, a Mitsubishi van with civilian plates. She sat in the backseat with a scarf wrapped tight around her head. The general's staff had found a flight leaving for Dubai just after midnight. He suggested that she take it and said it would be safer if one of his people made the reservation. She agreed.

The ISI chief sent a bodyguard with her, as well. He sat in the front seat next to the driver, cradling an automatic rifle across his lap. He didn't speak as they drove north from Shakarparian Park; he studied the terrain ahead, his eyes moving back and forth with the constant, synchronous oscillation of a searchlight beam. Marx asked his name; he answered that he was called Sergeant Asif.

"I am at your service," he said. Then he went back to scouting the road.

"Where are you from?" she asked.

"From Chitral, madam, in the north, where the snow leopards run."

"Do you miss home?"

"Never," he answered sternly.

Then he looked back toward her and softened.

"Always," he said. "My wife is here with me, and a daughter. But my father and mother stay in the mountains."

Lucky man, she thought. At least he has a home and people waiting for him.

When they arrived at the white concrete façade of the hotel, the bodyguard took charge.

"It is not safe for you," he said. He told Marx to wait in the lobby while he went up and checked the room. When she protested, he said proudly that it was his duty. She gave him the key card and took a seat on a brocaded couch amid the marbled expanse of the lobby, while Sergeant Asif went upstairs.

The explosion rocked the hotel with the fury of an artillery round. The bomb sucked in the oxygen and blew it out with a fiery roar. The building rumbled, and then shuddered, and the chandeliers in the lobby swung sharply on their moorings, adding the sound of tinkling glass. The alarm immediately sounded, too, like an air raid, and the sprinklers spurted jets of water onto the floor, and frightened hotel guests tried to run or hide. Marx moved toward the elevator, but a security guard stopped her and took her to a shelter in the hotel basement. She tried to call Cyril Hoffman, but she couldn't get any phone reception in the concrete bunker.

When they let Marx go upstairs, the medics were still working on the torn and bloodied form of the bodyguard. The bomb had blown out the windows of the room, and burst the plumbing so that the floor was awash in water. There was blood on the walls. The rooms on either side were barely touched. It had been a professional job—an attempt to kill one person only.

Sergeant Asif's mouth was still moving. They were taking him out on a stretcher now. The blanket covering him was already soaked with blood. There was an empty space under the blanket where one of his arms had been. The rescue workers tried to push Marx away so they could roll the gurney down the hall.

"I'm going with him to the hospital," she shouted. "This man was my bodyguard. They were trying to kill me. He was protecting me."

The Red Crescent attendants had no idea what the American woman was talking about, but she was so emphatic that they let her come along. Down in the lobby, a television crew from Dawn TV had already arrived. They photographed the American woman, now in a blood-streaked scarf, hunched over the body.

When the Red Crescent ambulance arrived at the naval hospital on Lalak Jan Road, a gaggle of television cameras was waiting. They all filmed the American woman escorting the body and later talking to the victim's wife, who had rushed to the hospital from her home in I-9, near the railway station.

Sergeant Asif died of blood loss an hour after he arrived at the hospital. A detail of ISI officers, who had found Marx in the family waiting lounge with Sergeant Asif's wife, now pulled her away and escorted her out the back door.

Among the millions of Pakistanis who watched the television images that evening was a research professor at the National University of Science and Technology. He didn't pay much attention to the newscast at first. The reporters were describing it as one more terrorist attack in Pakistan's long war, and speculating that it must be anti-American because it had taken place at the Marriott Hotel.

The professor suddenly took notice when the cameras showed the American woman who had accompanied the victim. His contacts had described the CIA operative who had arrived at the airport the day before. He knew that the target had survived the bombing at the Marriott. What surprised him was that she had accompanied the Pakistani sergeant to the hospital, and tried to comfort his widow.

The professor was confused. That image did not fit within his template of vengeance. He tried to put out of his mind the television picture of the American woman embracing the Pakistani widow as if she were her sister, but the image persisted.

Marx reached Cyril Hoffman two hours after the bombing, after the ISI had finally pried her away from the hospital.

"Somebody tried to kill me," she said. But Hoffman already knew that. He'd received a call from General Malik thirty minutes before.

"No more heroics," Hoffman said. "We are getting you out of there now, before you go out in a box."

Hoffman had already discussed with the Pakistani general the procedures by which Marx would leave the country. An ISI convoy would take her to the military side of Islamabad Airport, where she would be held in a secure VIP area. Then she would be driven in an armored car to the Emirates plane as it was about to leave.

"Won't that blow my cover?" she asked.

"I hate to break this to you, Sophie, but there's nothing left of it."

"I got what I came after," she said. "That's something, anyway."

"What's the short version?" asked Hoffman.

"We're screwed. I'll send you the details by cable. Have you told my boss?"

"Yes. I thought I really must. He was not pleased. He had some rather sharp words for me about your unauthorized trip. I believe the word 'betrayal' was used."

All the anger that Marx had been feeling toward Gertz suddenly broke the surface. She looked around. Nobody seemed to be listening, but it didn't matter.

"Oh, yeah? Well, fuck him. Tell him I said so."

Hoffman laughed, a high-pitched chortle. "Now, now. Chin up, my dear. Get on that plane and don't talk to strangers. Watch a nice in-flight movie, why don't you. Have a beverage. And for heaven's sake, be careful."

She composed her message for Hoffman while she waited at Islamabad Airport to board the flight. She sent it in her funny name, to his, as an encrypted email:

To: Marcus Crabtree
From: Doris Finn

Here's the bad news:

1. *The Hit Parade's network is compromised by Hostile Network (HN) that has used the public name Ikwan Al-Tawhid but is guided by a computer expert identified as "the professor."*
2. *The Hit Parade's financial transfers are being monitored by HN, in part by tracing SWIFT and IBAN account numbers. HN has a source at SWIFT HQ facilitating this analysis of financial flows.*
3. *The Hit Parade's credit-card and travel records have been accessed by HN, using data-mining and probably also human sources, identity unknown.*
4. *The Hit Parade's use of Alphabet Capital as a financial hub to coordinate money flows has been discovered by HN, probably prior to kidnapping of Howard Egan.*
5. *Identity of alleged HN agent in the SWIFT network: JOSEPH SABAH, Belgian national; residence Avenue George Bergmann 127, Watermael District, Brussels; cellular telephone 32-400-555-268.*

6. Request operational support when I arrive in Brussels. Recommend we take immediate action ref: item 5.

Here's the good news:

1. There isn't any.

Finn

Marx did one more thing, once she was in her seat on the plane. She called Thomas Perkins in London. He didn't pick up the first time. Rather than leave a message, she called twice more. The third time he answered.

"It's me," she said.

"Where are you?"

"I can't say. But I'm coming home. It got a bit nasty out here."

"That doesn't sound good. Can I come get you? Send the G5 or something?"

"No. I'm fine. I called to warn you about something. Alphabet is in trouble. You need to send your employees home for a few days. It's not safe. I can't explain now."

"It's a little late for that, sweetheart. The trouble has already arrived."

She froze. In her mind for an instant was the image of the trading floor in Mayfair, ravaged by the shrapnel of a suicide bomb.

"What do you mean? Tell me nothing terrible has happened."

"Pretty goddamn terrible, as far as I'm concerned. We had a visit from the Serious Fraud Office this morning. They cordoned off the place: files, computers, the whole lot. We had to shut down trading. I sent the employees home, told them not to come in tomorrow."

"Good," she said.

"No. It's a disaster. And I don't understand why it's happening. Is this what you were talking about? Is this the work of your friends?"

They were closing the door of the plane. The flight attendant was telling her, in the usual insistent way, to turn off her cell phone.

"I don't know," she said. "Just go home, and stay home."

"What's happening?"

"I don't know," she repeated.

The flight attendant had called the purser, who was wagging his finger at Marx. She said goodbye as the plane rolled back from the gate.

30
BRUSSELS, BELGIUM

When the Dubai flight landed at Brussels Airport, Sophie Marx was met by two security officers from the U.S. Embassy. They spotted her as she cleared customs and wordlessly flanked her on either side. She was happy to see them, though they were not exactly invisible. They had that overtrained look of security officers: big burly arms, and thick around the chest as refrigerators. The driver was waiting in the arrivals lane; when they were all seated in the armored Mercedes, the two security officers introduced themselves, Ted and Luis, or at least those were their work names. They were both from the station; they said that a team from Joint Special Operations Command was waiting at the rendezvous.

"How was the flight?" asked Ted. From bellhops to bodyguards, that was always the first question people seemed to ask any traveler. Marx said that the flight had been fine.

"I gather some folks are after you," said Luis.

"So it seems. But you never know until the bomb goes off."

"And you don't know then, either, if it's a good bomb," said Ted. "It's just lights out."

Marx closed her eyes. She hadn't slept well for days, and she dozed off as the Mercedes rolled toward the city. It was nice to have these big American men watching over her.

The meeting point was an apartment at the Citadines, a residence hotel off the Avenue Louise in the center of town. It was early morning, and the city was just coming to life, the sidewalks beginning to fill with gray civil servants heading to their jobs at the European Commission. As Marx emerged from the limousine, a frail beggar woman thrust forward her child and pleaded for money. Marx dropped into the cup some Pakistani rupees, which was all she had in her pockets, and the woman cursed her in a strange dialect.

Up in the apartment, three bulky members of the U.S. paramilitary team were already installed, looking at maps of the city. They were dressed in plain clothes, but the leader was evidently the man bent tight over the map like a human torsion spring. The others addressed him as Major Kirby.

"You're one tough lady," said the major after shaking Marx's hand.

"More lucky than tough," she said.

"That's even better. Hope it rubs off."

He pointed to his map of the city, laid out on the coffee table.

"We've had, like, twelve hours to work on this, which is impossible, frankly. But my boss talked to your boss, whoever he is, and I gather we have no choice but to move right away. And to do it unilaterally, without telling the Belgians, which is never a good idea, but what the hell, right?"

"Whatever you say, Major. I'm not even sure who my boss is anymore, but I think his name is Hoffman."

Kirby shrugged. He was wired and impatient. He wanted to get on with it.

"Look," he said, "we're here because the agency isn't supposed to do this anymore, interrogation and rendition and all that, and the military can do whatever it wants, so long as we call it 'force protection,' or 'tactical intelligence,' or 'preparation of the battlefield,' so the lawyers can say it's Title Ten. But basically, we're working for you, okay?"

"Sounds good to me. Any title you like."

"All they told us was that you have some kind of urgent security problem, which my boss says wasn't explained to him. Which must mean it's pretty damn serious, right, if they can't even tell us what it is?"

"Yes, Major, I promise you that it's extremely damn serious. Four of our people have been killed and more on the way if we don't get a handle on this soon. What's your ops plan?"

"The ID we have been given on the target is Joseph Sabah. Correct? For security, we are just going to call him Harry from here on. Okay?"

Marx nodded.

Major Kirby pointed to the lower right quadrant of the Brussels map, southeast of the city center. He spoke the place names very carefully, not wanting to botch them.

"Harry lives here, on Avenue . . . George . . . Bergmann. His apartment is a few blocks east of a big park called Bois . . . de . . . la . . . Cambre. Did I say that right?"

"Sort of," answered Marx. "Nobody would mistake you for a Belgian."

"Thank you," said Major Kirby. "Okay, Harry has a dog, a little yapper dog. What is it, Sergeant?"

"A miniature poodle, sir."

"Right. So every evening when Harry gets home from his job at this SWIFT place south of the city in, lemme look . . . La . . . Hulpe, he takes this dog out for a walk to do his business in the park, in this Bois . . . de . . . la . . . Cambre."

"You can just call it the park, Major, that's fine," said Marx.

"Roger that. Harry walked his dog last night, and we were able to get one of our friends to access the surveillance cameras in the park. He took the dog there every night for the last week, same route, pretty much. So, gents and lady, we are going to assume that he goes to the park every freaking night, and that when he gets home from work tonight he will take little bowser on that same route for his evening walk."

"And we will be waiting in the park?" asked Marx.

"Not exactly 'we,' ma'am, if that includes you. 'We' will be there, meaning me and my two JSOC brothers, plus Ted and Luis from the station. But you, meaning you, will be at the safe house where we are going to interrogate this clown, assuming we do this right."

"Okay, but I'm good luck. You said so yourself."

"We'll just have to live with that. Let's finish our pre-op. Ma'am, you may want to get some rest. There's a bedroom down the hall." He looked at the other four men.

"Okay, brothers. *De oppressso liber.*"

"Why did you say that?" asked Marx.

"Special Forces motto. Liberate the oppressed."

"Oh," said Marx. "Nice."

A voice piped up from the side of the room. It was one of the two other soldiers, who hadn't spoken yet.

"IYAAYAS," he said, speaking the letters quickly.

"What the hell does that mean?" queried Marx.

"Unofficial shooters' motto, ma'am," said the soldier. "'If you ain't ammo, you ain't shit.'"

"Please, gentlemen," she said. "Grow up."

The armored Mercedes returned to the Citadines at noon and transported Sophie Marx to a house in a leafy suburb south of Brussels, on the way to Waterloo. A member of the station was already there, preparing the room where the interrogation would take place. He had closed the blinds and the curtains and was moving furniture around, trying to make it look like Grandma's living room. The very word "interrogation" seemed to make him squeamish. He had been told to bring food for the "suspect" and the interrogators, as well as several cans of dog food.

Marx went upstairs to call Hoffman, but he didn't answer his phone. She rang Perkins again, and when he didn't pick up, either, she gave up trying. She knew she should call Gertz, but she didn't know what she would say to him, and if he ordered her home, she would refuse. So the best course, she decided, was to take another nap.

At 6:10, the surveillance team at SWIFT's headquarters on Avenue Adele in La Hulpe, south of the city, reported to the team in the Citadines that they had spotted "Harry" leaving work.

"Showtime," said Major Kirby. Two of the five men in the apartment had already set off, but the remaining three now departed and walked to the Metro station on Avenue Louise. They were carrying sports bags, marked with the symbols of Adidas and Nike, which contained their weapons: Three Heckler & Koch Mark 23 semiautomatic pistols with suppressors, the special operator's weapon of choice.

The three traveled by subway to Schuman station, melding into the wave of homeward-bound commuters; they found the Brussels railway line, which they took to the Watermael junction. They exited the station and walked west a half mile into the park, where they stationed themselves at the agreed watch posts.

The park cut a deep, green elliptical swath in the southern tier of the city. It was a smaller version of Paris's Bois de Boulogne: woods and meadows, with sandy paths bordering a kidney-shaped pond in the center of the park.

Joseph Sabah was driving north toward home in his gray Peugeot, meanwhile. He parked in the garage of his apartment building, changed out of his suit into a pair of blue jeans and hugged his dog, Émile, who had greeted his master's return by racing around in a circle in the living room of the apartment. The dog was now standing in the kitchen next to the leash, waiting for his walk.

Sabah fastened the leash to Émile's collar and descended the stairs to the street. It was still light outside, the sky illuminated on this summer day as if by a low-watt bulb. The dog couldn't wait to do his business; he dropped a turd a block from home. Sabah scooped it up in a plastic bag and continued on toward the park; he was carrying a second bag for later in the journey.

They walked along Avenue George Bergmann, the dog sniffing a few of his fellows along the way, and crossed into the park on the Avenue de l'Orée. The dog knew the route. He pulled Sabah south toward the pond on their left, stopping every few seconds when he encountered a new smell. Sabah tugged ineffectually at his leash.

Major Kirby was sitting on a bench along the Avenue de Flores, just inside the park. He saw "Harry" enter and spoke into the microphone in his sleeve to his colleagues, who were arrayed at other looking posts. It was light, and people were out strolling, so it wasn't easy to conceal their movements. It was so much easier to grab people in the dark.

The team slowly converged toward Sabah, two ahead of him, three behind. He was so slow, stopping and starting with the dog. The idea was to take him on his way back home, when it was darker, but it was still the soft half-light of a summer evening. The trees seemed to enfold the space; amid the green, the noise of the city fell away. You could hear birds calling to each other as they settled down for the night.

Sabah was crossing a wide expanse of grass now, entirely open, which took him to the northern edge of the pond. The dog relieved himself a second time; he was tired and ready to head home. Sabah took out his second bag and gingerly scooped up the droppings. The dog was tugging on the leash now, pulling his master homeward. They cut an arc across the lawn toward a path through the woods that would take them out via the Avenue Victoria.

"Now," said Kirby into his sleeve. "Close on him."

Two members of the team entered the wooded path and traversed it seventy yards to the end, where they waited. There were a few people along the path; Kirby had hoped it would be empty by that hour, but they had to work with what they had.

Sabah entered the canopy of trees, the two plastic bags swinging from his hand. Kirby and the other following members of the team were coming up behind. They were on either side of him now, keeping pace. Sabah looked at them, blankly at first, but then more anxiously as they matched his steps. They were in the middle of the wooded area. Kirby looked ahead and behind. He saw only two Belgians, sitting on benches, tired from their walks. This was their best chance.

"Go," he said. The two men astride Sabah continued to flank him, but now the two at the far end moved rapidly toward them. Sabah was looking anxiously, left and right and ahead, and the dog was barking. One of Kirby's men in the forward team bumped Sabah as he passed, jabbing him with a needle.

Sabah cried out and the dog yammered, but a moment later the target's body was crumpling and the two men astride quickly converged to prop him up, pulling his arms over their shoulders and putting a cloth to his mouth so he couldn't make any more noise. One of the Belgians looked up for a moment. But the team kept going, as if helping a friend home. The dog's yelps ended suddenly, thanks to another needle, and one of Kirby's men picked him up and cradled him in his arms.

Kirby called for the driver who had been idling just outside the park to meet them at the Avenue Victoria where it curved toward Franklin Roosevelt. His van was marked with the insignia of the Belgian Croix-Rouge.

The driver was there waiting, clad in the yellow vest of an emergency worker, when they emerged from the grove of trees: two men supporting a sagging body between them; a third carrying a small, furry animal. The door of the van was open, and the group quickly entered. Several passersby stopped to watch, in the curious way people do when they see something unusual happening, but they didn't attempt to intervene. The van pulled away. Fifty yards up the road, another car picked up the other two members of the team, and in an instant they were off, heading south on the N5 toward Waterloo.

31

WATERLOO, BELGIUM

It was a tidy locale for a messy endeavor: The house was on a quiet street near a suburban golf club. The residence had a wrought-iron fence, a plush, spongy lawn and ivy growing up the brick façade. The Brussels station kept a tenant there normally, so that the place wouldn't look empty and suspicious, but the tenant had been temporarily evicted so that this respectable Flemish address could momentarily serve as a "black site," where an undocumented and certainly illegal event could be handled discreetly.

Kirby's team had hooded the prisoner, as much to protect their identities as to frighten him. He had revived on the way, thanks to an antidote that counteracted the effects of the tranquilizer. His first query in the van was about his dog, and he seemed very happy when the curly-haired poodle was placed in his lap, even though little Émile was still out cold. He asked a few more frantic questions—where he was, who had taken him, what he had done—but Major Kirby had been instructed not to talk to him, and Sabah eventually gave up.

The ersatz Croix-Rouge van pulled into the driveway around eight p.m. The garage door cranked up to receive them, and the hooded man was gingerly removed from the vehicle and trundled indoors to the living room, where the hood was exchanged for a blindfold and he was offered food and drink.

The interrogator, who called himself "Sam," sat across from Sabah. He had flown in that day from the big CIA station in Paris. Sophie Marx sat in the next chair, a notebook on her lap.

Sam turned on a tape recorder. His voice was deep and insistent. He spoke stiff French, with a noticeable accent.

"Nous sommes prets a commencer, Monsieur Sabah. Si vous coopérez et vous nous donnez des informations correctes, ce sera un processus très simple, et vous serriez libre. Mais si vous résistez ou mentez, vous serriez en grand difficulté, je vous assure. Vous vous merderiez!"

He paused, to let the gravity of his words sink in, but Sabah was smiling.

"You are American!" the prisoner said in English. "I am not so frightened now. I thought you might be Al-Qaeda."

Sabah's smile widened incongruously below the blindfold. He looked genuinely relieved to have been abducted by Americans.

The interrogator looked at Sophie Marx. She shrugged: She didn't understand it, either.

"We are nobody," said the interrogator, speaking now in English. "The question is: Who are you?"

"My name is Joseph Sabah. I work at SWIFT, in the data processing center. But you know that, of course. I am your man."

Marx opened her hands, palms up, as if to say, *I don't get it.*

"We have some questions for you, Mr. Sabah," continued the interrogator. "Are you ready to talk with us now?"

"Yes, of course. Why not? Can I take off this blindfold?"

The interrogator slapped Sabah across the cheek, almost knocking him from the chair. His cheek reddened immediately as blood rushed to the skin.

"No questions from you, Mr. Sabah, just answers. Got that?"

"Yes, okay, sorry." He was sniffling away tears.

"How long have you worked at SWIFT?"

"Eleven years. No, twelve years."

"In that time, has anyone from outside SWIFT ever asked you for help in accessing wire-transfer records?"

"Yes, of course. Twice."

The interrogator looked at Marx again. She gave another shrug, then rolled her finger as if to say, *Let's keep going.*

"The first time was, I don't know, it was several years after September 11, maybe in 2005. There was a group of us at SWIFT. It was official. Secret, yes, but the management had agreed to help trace the money of Al-Qaeda. But you know this."

Sam looked to Marx for guidance. She motioned that he should join her outside the room. Sabah waited, mute in his blindfold, while they conferred. They returned a minute later.

"We know about the Terrorist Surveillance Program," said the interrogator. "The Treasury Department organized it. It was in the newspapers. But it was stopped. Is that what you mean?"

"Yes, that was the first time I was asked for help on wire transfers. It was very official, no problem. I was not important in that. They needed someone who spoke Arabic. I had a security clearance from SWIFT, so I was okay. I processed some requests, so I was cleared into the program."

Marx held up two fingers. Sam nodded.

"What about the second time? When did that begin?"

"About a year ago. I do not have the exact date, but I can get it for you."

"Tell me what happened."

"Okay, but you know. One of your people contacted me. His name was George. He said that you, America, were starting the program again but this time it had to be very secret. I could not talk about it with anyone at SWIFT. My contact said that he would give me account numbers and ask me to trace any transfers from them. That was it. I probably did twenty or thirty in the last year, maybe more."

"How did you know he was an American?"

"He said so. He had an American name. He was calling from an American cell phone number, "seven-oh-three," in Virginia, I think. And he knew about the earlier program. He said he had been a consultant before. He knew the names and procedures. That was how I was sure that he must be telling me the truth."

"Did you meet him?"

"Only once, in the beginning. After that we spoke by telephone or sent emails."

The interrogator shook his head. "You're a fucking liar," he said.

Sam looked like he was about to hit the prisoner again, but Marx raised her arm for him to stop and motioned that they should leave the room and confer again.

This time they took a little longer. When the interrogator returned, his tone was softer.

"I'm sorry for what I said before, Mr. Sabah. There was no need for me to swear at you. I apologize."

"Thank you, sir. I am not an enemy. Please do not treat me like one."

"Let's go back to the man who was your contact the second time. Where did you meet him?"

"In a hotel in Brussels. The Conrad, I think. It was on Avenue Louise."

"What did he look like, this man?"

"I did not see very well. It was dark in the room, and he was wearing sunglasses. I know you do that, you people, for disguise. I understand. His first name was George and his last name was very American, like George Washington or something. I forget. I assumed that was not his real name."

"Did he have an accent, this 'George' who you met in the hotel?"

"Yes, a little. He might have been from Britain originally, or India. I don't know. Everyone is from somewhere. That's what I thought."

"Is it possible that he was from Pakistan?"

"I suppose so. I am from Lebanon myself but I don't call myself Lebanese. I say that I am a Belgian. He said he was an American. And he knew things that only an American who was part of the secret program before would know."

"Things like what?"

"He knew procedures, code names, techniques, all of the little details. They were things that it would be impossible to know unless you had been part of the program. That was how I knew he was okay."

"Are you a Muslim, Mr. Sabah?"

"*Pas de tout.* I am a Maronite Catholic. My family fought against the Muslims in Lebanon. We hate the Muslims. That was one of the things that I talked about with the American man when we first met in the hotel. He said that he hated the Muslims, too, and all the terrible things that they had done. He made fun of the suicide bombers. That was another bond between us. He knew about my family, the village we were from in the Metn District. He knew all that. That was another reason I knew he must have been sent from the CIA, because he had all this information."

"When George called you after that, where would he be calling from?"

"Different places. Paris, London, Amsterdam. He traveled a lot. He had a Swiss cell phone, too, not just the American one. Different numbers. He was a technical man. He went to conferences. That was one of the things that made me trust him. We talked about science when we first met."

Marx was scribbling frantically on a page of her notebook as Sabah talked. She tore off the sheet and handed it to Sam. The interrogator read it and looked curiously at Marx, wondering if she really wanted him to ask those questions, but she nodded emphatically.

"Who is Perihilion, Mr. Sabah?"

The prisoner's jaw dropped in surprise.

"That is the code name of the man we have been talking about, sir, George. He used that name when he called me, so that I would know it was him."

"And who is Aphelion?"

"That is me, my code name. But you know that, of course. That is what I do not understand. Why are you putting me in a blindfold and asking me these questions when it is your operation we are talking about?"

Marx beckoned for the interrogator to follow her out of the room once more. This time the conversation lasted nearly thirty minutes, and then Marx called Hoffman back in Washington to get his approval for what she wanted to do. Hoffman had to consult someone, and then there was another long call. Then a Support officer from the station was summoned to put together simple disguises for Marx and the interrogator, Sam; wigs and glasses and makeup.

They sent in more food and water for Sabah while he was waiting. When they returned to the living room, the interrogator removed

Sabah's blindfold. The captive put his head in his hands. He didn't want to look at them at first, as if that might be taboo.

This time it was Marx who spoke first.

"I want to apologize, Mr. Sabah. I was here before during the interrogation, but you could not see me. We are sorry for the difficulty we have caused you. There were some things that we didn't understand, but now they are clear. Please accept our regrets for any pain or inconvenience."

"My apology, too, sir," said Sam in the most contrite voice he could muster. "I sincerely regret my behavior. I should not have hit you."

"Now we need your help, Mr. Sabah," continued Marx. "I know that's a lot to ask, after what we put you through, but I hope that you will be willing to cooperate with us. We would also like to offer you financial compensation for the injury we have done to you, if you are prepared to sign a release. But we can talk about that later."

Sabah had been rubbing his eyes after the blindfold was removed, like a mole emerging from his hole in the ground and adjusting to the light. Now he looked at them warily, especially at Marx. He had not realized there was a woman present during the earlier interrogation.

"Who are you, please?" he asked Marx.

"I am an American intelligence officer. So is my colleague here. My name is Edith Halsey and this is Mr. Samuel Potter. You can call the U.S. Embassy and ask for the regional security officer. He will vouch for us."

She handed him a piece of paper with her new alias and a telephone number at the embassy written on it. He put it in the pocket of his blue jeans.

"What do you want from me?" asked Sabah. "This is very confusing."

"It's been confusing for us, too, if that's any consolation. But I think now we understand it better. The man who contacted you, who called himself George and gave himself the code name Perihelion, is not an American at all. We think that he is a Pakistani Muslim and a very dangerous person."

"That is impossible. He said he was an American. He spoke of the earlier work. He hated the jihadists. He was working against them."

"It's called a 'false flag,' Mr. Sabah. A man from one country pretends to be from another, to get cooperation. Israelis pretend to be Americans. Americans pretend to be Canadians. It's part of the game."

"I don't like it. It's lying."

"I'm sorry, Mr. Sabah. But lying *is* the game."

The Lebanese-Belgian shook his head. It was too much to absorb in one evening.

"How could George know all the details of your programs, if he wasn't one of you?"

"We don't know. That's one reason we need your help."

"I'm not sure. I need to think. After all this . . ." He gestured to the room and, by extension, to the events of the last several hours.

"We don't have time for you to think about it, Mr. Sabah. This man is responsible for the deaths of some brave Americans, and he will kill more people if we do not find him. We can't wait."

Sabah was shaking his head.

"I do not know. *C'est trop.* This is dangerous for me, too."

"Let me show you something," said Marx. She removed a piece of paper from a folder and handed it to him. It was a copy of the list of four bank account routing numbers that Malik had given her in Islamabad.

Sabah studied the paper. This was a code that he understood well. He handed it back.

"I know what this is. I obtained this wire-transfer information for George. This was his most recent request. Is this a trick?"

"No. Not a trick. We know you were helping him, but we want to believe that you made a mistake. I want to show you something else."

She passed a second sheet to him. This was the transcript of the call between Sabah and his contact, shorn of its Pakistani ISI tailings. He looked at this one for a long while, and then put his head in his hands.

"*Haram*," he muttered, using the Arabic word that in Lebanon connotes wrongdoing, for Christians and Muslims alike.

Marx spoke now with a harder tone in her voice.

"I hope you can see now why it is so important that you help us, Mr. Sabah. These documents connect you with a man who is a terrorist. If you do not work with us, we will have to assume that you are working against us. You would not be happy with that situation, I'm certain."

Sabah sighed. He knew that he was caught, more tightly now than before when he had been hooded.

"So I do not have a choice," he said.

"No. Not really. There is only one good answer for you."

"I will do what I can," he said glumly. "What is it that you want?"

"We want you to help us catch him."

"You mean that I am the cheese, and he is the mouse?"

"Yes, that's the idea," said Marx. "But this man is no mouse. He is somewhere between a rat and a snake. He has a motive, and he wants to kill, and right now you are the only chance we've got. I hope that makes you feel better, knowing that you are important."

"It does not make me feel better," said Sabah. "Nothing will make me feel better until I am rid of all of you."

They took a break. Everyone was tired. Sabah's contact records and datebook were in his laptop computer at home. They needed the computer, and every digit of email and phone information it contained about the man who had posed as George. Sophie Marx would take Sabah to his apartment, where they could retrieve the computer files.

But right now the dog Émile was barking annoyingly in the hallway and Sabah went to check what was wrong.

32

STUDIO CITY, CALIFORNIA

Jeff Gertz had a two-part rule for dealing with trouble. It dated back to when he worked for the Counterterrorism Center traveling to Iraq and Afghanistan: First, always have a plan for what to do if something bad happens; and second, always be the first to move when danger strikes. Don't wait for others to run for shelter when a mortar round comes in, or to open fire at a hostile checkpoint, because by then it will be too late: Have a plan, move first. The threat in this case wasn't shrapnel or bullets, but it was deadly nonetheless. Gertz had one other rule. It was the cardinal precept of the rational man: Save yourself first, and worry about the others later.

The morning Cyril Hoffman called him to report that someone had tried to kill Sophie Marx in Islamabad, Gertz understood that the structure he had built was collapsing. He didn't know how or why Sophie Marx had been targeted, or even what she had been doing in Pakistan, but it was clear that every outpost of his network was vulnerable. It wasn't a matter of physical danger; he was deft enough to stay alive. His problem was more mundane: He needed to clean up the mess before it created an open scandal that would lead to his political and legal ruin.

He cursed Sophie Marx for her disloyalty and, more, for being smarter and tougher than he had expected. But he couldn't afford the luxury of personal animosity now.

Gertz called Ted Yazdi at the White House. There was no answer on the STU-5, so he sent a message to Yazdi's BlackBerry and got a quick, ostentatious message: *In Oval. Can't Talk*. Gertz responded: *We have trouble. Must see you in DC soonest to explain*. After five minutes, the White House chief of staff sent back his answer: *Meet me at ten tonight. Same place in Bethesda. Don't do anything stupid.*

Gertz called the Burbank airport and alerted the crew of the Gulfstream that he would be leaving in an hour for Dulles. Then he had his secretary send out a book cable to everyone in the system, saying that he would be holding an emergency staff meeting in twenty minutes. Overseas personnel could watch on secure videoconference.

That left just enough time to call back Hoffman at Langley. When they had spoken earlier that morning about Sophie Marx, Gertz had been angry and flustered, but now that he'd had some time to digest the news he was cold as a stone.

"We're shutting it down," he told Hoffman. "Fire sale. Everything must go. It will take about a week. Then, bye-bye birdie. *Finita la commedia,* as you opera buffs would say."

"Isn't that a bit rash, Jeffrey? We don't know how serious the damage is yet."

"Yes, we do. We know there's a leak. We know the boat is going to sink. It may take a week or a month or a year to go under, but we know how the story ends. You and Miss Priss can do what you want, but I'm not sticking around."

"What do your chums in the White House think about your liquidation plans? They seemed rather enthusiastic about this business enterprise."

"They don't know yet. I see them tonight. But they'll agree when I tell them the alternatives. They'll love me for it."

"Everyone loves you, Jeff. Always. We're just never sure what you're doing."

Gertz ignored the rebuke. He didn't have time to joust with Hoffman. The staff meeting was in ten minutes.

"Here's what I need from Headquarters. Number one, silence. This organization never existed. It doesn't exist now. So that will make it easy when it doesn't exist in the future. Do we agree on that? No statements, no briefings, no IG reports. Deaf and dumb."

"We will be silent as lambs. What's number two?"

"I may need help with relocation, severance, all of that. We have some decent people. I want them taken care of. Otherwise, they'll talk."

"I thought you had arranged all of that, dear boy. Weren't you supposed to be self-funding?"

"Nobody's perfect. And it appears that my funding mechanism isn't quite as airtight as I thought. Contamination problem. It could even involve fraud, the lawyers tell me. I put the Brits on the case a few days ago. Serious Fraud Office. They love catching rich Americans who have been gaming the system."

"Oh, do they, now?" Hoffman chortled. "It really is *sauve qui peut*, isn't it?"

"That's the Gertz family motto, Mr. Hoffman. Along with, 'Don't get caught.'"

"You are an unpleasant man," replied Hoffman.

"So what?" he said.

"I have one piece of advice for you in this self-demolition exercise: Don't leave any loose ends. They have a way of catching up with one, or should I say, with you."

"I won't. Speaking of which, where's my faithful employee, Miss Marx? I take it she works for Headquarters now. What's she doing?"

"Well, that's just it. She's looking for loose ends. Clever girl, Brave, too."

"She won't find any. But if she can figure out how this mess happened, more power to her."

"That's very generous of you, old boy. And unless I'm mistaken, she's well on her way."

"This is a fun conversation, Mr. Hoffman, but I've got to go. I have a staff meeting and then a flight to D.C. Give the director a kiss on the bum for me, eh? That's your specialty."

"You are a most unpleasant man," Hoffman said emphatically as he hung up the phone.

The double doors of the conference room on the third floor were open wide, but the staff trickled in single file, as if it were a TSA security line at the airport. People were mostly silent. They looked tired and on edge; many of them had been sleeping at the homes of friends of relatives for the past week; they had been taking the bus or borrowing vehicles from neighbors, instead of driving themselves to work in their own cars. Most of them had stopped using credit cards. The rumor mill had it that anything with a digital address, even in alias, was insecure, so people tried to protect themselves. Some had even sent their children away.

They were scared, plain and simple. Their boss, who was supposed to explain it all to them, had been away on unexplained travel, and when he was in the office, he was short-tempered and distracted. People didn't want any false assurances of security, they just needed to know what was going on.

The room was nearly full when Gertz arrived. He made a circular motion with his finger to the video technician, to the get the camera rolling for the secure videoconference. He waved to friends and coworkers and shook a few hands as he made his way to the podium. They were nervous, everyone fearing some new disaster, but the boss was smiling, so most of them smiled back. He had worn a tie to the office that morning, but had taken it off before the meeting. In his open-necked shirt he looked, if not quite relaxed, at least less uptight than in recent days.

When he reached the podium he tapped the microphone once, to make sure that it was on, and then started speaking.

"Ladies and gents, I want to share some good news," he began. There was a flutter in the room. The people who knew Gertz best didn't react at all; they understood that he was just clearing his throat.

"I want to report that we are taking decisive steps to protect our people, here and overseas. I know how difficult this period has been for everyone, and it would be wrong to ask you to live with continued uncertainty. That would not be fair to any of you, not after how hard you have worked."

That brought nodding of heads and some exhalations of relief. One woman who worked in Support actually said, "Amen." But Gertz was still priming the pump.

"Your security and safety have to come first. That's my point. I have been looking for a way to do that, while at the same time continuing The Hit Parade's mission and normal operating tempo. I am sorry to say that it cannot be done. You can't maximize two variables at once, as my economics teachers told me in college. The variable I have decided to maximize is your security."

Gertz paused, and people looked at each other, wondering what he was telling them, beneath all the fluff. But he was getting around to it.

"What that means, unfortunately, is that we are going to have to close down our operations, and we must do it in a hurry."

Now there were groans, and someone in the back muttered, "No way."

"Nobody hates this more than me, folks. This is my baby, and I have lived and sweated every minute of our time together. But we are losing people, with many more at risk, and I cannot rule out the possibility that our most secure procedures and systems may have been compromised. That puts everybody in jeopardy. We can't live like that. Am I right? Tell me if you disagree."

The docile souls up front who had been following along on cue nodded their assent once more. Of course he was right. He was the leader. He had the big heart.

"I had asked Sophie Marx, our chief of counterintelligence, to lead our effort to identify the security problem that has led to the deaths of your colleagues. Perhaps that was unwise on my part. As some of you cautioned me at the time, she is a relatively junior officer without much management experience. In any event, she has failed to make progress, and during this time The Hit Parade's risk profile has actually increased. She made an unauthorized trip to Pakistan, at a time when such travel was forbidden, and she was attacked, unsuccessfully. I blame myself for this poor choice of personnel. She has been relieved of duty, pending a more detailed investigation."

Marx had aroused so much envy with her rapid rise that people nodded in support for her firing, too, especially some of the women in the office, who might have been expected to back up one of their own. In bad times, every organization needs a villain on whom to blame bad events, and Gertz had given them one.

"We are going to have to move quickly now, and with good discipline. A retreat under fire is the hardest maneuver in warfare, as our ex-military colleagues know. So here is what we will have to do over the next few days:

"First, our cover company, The Hit Parade LLP, will declare bankruptcy the day after tomorrow. I asked the legal team to begin preparing the papers last week, as a contingency. Now they will be filed. We are a small company and very privately held, so that shouldn't generate too many ripples. In the meantime, we need to get all the secure paperwork and computers out of here. My deputy, Steve Rossetti, will coordinate this rapid movement with the associate deputy director's office at Headquarters. Some of you will have to stay late tonight and tomorrow to get everything bundled and on the trucks. Again, I leave the details to Steve."

Gertz turned to face the video monitor and the foreign staff. He was like an actor that way. He knew how to cheat to the camera, to establish an intimacy with his audience that was palpable, if also false.

"May I say to our brothers and sisters overseas, who have been taking the biggest risks without complaining or panicking: I want all of you home within a week. We will close all the foreign offices as quickly as we can. If you can't find a tenant for your office space or apartment, just leave it. We'll clean that up later. We will be bringing everyone home under false documentation. I want you to contact your nearest embassy or consulate and ask for the senior CIA officer. They will get you documentation and cash.

"No alias credit cards, please, no draws on your existing banks and if you haven't already left your current residences and offices, do so now, when this briefing ends. No bullshit, folks, there are no heroes in this movie. These movements will be coordinated by Tommy Arden in Support.

"Now let me come back to where I started, which is the good news. Everyone will be taken care of. There will be jobs in the system for anyone who wants them. You are all under cover, and I remind you that the secrecy agreements you signed are absolute, permanent and enforceable by U.S. criminal courts. Those who prefer to retire will get generous termination and relocation assistance. There will also be special 'hazardous duty' bonuses for everyone on the staff. They will be substantial.

God knows, you have earned them. Okay? Tommy Arden will be setting up a special HR 'help desk' to take care of the details."

Arden, sitting in the back, hadn't heard a word of this until now. But he stood up and waved his hand so everyone could see him.

Gertz looked around the room. People were dazed, basically, trying to take it all in. The circus was pulling down the tents and leaving town.

"Any questions?" he asked.

Before any of the bewildered employees had chance to raise their hands, Gertz was already moving away from the podium.

"Let's do it!" he said, with his fist raised in the air.

The applause was tentative at first, and then it petered out. They walked out, in silence and submission.

Ted Yazdi was waiting that night at his friend's house in Bethesda. It was a too-comfortable suburb, oversized homes set back in the trees. The houses were aglow from external lights that beamed up the pillars and porticos; the trees were alight, too, their branches illuminated by spots and floodlights. These people spent more on landscaping in a year than the average family did on food and shelter. Yazdi's rendezvous rested atop a green hill, across a moat traversed by a stone bridge. In the garage was a Lexus hybrid SUV with a sticker on the rear bumper that admonished: REMEMBER DARFUR.

Yazdi was sitting in the garden out back, fingering his BlackBerry and sucking down a Diet Pepsi. It was about 10:20 when Gertz arrived, escorted by one of the Secret Service agents on duty.

"You're late," said Yazdi.

"I had to fly across the country. Thunderstorms. I'm sorry."

"So fucking what? Not my problem. You're late, and you requested this meeting. That pisses me off. What's going on?"

Gertz surveyed the garden. It was a cool night, with a harbinger of fall in the air. The nearest house was a quarter mile away, and Secret Service agents were guarding the perimeter. Still, it was out in the open, not a good place for a sensitive conversation.

"Shouldn't we go inside?" asked Gertz. "Somewhere more secure."

"I like it here. I was inside at ten, but now I'm outside. Let's forget about the seating chart and do our business. I have to get up early tomorrow to help the president open a wind farm in Okla-fucking-homa. So what's this 'trouble' that you needed to see me about? It better be important."

Gertz was on his back foot. He had gotten off to a bad start. He needed to frighten the chief of staff enough to take action, but not so much that he panicked him into doing something that would make the situation worse.

"We have hit an iceberg, Mr. Yazdi. We are taking on water. I want permission from you and the president to close down the operation."

"Close down Operation Pax? The friendship payments, the whole thing? The president loves that stuff."

"I'm sorry. I know you were excited about those special activities. But they have become too risky."

"Risky for who? Not the president. And what's this iceberg you're talking about? I don't see any freaking iceberg. It sounds to me like you're covering something up. You'd better explain what's going on. Take it slower this time."

"You know about out security problem. I've briefed you on it before. You know that we have lost four officers. We nearly lost a fifth one the other day in Islamabad. It has gotten too dangerous out there. More people are going to get killed and the whole thing is going to blow."

"Whose fault is that? Not mine. Why is all this bad shit happening?"

"People have gotten hold of our address book, Mr. Yazdi. They know where we are. They're coming after us."

"But I thought you had that contained. We put out your total-denial, piss-off statement about Tawhid, and it worked, right? That's what you told me. So what's the squawk now? I never thought of you as the 'cold feet' type, but maybe I was wrong."

Gertz's soft sell wasn't working. Yazdi was too cranked up. He would have to try a different approach.

"Look, Mr. Yazdi, it's not just the attacks on our officers. That's part of the problem. But people are going to find the money trail if we don't shut things down quickly."

"What money trail? I thought you said there wouldn't be any trail. That was the pitch. This would be self-funding and self-liquidating. I don't know how many times I heard that from you. Was that bullshit?"

"That was the truth. We were self-funding, but now it's time to liquidate. That's what I'm telling you, Mr. Yazdi. We need to shut the operation down, bring everyone home. Turn off the money machine. In the process, we need to build a cover story to explain why billions of dollars have been bouncing around the world like Ping-Pong balls. And why people have been making fortunes trading on inside information."

"Too much detail. Just liquidate it. This is your problem, not mine."

"Just a heads-up, Mr. Yazdi: Our hub is in London. The British will take it down. It will look like a fraud investigation. We will keep it far away from you and the president, I promise you."

"What the hell is that supposed to mean? 'Far away from you and the president.' We don't have anything to do with this. What the fuck are you talking about? This is your mess. That's the deal."

Yazdi almost shouted these last words. Gertz put his finger to his lips, to get him to shush. He had him now.

"The president authorized these programs, Mr. Yazdi. There's a trail of authorities and permissions. Even where there were no formal presidential orders, there were subsequent memoranda for the file, and legal opinions. We don't do things on our own, Mr. Yazdi, as you well know. What's important is that this documentation should never, ever become public."

Yazdi stood up angrily, walked a few paces toward the house and then paused, weighing his options. He returned to his chair in the garden and wagged his finger at the intelligence officer.

"You are a cocksucker, Gertz. Don't ever threaten me or the president, ever. It won't work. Stop this bullshit right now and tell me how you're going to solve this."

Gertz's manner sweetened, now that he had his man locked up.

"I promise you there won't be any connection, if we do this right. No fingerprints. Clean as a whistle. But I need a free hand to close this down, quickly and efficiently, and do what I think is necessary. Do I have your authority? And I don't just mean now, but a year from now, if it takes that long. It will be complicated if you say no, because I've already started."

The chief of staff looked tired and deflated, a balloon that had lost its air and gone soft and rubbery around the edges. Gertz had scared him, and he was a man who made his living giving other people heartburn.

"Sure," said Yazdi. "What the fuck? Just make it go away."

33

LONDON

Thomas Perkins referred to the fraud investigation as "the witch hunt." From the first morning when the Metropolitan Police arrived in Mayfair Place with warrants and summonses, the campaign was conducted as much by insinuation and whisper as by hard evidence that could be put before the prosecutors and magistrates. Across Mayfair, people seemed to know that Perkins's firm was in trouble before they had any inkling why. A small crowd formed in Stratton Street behind the yellow tape in the first minutes after the fraud squad ascended the elevators. Where had they come from? How did they know?

When Perkins's employees asked him what was wrong that first day, he answered that he didn't understand what had triggered the raid. But that was not entirely honest. He had a good idea where this tangle began, but he could not speak about it to anyone who didn't already know.

The police set up a desk that morning in the entrance lobby of the building on Mayfair Place, before you even got to the elevator. On the top floor, where Alphabet Capital had its offices, the investigators took over a suite to coordinate their work. There were representatives from the Serious Fraud Office, the Financial Services Authority and, for good measure, a Foreign Office representative who was, in fact, an officer from MI6. The police cordon had the useful effect of providing security, though Alphabet's staff did not understand just how providential that was.

Perkins had been frantic the first day. He tried to contact the man he knew as Anthony Cronin. He called the cell phone number that Cronin had given him, and then another number to be used in emergencies only. On the cellular number, he received a message saying that the account was no longer in service. The emergency number rang and rang, but nobody ever answered. Perkins also sent emails to the account that Cronin had used, but they bounced back with an error message saying that it was a nonexistent address.

Sophie Marx's call from Islamabad, a few hours after the police had raided the office, had only confused Perkins. He called her back twice the next day, but each time it rolled over to voicemail, and he didn't leave a message. He didn't want to make a nuisance of himself, so he waited through the first twenty-four hours trying to make sense of what was happening.

On the second day of the securities dragnet, Perkins decided to contact Felix Stern, the representative at Fédération des Banques Suisses who handled his private, numbered accounts. These accounts had been created more than a year ago as "special-purpose vehicles" at the insistence of Mr. Cronin. They received a portion of the funds generated by Alphabet Capital from trades based on "the system," as Cronin liked to call it, of intelligence tips that generated arbitrage opportunities. Under the agreed formula, 20 percent of the firm's monthly capital gains would be skimmed into the Swiss special-purpose vehicle accounts, where they would be divvied up between Perkins and Cronin's team.

Felix Stern had handled all the details. The profits had been split into two accounts: The first was controlled by Perkins and was his money, to do with as he liked. The second was to be used by Cronin and his operatives, such as Howard Egan. The split was 25 percent to Perkins's account and 75 percent for Cronin and his network. That was an unequal division, but the flow of money was so substantial that until very recently Perkins had been entirely happy with the arrangement. His share of the proceeds was now approaching two billion dollars. Rather than manage it actively, the way he did with Alphabet's proprietary accounts, he simply let it sit in fixed-income securities, accumulating interest. Even at the low prevailing rate of about 3 percent, the fund was spinning off nearly sixty million dollars of additional cash a year.

Perkins had made a practice over the past year of checking with Stern once a week. The FBS officer held the documentation for the account himself, in his drawer, as it were. Perkins had always assumed the banker was Cronin's man, under some mysterious arrangement he did not need to know, and Stern had kept track of the sums well enough.

So Perkins, not sure now where else to turn, tried to contact this same Stern, the financial manager he had shared with the now-vanished Anthony Cronin. Rather than using one of his own phones, he borrowed a cell phone from his housekeeper at the townhouse on Ennismore Gardens. He dialed Stern's number at the FBS office on Quai Gustave Ador in Geneva.

A secretary answered. She said that Mr. Stern was unavailable, but that his accounts were being handled by a colleague, Mr. Traub, and Perkins asked to be connected.

"This is Herr Traub," said a very proper German-Swiss voice. Perkins identified himself and said he wanted to inquire about the status of his accounts with FBS. He read off the number of the principal account he had created, with Cronin's help, and gave other identifying details.

"Is this Mr. Thomas Perkins?" asked the banker, wanting to make sure that he had it right.

"Yes, I just told you that, for Christ's sake. Come on, Traub. I want to know the status of my account."

"I must advise you that I am recording this call, Mr. Perkins."

"I know, for 'quality assurance purposes.' Fine, very Swiss. Thank you."

"Your account has been frozen by order of the Swiss Financial Market Supervisory Authority. I am sorry. The order was executed this morning. I am happy to tell you about the account, but you cannot touch the money, I am afraid."

Perkins felt a chill. He put down the handset for a moment, then put it back to his ear.

"Why has my account been frozen? And how does anyone even know about it in the first place? This is a numbered private account. What the hell is going on?"

"That I cannot say, Mr. Perkins. You must ask the Swiss police or the FMSA. Maybe they can tell you, maybe not."

"Where's Mr. Stern? I want to talk with him. Felix Stern. He handles my account. Where is he?"

"I am sorry, but Felix Stern is no longer with the firm. I believe he has left the country. I have been instructed to handle all his business."

"Left the country? What about the other Alphabet Capital account that Mr. Stern was handling? It was much larger than mine. It was opened last year by an American named Anthony Cronin. I was a cosignatory. What about that account? Is that frozen, too?"

"I am very sorry, Mr. Perkins, but I cannot help you there, either. Any other accounts handled by Mr. Stern must have been closed or liquidated. I do not have any record of them. Let me look here on the computer to make sure . . . No, I am sorry, there is no record of any other account. Just yours."

"You mean the other money is gone?"

"Excuse me, please. I am not following you."

"Holy shit," said Perkins. "It's all gone."

"Could you repeat, sir? I did not understand."

Perkins ended the call. He was frightened, and he did not know where to turn or what to do.

Perkins remained in his office overlooking Mayfair, as representatives of the various investigative agencies came to him with their requests for documents. Keeping him company was his lawyer from Washington, Vincent Tarullo, plus a British solicitor named Jacob Gormley, who knew UK securities law. After the first two days of the inquiry, they discovered that there was very little they could do to prevent the pillaging of their files. The authorities had warrants and orders for every piece of information they sought, and they seemed to know what they were looking for.

A pressing problem for Perkins was dealing with his lenders and investors. By now everyone in Mayfair knew that Alphabet Capital was in trouble. Within minutes after the first police raid and sequestration of records, Perkins's own traders had been on the phone to their friends at other hedge funds and investment banks, asking if they knew what was going on. The rumors had spread in a viral chain. By the end of the first day, Alphabet Capital's swap arrangements at other firms had been suspended, and the next morning its credit lines were frozen by the firm's major lenders.

The credit squeeze wouldn't have been a problem by itself. Perkins's firm was well capitalized, thanks to its extraordinary profitability. But as word of its trouble spread, investors in the fund got nervous. There were calls all that second day from investors requesting redemptions, which was a polite term for pulling out their money. Alphabet Capital had a standard forty-five-day notification requirement, and many of its investors had signed one-year lockup agreements, which prevented them from withdrawing their money without severe penalties.

But the lockups and other precautions proved to be of little use. Late on the second day of the witch hunt, the Serious Fraud Office made a formal public announcement that it was conducting a criminal investigation of Alphabet Capital's trading activities. Lawyers for several of Perkins's largest investors were on the phone within minutes, saying that the lockup and notification agreements were nullified in the event of fraud. They wanted their money out.

Perkins instructed his managers to honor any valid redemption requests, and the firm massively sold off assets that second day, both fixed-income and equities. But it's in the nature of things in the financial world that bad news breeds more of the same, and the firm's distressed selling compounded its losses severely. By the third day, it had gone from the jewel of Mayfair to a firm that was perceived to be in a death spiral. No other major firm was prepared to act as a counterparty without a hefty risk premium, which accelerated the downward momentum.

Sophie Marx called Perkins back the second evening of his troubles. She was in Brussels then, with problems of her own, but she didn't mention them.

"Talk to me, Tom," she said. "What's going on?"

"I'm fucked. I didn't get out soon enough. Your friends have left me high and dry. They have pulled the plug on everything and disappeared. I am holding the bag. The British have their financial goons all over me. They've camped out here. It is a complete wipeout. Investors are running for the exit. So is anybody on my trading floor who can get another job. I don't know if I can make it another month."

There was a deadness in his voice that frightened her. In every other encounter with Perkins, he had been a resilient and buoyant personality. He had seemed to lead a charmed life. Now his voice carried the sound of exhaustion and despair.

"Hang on, Tom. These people aren't my friends. I've quit. I'm trying to undo their screwups. I can help you. You just have to give me some time."

"It's too late. They've taken me down, Sophie. They have all the cards. I'm ruined."

His words carried iron weights that were pulling him to the bottom. He was drowning.

"Stop it!" she said. "Stop feeling sorry for yourself. These people are professional manipulators, but they make mistakes. Trust me. Don't give up."

"I don't ever want to hear those words again, 'trust me.' You fucked me, Sophie, you and your friends. You have destroyed my life. Now go away and let me pick up the pieces."

"Listen to me. Get a grip. You're worrying about the wrong thing. People from Pakistan have been inside Alphabet Capital. They know all your secret money flows. That's why people have been getting killed. You have to be careful. There are more important things to worry about than getting busted."

Perkins gave a long exhale, a sound of ruin and defeat.

"You have not been listening to me, my dear. The people inside Alphabet Capital who have been stealing its secrets are your people. They have looted me and left me for dead. I don't want to hear any more of your crusader stuff. It's all over. I'm finished. If someone shoots me or sets off a bomb at Alphabet Capital, they will be doing me a favor, frankly. So leave me alone, all of you."

Perkins ended the call.

Sophie's eyes filled with tears. What he had said was true; she had been part of a ruinous, deadly process. She cared what happened to Perkins, and she wished she could give him some of her strength.

34
LONDON

On the third morning of the witch hunt, the chief of the Special Fraud Office himself, Herbert Crane, OBE, paid a visit to Perkins's office. He was in his late forties, young to be decorated, but he had distinguished himself in cleaning up the City of London, to the extent that was possible, after the financial meltdown. He had a chip on his shoulder; he didn't like the world of Mayfair, and he especially didn't like American interlopers like Thomas Perkins, who had used the relatively relaxed rules of the British financial markets to take risks and cut corners—and bring ruin on themselves and others.

Crane brought with him to the meeting a red-haired Scotsman named Angus Ward, who was his chief forensic accountant. Ward had been combing the files for the previous two days and had the eager, twitchy look of a hunting dog closing in on its prey. The investigators sat on one side of the conference table; Perkins and his lawyer sat on the other. The two British men had three briefcases lined up between them, a veritable archive. They both were leaning forward as if ready to spring.

Perkins and his lawyer were slouched back in their chairs, their body language advertising that they wanted to be anywhere but in this room. Tarullo's bulky frame and slicked-back hair gave him the look of a lounge singer on a bad night.

The fraud chief turned on a tape recorder, introduced himself and his colleague and asked Perkins to do the same. Perkins's voice, drained of energy, was barely audible, so Crane asked him to speak up. The American spoke again in the same flat voice, so the interrogator simply repeated the name loudly, for the record, and then began with his questions.

"I want to show you a series of trades made by your firm," said Crane, "and I would be grateful if you could affirm that these trades were, indeed, made by Alphabet Capital."

The SFO chief passed a series of papers across the table, while his accountant read a summary of what they contained. The first was dated in late 2007, and there were other trades in the succeeding months.

"UK gilts," intoned the investigator, as Crane pushed his document across the shiny tabletop.

Perkins studied it and nodded. Tarullo, the American lawyer, interjected that he reserved the right to challenge the accuracy of the document later, along with all the others, in the event that there was a formal legal proceeding. His reservation was noted and the inquisition continued.

"UK credit-default swaps, on four separate trading occasions, in March, April, May and June of 2008," continued the investigator. Four sheets passed from hand to hand.

"I get it," said Perkins. "You're just going after the old stuff, when I was on my own."

"Shush!" said Tarullo.

"Excuse me?" queried the fraud chief.

"Nothing," muttered Perkins. Now that he understood the game, he was losing interest.

Tarullo, the lawyer, objected that Crane was using copies of documents, and that unless the originals were produced they were useless as evidence, and this objection was also duly noted.

Crane rolled on with his recitation of suspect trades.

"British sterling, intra-day trading and futures, very large movements." Once again, the documents were transmitted, over legal protest.

So it went, as the investigators peeled off their deck of cards. The transactions all involved assets whose movement was affected by the activities of the Bank of England. Some trades involved the securities of certain large corporations that had been subject to British legal and regulatory proceedings over the period.

When they reached the bottom of their stack of papers, the representatives of Her Majesty's government collected them and set them in a neat pile.

"Now, Mr. Perkins, I want to show you affidavits we have received, anonymous for the moment. They link each of these transactions with specific insider information from the Bank of England that was relevant to the trade in question. My accountant, Mr. Ward, will read a summary of this information. You needn't respond to these crown exhibits, unless you choose to do so."

"I object to this procedure," said Tarullo. "You are presenting uncorroborated allegations with no explanation where the information comes from. That's outrageous."

"Of course you object. That's what lawyers do, but it won't make any difference. This isn't a trial. It isn't a formal hearing. It is an informal interview. So, please, don't be tedious."

Ward rehearsed the evidence of insider trading, without ever saying precisely how the information might have been transmitted. He noted central bank meetings that had been coincident with trades, news events at the bank's headquarters in Threadneedle Street that had followed Alphabet Capital's moves by hours or days. It was a devastating catalogue of inside information, from somewhere in the bank, which evidently had fueled trades resulting in many hundreds of millions in arbitrage profits to the firm.

Tarullo at first made a show of objecting, even though the fraud chief had warned him it would be useless. But Perkins waved him off. He knew they had the goods. He could remember most of the instances in question; the phone calls to his special cell from his "friend" in the parlors of the bank.

"I've heard enough," Perkins said eventually, with a dismissive wave of the hand. The recitation of his supposed "insider trading" had made him angry, all over again, at the people who had seen his weakness several years before and been manipulating him ever since.

"Why don't you go after my other sources?" Perkins asked.

"I beg your pardon?" said Crane.

"Shut up!" said Tarullo.

"This is all crap," continued Perkins. "I can't believe you would fall for whoever is dishing it out. You should be embarrassed, Mr. Crane. Someone is playing you. You're going to regret this, deeply, later."

"Not likely, that, Mr. Perkins, but brave try." The chief of the Serious Fraud Office wasn't quite done. He looked at his watch.

"I have just a bit more information that I would like to review with you, and then we can call it a morning. Then you can retire with your lawyer and say whatever venomous things you like."

The accountant opened a locked briefcase. Inside was a sheaf of banking files with detailed markings, noting the foreign provenance of the exhibits and the controls applying to them.

"These are Swiss bank records," said Crane. "We have obtained them under seal from the Swiss Financial Market Supervisory Authority. They have been transferred to us under the European Union's agreement to share information when there is evidence of money laundering or other illegal financial activity, such as insider trading."

"Big deal," said Perkins. He was tired of this show. Crane was an actor being manipulated by strings he didn't even see. It was a waste of time. This wasn't the main event; it was the shadow play.

"I object," said Tarullo. "Where did Switzerland come from?"

Crane continued with his narrative. He opened the folder and spread the records before Perkins, keeping a copy for his own reference.

"Do you recognize these documents, Mr. Perkins?"

"Nope. They look fake."

"These are records of the numbered account that is maintained on your behalf at the Fédération des Banques Suisses. I am informed that you inquired about this account as recently as yesterday."

"Prove it," said Perkins.

"I will prove it, I assure you. Now, these records show that the account was opened last September. As you can see from an examination of the records, the total sum in this account is currently one billion nine hundred eighty million dollars. And as you will further see, there have been regular monthly additions to this account. These deposits do not appear to have been declared properly to the Inland Revenue. That would be illegal, if true."

"This is all bullshit, Crane. You are a fool."

"Shhh!" said Tarullo, putting his hand on his client's shoulder. "No need for that."

"Okay. You're not a fool. You're a dupe. This isn't your fault. You don't even understand it. Where's the other FBS account?"

"I beg your pardon? What other account?"

"See? You don't even know your own case. There was another numbered account at FBS that had three times what was in this one, allegedly. What about that account? That's where the real money went, assuming for the moment that there was any."

"You are delusional, Mr. Perkins. There is no other account. We have checked with the Swiss authorities, and the only account at FBS related to Alphabet Capital is the one before you. You are shooting blanks, sir."

Perkins turned to his lawyer.

"This is a joke. Honestly. It would be funny if it wasn't such a serious goddamned menace."

"Serious it is. You are quite right there, Mr. Perkins. And I would advise you to consult with the most serious legal representation as to your situation. We will be making a presentation soon to the director of public prosecutions as to the proper disposition of these facts—yes, I would underline that word, 'facts'—by the crown prosecutors. It will require a most sober judgment on your part."

"Sobriety isn't my strong suit, normally, but I'll work on it. Now I want to ask you a question, Mr. Crane. Is that allowed?"

"Of course. This is an informal interview. You can ask whatever you like. That doesn't mean we will answer."

"Who's your informant? It's obvious that you have a snitch who's telling you all of this nonsense: trades, information, bank deposits. So who's your source? And I don't mean the poor dope at the Bank of England. I mean the person who put you on to him."

"That question is out of order, obviously. You can't expect me to answer it."

"No. But I would expect you to know the informant's identity. If you were doing your job properly, that is. But I would bet my last dollar that you don't know, in this case. You have an anonymous tipster who's sending you all these shit sheets. And maybe you have someone from the 'Foreign Office,' meaning MI6, who's whispering in your ear that it's legitimate. But you yourself don't really know. Am I right?"

Crane didn't answer. But there was just a touch of red on his pasty, pallid, high-born cheeks—the "tell" that the British have been unable to hide since the days of Jane Austen. They blush, the British. That is one of their few national weaknesses.

"Nonsense," said the fraud chief. "Sheer poppycock."

The "informal" interview was over. Crane and his accountant packed up their kit of exhibits and left the building. Perkins huddled in his office with Tarullo, who was furious that he knew so little about the case and the activities that underlaid it. But on that, Perkins wouldn't budge. He had done nothing wrong, he kept repeating, and that was all there was to say about it.

"Ask them in Washington about Anthony Cronin," Perkins told his lawyer. "He's the person who got me into this. Agency business, don't breathe a word, special financial relationship. That's where you have to begin, Vince. Start shaking that tree, and see what falls down. Cronin. C-R-O-N-I-N. He works out of an office in New York on Fifth Avenue, next to the Apple store. He's a member of the Athenian Club. At least that's where I met him once. Brown hair, six feet, gym rat, stars in his eyes. CIA standard issue. Find him and maybe you can graymail me out of this mess."

"You are an asshole, Peabody, really you are. Why didn't you tell me this a year ago, before you were up to your eyeballs in shit?"

Perkins removed his glasses and rubbed his eyes.

"Retrospective analysis is not a useful guide to current problems. It's a mistake to worry about 'sunk cost.' That's what we taught our economics students. If they didn't listen, we told them to pursue another course of study. Law, for example. Do me a favor: Find Cronin, then we'll have something to work with."

"Any other names?"

Perkins thought about Sophie Marx and the implicit pact they had made to help each other escape their situations.

"No," he answered. "Just find Cronin."

Perkins's bad day wasn't over yet. Late in the afternoon, as he was trying to negotiate a line of credit from some wealthy Saudi clients that would allow him to keep Alphabet Capital afloat, he received a visit from the senior Metropolitan Police constable who was heading the delegation that had invaded his workspace these past three days. Tarullo was down the hall, trying to fend off private litigants who were already preparing civil suits against Perkins. He raced back to Perkins's office when the chief constable arrived.

The chief constable, followed by two of his officers, entered Perkins's magnificent workspace. It was a glorious summer afternoon; the streets outside the local pubs were already filling with young people ready to drink away the summer's night. Across Piccadilly at the Ritz, they were finishing up with afternoon tea, tidying up the scones and jam and cucumber sandwiches.

The policeman looked sheepish, like a doctor who was about to perform a procedure that wasn't very dignified for the patient or himself.

"I must inform you that you are under arrest, Mr. Perkins. The Serious Fraud Office, in conjunction with my superiors in Scotland Yard and the crown prosecutors, have determined that there is a serious risk of flight in your case if you are allowed to remain at liberty. So I am afraid that we must take you into custody now."

The two policemen stepped forward. They weren't embarrassed in the slightest. They liked the idea of arresting a billionaire and frog-walking him down to the squad car.

"I object," said Tarullo. "Mr. Perkins is a U.S. citizen. I demand that the U.S. Embassy be informed."

Perkins laughed at this mention of the embassy, the first good laugh he'd had in three days. He put up his hand for Tarullo to be quiet.

"If you are prepared to come with us voluntarily, Mr. Perkins, I am willing to waive the usual formalities of handcuffs and the like. And we can take you down the freight elevator to the parking garage in the basement, where we have a car waiting. There won't be any unpleasantness with the media that way."

"I'll come voluntarily," Perkins said quickly.

"Wait a minute," said Tarullo, repeating once more, "I object, goddamn it."

"Shut up, Vince. A British jail is probably the safest place I could be right now. It will give me a chance to do some thinking."

He walked toward the constable, his arms outstretched.

"Take me. I'm yours," said Perkins with almost a laugh. There was something liberating about the act of surrender.

The two British cops were on either side of him now, grasping his arms. Perkins nodded to the constable, and they began walking out the door of the office, onto the trading floor. Most of the traders had gone home, but the ones that were left watched this little "perp walk" in astonished silence. What on earth had this brilliant man, seemingly impervious to bad fortune, done to bring about such a sudden and devastating reversal?

Perkins strode toward the back elevator, accompanied by his three escorts in their constabulary blue. As he passed the desks, he waved to several of his longtime employees. Though he had made them tens of millions of dollars over the years, they did not wave back.

35
MONS, BELGIUM

Joseph Sabah's dog, Émile, needed a walk. That was what got them out of the ivy-covered house in Waterloo in the first place. When the miniature poodle finally woke up from the drugs that had been shot into him, he did his business on the rug in the hallway. A security officer proposed to take Émile out for a quick walk, but his owner, Mr. Sabah, insisted on coming along, too, claiming that they would torture the dog if he wasn't present. Soon a small delegation had emerged from the house into the backyard.

The poodle inevitably started barking. That attracted the attention of the neighbors, who weren't used to a dog on the property. One of them, evidently a busybody, called the police to report that there were strange people in the house next door and that the quiet couple who usually lived there had disappeared several days before. The cops might have ignored the call, but for that.

A blue-striped Belgian police car arrived at the door. The CIA officer from Brussels station had to show his embassy ID and do some fast talking to convince the gendarme that a ring of kidnappers hadn't taken over the house, which was, in fact, precisely what had happened.

Sabah was quickly bundled upstairs when the doorbell rang. Major Kirby stuck a towel in his mouth as a precautionary measure. That didn't do much for rapport with the man who was the team's only channel of contact with the Pakistani mastermind behind the killing of American intelligence officers. They would have to move from the house now to another secure location, bringing along an angry and perhaps uncooperative source.

Sophie Marx proposed that she sit down with Joseph Sabah after the barking-dog incident. During the twenty-four hours that the group had been working together, she had emerged as its leader. She argued now that the only way to regain Sabah's confidence was to be honest with him, even at the risk of violating operational security. Otherwise, he would be useless to them. Nobody disagreed.

Sabah was in his room upstairs, still upset about how he had been manhandled, when the police arrived. Marx knocked, and when he didn't answer, she gently pushed open the door. She was bringing a cup of tea and a plate of cookies as a peace offering.

"It's me, Edith. I brought you a little something to eat, Mr. Sabah." She brandished the tray. "Do you mind if I come in?"

Sabah was scowling, but she was already well into the room, and he didn't turn her away. She set the tray down on the bedside table and pulled up a chair for herself.

"I'm very sorry for the way we have treated you," she said. "I don't blame you for being angry with us. I would be, too."

"I am absolutely furious," he answered. "Look at how you people behave. No wonder everyone hates America."

"You're right," she said.

She looked over at the plate of cookies. There were some Bonne Maman *gallettes* and a stack of chocolate-covered Petit Écolier biscuits. She took one of the dark chocolate biscuits from the plate.

"Do you mind?" she asked.

"Of course not. They're yours. You brought them. You can eat them all. I am not going to help you simply because you bring me sweet biscuits."

She ate the rest of her cookie and handed him the plate.

"Take one, for goodness' sake. They're delicious."

He took a Petit Écolier and had a small bite, then a bigger one.

"You are correct. This is quite delicious. But you did not come to bring me sweets."

"I came to explain something to you, Mr. Sabah. Maybe then you will understand why we have been treating you so strangely."

"Go ahead. But I will not change my mind."

"The man we were talking about before, the man who called himself George. There is something I didn't tell you about him."

"This is a surprise? Ha. You never tell the truth, any of you. Why should I believe you now? This is like Émile chasing his tail."

Marx ignored his comment. She leaned toward Sabah.

"This man George tried to kill me a few days ago in Pakistan. He planted a bomb in my hotel room, which was meant for me. Instead, it killed a Pakistani soldier who was acting as my bodyguard and trying to protect me. They took him out on a gurney. One of his arms had been blown off. When I close my eyes, I can see his body."

"I did not know that. I am sorry for you."

"That's not all. George killed four people I worked with. Two of them were my friends. They were good people, but they died bad deaths. That's why this is personal for me."

"I wish someone had said this before and treated me like a friend instead of an enemy."

"We should have. That was our mistake. I hope it's not too late."

Sabah was still scrolling his catalogue of victimization.

"Those men downstairs are ignorant. They put a towel in my mouth so I could not breathe. They hurt me, but why? What did I do?"

"They're just soldiers. And they are not in charge, Mr. Sabah, I am. That's what I wanted to tell you. This is my responsibility. I have to do something, and you are my only hope. I know you think that we're all liars, but I'm telling you the truth. If you won't help me, then this man will kill more of my friends. He may kill me."

"Is this true?"

"Yes. I need you. That's what I am saying. We all need you. Otherwise we are in a terrible situation, and I don't know how it will end."

Sabah lowered his head. He was a generous man, in his way. He wanted to be helpful to people who needed him. That was why he had been so easy for the Pakistani to manipulate in the first place.

"What do I have to do?" he asked. "You said before that you wanted to use me as the bait. Is that it?"

"Yes. I want you to contact this Pakistani who called himself George. Whatever channel you used before, I want you to use it again. I want you to tell him that you have new information that you need to send him. Can you do that?"

"Yes, I suppose so. But I told you before: The contact information is on my computer at home."

"Will you come with us now, so that you can get your computer from home and move to another safe place? We can't stay here now that the police have visited."

"Can Émile go outside at the new hiding place? He needs exercise. He gets depressed if I do not take him out, morning and night."

"Of course, and he's such a cute dog, by the way. So enthusiastic. But you have to promise to help me. No shouting, no calling out for help, no running away to the Belgian police. If you do that, then the men downstairs will get nervous again. That would be awful. So can you be a good helper for me?"

"I will help, but only for you. You are a trickster, too, but you are smarter. The others I do not want to see."

They took two cars, the van in the garage and a "clean" Audi sedan provided by the station. Sabah and Marx sat in the back of the Audi with Émile, while Major Kirby and the rest of the team crammed into the van.

Brussels station had been watching Sabah's apartment on the Avenue George Bergmann and they reported that it was clear. The Audi idled out front while Sabah and Marx went in together to collect his things. He found the laptop computer and bundled it into a case. Marx suggested that he should pack a change of clothes, too, and any medicines and personal things he might need.

"How long will we be away?" he asked as he collected his socks and underwear from his top drawer. He already had gathered Émile's dog dish and blanket, a bag of dry dog food and a leash.

"A day or two," she answered. "Assuming we catch him. By then you'll be a hero and we'll fly you to Disney World."

"I don't want to go to America, ever. When we are finished, I want to go home. How soon will that be?"

"Soon," she said, leading him back downstairs toward the car before he changed his mind.

The new safe house was a freestanding brick residence south of Brussels, on the military reservation in Mons where NATO had its headquarters. The location was secure and easily guarded. It had a large fenced yard where a dog could bark until he dropped dead without attracting attention. The house had just been remodeled for one of the NATO generals, who had been evicted on short notice.

Marx sat down with Sabah in a large study that had been set aside for them on the ground floor of the villa. He was guarding the computer bag on his lap.

"Do you want me to turn it on?" He held the laptop the same protective way he did his dog.

Marx knew it was urgent to get the information, but she also knew not to rush. Once Sabah turned over these secrets, everyone would be splashing about and the water would get muddy. This was a last chance to get a clear look at the man and what he knew.

"Not yet," she said. "Let's talk a minute first. Tell me how you got started helping us. Remind me what year it was? And maybe you can remember who contacted you and what they asked you to do. You probably think we all work together at the CIA and know the same secrets, but it doesn't work that way."

Sabah smiled and shook his head. America was a very strange country. It was a miracle they didn't have even worse problems.

"The program began in 2002, I think. But they did not ask for my help until three years later, in 2005. They were trying to follow the money flows of Al-Qaeda. They had developed software to look at patterns, you see. They would examine all the data electronically, so that they could follow anyone who had ever touched the bank account or credit card of someone in their database. Then they would look at that person's accounts, and run the traces all over again. It was simple link analysis. They told us that the digital space was our best weapon. Everything had an address, and every event left a signature."

"Why did they need you, Mr. Sabah?"

"Sometimes they had trouble with the Arabic names when they were doing their analysis. They needed people who were cleared into the SWIFT system who could help them make it work. We were consultants. We had to be approved by their security before they would let us into the program. One day we had a videoconference with one of the Americans back in Washington, the big boss who was running things. He gave us, what do you call it, a 'pep talk.' He was very loud."

"Do you remember his name or where he worked, Mr. Sabah? Maybe I could go back and talk to him."

"The name was a false one, I am sure. Mr. Smith. Mr. Jones. I did not take it seriously. But he told us that he worked at the Counterterrorism Center. That was real, I think."

"Yes, sir. The CTC was running that program, with the Treasury Department. What did the man look like?"

"He was thin, tough. He looked like a soldier. I can't remember the rest, really. The video wasn't very clear."

"That's okay. I'll try to find out who that was. Now, you said there were other consultants who were involved in this surveillance program. Do you remember where they were from?"

"All the places you would think. There was a man from Saudi Arabia, a man from Kuwait, one from Morocco, two from Egypt, two from Pakistan, maybe more."

Marx had been making notes as he talked, but she paid special attention now as he spoke of the consultants.

"Did you meet them, these consultants? Did you learn any of their names?"

"Oh, no. That was against security. This was a videoconference, remember. We were all watching from separate locations. I only know about the others because when they began the session, they gave an overview, so that we would know what a big thing this was. They wanted us to feel we were part of something important."

"But there was a consultant from Pakistan, you said."

"Two, I think. But I never saw them. They were trying to protect our identities."

"Do you think George could have been one of the consultants?"

"I didn't think so when he contacted me last year. He said he was an American, and that he had been part of the program, and they were restarting it. But when you told me at the other house that my George was a Pakistani, I thought maybe yes. He might have been one of the consultants. He seemed to know all the same things that I did, when he contacted me."

"We'll get to George in a minute. But what else can you tell me about this meeting with the man from CTC, by videoconference?"

"He was like a coach in one of those American sports movies. He wanted to get us excited. He told us we were part of the war on terrorism, and that people in every country were working with us. He said that by helping identify members of Al-Qaeda, we would help America bring justice to the world. They could not escape, he said, I remember that. He said Americans had big hearts, or strong hearts, or something like that. They could not hide. America would hunt them down and kill them."

Marx made a note to herself, and put a star next to it.

"Anything else?"

Sabah pondered the question a moment, searching his memory, and then came back to her.

"One more thing. He said America had a weapon called a Predator that could follow the Al-Qaeda fighters from the skies, by flying over the places where they were hiding in Pakistan. They had been using it since 2002, but now there were more of them. I had only read about these Predators in the newspaper, but here was someone talking about them. He said that with our help, America would take revenge for September 11, so that it would never happen again. They cannot escape justice, he said. It was supposed to make us feel happy and strong. "

"Did any of the consultants say anything, when this man from the CTC talked about the Predators?"

"Everyone was very quiet. We were all thinking, I suppose, about how powerful America was, that it could follow people and kill them from the sky."

They took a break. Sabah wanted to walk his dog and asked if there were any plastic bags. One of Major Kirby's men kept an eye on him and Émile as they circumnavigated the property several times.

Marx wrote a quick cable for Cyril Hoffman about the discussion she had just had with Sabah. She asked him for two pieces of information. First, she wanted a list of any Pakistani nationals who had been used as consultants during the SWIFT phase of the Terrorist Surveillance Program. She requested every shred of information they had on such people—phone numbers, addresses, travel records, security assessments, reports from liaison services. Second, she wanted a list of any senior officials from the Counterterrorism Center who had briefed foreign nationals involved in the SWIFT program in 2005.

She sent the cable in the restricted-handling channel, requesting an urgent response. But she thought she already knew the answer to her second question.

While dog and master were still outdoors, Marx tried to reach Thomas Perkins in London. His cell phone was turned off. A policeman answered his office extension and said that it would not be possible to talk to Mr. Perkins or leave a message for him at present. That was a relief for Marx, in truth, knowing that Perkins was under police quarantine.

Marx sat down again twenty-five minutes later with Sabah. He looked restored by his brief jaunt outdoors. There were grass stains on the seat of his trousers, from where he had evidently lain down on the lawn for a tussle with Émile. Sabah turned on his laptop computer as soon as he was seated, before Marx had a chance to ask him. He wanted to do his work now and get it finished.

It took thirty seconds for the machine to boot up and the screen to come alight. He opened his contact file and searched for names, mumbling to himself as he tried one, then another. Eventually, he voiced a relieved, "Ah," and called up the name.

"I was looking in the *g*'s for 'George,' but I had him listed by the last name he is using now on his emails, which is a *w*. I forgot that. Do you want the address?"

"Yes, please." She tried to sound at ease, as if this piece of information weren't something her life might depend on.

"It's George.White09@yahoo.com. That's what he called himself, George White. That's the address we used to communicate the last half dozen times. Before that it was GeorgeWhite17@hotmail.com. I still have that address but it doesn't work. He closed the account."

Marx asked for his cell phone numbers. Sabah had two, but he thought they were both dead. The U.S. number was 001-703-202-1211. The Swiss number was 4179-555-6548. She repeated the email addresses and the numbers back to Sabah carefully, digit by digit, to be certain she had them right.

"Do you mind if we take another little break?" she said. "I need to share these with my colleagues so that they can do some detective work."

She gave him a kiss on the cheek, which pleased and embarrassed him, and then excused herself and went into the control room, where they had set up a secure communications suite. Major Kirby brought in the dog to keep Sabah company, along with a sandwich and a glass of beer. Sabah drank the beer but fed most of the sandwich to Émile.

The communications officer helped Marx set the right designators for her message. She sent the cable to Hoffman, this time copying the Information Operations Center, which managed CIA exploitation of cyber-intelligence, and copying the operations center of the National Security Agency, as well. Then she waited.

36

MONS, BELGIUM

Sophie Marx was exhausted. It was only when she had completed her debriefing of Sabah that the fatigue enveloped her; she felt empty, depleted of every calorie of energy and desire. She wanted to collapse into bed, pull a white comforter over her head and sleep for a week. That fantasy of escape was punctured by the anxiety, and the satisfaction, too, of knowing that hundreds of people were counting on her now. She went into the kitchen of the safe house and made herself a double espresso, then drank a Red Bull.

That wasn't enough; she still felt groggy. Come on, girl, she told herself. Get your shit together. She asked Major Kirby whether there was a fitness room in the house, and of course the answer was yes. That was the first thing the Support team had organized when they secured the place, even before they finished the communications room. In the basement, they had installed a recumbent bicycle, an elliptical trainer and some free weights.

Marx spent nearly an hour on the elliptical trainer, striding like a space walker, listening to music on her iPod. She had eclectic tastes, but right now she wanted to hear music by tough women who had been lied to by manipulative men, such as her boss.

On her iPod she had a playlist she labeled "Revenge Music," and she selected it now. Top of the list was Carrie Underwood singing "Before

He Cheats," about a woman who takes a baseball bat and bashes in the headlights of her two-timing lover's car. Then there was Miranda Lambert's "Crazy Ex-Girlfriend," about an angry woman who walks in on her man while he's playing pool with a new girl and thinks of shooting her. For sure, she had "Goodbye Earl," by the Dixie Chicks. But her favorite song on the revenge playlist was Lambert's "White Liar," with its insistence that the truth finally comes out, even for liars. She turned up the volume and closed her eyes.

As the music played, Marx thought about her next steps. Jeffrey Gertz was in one compartment of revenge. But right now she needed to close on her Pakistani target—to flush him from his lair and into the open. The challenge was to think of a prize tantalizing enough that a supremely careful operator like this "professor" would take the risk to go after it. Her legs rocked back and forth on the trainer, keeping pace like a metronome. The more she considered this puzzle, the more obvious it was what she should do.

Hoffman called on the secure phone while Marx was working out. She rang him back a few minutes later when she had caught her breath. Her cheeks were flushed and beads of perspiration dotted her forehead.

"You've had rather a good day," he said. "You have opened the gates, I do believe."

"We don't have our man yet," she answered. "I'm scared we'll blow our chance to get him."

"You should be scared. He is a dangerous man. I called because we have a first cut from NSA. The cell numbers are all dead. We'll run patterns, but I think the links will be dead, too. This man is not a fool. The email address at Yahoo is still alive, but it hasn't been used since the last message to Sabah. So the question is, what next?"

Hoffman paused. He seemed to be waiting for her to pick up the thread.

"I have a suggestion, assuming that I'm running this, and not Headquarters."

"My dear Sophie, you *are* Headquarters. And yes, you're still running the operation. So far you haven't made any mistakes."

"I want to set a trap for the Pakistani. We can use Mr. Sabah to make contact, and we have a live email address, but we need some juicy bait. Otherwise this won't work. I've been thinking about it, and I have the right worm to put on the hook."

"Oh, do you, now? And who might that lucky invertebrate be?"

"Me."

"Preposterous. Out of the question. You almost got killed several days ago in Islamabad. Don't push your luck, my dear. It runs out, even for you."

"Don't you see? The fact that he went after me before will make me an irresistible target. He missed once. This is a very disciplined man. He doesn't like failure. He'll come out of his hole if the prize is big enough. I don't mean to be immodest, but I'm worth the trouble for him. Especially if Sabah sends him a message that will tell him we're up to something really big. He'll surface."

"How unreasonable you are."

"I will take that as a yes, Mr. Hoffman. We'll get to work here on preparing the email message. I'll need some help on details, to make the transfers look convincing. Can Information Ops get into Alphabet Capital's accounts?"

"Of course. We can get anything we like, if we know what to ask for."

"I need to know what accounts were used by Howard Egan, Alan Frankel and Meredith Rockwell, now deceased. Where the money began and where it ended. Send me those account numbers and routing codes."

"You are worthy colleague, Sophie."

"I'm a work in progress. What about the other traces I requested, about the CTC surveillance program and the consultants?"

"We are still digging on the consultants. The true names are originator-controlled, I'm afraid, very tight access. But the first part of your question is easy. The chief of CTC's Al-Qaeda covert-surveillance program at the time was a gentleman whose name will be quite familiar to you, painfully familiar: Jeffrey Gertz, former president of The Hit Parade LLP of Studio City, California, now defunct."

"Is that right?" she said blandly. Of course it was. She had known from the moment that Sabah described the videoconference by the CTC official, the earnest pitch, the bland amorality, that the speaker could only be her boss and sometime mentor.

"Where is Jeff these days? I've been wondering that."

"He has 'gone to ground,' as they say in the fox-hunting milieu. He is conducting a global disappearing act, shutting down anything that has any link with his former activity. He seems to have authority from 'the highest level,' as we like to say euphemistically. He is traveling, at present, but precisely where, I do not know. Do you need me to find him for you?"

"No, the opposite. I need for him to stay out of the way."

"That should not be a problem. I believe that Jeffrey's current preoccupation is saving his own skin."

Marx sat down with Joe Sabah, who seemed actually to have missed her company, and began drafting the email message she would send to "George White." To rouse the Pakistani's interest, she planned to transfer $50 million from an Alphabet account to one that had been used by one of The Hit Parade's operatives. To leave an unmistakable footprint, she decided that the transfer would move directly from Howard Egan's account at FBS to the account he had used in Dubai for his initial meeting with the Pashtun tribal chief Azim Khan.

She found Perkins's secretary, Mona, who was still ensconced in what was left of the office on Mayfair Place, and had her make travel arrangements just as she had only a few days before for Marx's trip to Islamabad. She advised Support to have one of its contacts at American Express make sure the payment cleared, regardless of any restrictions on Alphabet Capital.

Sabah let her examine all his previous messages to "George White," so that she could get the cadence right. He helped her encode the proper SWIFT wire transfer protocols, so the message would have the necessary detail. The final version, tweaked and massaged, was sent from Joseph Sabah's Gmail account to George.White09@yahoo.com, with the subject line, *follow up*. It read:

LARGE TRANSFER FROM PREVIOUSLY MONITORED ACCT FBS GENEVA. ORIGINATING ACCT: FBS AG GENEVA SWIFT BIC FBSWCHZH12A CH08 3771-7938-7155-8039-7. RECEIVING ACCT: CITIBANK NA/DUBAI SWIFT BIC CITIAEAD AE14-5300-5845-251. RECEIVER'S EUROCLEAR NO. 27593. TRANSFER AMT DLRS 50 RPT 50 MIL. APHELION.

The message vanished into electronic space. Marx alerted Headquarters that it had been sent. From that instant, all the surveillance technology available to the United States focused on the Yahoo account of an unknown recipient, and on electronic signals from Pakistan, Dubai and anywhere else that might be linked to any known operative.

Twenty-four hours passed without a nibble. But soon enough, there was a turbulence, a cascade of events, as the prey devoured the shining silver lure.

37
KARACHI

From the turreted windows of the members' lounge at the Karachi Boat Club at dusk, the light on Chinna Creek was a tawny pink. Dr. Omar was visiting one of his university colleagues, a man from one of the "good families" of this merchant city, who wanted to show off the old club. On the walls were yellowing photographs of the first regatta in 1881 and the early boat races against Calcutta, Madras and the other metropoles of the Raj. The people in these old photographs were all white-skinned Anglo-Saxons, the men in blazers and white duck trousers, the women "memsahibs" in enormous hats and lacy white dresses. There was not a dark face among them, but that didn't seem to bother the present-day members. They drank their gin and tonics and whiskeys and celebrated the lost world from which their ancestors had been so systematically excluded.

Dr. Omar was drinking nothing stronger than a Coca-Cola this evening. When he traveled to conferences abroad and wine was poured, he usually had a sip to be polite. He did not make a fuss about halal meat, either, the way some Muslims did. It was part of being a modern man, he liked to say, of living in the present.

Revenge comes in different flavors. Sometimes it is a swift act of rage that shatters the mask the oppressor has created for you. Other times it is a slow process in which the mask is an essential shield to cover actions that the oppressor could not imagine. Sometimes with a disciplined man, the act of revenge is all but invisible.

The professor did not appear to be angry; he was a protean figure who could assume whatever disposition suited the needs of the moment. That was one reason people rarely questioned his activities. He was an elusive personality, cleverer than his fellows. Since he was a boy, he had been off somewhere else, doing things that others knew they wouldn't understand, even if they tried.

The host asked Omar about the new research contract he had received from a European computer-security company. The professor explained modestly that he was only a small subcontractor: He had given a paper nearly a decade ago at a conference in London on encrypted search algorithms, and such papers had brought him a steady trickle of work ever since, enough to pay his bills.

It was almost dark now on the water. The last of the sculls was being hauled up into the boathouse. Across the creek were the dense mangroves of the low water shoals, and beyond in the last light of the evening the dark aquamarine waters of the Arabian Sea, stretching west to Oman and then the world.

Dr. Omar's friend asked if he should buy shares in the one of the Indian IT companies that was now a big software vendor in the subcontinent, and the professor replied no, it was not a wise investment. The future was not in boxed software, but in the "cloud," the applications that would be available on the Internet to all, even in South Asia. He suggested several American companies that would be better bets.

"The financial markets are treacherous," said Dr. Omar. "I was just reading today in the *Financial Times* online that one of the big hedge funds in London may go under. Alphabet Capital, it was. Solid as a rock, people said. Had investors here in Pakistan, too, I believe. But it turned out to be rotten underneath. Fraud investigation and all that, CEO arrested, horrible mess. Not really a surprise. They are too fancy in the West; too clever for their own good."

"Good advice, old boy," said the host. And a jolly nice evening, too, and time for another whiskey. But Dr. Omar had to excuse himself. He was working part of this summer term at Bahria University, near the club, as an adjunct professor of computer science. He had come from

Islamabad a few days before, and he had a bit more work to do that night at the lab. As he left the members' lounge, he admired the old photographs and memorabilia once more, the shots of men in flannel shorts holding their oars, and of men and women bathing together in the creek, before the water became polluted and the culture was transformed.

Traditions mattered, said Dr. Omar's friend, and the professor agreed that it was so.

Dr. Omar was tired. He did not like to admit that to his friend at the club, or to anyone, but it was a fact. He was a boat that was always moving against the tide. He had struggled as a boy to escape the flow of his tribal world, and to find a new set of connections in the West. And he had succeeded, visibly and invisibly. But once those attachments had become firm—visits and conferences and briefings—an event had taken place that compelled him to paddle back toward home, this time entirely in secret. He was never at home, even when he was at home. There was no place that was comfortable or safe.

The professor did not believe in permanent revenge, or in the permanence of anything that involved mortal beings. He had asked himself when it would be time to stop: How much blood would be enough? That was something his father had never explained when he talked about the tribal code. It was measure for measure, but how could you calculate the weight of an insult, or the commensurate volumes of honor and fear?

When he had seen the television footage of the American woman at the hospital in Islamabad, the face of someone he had intended to kill, soothing a Pakistani widow, he had thought: Perhaps it is time. But vengeance is a heavy weight, and the momentum of the thing had carried him forward.

Omar thought of his sister, the sole surviving member of his blood family, who was living in Peshawar. She had a son named Rashid who was now eleven years old. Omar had visited him six months ago, and brought him a small computer as a gift. The boy had pleaded for him to come back, but it was too dangerous to go more often. Too many people were curious about him, and he had worked so hard to erase his past.

It had been uncanny, but on that last trip to Peshawar, his young nephew had asked to play number games.

"I know all the perfect numbers," the boy had said. "Six, twenty-eight, four hundred ninety-six, eight thousand one hundred twenty-eight."

"Very good," Dr. Omar had said. "You are a bright boy."

"I know the prime numbers, too," the boy had boasted. "Two, three, five, seven, eleven, thirteen, seventeen—"

"Those are too easy. Tell me the primes over one hundred."

"One hundred one, one hundred three, one hundred seven, one hundred nine, one hundred thirteen."

"*Bahadur!*" Omar had exclaimed, which means brave man. "Over five hundred."

"Five hundred three, five hundred nine, five hundred twenty-one, five hundred twenty-three . . ."

"*W'Allah!*" Omar had said, patting the boy on the head. As he listened to the numbers spilling out, he had felt himself falling through time. He had rung that same scale as a boy, saying the primes out loud to himself because his father couldn't understand. This boy Rashid would not be caught between two worlds: He would live only in one.

And Omar had thought to himself that day as he finished his visit to his sister's home and said his goodbyes: Perhaps we have come to the end. Perhaps this is the balance.

Dr. Omar walked to the university compound, a half mile from the Boat Club. He passed the cantonment where the senior naval officers had their residences, and then entered the gate of Bahria, which was itself a creation of the navy establishment. The naval engineers had been interested in Dr. Omar's work, like so many others. The porter waved him through the gate and he climbed the stairs to his office, which overlooked a lawn that had faded to a sickly lime-green in the summer heat.

He turned on his computer and checked his mail, account by account. The computer he was using at Bahria was a university machine whose IP address had no connection with him. The professor had nearly a dozen email identities, each with a different name and set of secrets.

Near the end of this session, he visited a Yahoo account that he checked daily on the chance it might contain a new bit of information.

What he saw in the Yahoo account this evening astonished him: The mischief-maker was persistent. You cut off this creature's head, and still it kept moving. You closed down its financial hub and it found another way to move money. And back to Dubai, the same bank, too, and fifty million this time, to pay more bribes. This was arrogance, surely.

The professor had imagined the time when he might be satisfied in his hunger for revenge, but this was a special opportunity. He sent his Belgian correspondent a brief reply in Americanese:

Good stuff. Take care. Perihelion.

The professor moved quickly to exploit this gift of information, using the confidential network he had assembled over the past year. He sent a message to a Pakistani who worked at the Citibank branch in Dubai, and asked him to monitor the receipt of a large transfer coming from an FBS account in Geneva. He emailed another Pakistani who worked for the UAE aviation-security authority in Dubai and asked him to forward the names and credit card numbers of all tickets purchased for travel to Dubai over the next week.

It did not take him long to find a match. By late that night, Dr. Omar knew the identity of the woman who was coming to Dubai and when her flight would arrive. It was a paradox: This very person had appeared to show mercy, and yet she continued her evil work. He could only wonder at the cruel determination of the Americans. Their front company in London was collapsing, and still they continued with their meddling. That was why their adversaries would triumph; this America marched ever deeper into folly. It did not know when to stop. He wanted to go to Dubai himself to settle this account, as it seemed to him. But that would be unwise. Better to contact one of the members of his network.

Dr. Omar sent all his messages and left the computer lab after midnight for his lodgings to catch a few hours' sleep. He rarely communicated in such a burst, but he was impatient.

The watchers and listeners were in place when the mysterious professor surfaced on the Internet. Cyril Hoffman had done his work: Small teams were on the ground waiting in Karachi, Peshawar and other Pakistani cities. Half a world away, people saw the messages, and they carried out the operations that had been planned. They were impatient, as well.

Dr. Omar drifted in and out of time when he put down his head on the pillow. He was sleeping at the apartment of a new friend, Aziz. The professor was changing lodgings every few nights now, to be safe. This man Aziz was part of the network that supported Dr. Omar's work. He was a "connected" man.

Omar awoke suddenly, bathed in sweat. He had felt a sense of vertigo, not just stumbling as we do in our dreams sometimes, but falling through space as if from a great height, with nothing to break his fall. He tried to go back to sleep but he was roused after an hour.

"There is a call, Ustad," said his host. "A man wants to speak to you."

"I am not here. Tell him that it is a wrong number."

"It is one of the brothers. He says he must talk now."

Omar put the phone to his ear. He listened to the voice. He cried out, as if a blade had punctured his skin.

"Call me back, sweet brother, when you know," he said, tears filling his eyes.

Then he dropped the phone. He put his hands to his head and then across his chest. He bowed and tried to kneel in prayer, but his legs were too wobbly and he fell.

"What is it, Ustad?" asked Aziz, reaching out to his guest and steadying him.

"There was a bomb this night in Peshawar at the home of my sister. I do not know if she and my nephew have survived."

He turned to his host, his eyes wide with the horror of this new twist of the tourniquet of vengeance.

"I am not a good Muslim," said Omar, taking his host's hand. "You must help me pray for my nephew."

The two men held hands and prayed together through the last hours of night. At length the phone rang again. Omar could not bear to answer it. He left it for Aziz. The host answered. He smiled and turned to Dr.

Omar. He was still smiling as the tears formed in his eyes. That was how Omar knew that his nephew Rashid and his sister had survived.

"God is great," murmured Omar.

Aziz nodded, but he was puzzled by what had happened.

"They wanted to kill me," said Omar. "I have slept in that house in Peshawar. Instead, they nearly killed this innocent boy and his mother. But this plot failed. Perhaps it is enough."

Dr. Omar put his head back down on the pillow. He had made a promise to God, in his prayers, when his young nephew's life was in the balance. It was one of the promises that we all make when we are trying to bargain with God. *If you spare this one I love, then I will stop. Give me this, and the score is even.*

There was another message sent the next morning. A small bomb detonated at Bahria University just before dawn. The explosion shattered most of the windows in the engineering department, where the computer science faculty had its offices. No students were killed, mercifully. If the bomb had detonated several hours later, as they were coming to class, some of the young men would surely have been wounded.

Dr. Omar thought about his own graduate students when he heard the news. They were young men who had come to the city to do their studies, just as he had years before, the flower of the youth of Pakistan.

"It is a blessing," Omar told his host, who brought him the news.

"But surely it is a curse from the evildoers," replied Aziz. There were fresh tears in his eyes. He was angry. "They meant to destroy you with this bomb, too, Ustad."

"No, it is a blessing, you see, that no one died. There is no more *badal.* We shall not argue about this anymore. I have had enough argument."

Dr. Omar thought: I have brought this danger to people who were innocent. This is what wars do. They destroy the guilty, yes, but also the innocent. That is why all wars must end.

When he bathed and dressed that morning, the professor's ruminations had hardened into a decision. It was time to resolve his business, to go back to the center point. He had been living on two sides of the world, on two sides of the knife. He could not do that anymore. Now it was time to close the double-edged franchise, for the project was nearly complete.

He was exhausted, in his head and heart. It had been more complicated than anyone could imagine. He had conducted his campaign of vengeance, as was required. But he had never stopped the other life, of providing advice and guidance. He had thought of himself as a giver and avenger, combined. He named the beneficiaries of the enemy's largesse, so that these eminent persons were showered with money. Then he arranged to kill the courier-spies who came to deliver the payments. It had the simplicity of the balance wheel in a watch, flicking from side to side. But it could not continue.

Omar sent a message, to an account that he had not used for a very long time, to a man who had once been his mentor, for whom he had acted as a consultant, in fact, in the time before his world went dark. The man did not answer his message, so he called him by phone, using a cellular number that he had been told was only for the most unusual emergencies. It was a clean number; a phone to be used for this one purpose only.

The man answered in the comfortable, noncommittal way that Americans do. Yes, of course he remembered the professor. His consulting help had been invaluable. It would be a pleasure to see him again, indeed. A trip to Pakistan was impossible, but perhaps they could meet in London, where he had business. They would have to meet discreetly, leaving no electronic traces. It is always good to visit with an old contact, said the American, and close a circle.

Just so, said the Pakistani professor. Close a circle. They discussed where they might meet. Neutral ground, where they would both feel secure: a park outside the city. The American suggested Kew Gardens, at the far western end of London, a particular remote area of the park that he named.

The Pakistani made several other requests of the American, naming other people who should be part of their meeting. It was a question of *gundi,* he said. He did not bother to translate the word, and the other man did not ask, but it meant "balance" in the Pashto language.

38
WASHINGTON AND LONDON

Cyril Hoffman's office was on the celestial seventh floor at Headquarters, but not on the fashionable side that looked out over the trees toward the Potomac. That view was afforded to the director and his deputies for operations and analysis, but not to the humble cleanup man, the associate deputy director, the one who kept the place running while the high-flyers and the A-students were off taking credit. His office looked the other way, toward the cafeteria and the dull façade of the new Headquarters building and beyond to the acres of parking lots, cutely named in bright colors: blue, green, yellow, purple.

Hoffman gorged on his unfashionableness and indispensability. He knew the real secrets that kept the place running—where the money flowed, how the safe houses were acquired, where the air assets were sheltered, how their tail numbers were disguised. He understood what his flamboyant relatives in the agency had never realized: Power was not one big thing, but an accumulation of little things.

This was a good day for Hoffman. The systems that he and Sophie Marx had set in motion to track their quarry had worked. For as Hoffman liked to say: Finding a needle in a haystack was not as hard as it sounded, if you had a thread tied to the needle. It was a matter of fusing the lookers and the finders—or, in intelligence parlance, the analysts and the operators. Hoffman had launched this process of location and discovery when he received the operational plan from Marx in Belgium.

This CIA did many things wrong, but it understood this humble job of identifying targets. The targeters were not the "chosen ones" from the Clandestine Service, or "knuckle-draggers" from Ground Branch, but Hoffman's people, the nerds and geeks in the Science and Technology Directorate who thought up the gadgets, the clods in Support who put them in the right places, and the analysts from the Directorate of Intelligence who figured out what the information meant.

Every day, teams of analysts prepared lists for the Joint Special Operations Command. They could map a country's entire telephone network, and overlay the patterns of who had called whom until the Al-Qaeda pockets glowed like Christmas tree lights; they could find the location of a particular cellular handset "of interest" down to the meter, and once they had located the target, they could track it with persistent surveillance and strike when the moment was opportune.

For a few deadly weeks, this process of discovery had eluded the agency because it lacked the right coordinates to program into this architecture of discovery. But now the pieces had combined. The email message from "George White" at Yahoo was monitored instantly through a Yahoo server in the United States. It had taken a little longer to locate the computer in Karachi where the message had originated, but soon enough they had it, and the Information Operations Center in Langley had been able to monitor other messages being sent to and from that computer. Calls to U.S. cell phones were harder to track because of legal limitations, but the rest was easy.

When the analysts called Hoffman to report that they had identified their target, he knew that it was essential to take action to remove this target as quickly as possible, but also in an appropriate way. He roused his CIA colleagues in Karachi, Islamabad and Dubai. He alerted the JSOC liaison at Headquarters to get military assets ready. He had one more essential call, but it could wait a few minutes. First, he wanted to reward himself for his unsung mastery.

He sent his secretary down to the cafeteria to purchase a cup of soft-serve ice cream, a chocolate and vanilla swirl. Some men, when they want to celebrate, might do something reckless—buy themselves a night with a fancy hooker, or get fall-down drunk in public. But Hoffman's pleasures were gentler. When the ice cream arrived, he took from his desk a package of oatmeal cookies and crumbled one on top of the ice cream, to add a crunchy texture to the cool on his tongue.

When he finished his ice cream, Hoffman placed the call to Sophie Marx in Belgium. She was still at the villa on the edge of the NATO compound, awaiting approval to travel to Dubai. She had been dozing, allowing herself the pleasure of an afternoon nap, but she braced up when she heard the voice on the other end of the line.

"We've got him," said Hoffman. "You can unpack your bag and relax."

She was speechless for a moment. When you've wanted something badly, it's hard to believe that it has really happened.

"Thank God," she said. "Who the hell is he?"

"He's a Pakistani computer scientist named Omar al-Wazir. The analysts are still assembling the file, but from what we know he's a Pashtun, some kind of a computer genius. He travels all over. He's in Karachi now, working out of one of the universities there, but he's based at the National University of Science and Technology in Islamabad. I don't think you're in his sights anymore. His main concern right now would be staying alive, I would think."

"Can we grab him? I want this guy in a box."

"I don't think capture would be the right solution here. We're doing a little of this and that. The consulate sent a team last night to the university. Surveillance-plus, shall we say. Islamabad station found another spot where he stayed in the past and sent a team there. We fired a few warning shots, you might say."

"Have you told the Paks?"

"Goodness, no. I make it a rule never to tell General Malik anything unless it's for the purpose of deceiving him. That's the way he treats me, invariably. I will have to tell him something, sooner or later. We need help in dismantling the good Dr. Omar's underground network. We can't kill them all ourselves."

"What have you got on the network?"

"We have identified two people in Dubai, thanks to his messages. The UAE will arrest them at dawn. We're analyzing old message traffic, from Professor al-Wazir and anybody he has touched. Each time we get a good name, we will take them down."

"You are the ayatollah, Mr. Hoffman."

"Thank you, but I haven't told you the most interesting part. We have been running checks on Dr. Omar's contacts with Americans, and guess who turns up in our first run-through? It's a bit upsetting, I have to warn you."

She knew the answer. She felt as if she had known it for days, maybe weeks.

"Jeff Gertz," she muttered.

"Clever girl! How did you know, pray tell?"

"It had to be him. From what Joseph Sabah told me about the consultants, I figured there must have been contact between Gertz and the Pakistani. I just didn't want it to be true."

"Well, believe it," said Hoffman. "Jeffrey has stepped on a rather large turd, I'm afraid."

"What have you got on him?"

"Not much as yet. The analysts have just started looking. But there were regular chats, it seems. This is rather sensitive, as you can imagine. It's embarrassing for us; the White House, too. But we'll pry it loose, and then take a look at it. The White House will want to limit damage, no doubt, and I'm sure they will understand better the case for strengthening the agency that I have been making on behalf of the director."

"Where is Jeff now? Is he still in L.A.?"

"Heavens, no. He closed that operation down, kaput. Your beloved office has probably been turned into a tanning spa or a manicure salon. Jeffrey is on the move, tidying up this, shutting down that. And no wonder. Last I heard, he was on his way to Britain."

"That's my destination, too, Mr. Hoffman. Now that we have our man al-Wazir, I want to go back to London. I left all my things there. I'm sick of wearing the same clothes. And honestly, I'm worried about Tom Perkins. I want to see if there's some way to talk with him. Maybe I can help him out. Do I have your permission?"

"I don't think you need my permission, actually. It's not really clear who you work for. But I would never want to separate a lady from her wardrobe for too long. And if you're going to London, perhaps I'll just come along, too. We can have a reunion, what?"

"A cast party," she said. "Like on the night when they close down a show."

"Not at all, my dear. This show has a way still to run. Just a few cast changes."

39
LONDON

The Metropolitan Police took Thomas Perkins first to a holding cell at the West End Central Station. It was on Savile Row, a few doors away from Perkins's tailor, as it happened. The station was a flat brick box, constructed in the bland, suppressed style of British public buildings of the 1960s and '70s when there never seemed enough money to decorate a façade or build a proper-sized room. The police held Perkins overnight in the lockup downstairs, not sure what to do with him. There was high-level interest in the case, not just from the Serious Fraud Office, but from a young man who claimed to represent the Foreign Office and camped out in the squad room with the sergeant on duty.

That first evening the superintendant's office at New Scotland Yard issued a directive saying that the new prisoner at West End Station was a security risk. The order didn't specify whether the risk was to others or to the prisoner himself, but an extra detail arrived at the lockup to keep an eye on him. The security officers were mum about who had dispatched them, but the sergeant on duty was told by one of his mates at headquarters that they were from the counterterrorism command known as SO15. They established a cordon around the station and banned parking on upper Savile Row and the adjoining Boyle Street.

Perkins himself was quite content. He ate a hearty dinner of spaghetti and meat sauce, and tried to converse with the other two overnight prisoners in the lockup. That was not productive, since both had been arrested for drunk and disorderly conduct. The first was raving piss-drunk and the second passed out.

After thirty-six hours, Perkins was moved on order of the crown prosecutor to an old Victorian-era prison in North London called Pentonville. This was a much bigger and more imposing establishment, built in Victorian times as a model penal institution. Its entrance was a creamy white façade that might have belonged to a Georgian townhouse; inside were facilities for fitness, wellness and the modern range of therapies. A plaque outside the gate noted that inmates over the years had included such luminaries as Oscar Wilde and Boy George.

Perkins was nervous at first when they put him in the police transfer van, worrying that the CIA might be planning some form of secret extradition. But through the barred windows he saw that the van was not moving west, toward Heathrow, but north, past King's Cross and St. Pancras stations and up Caledonia Road toward Islington.

The prison warden, a tall man with a long nose and fringe of white hair, greeted Perkins personally and issued him a set of gray coveralls. He was assigned a cell in A-wing, where new arrivals were housed. But after an hour, an order came that he should be segregated from other prisoners, so he was moved to an empty corridor of D-wing, which was reserved for "enhanced" prisoners who were thought to be nonviolent. They gave Perkins his own television set and a stack of back issues of a celebrity magazine called *OK!* that featured pictures of big-breasted actresses and members of the royal family.

Perkins's lawyer from Washington, Vincent Tarullo, came to visit him the first afternoon he was at Pentonville. He was accompanied by the dough-faced British solicitor who had been negotiating with the prosecutors. They were given an interview room in the entrance wing, near the warden's office. Tarullo was a big man who usually walked jauntily on the balls of his feet, but today his body was slumped. His eyes were rimmed with fatigue from his fruitless efforts on two sides of the Atlantic to secure his client's release.

The attorneys were seated at a wooden table when the guards brought in Perkins, who was smiling and looking relaxed. Tarullo had an unlit cigar in his mouth, which one of the guards told him to put away.

"Hi, Vince," said Perkins. "You look absolutely awful. That must be my fault. Sorry about that."

"What are you so cheery about? You are in very deep shit, my friend."

"I like it here. I get three meals a day and my own toilet and a nice bed. I haven't slept so well in months, actually. You should try it."

"Don't get used to it. I am busting you out of here, whether you like it or not. I brought along Mr. Chumley, here, who will be filing motions and petitions."

"Gormley," said the solicitor. "My name is Gormley."

'I have a question, before we go any further," said Perkins. "Did you find Anthony Cronin?"

Tarullo shook his head.

"Jesus, Vince! The last time we talked I told you to squeeze everyone you knew until you found the guy. He's the one who got me into this. He's the way out."

Tarullo sighed. He shrugged; he took his cigar out of his breast pocket, put it in his mouth again and then laid it down on the table between himself and his client.

"There is no Anthony Cronin, at least nobody who matches your description. I turned the government upside down trying to find him. Called in every chit I had, with the agency and the bureau, too. I paid consulting fees to two former chiefs of the CIA station in New York. I even paid some dope to look at the membership roster of the Athenian Club. Sorry. No such person."

"Of course there is. I talked to him, repeatedly. We signed papers. We set up joint accounts at FBS in Geneva. Anthony Cronin was my freaking business partner."

"It's a false name, brother. Sorry to break it to you, but they do that. Whoever he is, he's gone with the wind."

"Then have the agency find the person who was using that cover."

"I tried that. They claim there was no such operation. No Cronin, nobody with that work name, no connection with Alphabet Capital. Nothing."

"But that's bullshit, Vince. These people are paid to lie."

"Maybe so, but they've been lying to everyone in town, in that case, because nobody knows shit about any of this. I even went to the congressional committees—that's how much I love you. I got one of my buddies on the House side who is the ranking member, a gentleman who owes me a favor, owes me his fucking seat, to be honest. He has all the clearances. He went up to the vault and asked to see all the covert-action findings and proprietary operations involving U.S. financial companies overseas. They did a special search for him, and he didn't get diddly squat. It's not there."

Perkins pounded the table, causing the cigar to roll toward the edge, where Tarullo caught it.

"Those fuckers! They are squeezing me, Vince. I'm the fall guy. They're closing out the operation they were running through my firm, and now they are taking me out, too. They're finished with whatever they were doing. I'm expendable."

"You got it. That's their game. The question is, what do you want me and Chumley to do about it?"

"Go to trial. Win the case. Get me off."

"Not so easy, big boy. The Brits have gathered enough evidence to nail you: fraudulent statements to the regulators; insider trading; numbered Swiss bank accounts not declared to the Inland Revenue. They have a lot of shit, my friend. And I have some bad news for you: Juries don't like billionaires, even in England. They want to crucify them. You'd have trouble finding a respectable barrister who would argue the case in court."

Perkins listened to this litany of misdeeds and then shook his head.

"It's all crap. They used me as long as it suited them, and then they ratted me out to the Brits. This is a setup, first to last."

"Look, Tom, do you want my professional opinion?"

"No."

"This case is a loser. If you take it to trial, you're going down. Now, Mr. Chumley here has been talking to the prosecutors, which I am not allowed to do. And I think you should listen to what he has to say."

"Can he get me off?"

"Sort of. Hear him out."

"Fine. And stop calling this man Chumley, for god's sake. He already told you it's Gormley."

The British solicitor looked relieved.

"Thank you. What Mr. Tarullo said is quite accurate. I have been in discussion this morning with Mr. Crane of the Serious Fraud Office, who was accompanied by a rather aggressive gentleman from the Crown Prosecution Service. We discussed the possibility of your entering a guilty plea to reduced charges. That would avoid the risk of going before a jury, which as Mr. Tarullo said would carry risks, given the current public mood toward, um, finance."

"What would I plead to? Assuming that I was willing to pretend I did anything wrong."

"That is still under discussion. But I was given to believe this morning that a possible arrangement might involve pleading guilty to a low-level count of banking fraud and a similarly low-level count of revenue fraud."

"What would the sentence be?"

"That would be at the discretion of the judge. The guidelines suggest there should always be some reduction in sentence for a guilty plea. But there might still be a brief prison sentence."

"How long is 'brief'?"

"For the simplest banking fraud conviction, the guidelines recommend twenty-six weeks. For revenue fraud, it is twelve weeks. So let us imagine something well under a year. It could be more or less, of course, or nothing at all."

"Take it," said Tarullo. "It's your best shot."

"Shut up. Now, suppose I don't accept this plea deal and I get convicted, what would I be facing?"

"Goodness, hard to say, but it would be quite unpleasant. The judge would not be amused by your subornation of an employee of the Bank of England."

"How much time?"

"For major banking fraud, the recommendation is five years, plus five more years for major revenue fraud, plus ten years for false representations, plus seven years for false accounting, plus five years for obtaining services dishonestly. So it could add up to, let me see, approximately thirty years. But that would be a very hard-hearted judge."

"Thirty-two years, to be precise," said Tarullo. "Don't be an idiot."

"Okay, suppose I listen to my lawyers and agree to plead guilty, Mr. Gormley, would I be able to work in the investment business again?"

"Probably not, I'm afraid, certainly not in the United Kingdom."

"And would I be liable for civil suits from investors?"

"Yes, sorry to say, there would be no stopping that. The guilty plea would be dispositive, your plaintiffs would argue, so you would be rather vulnerable."

He turned back to the burly American counselor.

"And the same would be true in the States, isn't that right, Vince? We would have to settle with the SEC, and at a minimum they would bar me from being a broker-dealer or an investment adviser. The evidence from the British court could be used as evidence in civil cases in America, and every shyster lawyer who wanted free money could file a strike suit. Am I correct?"

"We would fight the suits, obviously," said Tarullo. "Maybe we could talk national security with the judges, but I doubt it would work."

"So basically I'm screwed. That's what you're telling me. Either I go to court and run the risk of a ridiculously long prison sentence on multiple fraud charges, or I make a deal for a short sentence, but I still get bankrupted with damages from civil suits that I can't pay because I can't work in finance again. Is that it, more or less?"

"Hey, Tom, it is what it is. Not a great situation, I admit. Should you take the deal? Depends on your tolerance for getting ass-fucked for the next thirty-two years at Brixton."

Perkins put his palms to his head, so that they covered his eyes and most of his face. He murmured to himself as he thought about his options. When he removed his hands, he was smiling. It was uncanny, a big grin, as if he had been released from his cell and sent home.

"No fucking way. That's what I've decided. Let them try to prosecute me. You know what? They won't dare. They think they can nail me for stuff that happened before they got in deep. But I'm not going to play. This evidence is all tainted by the fact that I was involved in secret intelligence activities the CIA may be claiming don't exist, but which they will never, ever allow to come out in open court. And the minute they ask the judge to go in camera to discuss secrets, I've made my point, I've won."

"So you want to roll the dice?" asked Tarullo.

"Gambling is for suckers, Vince. This is a no-brainer. I've made my career knowing when to take risks and, honestly, it's not even close in this case. These people are bluffing. They will fold. Mr. Gormley, tell the Crown Prosecution Service, 'Thank you very much for the offer, and we'll see you in court.' But I promise you, it will never get there."

"Bracing words, Mr. Perkins," said the solicitor. "I will convey your message. I do hope you're right."

Perkins said he wanted a few words alone with his American attorney before they left. The prim British solicitor padded off down the hall to wait in the entryway.

Perkins leaned close to Tarullo and spoke as quietly as he could.

"This will work, Vince. You have to believe me."

"If you say so, Tom. What do I know? I'm just your lawyer."

Perkins lowered his voice another few decibels.

"I want you to do something for me. I want you to go see the CIA general counsel. Get all the records you can find of my accounts at FBS. Tell them that the CIA, or some spinoff somewhere, has been using these accounts to fund operations and using my firm as cover for its people. And I can prove it, if they make me. Will you do that?"

"Sure. I know the general counsel. He was an associate in my firm a long time ago. He told me I was all wet when I asked about Anthony Cronin a couple of days ago. But he'll see me."

"Tell him that what they're doing is illegal, Vince. There is something called the 'Anti-Deficiency Act.' Do you know what that is?"

"Of course I do. I'm a lawyer. It means that government agencies can't spend money that hasn't been appropriated by Congress. But how do you know?"

"I've been doing my homework. I've known I would need to break with these people, eventually. The point is, somebody has been using me and my firm to violate that law. That's what they were doing, running a fund off the books to provide money for their operations. And I want you to tell the general counsel that if they do not back off, I am going to say this in open court in Britain, and they are going down!"

Perkins's stage whisper had grown so loud the guard or anyone else listening could surely hear it. But he didn't care.

Tarullo got up to leave. He gave Perkins a kiss on both cheeks, Italian-style, and the heavy body lumbered out the door.

Perkins leaned back in his chair, his hands clasped behind his head. He put his feet up on the wooden table for a moment, savoring his act of defiance, but the guard pushed them away and ordered Perkins back to his cell.

40
LONDON

The Eurostar arrivals hall at St. Pancras station was thick with well-dressed young men and women, their computer bags slung over their shoulders and rolling their luggage behind them. There was the faint sound of a thousand tiny wheels clicking across the floor as they busily sped off to their London destinations. They were bound for Euro-Britain, a nation of espresso bars and gourmet sandwich shops that seemed barely connected to the old country of dingy corridors and cigarette butts.

Sophie Marx was traveling on a new diplomatic passport, supplied by the embassy in Brussels, so she avoided the queue at Immigration. She took a black taxi to the Dorchester Hotel, where she had left her luggage in storage when she had decamped suddenly for Islamabad a week before. The doorman tipped his black top hat, and the concierge in his morning coat welcomed her "back home," as if she'd been off sporting on the Côte d'Azur these past few days. Nothing in her appearance gave her away; she wore a pair of well-tailored slacks and her snug leather jacket and she did look, at a glance, like someone who belonged on a yacht rather than in a safe house.

Marx asked the man at the front desk for a simple room that would fit her new budget, but she was family now, and they gave her a big room with a four-poster double bed and windows that overlooked the park.

She rang Thomas Perkins's numbers again when she got upstairs. She had been calling him for two days without success, at his office, home and cell numbers. It was evident that something bad had happened to him but she didn't yet know what, and she blamed herself.

She unpacked her things, took a long shower and collapsed on the bed. She wanted to hide for a while, from the people who were pursuing her and from thoughts about the people she had placed in danger. She unhooked the chintz curtains that surrounded the bed and let them fall, so that she was enclosed in a doll's house of floral print fabric and down pillows. She hugged a pillow tight against her chest, the way she had as a girl in her first weeks at boarding school, fighting the loneliness of separation from her crazy parents. Sleep came quickly; she was awakened ninety minutes later by the insistent ring of her cellular phone.

Marx fumbled for the handset, uncertain where she was in the dark of the bed. It was odd to hear the ring at all; so few people knew how to reach her. She looked at the number of the incoming caller; it was a London mobile phone she didn't recognize, and she thought at first that it might be Thomas Perkins.

"Hello," she answered. "Who is this?"

The answer was the clipped, emphatic and all too familiar voice of Jeffrey Gertz.

"It's your boss. Or should I say, your former boss. I gather you've gone over to the parent company."

"I don't want to talk to you," she said. "You're hazardous to my health."

"I need to see you. We have to talk."

"Wrong. We have nothing to talk about. You are a menace. I mean it. Don't call again. Goodbye."

She pressed the red button on the phone and ended the call. The phone rang again, twice, from the same number, and she let it roll over to voice mail both times. Ten minutes later, there was a call from a "private number," not otherwise identified. She ignored that one, too.

Marx put on her jeans and black leather and walked the half dozen blocks across Mayfair to the handsome building that housed Alphabet Capital. It was a Friday afternoon and the pubs along the way were already crowded with merry-makers, spilling onto the sidewalks with their pints of beer and their wine coolers. As she threaded the crowds, several men offered to buy her a round.

The police had departed Perkins's building. When the elevator door opened at the top floor, the Alphabet offices looked depopulated, with perhaps a third of the normal contingent on the trading floor. The boisterous feeling she remembered was gone, too; it had the dazed and enervated look of a business in liquidation. Marx walked toward Perkins's office. The door was shut and the windows that looked out on the trading floor were curtained.

Perkins's secretary, Mona, was sitting alone at what had been a bank of three assistants. Her eyes were red from days of sleeplessness and crying. She saw Marx approach and pulled back at first. The American woman was part of the problem that had capsized her boss and his firm.

"Where have you been?" she asked Marx. "You missed all the, what, action, but that's not quite the right word. More like a typhoon."

"I was away. What happened? It's so quiet. It looks like they just had a funeral here."

"Might as well have been. There police were here all week. They just left this morning. Shut the place down, you might say. Took whatever they liked: half the files, and the proprietor, too."

"Where's Mr. Perkins? I've been trying to reach him for two days. He doesn't answer my calls and he doesn't respond to messages."

"Don't you know what happened, miss?"

"No, Mona, I have no idea. I told you, I've been away. Where is he?"

"He's in prison, ma'am. They took him off two days ago. He's in Pentonville now, or so they say. Mr. Tarullo has been up to visit. He's the only one."

"I need to see him. It's really important. Can you contact him for me?"

The secretary shook her head sorrowfully. Her life had been devoted to making arrangements for people to see Thomas Perkins, and now she was useless.

"I told you, he's in prison. No phone, no mobile, no visitors that aren't on the list. You have to apply to the warden. And he isn't seeing most people, I should warn you, only his attorneys. He thinks it's better that way, or at least that's what Mr. Tarullo told us."

Marx got Tarullo's number from the secretary and called him. The American lawyer sounded harassed and grumpy. Marx gave him her name and said she needed to visit Perkins in prison, but Tarullo sounded uninterested. Perkins, in his desire to protect her, had never mentioned her name to his lawyer.

Tarullo said he was preparing to leave for the States that night on the last British Airways flight, to "shake the tree," as he put it.

"Who the hell are you, anyway?" he asked. "I never heard of you. Who do you work for?"

Marx thought a minute. She didn't have time to play games and neither, evidently, did Tarullo.

"I work for the U.S. government. That's all I want to say on the phone. But I'm a friend of Mr. Perkins's, for real, and I suspect he doesn't have too many right now. I need to see him."

Now Tarullo was a little more interested. The busy lawyer's go-away tone changed to something more solicitous.

"You work for a part of the government that doesn't like to say that it's the government. Am I right?"

"Yes. 'I could tell you more but then I'd have to . . .' You know the line. Can we talk?"

Tarullo decided to take a flyer. He had to leave for the airport soon, and he needed to know if this call was worth his time.

"Let me ask you something, whoever you are. Do you know anything about someone named Anthony Cronin?"

"Yes. I know all about him."

"You're shitting me. For real?"

"Yes. That's why I need to see Mr. Perkins."

"Not so fast, sister. Before you see Tom, you're coming to see me. Can you get over to my hotel right now? I'm catching the eight o'clock flight to JFK, and I have to leave for Heathrow in an hour, max. I'm at the Park Lane Intercon. I'll be in the bar. Ask the concierge for Mr. Tarullo."

He was there, waiting impatiently, when she arrived ten minutes later. She didn't have to ask the man at the desk. It was obvious that the big guy staring at his watch, the one with the slicked-back hair and the look of a superannuated pop star, must be Vincent Tarullo. He had already packed and was dressed for the flight in baggy slacks and a velour jacket. His eyes lit up when he saw her walking toward him.

"Howdy do," he said, sticking out a meaty hand. "Buy you a drink?"

"I think we're better off taking a walk," said Marx, taking his arm. "A lot of people would like to hear what we're going to talk about."

They exited the hotel and took the underpass beneath Hyde Park Corner that led toward the green oval of the park. If there was surveillance, it was well organized; there was no sign of anyone following or watching.

"I need to see Tom Perkins," she began, taking his arm and leaning in close. "I'm part of the reason he's in this mess, and I think I can help get him out."

"Where were you when I needed you, lady? The poor man is in prison now. They're about to nail him with enough fraud charges to put him away for a long time. You picked a strange time to get in touch."

"I was traveling. I can't explain any more, except that I was dealing with the fallout from the same mess that got your client in all this trouble."

They emerged from the tunnel into the light and turned north, heading up a pathway that traversed a bower of trees along Park Lane.

"My client thinks he can get off," the lawyer said. "He says they're bluffing. The CIA will never let them prosecute this case because of all the secrets that would come out."

"Your client is right. This is all a house of cards. He was the cover for something very secret. They used him, and now they want to make him the fall guy. But it won't work."

"Oh, yeah? It seems to be working pretty good so far. Why is that going to change?"

"Because I'm ready to talk. I'll testify in court if I have to. You can tell that to people in Washington tomorrow. Sophie Marx is prepared to testify about everything she knows concerning Tom Perkins and his firm, and its connections to the U.S. government. How's that?"

"Pretty damn good."

Tarullo looked at his watch. If he wasn't in the cab and on the way to Heathrow in thirty minutes, he would miss his flight. He spoke quietly, even in the hush of the wooded glen.

"Level with me. I'm running out of time. Who's Anthony Cronin? You said on the phone that you knew about him. Where can I find him?"

"You can't. He doesn't exist. His real name is Jeffrey Gertz. He's the one who contacted Tom in the beginning and arranged to use Alphabet Capital as a front company. He's the one who's taking it apart now, to cover his tracks."

"Shit! No wonder nobody had heard of him. Can I use his name when I talk with people in D.C.? It's G-E-R-T-Z, right?"

"Yes, but be careful. This man is toxic. I mean it. Don't use his name with people unless you trust them."

They were moving west now, out of the trees and across the grass toward the Serpentine. Tarullo looked at his watch again.

"Listen, I have to head back now or I won't get out of here tonight. What can I do for you before I go? What do you need?"

"I want to see Tom. Can you put me on the visitors' list and get me into the prison?"

"Sure, why not? It's too late today. Tomorrow morning. Remind me your name, and not one of those bullshit spook names, please."

She repeated her name, Sophie Marx, the one that Perkins knew her by, not the one on her new diplomatic passport.

Tarullo popped open his cell phone and called the warden's office at Pentonville. He gave the clerk Marx's name and asked that she be allowed to meet with Thomas Perkins the next morning, at the special and urgent request of his attorney. He was put on hold for a moment, and then the warden himself came on the line and quizzed Tarullo to make sure this was indeed his special and urgent request. They haggled over dates and times, and then Tarullo ended the call.

"You can see him the day after tomorrow," he told Sophie. "It's too late for tomorrow. The list is already set. Sorry. Best I could do. In the meantime, I'll be chumming the water in D.C. See if we can make some people nervous."

Tarullo was walking faster now, gesticulating as he spoke on the phone and nervously checking his watch every twenty seconds.

Sophie strode along with him, determined to get him to the airport on time. Rather than take the tunnel, they bolted across Park Lane, waving down the traffic so that the big man could make his way across the busy thoroughfare. He lumbered into the hotel as quickly as he could, retrieved his bag and had the doorman hail a black taxi from the queue.

Tarullo gave the cabbie a forty-pound tip, in advance, and said he had to—*had* to—make the eight o'clock British Airways flight from Terminal Five. Marx watched him go and then walked the hundred yards up Park Lane to her own hotel.

At the entrance to the Dorchester was a concrete island that served as a turnaround for vehicles approaching the front door. A neat wrought-iron fence protected a fountain in the middle, where passersby liked to sit in the sun in the late afternoon and watch the famous people go through the revolving door of the hotel across the way.

Sitting by the fountain as Sophie Marx approached, scanning the entrance with the eye of a man trained in surveillance, was Jeffrey Gertz. He was wearing sunglasses, and he had a full beard now, but he was unmistakable.

When Gertz saw Sophie, he sprang to his feet and walked toward her. She thought of running away, but that would attract the attention of the police who were parked in a squad car on Mount Street, just to the right, and Marx wanted to deal with the London police at that point even less than she did with Gertz.

He was smiling as he walked toward her, with his hand extended in greeting.

"You've been ignoring me," he said, still smiling. "I don't like that."

"Get over it," she answered. "As you said, I'm a 'former employee.' And I don't feel safe around you. I wonder why that is."

"Don't be melodramatic, Sophie. It doesn't suit you. We need to talk. Let's go someplace quiet."

"The only place I'm going is into my hotel. How did you find out I was still here?"

"You're noisy. You move like an elephant. Come on, buy me a drink."

Gertz walked toward the revolving door. Sophie followed along behind. She was curious what Gertz would have to say for himself after his imaginary world had come crashing down.

The doorman gave Sophie a concerned look as Gertz entered the hotel lobby, as if to ask whether this bearded roustabout was really a guest of Miss Marx, a member of the hotel family. She nodded that he was okay.

Sophie led the way to the bar, which flanked Park Lane. It was just beginning to fill with drinkers in the late afternoon. She found two chairs at the end of the long, curved counter. The martini glasses and bottles of liquor were lined up against the mirrored glass like an army at sunset. Sophie took her seat and told the bartender she wanted a kir.

"Don't we want somewhere a little more private?" asked Gertz. "We have a lot to talk about."

"Privacy is the opposite of what I want with you," she answered. "I want a public place, in my hotel, where everyone knows me. It's the only way I would feel remotely safe in your company."

"Suit yourself," said Gertz. He ordered a gin martini and began popping pistachio nuts into his mouth from the silver-plated dish.

"Nice spot, the Dorchester. A rich guy must have set you up here. But I guess he isn't so rich anymore. From what I'm hearing, his hedge fund is about to go bankrupt. Let's see how nice people are to him now that he's an ex-rich guy trying to stay out of prison."

"It won't work, Jeff. Maybe you think you can hang it all on him, but it's going to come out."

"It doesn't matter to me either way. My fingerprints aren't on anything. I'm invisible. But you need to be careful, sweetie. You're still a target. And a very bad person is coming your way. That's why I tracked you down. I wanted to give you a warning. He knows where you are. He has all your aliases."

"The Pakistani? We're shutting him down. Mr. Hoffman told me so.

We're rolling up him and his people. His network wouldn't exist, as near as I can tell, without your help."

Gertz laughed and knocked the bar with his fist.

"That's rich. 'Mr. Hoffman told me so.' I love that."

She was angry now, at his arrogance and the dismissive tone. She had forgotten how compact and self-assured Gertz was.

"How could you do it, Jeff? This man was your 'consultant.' You let him see into your operations. How could you be so stupid?"

Gertz ran his index finger along the edge of his glass until it began to hum. He took a swig, and then another.

"What do you know?" he said. "Nothing."

"I know his name. Omar al-Wazir. I know you used him in 2005, and that you stayed in contact with him. I know . . ." She paused, trying to think of the word that would sting him the most. "I know that you are a fuckup."

Gertz muttered a curse of his own in response, but that wasn't enough. He was a man whose inner balance required that he be needed and respected by others. That was his vulnerability. He had to prove he was right.

"You don't get it. This isn't 'Tradecraft for Tots' like they teach at the Farm. This is the real world. He was my asset. He helped me pick my targets for recruitment. He knew the pressure points in Pakistan. He helped me move money to them. He helped set up the network. The operation wouldn't have been possible without him. He did a lot of good. It turned out he had flipped. He became dangerous. That wasn't my fault."

"Are you crazy? You got your own people killed, Jeff. How could there be anything worse than that?"

He took a sip of his martini, liquid ice on his tongue. He shook his head.

"I feel sorry for you. You're a sucker, and you're about to walk off a cliff."

He stood up from his stool and dropped twenty pounds on the mirrored counter of the bar.

She stared at him, her eyes angry and defiant, but with just a flicker of uncertainty.

"Piece of advice," he said. "Parting shot. Don't trust Cyril Hoffman. Who do you think told me about the Pakistani professor in the first place? How do you think I know he's on his way to London? From Hoffman, that's how. You're getting played."

He turned and walked away, back toward the hotel lobby.

"You're lying," she muttered. But she wasn't sure that she knew where the truth lay anymore. Sometimes it was indeterminate; the closer you got to it, the more you disrupted its pieces, so that it changed its shape and position. The truth wasn't straight. It had bends and curves.

41
ISLAMABAD

How do wars end? That was the question that had vexed Omar al-Wazir since he was a boy, when the time of the big wars was beginning in his part of the world. He could see well enough how they started, but how did they ever stop? He thought about it now as he sat in an air terminal waiting to board his Pakistan Airlines flight to London. It was a jumbo jet, and the waiting room was hot and crowded with Pakistanis of every age, old grandmas off to see their children in Manchester and young families going home to Neasden or Wandsworth, all tired and sweaty in the gritty seats of the boarding lounge.

The professor's face was clean-shaven, as always. He was wearing a gray suit of light summer wool and a white shirt. His glasses rested on the top of his big nose. It was the face of a doctor of computer science, a modern man, as he always insisted. In the simplicity of his demeanor, there was an invitation to trust. That was why he had been so adept at recruiting others: They wanted to believe that he was their ally; they felt more confident in battle if someone like him was on their side.

A part of the answer to this question of ending wars, the professor thought, was that the fighters on both sides got tired. They were exhausted by battle, bled white from their wounds. They had run out of troops and money, and so it was time to go home. That was what had happened to the Russians, certainly. Their Afghan war ended because the nation was bankrupt, economically and ideologically. A regime fell because of an unwinnable war, just as had been the case in 1917. Other wars ended because of political exhaustion or simply impatience; a nation still had the money and the weapons to fight on, but its will was gone. That was the story of America in Vietnam, the books all said. The war had been lost back home; events on the battlefield were of secondary importance.

But wars that ended in such ways did not bring a good peace; the professor knew that from his study of history. They brought dishonor, shame, a simmering desire for revenge. The Germans had gone from the humiliation of Versailles to the brazen assaults of the Nazis in less than two decades. The start of the second war was contained in the end of the first. That was what people in the professor's part of the world understood better than more "civilized" people: The victor in war must find a way to salve the dignity of the vanquished; otherwise, there would just be another war.

An old grandfather sitting next to the professor in the waiting lounge had fallen asleep. He was snoring loudly, and some of the children nearby were pointing at him and laughing. It was undignified. The professor gently nudged the old man until he was awake and the loud nasal percussion ceased. He went back to his reverie about war and peace, which helped him to forget about the unpleasantness of the airport waiting room.

The tribal code for restoring harmony was called *nanawatay* in the Pashto language. That was how wars ended among honorable men. The vanquished party would go to the house of the victor, into the very heart of his enemy, and look that man in the eye and request forgiveness and peace. The defeated man was seeking asylum, and the victor could not but grant him this request. To refuse would be dishonorable and unmanly. When a man is asked to be generous, he can unburden himself of his rage toward his enemy. He can be patient in forgiveness and let go of the past. The defeated man will have brought a buffalo, or some lambs and goats for slaughter. In this gift is his dignity. A feast is held. The war is over.

There were shouts in the terminal suddenly, and a frantic rush. They were calling the flight now, and people were crowding toward the door, pushing and shoving. The professor sat where he was. He had his ticket in his hand, with the seat number printed on it clearly. The plane would not leave without him. It was a sign of the immaturity of people in the East to jostle like this every time there was a queue. A Pashtun man would never do this. Better to miss the flight than to act like a woman.

The professor thought again of his problem: In the old days, it was said, the defeated man would come to the house of the victor with grass in his mouth and a rope around his neck as a sign of his humbleness. He was as meek before the victor as an animal of the field. Other times, the supplicant would attend a funeral for someone in his enemy's family. He would come to his rival's village and somberly enter his house, to share the grief. And once inside the house, he could ask for asylum and forgiveness. It was unthinkable to refuse such a plea; only a coward would do so.

The professor thought of the Americans. This culture of asylum was what they had never understood: They had made war in the years after 2001 because the Pashtuns would not refuse the asylum request from the Arabs fleeing across the mountains. The Americans demanded something the people of these mountains could not grant without great shame. You could say that it was a war about hospitality.

Even smart people could be stupid in this way. It was true of the British. The professor had at home somewhere a history of a terrible war the British had fought in the 1870s with the Jowaki clan, which was part of the Afridi tribe. The Jowakis had given asylum to two fearsome outlaws. The British demanded their return, but that was impossible for the tribesmen; better that they all should die. So they fought a bloody war, and it was reported by a British historian of the time, George Batley Scott: "Every glen and valley of the clan was occupied, every tower destroyed, many cattle died, the families suffered in the wintry cold, only then did the chiefs come into camp and ask for terms."

But the British hadn't understood how wars end. They had proposed what they thought was a proper settlement—payment of a fine, giving over weapons and, of course, return of the outlaws. The Jowaki chief answered in the only way that was consistent with tribal honor: "We will pay the fine, we will surrender our arms, but those two men who have taken refuge with us, we will not give them up. You are in possession of our country. Keep it, we will seek a home elsewhere, but those men we will not give up. Why will you blacken our faces?"

History was a recording that played continuously, so that you did not realize it was the same song, over and over.

The waiting lounge was nearly empty now. It was possible to board the airplane in a dignified way. Professor Omar collected his computer bag and the book he had been reading and walked to the gate, where a frazzled attendant collected his ticket. When he thanked her for this service, the woman looked astonished.

On the plane, there were families with young children in front of the professor and behind him. He put the buds of his music player into his ears so that the world would disappear and he could listen to Kinan Azmeh, a Syrian clarinetist who played in the classical way of the traveling musicians who had visited his town when he was a boy, who could make their instruments sound like human voices, but sweeter.

The professor was not flying to London with grass in his mouth or a yoke about his neck, it was true. And it could not be said that he had been defeated. But in traveling to Britain, he was entering the house of his enemy, certainly, or his enemy's best friend. He was seeking the balance, as he had come finally to understand it. He was giving his counterpart the opportunity to forgive—and thereby regain a measure of honor. Surely that would be understood: Just as it was necessary to fight, to avenge the insult, so it was also necessary to forgive. Otherwise the wars continued until there was no one left.

The plane was taking off. The professor could hear the roar of the engines against the sinuous notes of the clarinet. He fell asleep thinking of his favorite word in the Pashto language, *melmastia,* which meant "hospitality." That was the way wars ended.

Another plane was waiting to take off to the north, in Islamabad, heading for the same destination of London. This one was a military jet carrying Lieutenant General Mohammed Malik, the director general of

Inter-Services Intelligence. It was an unlikely journey, in some respects. The general normally did not like to travel to foreign countries unless he had official business with their intelligence service chiefs. He was not a mere case officer or a brigadier; there were questions of protocol and status. But in this case he felt he had no choice.

General Malik had a private cabin on the military plane. It was a small compartment, with a portrait of the president on one wall and one of the chief of army staff on another, but it had a bed and a desk, and a door you could close, so that you did not have to make conversation when you had nothing to say.

The general was a fastidious man. His orderly had packed his uniforms in the hanging locker, protected in their zippered suit bags. His dress shoes were already polished to a high shine, but they would be buffed again before the plane landed. The orderly had laid out his pajamas, too, on the bed, along with his felt slippers and his dressing gown. The general would change after the plane had taken off. It would be undignified to be dressed in bedclothes if the steward knocked before takeoff to offer tea or a cold drink.

General Malik had been contacted by his old friend Cyril Hoffman the day before. Usually there was a roundabout indirection to Hoffman's manner; he could be as Oriental in his ways as a pasha. But this time he was more direct. When the phone rang, the general had been in the garden adjoining his headquarters in Aabpara, sitting in his Adirondack chair, having his tea in the late afternoon and reading his cables, and trying to sort out the tangle of operations that was knotted too tightly now to be easily undone. The duty officer said that Langley was on the line, and that was a call he could never refuse.

The Pakistani general left his garden chair and walked up the stairs through the open doors into his office. It was Hoffman on the line, coming immediately to the point without the usual patter.

"We know who he is," said the American. "So do you."

"That is an unpleasant way to begin a conversation, Cyril, out of the blue. Whatever do you mean?"

"We know the identity of the bomber who has been killing my

American colleagues. The gentleman's name is Dr. Omar al-Wazir, as you surely must be aware by now. He's on our target list. But I don't think the time is ripe quite yet."

"I am the one who should be making the protests, Cyril."

"About what, pray tell?"

"There were bombings last night in Peshawar and Karachi. Our analysts think they were connected to the gentleman you mention, a distinguished scientist, I might add, well known to our military service. If we thought there was the slightest connection between those bombings and the United States government, it would have the most serious repercussions."

"You won't find any connection, I assure you."

"Less than a ringing denial, but certainly welcome. Let me repeat that the government of Pakistan will not tolerate any violation of its sovereignty."

"Noted."

"As for Dr. al-Wazir," the general continued, "present us with the information of his culpability, if there is any, and we will as always be prepared to take appropriate action."

"That's why I'm calling, actually. We've learned some things about Dr. al-Wazir that I thought you would want to know. Not that you have any interest in him, other than as a Pakistani citizen."

"That is the second time you have made the insinuation that we have some kind of illicit contact with the man, Cyril. I will ignore it, again, but it is tedious. What is the information that you wish to share?"

"I thought you might want to know that Dr. al-Wazir has been in contact with a certain rogue element of American intelligence; the very element, as it happens, that has been seeking to bribe your good countrymen. The professor is not what he appears. He is spreading the money, and also killing the people who distribute it. He thinks he's a Pakistani Robin Hood. This is getting much too complicated; it's trouble all around. It needs to be set right, don't you think?"

The Pakistani general put the phone away from his ear. Of all the things that Hoffman might have said, this was one he could not have anticipated. Surely it was a ruse or a trick; that was so often the way with Hoffman.

"I don't believe you," said Malik. "He is a Pakistani who, according to you, is part of a terrorist plot to kill Americans. How could he possibly be in touch with your intelligence agencies?"

"Yes, I know what you're thinking: How can he be one of yours? He's one of ours."

General Malik snorted. "This is all bosh."

"Stranger things have happened, Mohammed. Good and decent Pakistani patriots share information with the United States. Why not terrorists? I don't want to get personal. But you, of all people, should know that the United States of America has a long reach."

"Whatever are you talking about?"

There was an edge of anxiety in the Pakistani's voice. He wasn't used to the normally genial American speaking this way.

"Let's be honest, for once, Mohammed. I am thinking of a young Pakistani Army officer in the United States for training, at Fort Leavenworth, Kansas, to be precise. That gentleman certainly enjoyed the hospitality of the United States, yes, he did. It was good for his bank account, too, helped get him started up the ladder. You should see his 201 file. I have, and I can tell you, it makes very interesting reading after all these years."

General Malik put the phone down for a moment. His hand was trembling slightly, and his face had gone ashen. He was a military man, and his life had been an exercise in self-control.

"This is intolerable, Cyril. You are a scoundrel."

"You flatter me. I'm just doing my job, a humble civil servant; I'm a patriot, too, like yourself. But I got off the subject. I was talking about the good Dr. al-Wazir and his surprising contacts with the United States. I thought that might concern you."

"It certainly would, if it were true. Any contact by a Pakistani national with a foreign intelligence service concerns me. I have been on watch for that very thing, sir."

"Yes, right. Well, listen to this, my friend. In a matter of hours, the duplicitous Professor al-Wazir is going to be on a flight to London. And while he is there, I have reason to believe that he intends to meet secretly with an official of the United States government. And I just thought that was something you would like to know."

"This is another of your tricks. How do I know that you are not lying?"

"You don't have to trust me, Mohammed. I agree that's never a good idea. Have your people check the manifest of flights leaving for London. The man will be on it. I suggest you get to London, too. Please don't try to stop him from going. Then you'll never know what his real game was. You'll miss the party. Follow me?"

"Yes, I follow you, to the extent there is any path here that a sane man could discern."

"Good. And since you've been such a friend to the United States all these years, I'm going to give you another tip I've picked up from one of my sources. How would you like that?"

"I never refuse a tip. Bad practice in our business."

"The meeting between the esteemed doctor and his American friend is going to take place at Kew Gardens on Saturday, at four o' clock in the afternoon. The meeting will be in the far western corner of the park. I can send you a map in a few minutes. What do you think about that?"

"How do I know this isn't a trap?"

"You don't know, Mohammed. That's why I would come armed, if I were in your position. That way, if you don't like what you see, you can do something about it. But don't bring an army with you. The Brits won't like that. Just bring a bodyguard. A good shooter."

"I'll think about it," said the Pakistani.

"Don't think too hard. Bad for your health. Makes you stay up late at night worrying about things you can't change. What's done is done; overdone, in this case. So I'll assume we have a date, until I hear otherwise."

Now General Malik was sitting in his cabin on the airplane. The steward arrived and offered a beverage before takeoff. The general had a whiskey, and then a second one when they were in the air. It was a long flight, and they would have to stop and refuel in Turkey, which was a nuisance. The general had brought along one of his favorite books, *Vanity Fair*, by Thackeray, which he liked to reread every half dozen years or so. He especially liked the battle scenes. But he found this night that he was unable to concentrate.

He put on his pajamas and took a draught of powder. He wanted to sleep. In the minutes before he was enveloped by a heavy, dulling slumber, he thought of the Americans: They were on all sides of every deal they made; they were the gambler at the table, and they also owned the casino. Even when you thought you understood what they were doing, you couldn't be sure, because they didn't know themselves.

42
LONDON

It was a beguiling Saturday afternoon for an outing in the park. Summer was at the cusp; a cool breeze rustled the trees in a shimmer of green. There had been rain overnight, and the well-nourished grass sparkled in the sun like a glistening jewel. The motorways west had been crowded in the morning, but by afternoon the traffic had thinned out, especially south of the Thames on the way to the Royal Botanical Gardens.

Kew was a trophy of imperial days that had survived into the post-colonial age. It had been built with the explorer's spirit that had sent the East India Company off to Calcutta and Karachi. It was filled with imperial kitsch: a pogoda, a glass house fit for a maharaja, a conservatory sculpted like a Greek temple, exotic flowers and trees from every point of the compass. It was, you might say, the perfect place to assemble a group from the former empire.

Jeffrey Gertz was the first to enter the Kew compound. He had prepared for battle, just so, but nothing ever goes as planned. He had organized a half dozen shooters, dressed like Saturday tourists, but there was trouble at the gate. British security was tight, and the weapons were found at the entrance. Gertz's men were detained and taken to Richmond for questioning. They would be there all afternoon, the detective sergeant at the station had advised. Fortunately, Gertz had planted a weapon for himself near the meeting site the day before, with help from a British security officer who had contacts in the Metropolitan Police.

Gertz would manage on his own. He had a big heart, and anyway, relying on other people always created problems. He entered the gardens at Victoria Gate, on the southeast side. Ahead of him was the curved glass façade of the Palm House, ribbed with white metal stays. It enclosed the tall palms like a giant hatbox. Gertz skirted the pond behind the Palm House and lingered by the rose garden, to make sure he wasn't being followed. Then he moved west toward the meeting place.

The meeting with Dr. Omar was to take place just past the Badger Sett, a Christopher Robin sort of place carved out under the roots of a giant oak tree. That had been a strange choice, Gertz had first thought, but when he looked on the map he saw that it was the farthest landmark from the main gate, and thus the best venue for a clandestine contact. That had always been one of Dr. Omar's talents, Gertz knew. He was meticulous about his tradecraft. That was why he had survived so long.

Gertz continued down the long promenade. The lake, narrow as a fjord and shining crystal-blue in the afternoon sun, was on his right. To the left was the grand Victorian structure known as the Temperate House, a name you could give to this whole damned country, as far as Gertz was concerned, so cool and well put together, never a hair or a shingle out of place. It was a wonder that they had managed to field a good army for so many centuries, but that was pretty well gone now.

The American continued on past the catwalk that connected some of the treetops in this western part of the gardens. He had intended to put some of his shooters up there on the arbor way, with a perfect line of sight out over the lawns toward the rendezvous. That wouldn't work now, but it had been a sweet idea. Eventually Gertz reached the Badger Sett. It was empty, save for a few kids shouting at the critters they hoped were down there somewhere underground. The meeting site was a little farther on, hidden behind the next grove of trees

Gertz continued another fifty yards past the rendezvous point to a stand of trees ringed by dense ferns. He slipped into this natural hideaway, found the weapon he had hidden there and sat down to wait.

Next into the fold was Lieutenant General Malik. He was in mufti, as was the sturdy Pakistani soldier who accompanied him, following several steps behind. The general had thought to contact the MI6 liaison officer at the British Embassy in Islamabad before leaving. He said that he was traveling to Britain for a little personal holiday and that, as always, he planned to bring along a personal security detail, in this case just one chap. But the man would be carrying a firearm and he would need the necessary permissions. The general had even mentioned that he was thinking of doing a little sightseeing at Kew, and that he hoped his man wouldn't have any difficulty at the gate.

The general stopped to look at the flowers: aloe, oleander and golden lotus. He was a horticulturalist, in his own modest way. As a young intelligence officer, he had read that the celebrated James Jesus Angleton cultivated orchids. That was a bit much for the general, and expensive, too, but he had an enlisted man who watered and fertilized his roses, and sprayed them when the bugs were out.

He was dressed in a blue blazer and charcoal slacks, and a pair of slip-on loafers that he disdained back home as too casual. Even after the long flight, he looked trim and taut, his face nearly free of wrinkles and his mustache clipped to the millimeter. He walked with a military bearing, so that a person would know, whether the general was in uniform or not, that he was a substantial man.

General Malik tried to be inconspicuous as he made his way toward the Badger Sett, but it wasn't easy, for a man of his demeanor and self-regard. He liked to be looked at by others. That was any officer's vanity. When children skittered noisily on the walkway between the general and his bodyguard, he gave them pats on the head, as if that were the normal thing to do, but he looked like the headmaster of a school.

When he saw the Badger house, the general turned and walked away. He was early; he didn't want to hover conspicuously. He discovered a lily pond, on the other side of a thicket of pine trees, and sat on a bench gazing at the water plants while his bodyguard tried to keep still.

Omar al-Wazir, the man from the washboard mountains of Waziristan, oddly looked the most like a man out for a Saturday afternoon walk. He had come unarmed and penitent, with the grass of humility in his mouth, figuratively if not literally. His trip had been long and uncomfortable, with none of the special perquisites of the general; he wasn't staying in a fancy hotel; indeed, he had barely found time to wash and shave at a small bed-and-breakfast in Kensington favored by Pakistani travelers. But there was a serenity about the Pashtun man that was genuine. He knew why he was in London. He had done his business, and now he had come to make a dignified ending of it. He would meet with his enemy, come into his house, find the *gundi* where life and death are in equilibrium.

The professor had arrived at the gardens half an hour before the appointed meeting. He did not need time to plan or reconnoiter. He obtained a map at the entrance, just inside the Victoria Gate, and was informed by one of the staff that it would take him ten minutes, walking briskly, to reach the Badger Sett, fifteen if he strolled at a more leisurely pace. He set off on a dogleg along a row of cherry trees, past the Greek temple built to commemorate King William, and then north through a corridor of cedars that made him homesick, just for a moment, for the deodars that stepped up the hillsides of Makeen.

The last to appear was a man in a voluminous summer suit, in a pastel color that did not occur in nature but was closest to green. He was wearing a white silk tie with small blue stripes, and he might have been the groom at a midsummer wedding, for the jaunty way he walked on his toes, almost prancing as he traversed the path toward the hidden clearing just past the Badger Sett.

This gentleman had actually been in the gardens since the morning, resting a quarter mile below the meeting point in a cottage that had been the haunt of Queen Charlotte, the handsome wife of George

III who had loved these woods. He wanted to be ready, but also out of the way, so that he would be invisible for as long as possible. But when one of his spotters saw Dr. Omar arrive at the gate, and then another reported that he was moving up the Cedar Way, he knew that it was time to move. He left the cottage then and made his way to the rendezvous.

The big man arrived at the appointed spot at precisely four o'clock. This was his theater, for it was he who had set the meeting. At that same moment, onto the crest of lawn stepped the man he had planned to meet, Dr. Omar al-Wazir, punctual and precise as ever.

Cyril Hoffman, the concertmaster, embraced the Pakistani professor. He kissed him on both cheeks, and took the man's hand.

"You came," said Dr. Omar. "I was not sure you were ready to see me, after everything that has happened."

"Of course I came," said Hoffman. "I could not refuse a request from a man who has suffered, even if that man has made mistakes. For we all make mistakes, don't we? Yes, we do."

There was movement in the woods, but the professor did not hear or see it.

"I have been thinking," said Dr. Omar, "that it is time to find an ending. There are so many dead, so much *saz*. It is enough, now. I come to ask forgiveness and asylum. I pray that you will be an honorable man and grant my request."

Hoffman was about to speak, but he did not have time. Events moved more quickly than he could express the words. But what he wanted to say was, *Yes, I grant your wish. It is over.*

The other two men who had been awaiting Dr. Omar 's approach had moved into the clearing, too. They watched this greeting with utter astonishment and rage, in the case of General Malik, and a grim appreciation of the concertmaster's art, on the part of Jeffrey Gertz. But they had come for their own reasons, these two, and they were not to be deterred.

General Malik walked toward Dr. Omar. There was a look of recognition in both men's faces. They had been circling each other for so long. Each had tried to imagine the other's motivations, and each had been wrong.

The general was the first to speak. He turned to his bodyguard.

"Execute this man," he said, pointing to Dr. Omar. "He is a traitor. He is an American spy."

The general's bodyguard fired his service revolver. The sound was muffled by the silencer.

Gertz had drawn his own weapon. His eyes had been fastened on Dr. Omar, his sometime adviser. The Pakistani was the last piece of Gertz's botched conspiracy that needed to be cleaned up. Gertz had been prepared to do the necessary job, as soon as Hoffman had told him about the meeting, but now it seemed that he was redundant.

Gertz watched the Pakistani professor fall, and saw the blood spurt from his shattered skull. He crouched and swiveled his body in a quick turn, aiming first at the bodyguard, then at General Malik, then at Cyril Hoffman—uncertain who was the enemy. Always have a plan, and always make the first move. That was his rubric, but it failed him now. He didn't have a plan for this bizarre situation, and he hadn't moved first.

There was a muffled sound of impact, like a fist hitting a pillow, and again. Two more gunshots had been fired. The first took down General Malik's bodyguard. The second struck Jeffrey Gertz. These shots came from a different direction, from the nearby woods. The concertmaster had brought along a shooter of his own, with very precise instructions. They were clean shots to the head, both of them meant to kill.

Hoffman pulled at General Malik's arm.

"We need to go now," he said.

The Pakistani general surveyed the scene and made a quick decision. He took a handkerchief from his pocket and used it to wipe clean the prints on Gertz's gun, and then put it into the hand of Dr. Omar. Malik was good at that sort of thing. He knew how to compose the frame.

"He was a stupid, dangerous man," said Hoffman, staring at Gertz's body as the life slipped away.

Hoffman led Malik away toward the cottage from which he had emerged minutes before. It was at the far end of the park, along Kew

Road. A car was waiting for Hoffman, but he gave it to the Pakistani general and sent him away. He summoned another car for himself, and it was there in thirty seconds. If there was one thing Hoffman understood, it was logistics.

They exchanged a few words before they parted, about money. Oddly, on such a grim afternoon, both men were smiling as they said farewell.

43
LONDON

Sophie Marx arrived at Pentonville the next afternoon at the appointed time. The guard asked her to take a seat in the reception room outside the warden's office. She had been up much of the night, unable to sleep, but she had dressed up for Thomas Perkins in a bright new frock, the color of toasted almonds, that she had bought on New Bond Street the day before. She thought it would cheer him up, but it wasn't just that. She wanted to look nice. After she had waited nearly an hour in the visitors' lounge, she knocked on the warden's door and asked his assistant if something was wrong.

The warden's deputy apologized that there had been some last-minute discussions involving Mr. Perkins's case and asked Marx to wait a bit longer. She returned to her chair in the spartan reception room, certain that something bad had happened. The guards changed shifts at four and a new group came in, but still she waited. The only reading matter in the room was the newsletter of the prisons bureaucracy that carried the anodyne name National Offender Management Service.

She didn't want to close her eyes, despite her fatigue. Every time she did, she saw the face of Jeffrey Gertz. She had wanted him dead, that was the grisly part of it; she had said as much to Hoffman. And now that he was dead, she wondered if it was her doing.

It had sounded impossible, when Cyril Hoffman first hinted at what had happened in a phone conversation the night before. But the late newscasts had bits of it, and she had spoken at length with Hoffman that morning, before he caught his flight back to Washington. He had asked her to come to breakfast at the Travellers Club on Pall Mall. It was his home away from home, he said: lots of food, badly cooked, and eccentric old men who appreciated the medicinal benefits of alcohol.

He told her the outlines of the story, at least the version that was being fed to the media with the cooperation of the ever-pliant British. A former CIA officer named Jeffrey Gertz had gone to a rendezvous in Richmond upon Thames the previous afternoon, at the Royal Botanical Gardens at Kew. Gertz was now a private contractor, according to the version for public consumption, working for a Blackwater-type firm. He was pursuing a Pakistani terrorist named Omar al-Wazir, a renegade academic who had been linked with the recent killings of American citizens overseas. Gertz had been hired by one of the victims' families to track him down, that was the cover story. The terrorist had brought along an accomplice, a Pakistani soldier who was in his pay. There had been a shoot-out, and all three were dead.

"How useful for you," Sophie had said when he finished. "No loose ends."

"None whatsoever." Hoffman smiled. "It even makes Jeffrey look heroic. And it avoids that awkward business about his 'consulting' arrangement with the enemy."

"Why were they meeting? Explain that to me."

"It's quite scandalous, actually. I suspect that Jeffrey was stealing money, with help from this Wazir fellow, and diverting it to bank accounts around the world. Greedy little bastard, it turns out. He fooled everyone. Perhaps it was a dispute about money. Perhaps they truly wanted to kill each other."

"Is any of that true, Mr. Hoffman?" Sophie had asked.

"We'll never know, will we?"

Sophie had looked into Hoffman's catlike eyes. What he had said was mostly nonsense, but it would hold up. He was so easy to underestimate. That was how he had survived and prospered.

"Gertz didn't fool you, did he, Mr. Hoffman? You knew his operation would go bad. That's why you kept tabs on him, always."

"I had my doubts, that's a fact. It's well documented in the cable traffic, I'm sure. I thought this covert-action capability he and his White House chums were creating was bound to get us all in trouble. I'm glad that it has been dismantled, so that we can go back to normal order. The doctrine is affirmed: Outside the Church there is no salvation. But it's no satisfaction to have been proven right, believe me."

"And what about the money that Jeffrey stole? Where's that?"

"Goodness. Hard to find now, I'm afraid. Not clear even who it belongs to."

Sophie laughed. She didn't mean to, but she couldn't help herself. He might as well have stuffed it in the pockets of that lime-green suit.

"I like a good yarn as well as anyone, Mr. Hoffman, but please tell me the truth. What did you know about Omar al-Wazir? Gertz told me you were the one who set this all in motion. Is that true?"

"Don't be silly, my dear. Of course it's not true. If I had been running this, it never would have gotten so messy. Be very careful not to spread that sort of malicious gossip. It will do no one any good."

Hoffman excused himself to go upstairs and pack. Otherwise he would miss his flight. He invited Marx to come visit him at Langley as soon as she returned to Washington. There was an opening for a senior job on the seventh floor, he said, and Marx would be an ideal candidate.

It was nearly six when the warden's door finally opened and out walked Thomas Perkins, a free man. He was dressed in the pin-striped suit he had been wearing when he was first taken into custody and sporting a pair of handmade shoes from John Lobb. The pencil-nosed warden was shaking his hand and apologizing strenuously for the inconvenience of the last few days.

When Perkins saw Sophie in the waiting room, a smile rolled across his face like a gentle wave breaking on the ocean. She leapt from her chair and, without thinking about it, embraced him and kissed him on the cheek. The warden handed over a manila envelope that contained Perkins's wallet, gold cuff links and other valuables that had been collected when he was first taken prisoner.

"That's it?" Perkins asked. "I'm really free to go?"

The warden nodded in a proprietary way and walked him out the gate onto Caledonian Road. He offered to send Perkins home in one of the vehicles of the National Offender Management Service, but Perkins said he would rather walk with his friend and savor his new status as a free man.

They ducked into the first pub they saw. It was early evening, and the summer sun was low in the sky. They brought two pints of beer out into the courtyard. Perkins had purchased a pack of cigarettes. He hadn't smoked one in more than twenty years, he said, but he had promised himself that if he was released from prison, the first thing he would do would be to have a cigarette. He lit it up, breathed the smoke in deep, coughed, took another puff and threw it away. He looked like a man who had awakened from a nightmare and realized that none of the horrors he had been experiencing were real.

Sophie demanded an explanation. Why had he been freed, after so much thunder and rage? Had he bribed the prime minister, or just the home secretary?

"I frightened your friends at the CIA," Perkins answered. "They thought I was going to tell the truth, and they panicked. They contacted the British government last night, and they negotiated all morning. Hush-hush, the warden told me. By the time the meetings were over, they had decided they wouldn't bring any charges. Terrible misunderstanding, they told my lawyer, frightfully sorry."

"What are you going to do now? Go back to being a billionaire?"

"I'm not a billionaire anymore, sweet girl. Not even a tiny fraction of one. The run on my firm was like a fire sale. I'll be lucky to avoid bankruptcy."

Sophie took his hand. She wanted to be supportive, but she wasn't sure how. She had never been very good at relationships.

"You can build it all back up, if you want."

"That sounds boring. I've done that. I want to try something new. I want to see what's on the other side of all those things that we're supposed to want."

Sophie thought of the dreams she'd had as a young intelligence officer, the places she had been and the risks she had taken. What had all of this produced?

A string of lies, near as she could tell: colleagues who lied and cheated and only got upset if it seemed that someone was about to blow the whistle. They had been dropping bombs on people for so long, it had begun to seem natural. That was the corrosive part: If you killed someone at close range with a knife, at least you knew what it felt like to have blood on your hands. But if you did it from ten thousand feet, looking at a picture on a television screen, you forgot that there were real people down below. It wasn't that the cause was wrong, but that it wasn't an honest fight.

"I want to see what's on the other side, too," said Sophie. "I've had enough dishonesty to last a lifetime. I want to see what it's like to tell the truth."

"Want some company?" asked Perkins.

She nodded and took his hand. They finished their beers, and had another round, and eventually they caught a taxi on Caledonian Road and went off to find a restaurant in Camden Town where, Perkins assured Sophie, there would be nobody that either of them knew.

ACKNOWLEDGMENTS

This book is dedicated to Garrett Epps, a professor of constitutional law and novelist, and my closest friend since we met at college more than forty years ago. Each of my novels has included a nod of appreciation to Garrett as a reader and critic, but my debt is greater than that: I would not have written any of these books without his generous and patient help. Garrett's assistance was especially valuable with this novel.

This book is set largely in Pakistan—not in the real country but one of my invention. Similarly, although the book describes a fictional Inter-Services Intelligence Directorate, it should not be confused with the real organization by that name. This is a work of fiction, and the characters, events and institutions have no connection with actual ones. There are no real people or intelligence operations in these pages.

I have tried to paint my fiction using colors that are true to life. I was lucky enough to visit South Waziristan, Dushanbe and many of the other places described in this book. My most important guides and advisers are best left unnamed here, but I am deeply grateful to them. I owe a special debt to Pakistan scholar extraordinaire Christine Fair of Georgetown University, whose knowledge of Punjabi curse words is surely unmatched this side of Lahore. I have drawn on many written sources, but the most helpful was the Pashtun cultural material collected by the website khyber.org.

A second locale for this book is the domain of hedge funds centered around Mayfair in London. Here again, my primary consultants are best left anonymous. But I would like to thank my friend Carla Rapoport for her hospitality during a week of research in London. I also thank, once again, my friend Jonathan Schiller, who gave me a hideaway at his law firm, Boies, Schiller & Flexner, during the early months of composition. And I thank my friends Lincoln Caplan, Jamie Gorelick, and Candy Lee for their steadfast support.

I am grateful to those who read and commented on early drafts: my wife and first reader, Dr. Eve Ignatius; my esteemed literary agent, Raphael Sagalyn, and his colleagues Bridget Wagner and Shannon O'Neill; and my agent at Creative Artists Agency, Robert Bookman. It is my good fortune to be published by W. W. Norton, and I owe special thanks to many people there, starting with my superb editor, Starling Lawrence, and including Jeannie Luciano, Bill Rusin and Rachel Salzman.

My greatest luck, for twenty-five years, has been to work at *The Washington Post*, and I would like to thank all my colleagues there, especially Don Graham, Fred Hiatt, Steve Pearlstein, Alan Shearer and James Hill.

This book is ultimately about how wars end, and I pray that such a process happens in real life in Pakistan and Afghanistan.